# Ace

*The Deuces Wild Series*
*Book 4*

# IRISH WINTERS

# Ace
## Deuces Wild, Book 4


You can find Irish Winters

On Facebook
https://www.facebook.com/IrishWintersAuthor/

On Twitter
https://twitter.com/irishwinters1


Sign up for Irish Winters' Newsletter at:
http://www.irishwinters.com/newsletter.html


For more information about all of Irish Winters' books, visit:
http://www.irishwinters.com.

# The Dead Man's Hand

Old West lawman, gambler, gunslinger and showman, James "Wild Bill" Hickok, was murdered on August 2, 1876, while playing five-card draw at Nuttal & Mann's Saloon in Deadwood, Dakota Territory. Jack McCall, a disgruntled gambler, approached Hickok from behind and shot him at point-blank range in the back of the head, killing him instantly. McCall was later hanged for the murder, but by then, America had lost one of its premier Wild West heroes.

Legend tells us "Wild Bill" held two pair at the moment of his death, black aces and eights—the *dead man's hand*. The identity of the fifth card has been the subject of conjecture for years. For the purpose of this series, I've chosen a deuce of hearts for that card-in-the-hole, in honor of a little boy named Devlin who loved to play the violin. In honor of a father's undying love for his son.

Some players think wildcards are amateurish and juvenile. Others believe the more wildcards in the game, the greater their chance of winning. I only know that one Deuce and a pair makes three of a kind, and that sounds a lot like a family to me. You be the judge.


*Deuces Wild.*

# Chapter One

There was something in the stuffy, filtered office air that afternoon. Something unsettling and unseen. Something dark. The moment Special Agent Keller Boniface returned from meeting with the District's police chief about a prostitution ring that crossed state borders, he felt a sinister presence tap, tap, tapping at his double-reinforced psychic perimeter. From the get go, he'd developed a hands-off boundary to protect his inner self from prying by his new associates, aka the not so subtle geniuses of the Bureau's only psychic team, Deuces Wild.

A relentless migraine commenced throbbing deep in the muscles at the base of his skull at the mere thought of the stupid moniker. Keller willed the pain away as if he truly possessed that kind of power. How he wished. He would've willed himself away from this team months ago.

Keller didn't like his new assignment, plain didn't want it. Until Candace-the-Psycho Bratton murdered her father-in-law, Chester Bratton, aka the father of one of her two kids, Keller's life had been on track. He'd been in control and able to hide his unique brand of empathy. He'd lived as close to a normal life as any empath could. Off the radar and out of sight.

It'd taken years to learn how, but he'd kept his head down and he'd worked hard, racked up enough trust to be deemed reliable, earned more than enough awards, garnered only the right recognition to be considered indispensable. A team player. One of the guys.

Not anymore.

Since the fateful day he'd seen, as in psychically seen, Candace stabbing her father-in-law and lover, Chester, to death, well, now the proverbial lid was off. Because Special Agents Isaiah Zaroyin and Tate Higgins had been in that abandoned garage near the Navy yards that day, too. They'd seen the same vision and were savvy enough to know who and what Keller was. His days of normalcy evaporated, and now everyone in the Bureau knew Keller was different. Weird. An empath who saw things most people couldn't. Everything Keller never wanted to be. Everything he'd hidden from the world.

But like the obedient civil servant he was and would always be, FBI Special Agent Keller Boniface now boldly stared at his new boss, the bombastic and most pretentious man alive. Tucker Chase, Supervisory Special Agent and Director of the FBI's one and only Psychic Team that he himself had named Deuces Wild. Like anyone cared what Chase called his team of misfits. Jesus Christ, look at them. All busy little bees tapping out reports Tucker probably didn't even know how to read.

The last rays of spring sunlight faded from the panoramic view of this tenth floor open office. Normally Keller wouldn't have noticed, but the way it had faded from yellow to gold to orange, now red, seemed prophetic in a backward kind of way. Red sky at night, sailor's delight...

It'd been a damned long time since he'd known one second of sailor's delight. Rolling his neck, Keller strived for patience to endure this forsaken group of wannabes. *Former SEAL, huh?*

Tucker cocked his head as if...

*Damn, maybe he really can read my mind.*

Tucker's head canted to the other side, as if...

*Shut the fuck up,* Keller commanded himself. *He* can *hear you. Stop. Thinking.*

Even that earned him one of Chase's infamous smirks.

*Guess he heard that, too.*

Which explained why Ky Winchester and his sidekick, Eden, chuckled as if they'd shared a private joke. Because they probably had, and no doubt that joke was Keller.

*Well, har dee, har, har.*

"No, it wasn't. Honest," Eden piped up, her pretty green eyes bright against her creamy complexion.

Blonde, forever smiling, and one of those terminally cheerful morning people, Eden could read most people's minds, as well as influence their decisions. The story was that from her kitchen in Virginia, USA, she'd *'heard'* Ky's psychic plea to die from a prison cell a world away in Afghanistan, where he'd been tortured for days. She was the psychic who'd then influenced the big bruiser of a Marine in the cell next to Ky's to escape and help him.

It was USMC Lee Hart who'd saved a few other American soldiers that night, but it was Eden who'd truly saved Ky. He was blind back then, his face beaten and unrecognizable, his will to live gone. Lee might've given him the knife to defend himself, but Eden gave Ky what he'd needed to live. She gave him hope. Yeah, that was Eden Winchester for you, terminally hopeful.

But she was talking too fast now, tripping over her words. "Ky made a funny face, that's all, Keller. He does this thing with his nose, and then he... Oh, my gosh." Her eyes grew wide when she realized *she too* had mentally eavesdropped. She slapped a hand over her mouth but chuckled through her long, slender fingers. Her shoulders scrunched, making her even more adorable. Damn, she was pretty. "Oops, you're right. I'm sorry. But Keller, you might as well get used to us. We are psychics, after all. It isn't easy to *not* listen."

Even Ky's face split with a big, cheesy grin. "Yeah, big guy, mellow out. We're on your side, you know."

Keller kept his big Ranger mouth shut. Why shouldn't Ky be happy? He had Eden to go home to. Keller had shit to go home to.

But apparently Tucker had something to say. He nodded to Keller, then at his office.

Keller followed, certain he was on his way off this *team*, which would suit him fine.

"Sit," Tucker ordered the moment he cleared his door.

Keller took the chair nearest the exit, his eyes straight forward, his butt ready to be reamed.

"At ease, damn it. You're not Army anymore."

"Why not? You're still Navy," Keller said as evenly as he could manage without sarcasm. The sooner Tucker fired him, the better. He could get back to his carefully controlled life, and if he was lucky, another position within the Bureau. "Don't you guys always say, *'Once a SEAL, always a SEAL?'* Well, I'm still a Ranger." *So back off.*

"Shut the door," Tucker ordered.

Keller complied, not that closing the door prevented his psychic teammates from listening in.

Pursing his lips, Tucker assumed his position behind his desk, his ass in the chair, and his nose in the air. Lifting one hand, he scrubbed it over his big square chin, while Keller waited for USN words of wisdom he didn't want to hear.

To be fair, the rugged, unpolished man did have a well-deserved rep. Built like a brick wall, Tucker Chase *was* one of those tall, dark, and handsome hero types.

Over and over again, he *had* saved countless American servicemen and women while he'd served. After he left the Navy, he'd joined the Federal Bureau of Investigation. There, he'd accomplished something no one else could have when he pulled the Bureau's first team of psychics together, slapped a catchy handle on them, and made it work.

Keller just didn't want to be part of Tucker's Deuces Wild team. He didn't want to be that kind of 'special'. He wanted to be normal again, just one of the guys. Just not these guys.

"You're an empath," Isaiah Zaroyin said quietly from the corner opposite the door.

Keller's head jerked up at the unexpected comment. *Man, these psychic types are creepy. Just when you think you're alone, you aren't.* "Didn't know you were there."

Isaiah shrugged. Dressed professionally as usual in his stereotypical Men in Black's crisp black suit, white shirt, and black tie, the Tucker Chase look-alike seemed particularly gaunt this morning. Tired. Shadows rimmed his eyes and his cheeks were hollow. Gray.

That head of dark, curly hair and his blue eyes made Isaiah look younger than he was. But in fact, Isaiah Zaroyin was the old man of this team of mavericks. The only Level Ten psychic in the country, he was the real genius behind Deuces Wild. Eden, Ky, Tate Higgins, and Tucker Chase were just wannabes by comparison. Hell, so was Keller, only he'd never wanted the notoriety that came with this job, when people knew you were gifted. He worked best from the shadows, unknown, unseen, and unappreciated. That was who he was, just an average Joe doing his job, controlling the scene, and doing it right.

But Isaiah was the real deal. He actually could move mountains. Since he'd married Roxy Thurston, he'd changed from a nervous genius to a genuinely scary adult male with crazy psychic abilities. Tucker said his powers were growing. Keller didn't want to know what that meant.

"Unfortunately, it means I'm still scary," Isaiah offered a sincere but faint smile, tapping one elegant brow with a long finger as he met Keller's gaze.

"You heard?" *Of course, he heard.*

With a gentle nod, Isaiah closed his eyes and exhaled a controlled breath. He sank deeper into the chair, one arm cocked, one hand holding his forehead. Superman. That was who he looked and acted like. Make that Clark Kent. Mysterious but humble. Good-looking but capable of inflicting complete control on the psychically impaired—politically correct speak for normal folks.

Keller's antagonistic opinions fled as an empathetic wave of heartbreak, so bleak that it dimmed the bright ceiling lights, washed up from the floor like a flood. Make that a tsunami, the waves cresting up the length of his body and ending high over his head. Turning in his seat, he angled his shoulders and zeroed in on the source of the pain, Isaiah. What the hell was going on?

Isaiah seemed barely in control. Keller got the weirdest sensation he doubted himself, that he was afraid. But mostly? Isaiah's love for his wife battered Keller, nearly knocking him out of his chair to his knees. It wasn't Isaiah's sadness choking Keller, though. It wasn't anger. It was the raw, frightening pain of leaving her behind. Like the air and the stars in the sky and night and…Isaiah didn't want to leave this mortal life, especially Roxy! It clawed at him, and now it clawed at Keller, too.

"Where are you going?" Keller asked as evenly as he could. The rest of the room faded away as he focused on Isaiah, but damn. The bleakness radiating off the Level Ten filled Tucker's office to overflowing. Suffocating and dark, it was as thick and stiff as tar, and Keller was Uncle Remus's tar-baby. Stuck, his gift of empathy holding him fast.

Isaiah nodded that he now knew Keller was on board, that Keller sensed the real reason for his discomfort. He closed his eyes, and the stifling sensation evaporated. "Sorry. I can't always control it. Now you know what I'm up against." He cleared his throat, the muscles in his neck rigid. "At the moment, I'm going nowhere fast. Just like you, I'm stuck. I can't do the job I love, and I've become a danger to everyone around me."

"Including your wife and unborn child." Keller understood perfectly. That was the only good part of this extraordinary *gift* he'd been blessed with. Psychic empathy filled in the blanks when words failed.

Isaiah cupped his chin, his elbow still on the armrest as if his neck wasn't strong enough to hold his head. "But that's not the real problem. Most people's bodies fuel their brains and minds, but mine works in reverse. I think it pulls energy from the universe. I can't control it. It's an automatic reflex, like blinking, breathing, and heartbeats. Because of that, my brain never shuts off, and by default, my mind can't. What I can't deal with is the negative energy my *genuinely scary adult* mind produces. That's what you just felt. I can't sleep, and most times, I don't eat. I can't. It'll take over if I do."

"You're over-energized?" Keller murmured. *Whoever heard of that?* "Um, sorry. Didn't mean to—"

Isaiah tilted backward, bumping his head against the wall behind him. "Tell him, Tuck."

"Tell me what?"

The narrow empathetic tunnel between Keller and Isaiah expanded outward to include Tucker Chase.

Tucker huffed, blinking like he had something in his eyes all of a sudden. "There's a woman in Louisiana near New Orleans. You're going to visit her. She's a hundred and three, but word on the psychic street is she's got the same condition and power as Isaiah. She's a Level Ten, only she knows how to handle it."

Keller's hand lifted automatically to the back of his neck where a migraine had just mushroomed like an A-bomb over the Pacific. Empaths worked that way.

They suffered the same physical, emotional, or spiritual pain the person transmitting did, oftentimes more acutely than the transmitter. Mother Nature had a knack for enhancing the most peculiar traits in her prodigy. While Isaiah was transmitting one helluva mental cocktail, Tucker's pain was worse. He wasn't just angry at himself. He was pissed at not being able to fix Isaiah's problem, for being as helpless as Isaiah.

Keller bowed his head to shake the powerful sensations lapping at him from his boss and friend. If empathy was a gift, he didn't want it.

"I get why you're angry all the time, Keller," Isaiah said quietly, his voice softer than Keller had ever heard. "I know you don't want to be here. You don't like us. I understand. I do. One day you were a normal guy doing a bang-up job for the Bureau, and you had the world by the tail. Then lightning struck, and the next thing you know, you're tagging along with us like a newbie instead of leading the way. You're learning there's an entirely different, invisible world out there, one you still don't believe you belong in. Yet you never fit into that other world, did you? Not even when you were active duty and hiding what and who you were."

Wasn't that the truth? Keller stared at Isaiah instead of answering. But yeah. He'd had no idea how powerful his reaction to his first Army kill would be until the repercussion—his damned empathy for the bastard aiming a fifty-caliber rifle straight at him— slammed over him that day in Afghanistan. Self-defense hadn't made shooting that enemy sniper—a kid, for the love of God—any easier. And puking his guts up afterward had only made Keller look weak in front of his men.

But that day, he'd felt every barb of the twisted hate emanating from that teenage killer. Stupid kid was clutching a fully loaded, beat-to-death Kalashnikov in his sweaty hands. But deep inside, the hatred he'd been taught mingled with liquid yellow fear that ran down the kid's legs beneath those dirty pajama-like trousers. Only thirteen, he'd been promised he'd see Allah if he followed through with his divine, holy mission. There was nothing on earth worse than an overzealous, homegrown martyr, peeing himself and crying because he knew he was going to die.

*His name was Ahmed...*

Keller swallowed hard, remembering. Ahmed had been told to kill American soldiers. That was his mission. He'd meant to be brave and courageous. He'd meant to die a martyr's death to honor his parents. But he'd hesitated...

In the end, it all came down to the law of the jungle, kill or be killed. There'd been no other choice. Not for Ahmed. Not for Keller. The kid was armed, twitchy, and dangerous. There wasn't time to talk him out of his death wish. It was either him or Keller's men. So, Keller granted the wish. Ended the threat. Saved his men. Became a hero. Yeah, right. Killing a kid with a gun was the worst kind of hero to be.

But that was also when Keller discovered just how different he was. That no matter how he tried, he would forever share the last few moments of his target's terror, especially good kids or men like Ahmed. Which was why Keller had hidden his so-called *talent* for years. Didn't want it now. A fat lot of good empathy did in a world gone batshit crazy, when a man had to kill a kid.

Keller shot Isaiah a look from the corner of his eye. "I'm not mad at you." Which clearly targeted Tucker, but so what? Most of the world couldn't handle Tucker's brash, in-your-face, Navy SEAL ego.

"You just don't want to be here. I get it. You think we're a bunch of freaks, and you don't want the stink rubbing off on you," Tucker stated as undiplomatically as ever. He tipped back in his swivel chair, his elbows on the armrest, his long legs stretched forward for balance, and his fingers steepled beneath his big, square chin. Always the predator, his dark brown stare beneath intense thick brows seemed to see right through Keller.

He squared his shoulders and anted up. "What the fuck do you want me to do?"

Tucker opened his mouth, but Isaiah interrupted with, "Talk to her, Keller. That's all. Just go see her and learn what you can from her. If she's the real deal, you'll know the moment you shake her hand. If she'll let you. She may not. Psychics are funny about touch."

Yeah, whatever. Keller's need to get away from Tucker was growing stronger. "You got a name and address?"

"I'll text you what you'll need, only—" Tucker rolled forward and stuck his elbows on his desk. The vein that ran across his forehead when he lost his temper bulged thick and dark and tense.

"Only what?" Keller asked, impatient to be gone.

"Only I need you gone now. Grab your go-bag. It's late, but I've got a pilot on standby. He'll get you there by morning. Call when you touch down, the moment you make first contact. She lives east of New Orleans. I want hourly Sit Reps. I need to know what you know, as soon as you talk with her."

Who'd ever heard of hourly situation reports? "Why the rush?"

"Because I'm dying," Isaiah murmured from the darkness swelling around him. "And you're going to save me, Keller."

# Chapter Two

Savannah ran, her heart in her throat, wings on her bare feet, and her red rosary slapping like Mardi Gras beads around her neck. Today was the day. She could sense it. The willows whipping at her bare legs and arms as she ran through them declared it. The wind breathed it. Her beloved Gran Mere was dying. Worse, she'd predicted she'd be leaving today. Savannah just hadn't wanted to believe that the one-hundred and three-year-old matriarch of her family could actually foresee, much less predict, her own death. She'd predicted dire consequences before, even death, but those had all been more like curses cast upon others. Sure, they were still foretelling, and they came true, but choosing your personal day to die? Who did that?

So Savannah had refused to believe, and because of the pig-headed, stubborn denial she'd been born with, she'd wasted the morning feeding the scruffy cat that had arrived last night looking for clean water and a dry bed. Sanctuary. The name of Savannah's unwanted pet rehabilitation center that saved as many unwanted pets as she could manage. Just not her great grandmother.

She rushed up the gangplank to the houseboat Gran Mere called home. Back in 2005, Hurricane Katrina had capriciously grounded the boat three miles inland, far from the backwoods bayou where Gran Mere had lived most of her life. But oh, how she'd loved it here.

The air hung hot, humid, and heavy in these remote parts of Louisiana. Frogs and crickets chirped from the shade all day long. Katydids droned overhead in their relentless, grating way. An alligator rumbled somewhere off in the stands of drowned sycamores and oaks. Down the lane and just past the road, dying trees still stood knee deep in more water than they could handle since Katrina had cast her evil magic. Feathery fingers of silvery-gray Spanish moss dangled in the breeze from gnarled cypress trees. The giants of the bayou, their roots were forever planted in brackish swamp water, their twisted, scratchy branches reaching like arms and fingers to the sky.

Savannah loved this eccentric hideaway with every last bit of her wild and reckless heart. Everything about it was imbued with the life and love of the sassy lady who owned these few parcels. Gran Mere might not look nor act the part, but she was a proud property owner, and here in the South, that meant something.

Calming herself lest she burst into the houseboat like the reckless child she could still be, Savannah knocked quietly at the door that Gran Mere painted a vivid red only months ago.

*'Always choose to be a lady,'* Gran Mere would say. *'Even when folks are nasty to you, look them in the eye and don't stoop to their level. Don't be anything less than the true woman of worth you are. The world doesn't need any more crazy.'*

Wasn't that the truth?

"Come in, cher," came the weak reply from within.

Frightened now, because Gran Mere had never sounded so small nor so frail, Savannah stepped out of the messy world Nature created and into the refined, clean, and orderly world of a generation past. The scent of lavender, along with the lemon cleaner Gran Mere used religiously, suffused the welcome cool air that filled the cramped interior of the houseboat. Central air was what separated civilized folk from the rowdy Cajuns who also lived in the shadows of these same trees. Not that Gran Mere looked down on anyone. She would never. She just liked her comforts, and not sweating all day long was a big one in her book.

From the outside, the home still looked like a houseboat. But inside, it was magic and potions and the witchcraft Savannah had grown up with. Chantilly lace doilies, French antique china, as well as a human skull, raven feathers, and bundles of white sage smudge sticks adorned the two piece, mid-nineteenth century Louis XV china cabinet that dominated the small dining area, what sailors called a galley.

Opposite the cabinet, a triple back settee of the same French era boasted cut velvet, moss-green scroll work and rose-colored flowers on ivory silk filigree. Elegant. Gran Mere might be eccentric, but she was the most elegant woman Savannah had ever known.

Curled up in her red and black brocade bathrobe on the green settee, she was the epitome of elegance. A blood red boa draped her neck like a regal queen. Even in death, Gran Mere strived to be that Southern woman who would never be seen as anything less than proper. But her skin was too white this morning and her eyes too bright. Covering her mouth, she coughed politely into the white handkerchief clutched in her slender but bony fingers, then dabbed her lips and her nose to be sure she wouldn't offend.

Ever the genteel lady, she'd nonetheless raised two rowdy boys singlehandedly, then lost them both; the oldest, Stanley, to the Army, then to the Vietnam War. The younger, Gene, to the Navy, then to the road after he'd come home from some covert affair in Africa. By then he was older, yet he'd fathered Savannah's mother. When she succumbed to ovarian cancer when Savannah was a mere babe, Gene'd had enough. He dropped his only grandchild at Gran Mere's place and never looked back.

Since then Gran Mere had provided sanctuary for her orphaned great granddaughter, instead of letting the state, with its eternal lack of wisdom, take the little girl. It was also when Savannah began to learn the ways of what folks around here called the witch.

"It's time," Gran Mere whispered bravely, her voice as dry as an autumn leaf. "Come here, cher. Kneel beside me one last time. There are things you need to know."

Promptly, Savannah ran to the settee, dropped her knees to the soft cashmere Turkish carpet and obeyed. She sat back on her heels in case she needed to run if Gran Mere asked her to get something. Maybe one of her homemade potions. One of her scrolls where she'd written recipes of her brews. Or her doctor. Surely Doctor Rudy John would run to Gran Mere as quickly.

"Silly girl," Gran Mere said softly as she reached out and cupped Savannah's chin. Her hands were cold, but her eyes were as sharp as ever. Still seeing all. Still reading Savannah's thoughts as if Savannah had spoken them out loud. "I don't need a doctor. Not anymore. Wouldn't bother with one if I did. It's too late for worldly nonsense, and that man might think he's smart, but he hasn't a lick of the wisdom you do. You know that."

"I do know," Savannah murmured, her heart caught high in her throat, choking her. But still a silly enough girl to fear losing the only mother she'd ever known.

"I am going to miss you, cher," Gran Mere murmured, her beautiful blue eyes gone distant, the sparkling light deep within them dimming.

It was happening. Savannah pushed inside the safe circle of her great grandmother's arms, holding onto her one and only refuge although she knew she couldn't stop Death from stealing Gran Mere away. She was losing everything. Her world and her best friend. She swallowed hard, ashamed that now Gran Mere would know she wasn't strong enough to hold back her tears. Gran Mere had never cried. Not once.

Her fingertips tapped weakly at the back of Savannah's head. "Promise me you won't linger here once I'm gone, baby girl. I'll be with my Antonio. Let me go, Savannah. Look for the wild roses that grow deep in the bayou. Watch for the warlock. He holds a black magic in his heart, one only you can overcome. You alone hold the key to bring him down, my dearest. Whatever happens, be fearless and strong. Be the blessing the world needs more than it ever needed me."

"But I need you," Savannah cried out as her heart broke. "I'm not brave. I'm not! And I don't know enough. Not yet. I'll never, ever know enough to let you go!" If that whiney rant didn't make her sound like a petulant child, nothing would. How her fingers ached to cling tightly to the only mother she'd ever known, who even now, was slipping away.

But that was not how life worked, and Savannah knew full well she wasn't strong enough to hold back the grains of sand in the unforgiving hourglass called Time. Grain by grain. Breath by breath. She knew the instant Gran Mere's spirit fled her tired, old body. It just lifted out of her like a spirit set free. All the stiff, uppityness Gran Mere was known for throughout the parish drained out of her on the quietest sigh. Her last breath.

As if she could stop the inevitable, Savannah pulled Gran Mere's frail body against her one last time. But it was too late. Like the wind on an old tin roof on a hot summer day, Gran Mere was gone. Her body was still warm, but with the kind of warmth in the jacket you'd taken off and set aside. The cooling down kind of warm.

*Rap! Rap! Rap!* A snappy knock at the front entry crashed the deafening stillness of the tender, tragic moment. Squeezing her eyes against the deluge of tears lurking in her heart, Savannah began the chant to expel the idiot from Gran Mere's narrow porch.

"Leave and never come back," she murmured as she pressed her nose into her great grandmother's cheek and cried like the lost child she was once again. The lovely scent of rosewater filled her senses, but this time hope did not spring eternal. The deed was done. The woman who'd brought those roses to life on her skin was eternally gone. Gran Mere had left them behind, too.

*Rap! Rap! Rap!*

Savannah's eyes narrowed. "Leave and never come back," she repeated, then repeated it again and again, banishing the troll who would dare disturb this sacred place, now of all times. "Leave and never—ever—come back."

# Chapter Three

Keller cocked his head, sure he'd heard voices coming from inside this bizarre excuse for a home. It was too damn early in the morning, and the air was already sauna hot. He'd flown straight from Reagan National Airport in Virginia, to Louis Armstrong International Airport, New Orleans, well after midnight. From there, he'd rented a fast car, a Camaro of all things, hooked onto I-10, and raced across the southernmost portion of the mighty Lake Pontchartrain to the city of Slidell.

The woman he'd been sent to retrieve, one Mariposa Church, lived east of Slidell, near the western edge of the Pearl River Wildlife Management Area, which put her damned near in Florida. Which meant ticks, chiggers, mosquitos, and fleas aplenty, not a pleasant homecoming for a Southern boy who'd been away too long, and who, if not for Isaiah, wouldn't be here now. But here Keller was, standing in early morning sweltering humidity of St. Tammany Parish at Mariposa Church's front door, trying to maintain his customary professional demeanor while sweat trickled down his neck, his back, and into the back of his pants. It didn't get any better than this.

More derelict than home, the boathouse lacked the slightest hint of proper maintenance. The paint had long since peeled fore to aft. Moss crept up the rotting gangplank like an encroaching green army. On the southern side, the several pecan trees leaning into each other needed staking and serious pruning before they'd produce any pecans, which was too bad. Keller loved fresh pecan pie. Gaunt and gangly, their branches sported barely any signs of life, certainly no tender sprouts, which they should have by now. It was spring after all.

But that mighty oak on the north side, the one dragging its brittle branches over the houseboat's roof like wicked witch fingers? That poor old thing had to go, sooner than later. It'd probably drowned when the last hurricane to make land pushed inland. The old guy's impressive deep tap root hadn't been able to handle saltwater. Even the smallest tidal surges would've been enough to kill it, though there was no standing water nearby that Keller could see now. Not like it mattered. The damage was done. It'd only take one stiff wind to bring that giant down on this derelict, wannabe houseboat and crush everyone inside.

Things would be different if Keller owned this piece of junk. He'd renovate the houseboat, landscape the surrounding acreage, and he'd trim those trees. Hell, he'd plant new trees. He'd control Mother Nature even as he let her close in and block out the rest of the world. That was what he'd do. But this wasn't his land and he didn't have time for pipe dreams.

Pursing his lips in frustration—because he had heard voices inside, yet no one had answered—Keller knocked again. Louder. Brasher. Determined to get whatever secret this old woman possessed back to Isaiah in time. Damn, it was hot. Washington, DC knew sweltering heat, but spring in the District was nothing compared to spring in the bayou. How did people stand to live where merely stepping outdoors could parboil them at the crack of dawn?

Known as the '*Northshore*' because of its location on Lake Pontchartrain, affluent St. Tammany Parish was where the high class, well-to-do folks, those who wanted to stay near, but not in New Orleans, lived. Here they could avoid the riffraff, hucksters, gangsters, and the drama of living in the high-powered, take-your-chances, watch-your-step Big Easy. But enough common folk lived here too, especially along the undeveloped shores of the bayou.

"Damn it, talk to me. I don't have all day," he cussed as he glared at the lackluster surroundings he'd trudged through since parking his rental nearly a mile away.

Virginia creeper, moss, and kudzu had taken over everything around this shabby house. Weeds even covered what he suspected were two Adirondack chairs on what might have at one time been a decent concrete patio. The lumps under all those vines could've been chairs. Hell, they could've been Chinese stone temple dogs for all he knew, the weeds were that thick.

But just like back at the Deuces Wild office with Isaiah, there was a malevolent presence here. The feeling at the back of Keller's neck was eerie, as if someone were standing in the dark shade of the cypress trees. Watching. Warning. Urging him to run. To hurry and leave and never come back.

He shook it off and once again raised his fist to knock when the door swung open. Caught off guard, Keller all but fell into the deepest, angriest, chocolate eyes he'd ever seen. The young woman standing there was dressed in a skimpy, pink tank top pulled over faded denim shorts that enhanced her already long, glamourous mocha-colored legs. She was one of those incredibly welcome sights for sore eyes. Red crystal beads hung around her neck, leading to a crucifix tucked between her breasts. A rosary. Didn't it figure? He huffed at the sight. Louisiana's culture was a crazy mix of heathen voodoo and Christian.

But she wasn't happy to see him. Her chin jutted forward. Her slender fingers came to rest over two softly-rounded hips that shouldn't have gotten past Keller's professional, guarded perimeter. But they did. This lush woman was stark, raving beautiful in a way he hadn't expected. Gorgeous, came to mind. Right on its heels, *goddess*. And something else he couldn't put his finger on. Childlike? Nah, that couldn't be it. The anger humming off this woman like electricity from a downed powerline raised the tiny hairs on the back of his neck.

Her bare feet were spread in outrageous defiance. Her chin, though elegant, tipped up like a wall. Even her tiny, straight toes, the nails painted a delicious blood red that reminded him of cherries and further accentuated her richly tanned skin, were tapping out a storm warning.

*Day-um.* This wasn't the old woman he'd expected to answer the door. Uh uh. This gal was a thousand times better. Prettier. Younger. Full of life and hair-raising vitality that reached out and all but slapped him across the face. Hard.

Long, athletically-toned legs. Tiny waist. Lord-help-me-cleavage that tested the fabric of her cotton top to its limit. Straight black hair hung to her shoulders, while blunt cut bangs framed a hostile but intelligent face. She was a melting pot of ethnicities all by herself.

The rich, deep color of her skin bordered on coffee with a good dose of sweet, rich, melt-in-your-mouth cream. All by itself, it bespoke a mixed heritage Keller couldn't precisely define. Perhaps Asian? Her eyes were more almond-shaped than round. Perhaps African too? Her nose flared just enough to make him wonder. Perhaps both with a dash of Caucasian thrown in as well? Not that he cared. Keller had learned long ago how little bigotry meant.

He knew the second her expressive brows narrowed and the thickest, blackest lashes he'd ever seen blinked out a definite, *'Get the hell off my porch!'* This fierce woman was not to be toyed with. He should've backed off. He certainly should've known better. But his cock chose that precise damned second to stand up and take notice. The damned thing wanted an introduction. *Really? Now?*

He hadn't had that reaction in, well, years. For reasons he didn't want to analyze, Keller took an involuntary step backward. He wasn't intimidated, but he was smart enough to recognize a mental push when he felt one. Okay, so this young thing was not only gorgeous but psychically gifted. He was used to folks like that.

Shaking off her gentle push of impending doom—because he'd never backed down from anyone or anything in his life—Keller spread his feet and steadied his stance, not willing to be pushed any farther. Determined to do what he could to help Isaiah sooner than later, he stuck out one hand and relied on standard, every day FBI protocol. "Good morning, ma'am. Sorry to disturb you, but I'm from Washington, and I've come a long way to speak with—"

"Don't care where you're from and don't want what you're selling, mister," she bit out as she crossed her arms, drawing his attention to two small breasts now pleasantly plumped together and pointed directly at him. "This here's private property. You're trespassing. Beat it."

Hot damn. It'd been years since Keller had been distracted by the mere sight of a woman's body, but that tiny, pink tee was way too small for even the hand-sized packages beneath it. And those soft, warm packages would fit his palms. Nicely.

The sparks flying out of those wells of mystery were too much to ignore. Of all the things he'd never expected, his damned cock sprang to standing-room-only in his briefs. Clearing his throat, Keller tried again, his hand still extended even as he willed his body to, *'Stand the fuck down already!'*

"FBI Special Agent Boniface, ma'am. If I could just talk to you, I'm sure—"

"I'm busy. I said go, and don't come back."

"That was not a request," he told her just as adamantly, pulling his hand back since courtesy hadn't gotten him anywhere. "I have business to discuss with Mariposa Church, not you. This is her place, right?"

"This is not a good day," the young woman declared, a definite edge in her tone. "Mizz Church, she... she doesn't have time for whatever you're peddling."

There was something soft and plaintive in her tone, but Keller was task-driven, and bottom line, Isaiah didn't have time to waste. "Sorry ma'am, but this is the only day I'll be in town. I have business to discuss with Miss Church, not you, now please. Either take me to her or get out of my way."

The cold disdain shadowing this woman's countenance called his bluff. Thrusting her chin forward, she enunciated, "I. Said. No. Leave this place and don't come back."

Why did those words feel familiar, as if he'd *felt* them before? And why did he get that same eerie, *I'm-watching-you* sensation, as if this little thing could pack a punch behind that angry command and make him leave if she wanted to? "You did hear me say I was FBI, didn't you?"

Her eyes popped. "Are you threatening me?"

He raised the ante. "Do I need a warrant? Is that what it'll take just to talk to Mariposa Church? Because I can do that if you won't listen to reason."

"You wouldn't dare," she hissed even as she wiped the corner of her eye and...

*Aw, shit. She's crying.* Keller took a voluntary step back that time, pissed at himself for not catching onto what was going on. He was a psychic empath. He should've recognized her pain. He should've felt it. This woman wasn't angry. She was defensive and sad and... so beautiful it nearly hurt to look at her.

"I can help if you let me," he offered quietly. "Trust me. Whatever you're up against, I can help. That's my job."

Her nostrils flared even as her full lush lips pinched into a thin line. "I don't need your help, mister, now please. Just get off Gran Mm-m-m... I mean, m-my porch and..."

He couldn't make his eyes move away from the pain he now clearly saw. This woman was tender yet fierce, gentle but determined and stubborn, not traits he usually cared for in the fairer sex. But they lit her from the inside out like candles glowing behind the loveliest stained-glass windows.

Awareness came to him on a stifling wave of Louisiana humidity. Keller's hand went automatically to his chest where a black hole was now sucking the sunlight out of the day. He sensed bottomless grief hollowing her soul even as she stood there brave and ready to fight him—the last thing he wanted. He wasn't there to fight, especially not her. He reached out his other hand, needing to touch her. This young woman was barely holding it together, and empathy demanded he help her—if only to alleviate the same pain now hollowing him like a razor-sharp melon baller.

But she stepped back. Damn it.

Yes, that contact would've been devastating—to him—but touching her was the only way Keller could complete the connection between them. At the moment, he was an overloaded circuit with no release. All the negative power channeling from this woman was on a one-way, dead-end track that would fry his circuits.

He'd learned the hard way. He was the receiver and she was the transmitter. Only as usual, his mind wasn't strong enough to contain all her negative energy. It was too much. He had to give something back—and soon—or risk an overload that would manifest one ungodly killer migraine. He'd end up incapacitated for days. Empathy was never a one-way street. Like karma, it was a giver and taker. It demanded balance. In one way or another, comfort had to be exchanged for grief and pain. Forgiveness for sin. Sooner than later. Before he lost his mind.

Keller faltered as the son-of-a-bitchin' auras that preceded his migraines began their inevitable dance of agony at the edge of his peripheral. "Please. Let me help," he said as evenly as he could. "Tell me what your great grandmother needs." *Before I go blind from this headache and embarrass myself.*

The instant those words fell from his lips, the details of his intended subject's life came back to him. Oh yeah. Mariposa Church. One hundred and three years old. Born in New Mexico to a wandering Cajun alcoholic. But Max Butterfield never married her mother, Grace Finley. They gave birth to three daughters before he killed Grace one particularly dark and drunken night, turned his bloody knife on Mariposa's two older sisters, then killed himself as well.

Mariposa was the only survivor of the bloody crime. She'd spent years in a loving foster home before she'd married Antonio Church and moved with him to his hometown, New Orleans. After he died an early death, she took to the brackish waters of the deepest bayou. Known as a gifted, sighted psychic, she read palms and tarot cards for a meager living. When her two sons passed, she took in the last of her dismally sad line, her great granddaughter, one Savannah Charisma Church.

Who had to be the beautiful woman confronting Keller now. The one whose bottom lip quivered as a sheen of unshed tears extinguished the fiery sparks in her eyes. "No, you can't help," she murmured, her voice soft and broken. "It's too late. No one can help her now."

Which meant the old woman was dead, and Isaiah was screwed. Talk about bad timing. Keller had arrived on what had to be the worst day of the young Miss Church's life.

He stepped forward when she wiped her face again. "May I?" he asked politely as he reached for her hand, desperate to release the thrumming energy dammed up in his head, but just as desperate to lessen her pain. Migraine be damned, he could help this woman if she'd just let him. That was his true gift, helping the broken hearted when no one else could.

But she said, "No." Standing there like a teary stone wall, yet falling apart at the same time, needing someone to lean on, but not willing to let it be him, Miss Church resisted his help.

Once again, Keller pulled back and stopped being the hero. Kindness wasn't getting him anywhere, not today. He had to get out of there. It might already be too late. He mentally tallied the pain meds this migraine would demand. The ice packs. A pitch-black cave to hide in until his retinas could tolerate light again would be a blessing, but he doubted he could find one before the suffocating pain took over. If big, brash Tucker Chase only knew what a pansy he'd hired...

"I'm sorry I bothered you," Keller said sincerely as the first lightning strikes of what would soon be pure agony lanced from left to right across his frontal lobe. The aura now dominated most of his line of sight, all but blinding him. He was operating on empathy alone. Vomiting would soon follow. "And I'm sorry for your loss. I'm sure your great grandmother meant everything to you."

Reaching inside his jacket, he fingered a business card up from an inner pocket and handed it over, fighting to control the tremor at his fingertips. "I'll be in town until tonight if you change your mind. If you need anything, please don't hesitate to call. That's my cell number. As I said, I'm FBI Agent Boniface. Call me anytime."

Mental note to self: *Sleep with your damned cell under your pillow in case she does call.*

Savannah Church took the card. But when it crumpled in her fist like so much garbage, Keller's last hope for sweet relief died. He turned to leave before he was too blind to walk or before he threw up. Empathy migraines struck hard, and they were brutal. He forced his feet not to run even as he knew he was out of time. Retreat, especially on his hands and knees, was not his style. His heels had barely hit the end of the gangplank when he heard a whispered, "Thank you for your service."

How did she know? Unlike the rest of his team, Keller couldn't read minds, only feelings, and this woman was a cast of thousands. Even an ungifted man would've felt the boundless sorrow washing off her and spilling into him. She was that overflowing pitcher of sorrow, and it was cold and black, and it was killing her. He truly was an overflowing cup. Only his cup overflowed with other people's darkness, pains, and sins.

The grief he could understand, but the fear quivering inside this woman like a hiccup she couldn't expel, was something else again. Might be the unknown future all survivors faced. Losing a loved one pushed vulnerable people into uncharted waters where they didn't want to go. Women who'd never worked were forced into a dog-eat-dog workforce to take minimum wage jobs, to learn how to handle home finances and auto repairs. Men who'd never learned to cook, well, they usually starved until they acquired numbers or apps for every pizza parlor in delivery distance. Children too young to care for themselves went to family that often didn't want them or worse, handed them over to state institutions for any number of sniveling 'good' reasons.

His migraine roiled like a living beast inside the cramped confines of his skull, beating him for what he'd lived through when his wife had died at the tender age of twenty-two. Life was incredibly unfair. Why should it be any different for this young woman?

*But why did it have to be as tough?*

He couldn't just leave. "You have psychic skills," he said as he turned around.

"W-what?" she asked as her big brown eyes widened with disbelief and her ever-ready dose of hostility hit an all-time high. "I've got skills? That's all you've got to say?"

Interesting. She hadn't denied her psychic talents, just didn't like him mentioning them.

"I also said I was sorry for your loss," Keller reminded her gently. He ached to rush back up that gangplank and hold this woman, but not for his gratification. The migraine he could live with. He'd survived enough of them before. Only most times there'd been no way to complete that demanding cosmic circle of give and take. Evil men and women simply did not want to be touched, but if he'd had to kill someone in the line of duty, well. He could kiss that much needed psychic connection goodbye, and *'Hello Excedrin headache number one million forty-five.'*

But this was different. This was Mariposa's great granddaughter. More than anything, she needed to know she wasn't alone, that someone who'd shown up on the worst day of her life, even a hard-nosed, pain-in-the-ass Ranger, could genuinely care for the stranger he'd just met.

Keller played it cool and stayed put, not wanting to frighten her more than he already had. "Is there someone I can call for you, ma'am? At least let me do that before I leave."

Swallowing hard, she shook her head. "I'll be fine."

"I doubt that, but okay," he said, summoning the strength to maintain a professional FBI vibe. It was early morning, but the day was already so hot and humid, he could barely breathe. A steady trickle of sweat ran down the center of his back, and his pounding head felt heavy, ready to implode. "Well, you've got my number."

"Thanks. Yes. I'll call if—"

*'If and when hell freezes over,'* Keller thought as he shook off the oddest sensation of sparks beneath his skin. Once again, he began the trek to his car and its air conditioner. The cool air might stall the migraine until he made it to a hotel. It could work. If he hurried.

"Bacon."

Keller froze at that softly spoken word. Was it a lure or a threat? Did she plan to feed him or turn him into dinner for some nearby alligator? Allowing the smallest smile to breach his dry lips, he cranked his stiff neck and turned one last time to face Miss Church. "Excuse me?"

Still at her front door, she lifted her chin and declared, "I said bacon. Listen, Mr. Secret Agent Man, if you help me get through the next couple hours, I'll... I'll..." The cords in her throat worked extra-hard. "I'll fix breakfast, and, umm, well, all my dogs come when I say bacon, so I figured..."

*That I could be lured with bacon, too.* Keller let the insult hang. Being called a dog by anyone else would've offended him, but dogs *were* better than most people he knew, and maybe soon this stubborn woman would let him at least shake her hand.

"I accept," he replied as the first of what would soon become many opaque spinning vortexes completely obscured the rest of his twenty/twenty vision. This migraine promised suffering. But if the reprieve the younger Mizz Church had just offered allowed the smallest chance to get her through this day, he'd suck up the pain and endure.

# Chapter Four

The second she invited him inside, Savannah knew she'd made a mistake. This black-suited FBI agent took up all the air in the place even as he filled it. It seemed to hiss around his frame in its hurry to escape when he ducked through the narrow front door and into Gran Mere's home. Tall and lean, he was as tawny as a lion. Probably as deadly, too.

Her hackles lifted.

"I am sorry for your loss," he repeated, his voice an odd blend of control, concern, and something she couldn't yet define. "When did she pass?"

"Just before you, umm, knocked," Savannah admitted as she took a moment to size him up.

The mental push she'd flared a few minutes ago should've knocked his ass off her porch, but it hadn't. That by itself was concerning. Her mental pushes worked on everyone else 'round these parts. Why not this guy? Maybe FBI agents had special training for that kind of thing? Were they psychic too? Because Agent Boniface wasn't just smart. He was—something else.

He did carry himself with a certain lethal charm, though. Shoulders back. Former military if that closely shaved head of his meant what she suspected. There was just enough stubble to prove the color was dark blond. Not brown. Not gold. Dusty. As if someone had sprinkled gold over sand and called it hair.

His black striped suit looked expensive. Pressed and immaculate, it was completely and utterly out of place, just like his white shirt. Silly man also wore a cotton t-shirt under that shirt. In this heat, he'd soon be pit-stained and sweaty.

His trousers were pleated but not rumpled despite the humidity of the day, the norm for Louisiana this time of year. Which was odd. He had to have walked through plenty of brush and weeds to get here, yet his black shoes still shone to a luster. If she cared to, Savannah expected she could see her reflection in that leather. Stuffy, uptight man must've dusted them off before he'd banged on the door.

Which made him interesting in an outdated, pretentious kind of way. Special Agent Keller Boniface was Gran Mere's favorite rerun all over again. He was Sergeant Friday, the stuffy cop from her beloved *"Dragnet."*

Which set off Savannah's radar all over again. He was everything she wasn't, a by-the-books, *just the facts, ma'am'* kind of guy. Uptight. Masculine. A veritable straight arrow. And he'd been in control since he'd knocked on her door. He'd taken charge.

That disturbed Savannah more than anything, because Special Agent Boniface also seemed extraordinarily sincere. She'd tried to disguise her feelings, but this guy had a way of looking through her, as if he knew precisely how badly her broken heart hurt. How fragile and vulnerable she was now that Gran Mere was gone. Not only interesting, but darned disconcerting. Used to controlling most situations, Savannah wanted him gone before he looked any closer.

"I am sorry I disturbed your last moment with your great grandmother," he said gently. "I shouldn't have bothered you so early today, and I certainly shouldn't have knocked as hard as I did."

"No, she was already gone, and I... I..." Gulping at what she'd just admitted, Savannah stared at her great grandmother in case she—needed anything? "Gran Mere said this would happen. She knew she was leaving today, but she never mentioned..." *Y.O.U. Not unless you're the warlock she warned me about, in which case I have no idea what to do with you.*

He made a sound in the back of his throat. "But you chose not to believe."

It was clear he'd dealt with death and disbelievers before. Were all FBI agents this observant? This over-the-top in charge and this... this handsome? She could barely tear her eyes away from him. They seemed bewitched or bedazzled or—something.

"No, I... I..." What could Savannah say? That her great grandmother had always been prone to wild prognostications and dreams as well as blessed with vivid sight? That she could tell the future as accurately as a learned historian could recite the past? Who in their right mind would believe that? "It's just that she told me so many incredible things over the years, that I—"

"You chose to believe what was the easiest to swallow. So to speak."

She answered with a noncommittal shrug even as she struggled to catch her breath. This ruggedly handsome Yankee seemed able to read her mind, not what Savannah needed when her only living relative had just passed away. Why was it suddenly so warm in here?

"We should let her doctor know she's gone," Sergeant Friday advised. "Do you want me to do that for you or—? Excuse me. I'm sorry, but you are Savannah Church, right?"

"Just Savannah," she breathed, her gaze riveted on Gran Mere to keep from asking this stranger if he was real or magic, if he was the warlock, or if he knew who the warlock was.

"Mariposa was your grandmother?" He already knew that, and she had a feeling he'd already known her name, too. Why'd he ask?

"My great grandmother. M-my Gran Mere." She swallowed hard at the quandary she found herself in. At one hand, her precious Gran Mere lay in peaceful repose like an angel. At her other hand, stood this breathtakingly beautiful, but extremely capable stranger, who was so not her type. Not that Savannah had a type. She wasn't experienced. She didn't have a type or preference.

But Special Agent Boniface was intensely male. His stone face bore the requisite square Superhero chin, while those piercingly perceptive amber eyes betrayed barely concealed emotions beneath their calm surface. Still waters, that was what he was—the stillest waters in the bayou where the oldest living alligator cached its prey. Where it would lie in wait for hours until some unsuspecting catfish, long-legged bird, or land animal strayed.

He removed his jacket and hung it on the back of a nearby chair. His tie went next, tucked into his pocket. Then he folded up those long legs, and crouched at Gran Mere's side. *Oh, my my my.* Not only was he handsomely attractive, but Agent Boniface was also armed. His jacket had concealed a leather holster looping over his shoulders. It ended with two hefty pockets positioned securely under his arms, both sporting identical pistols. That were probably loaded.

Not that Savannah was afraid of guns. She knew how to shoot the double barrel shotgun stashed behind Gran Mere's front door. She had to. Everyone in these parts carried when outdoors, and most of the time, indoors as well. You didn't call the bayou home for long if you ascribed to the liberal agenda of waiting around for the police to come protect you. Alligators, panthers, and the occasional Anaconda slithering across her porch or sunning itself in the weeds didn't wait before they ate you alive.

Yet as surprised as Savannah was to see those two hefty weapons, she wasn't fearful of this guy or his guns. Despite his size and bulk, Agent Boniface had been nothing but a gentleman so far. A handsome, remote gentleman whom she still wanted to leave.

She couldn't make herself stop looking at him as he knelt beside Gran Mere, though. It happened slowly. Sergeant Friday reached for Gran Mere's wrinkled cheek. Savannah held her breath. His confirming what she already knew—that Gran Mere was gone—would hurt.

He did have nice hands. Big, wide, and callused, both ended at neatly squared-off fingers. His nails were clean and trimmed, with perfect half-moons at the cuticle. But when he touched Gran Mere...

When he cupped her jaw tenderly as if she were a precious treasure...

When he whispered, "Be at peace, Mariposa. Your work here is done. We've got the watch now..."

Savannah's heart collapsed into a soggy lump of grits. The exquisite tenderness in that single contact revealed a true gentleman and a man who valued the fairer sex. Who was, or had once, been loved by a lady. This wasn't just a distasteful job for Agent Boniface. It wasn't something to get over and done with as quickly as possible. No. He'd treated Gran Mere as if she were not only a person, but a queen. Perhaps the same way he treated his mother. Or his wife.

Sadness washed over Savannah like the gentle tide at the end of a hard day. Agent Boniface wasn't anything like Sergeant Friday after all.

His index finger strayed to Gran Mere's cheek and tucked that perpetually unruly strand of long gray hair behind her ear. "How long has she lived out here in the middle of nowhere?"

That got Savannah's heart, too. "She... she owned this houseboat all my life, but it wasn't here until a few years ago."

His brow spiked. "Hurricane?"

Savannah nodded. "Katrina. Tidal surge. You know."

"I suspected as much," he said as his sharp eyes scanned Gran Mere's deathly pallor.

She lay there on her lovely settee with her lips curled into a small smile, as if passing away had been everything she'd expected it to be. By then, a lovely golden glow infused every bit of her skin. With her long white hair spread over her shoulders like a mantle, she looked otherworldly. Peaceful. Almost angelic. As if she still knew precisely what she'd done and where she was going. As if everything would be okay.

Savannah dashed a tear away before Agent Boniface saw it. She didn't need pity from a stranger. But why was his chest heaving? Tiny pinpoints of sweat beaded his brow and dotted the clean-shaven skin above his upper lip. His cheeks were flushed, too. *My goodness, is he hyperventilating?*

"Are you thirsty? I've got lemonade or ice water if you prefer." *Or will you faint like a girl?*

"No, thank you, I'm good," he replied quickly. But his voice had changed from businesslike to a deep and ruggedly gruff growl. His tan had faded. He wasn't anywhere near feeling '*good*'.

"Then what's wrong?" she asked, projecting a calm energy she didn't feel, but which usually worked on her dogs. Most guys were no different. This man was suffering nearly as much as that pittie she'd recently rescued from Wilford Duckett's illegal dogfighting ring. Scarred, wounded, and ready to fight anyone who came near him, that poor boy had snarled and lashed out at everything and everyone, including the metal crate Sheriff Douglas transported him in. By the time he was safe inside a clean kennel at Sanctuary, his entire body frothed with sweat and he'd foamed at the mouth.

Everyone else that day had labeled him unfit for human company. Everyone but Savannah. They'd wanted him euthanized immediately, and that day, they were right. Sir Galahad was a vicious dog back then. Unpredictable and feral, he'd been kept penned and forced to fight ever since he'd been a puppy. He'd been mistreated and starved. But if any of those people took the time to come visit him today—which no one ever did—they'd know they'd judged him by just one slice of a pitiful life that, until Sanctuary, had been sheer Hell.

*One puzzle piece does not the whole picture make.*

While Agent Boniface wasn't frothing or foaming at the mouth—yet—Savannah could tell by the energy he projected he was fast reaching a breaking point like Sir Galahad had back then. Which begged the question, why was Agent Boniface here if he was under so much stress? Was he scared? A coward? Or was the FBI so desperate that they sent just anyone who was available? To make matters worse, she still didn't know what he'd wanted with Gran Mere.

A tiny groan escaped him. "How...?" He sucked in a deep breath. "Damn it. This is all wrong. I'm supposed to be helping you."

Which meant he did need help. Savannah stared him down. "Me? You're the one in pain, Agent Boniface. What's going on with you? Is it the heat? Are you sick?" *Are you going to die on me, too?*

"I'm not sick." What a bold lie. He was too sick. "This isn't about me. It's—it's about your great grandmother."

Like heck it was. Savannah touched him then. She reached out and laid her hand on the masculine, overheated forearm beneath that pressed, white shirt and—

*Whoosh!* Pure white energy sizzled up her fingertips and through the bones in her arm. On its heels, an unlikely shot of lust blossomed in her core. Her nipples hardened. She could barely catch her breath at the blinding deluge of... of... sexual arousal that came out of nowhere.

This guy was burning hot in every possible way. Physically. Psychically. Emotionally. Maybe even spiritually. Worse, he knew! Special Agent Boniface knew everything she was feeling the second she touched him!

Savannah jerked her hand back as quickly as she would from a hot stove. "You're him. You're the warlock Gran Mere told me to watch out for. You're him. You're real."

"That's the dumbest thing I've ever heard," he groused, though he was obviously on the verge of passing out. Still crouched by Gran Mere, he rested one elbow to his knee and cupped his forehead. "It's just a migraine," he said to the floor. "It comes and goes. Makes it hard to see. Maybe I will have that drink."

"Maybe you should." The man was not telling the truth. He didn't need a drink, but Savannah understood. It wasn't that he'd meant to lie to her. He just didn't know her well enough to admit to weakness in front of her.

Hurriedly, she walked over to the kitchen which, despite the grand antiques that dominated Gran Mere's home, comprised the same open space where she now rested in peace. For all her eccentricities, Gran Mere had never ascribed to the logic of building a real house to accommodate all of her abundant, outrageous lifestyle. She'd believed in squeezing everything in, making do, and wearing out. Which she had certainly done with herself.

Running the faucet until the water turned cool, Savannah filled a blue metal tumbler and returned to his side. "Here. Drink slowly. You might want to sit down, too." *Before you fall down.* The last thing she needed was a guy the size of Agent Boniface passed out on the floor when Gran Mere's doctor arrived. How would she explain that to RJ? "I've got aspirin if you need any."

"No. Please. I'm fine. It'll pass. Don't be afraid," Agent Boniface murmured, even as he tipped his head back and gulped the water. His gaze hit the carpet as soon as he drained the glass.

Wasn't that interesting? He couldn't bring himself to look her in the eye, but he expected Savannah to trust him. "You are not well, sir."

"No, I'm fine. Really. I just tend to get, umm, emotional, when I see things like this." He nodded at Gran Mere. "Tell me about her."

"Then look at me," Savannah demanded. He might as well. She was the one who'd just lost everything.

Yet when he lifted his chin and met her gaze, his amber eyes glistened like he was the one suffering. Heat flushed his cheeks. Moisture, not sweat, spiked his long, lush eyelashes. Tears. This man was hiding tears. It was as if Gran Mere's passing was his loss, too. As if he felt every bit of Savannah's pain.

"You can't see me clearly, can you?" she asked. "I'm fuzzy. Out of focus."

He looked away, and she understood. Agent Boniface had lost control. He was embarrassed and angry that she'd seen him in less than macho condition. Which gave her the edge. "You certainly have a tender heart for a federal agent."

"No. I don't," he stated unequivocally, blinking, probably to get himself under control. He took a quick swipe over his eyes and set the glass on the end table near Gran Mere's head. "Listen. Someone needs to take care of your great grandmother before I leave. I can call the police or a doctor. I'll wait here with you."

"I never knew my mother," Savannah said. It was time he knew. "Gran Mere raised me since I was a baby."

"I know. She was the reason I came here. Had she been ill long?"

"She was a hundred and three. What do you think?"

"I think people tend to pass from actual illnesses even at her age."

"Not Gran Mere. She planned to die on the fiftieth anniversary of her husband's death, so she did."

Agent Boniface canted his head. "She did? Just like that—" He snapped his fingers. "She set a date and then... she died?"

*Died...*

*Died...*

*Died...*

The finality in that word reached out and bitch slapped Savannah square in the heart. She couldn't breathe. It was true. Her beloved Gran Mere was gone. She'd never teach Savannah another one of her potions, teas, or brews. There'd be no more of her special spicy crawdad stir-fry with turnip greens, sunchokes, and bok choy. No more late night sleep-overs. No giggles or laughter. No ghost stories and no phone calls just to hear her sweet voice. No more afternoon fish fries. No more deep-frying gator nuggets on the back-porch fryer. No more midnight trolling for largemouth bass on Lake Pontchartrain.

The houseboat would never again fill with the scent of the chicory coffee she'd ground from scratch. There'd be no more gigging frogs on moonless nights, nor feeding gators that came like trick-or-treaters at Gran Mere's beck and call.

*One door closes. Another door opens.*

Suddenly, everything was too hard. The room tilted, and Savannah found herself caught in Special Agent's strong, and oh, so capable arms. On his feet now, he rested one big hand at the small of her back, keeping her from falling. The other grasped her bicep as he pressed her into full body contact. His chest to her breasts. His pounding heart to her pounding heart. A full breath of air hissed out of him, but there was that feeling of safety again. Of having been caught. Of being found.

Breathing hard through her nose so she didn't pass out, Savannah pressed her palms over his strong collarbones and tipped her forehead to the center of his shirt and the sculpted, muscle beneath it. This man was a wall of comfort, not just physically. That 'something else' she'd sensed since the moment he'd shown up was an amazing deep well of empathy. She'd never met another who shared her gift.

Yet his version was different. Disjointed, like a chain missing a link. Aware that his pulse had quickened along with hers when she'd touched him, Savannah sent another push into him, this one of empathy and understanding. That was when she knew what it had cost him to enter Gran Mere's humble home. He'd been nearly blind when he'd crossed the threshold, going on instinct. That he'd offered genteel compassion when he'd been on the verge of collapse spoke volumes. Yet Agent Boniface had handled himself as if nothing was amiss, his other senses on alert, masking his frailty. He was a rare man indeed.

As she let herself be comforted by the sheer size of his body and his unique empathy for her loss, Savannah gave back the same understanding to the strong, yet vulnerable man in her arms. Within seconds Agent Boniface relaxed, which was precisely what she'd intended. Because she very much needed the gentle strength pouring out of him, enveloping her like a soft, warm blanket. Why not? He was here to help, wasn't he? He might as well start with her, and he might as well find strength in the giving.

*Wonder what Gran Mere would say about this. About him.* Savannah glanced over her shoulder at the peaceful lady reclined on the settee. Was this why she seemed to be smiling? Had Gran Mere known Special

Agent Boniface was coming today? Was he why she'd decided to leave or was this truly the fifty-year anniversary of Great Grandpa's death? Had Gran Mere seen Special Agent Boniface in Savannah's future? Did she know how much her great granddaughter would need a knight in shining armor to get through this day? For that was what Agent Boniface was, a strong, capable man of untested power. Savannah would know.

"It's okay," he whispered as he kept her from falling, his hands warm and steady, his arms bands of solid, unwavering support now that he was breathing evenly. "This has been a hard day for you. I shouldn't have said what I did. I was insensitive."

She let him talk as he stood there being a sorry, tense and uptight male. He was right. This was the hardest day of her life. But she stayed put, because for the first time since Katrina rolled in and drowned the once lovely tree beside Gran Mere's houseboat, Savannah found herself engulfed by the same sheer, brute strength as that tree. Agent Boniface had even bent his knees and waist to hold her at her height instead of stretching her to match his. He'd seen to her needs instead of expecting her to meet his. How sweet was that?

Besides, Agent Boniface smelled too good to move away from. She closed her eyes and drew in the crisp notes of black silk ties and starch, of bourbon and tobacco. Minty toothpaste and tangy deodorant. Manly smells. Civilized, deliciously masculine smells.

They filled Savannah's body with a steady, pulsing thrum, and were fast becoming an intoxication she didn't want to resist. Or give up.

She glanced at Gran Mere again, wishing she'd thought fast enough that she'd asked precisely who the warlock was and what he looked like before Gran Mere slipped away. Because Savannah was no shy, fainting, Southern Belle. In a couple minutes, she'd be capable of distancing herself from Agent Boniface. Soon in fact. Very soon. Just. Not. Yet.

Was he the warlock Gran Mere had warned her about? Savannah wasn't sure. He surely carried himself with a definite lethality. But Special Agent Boniface seemed more mystery than menace. Her instincts told her he was a good man, but wary. Perhaps that explained why he'd panicked and asked for a drink instead of remaining suavely professional as he had at first sight.

*First sight.* Gran Mere had always told Savannah to trust her first sight. First impressions were the purest reflection of a person's soul. They were the moment you saw someone before they saw you, before they had a chance to hide who or what they really were. Before they could throw you off track with bravado or slap on a mask to cover their sins.

With her eyes still closed and her nostrils flared wide, Savannah did what she did best. Gran Mere was a witch, as the Cajun folks called her, a witch of many sights. But Savannah was not without skill or sight. And this uptight man from...

*Wait for it.*

Unleashing her one true gift, her sight, she probed the universe for the detail she needed, the name of his hometown. Wasn't that interesting? Agent Boniface had a solid network of mental defenses in place. As hard as she tried, probed, and pressed, she couldn't reach far enough into his psyche to uncover the city or state he hailed from. No matter.

If she could tame Sir Galahad, she could certainly tame Special Agent Boniface.

# **Chapter Five**

*'I am such an ass!'* Keller stood there in that poor dead woman's houseboat, berating himself for letting the tiny creature in his arms get the better of him, and trembling. Him. Trembling like a woman! Of all things, he was holding Mariposa's great granddaughter, not so much because Miss Church might pass out, but because *he* might. Damn this unpredictable, psychic bullshit. And damn Tucker Chase for sending him here to the land of witchcraft, voodoo, and gris-gris.

The moment Miss Church touched him, she'd set off an avalanche of emotions that damned near floored him. Her great grandmother became his Gran Mere. He was the one who'd just lost everything. His heart physically ached because an elderly woman he'd never met was gone. How the hell did that work?

Like a wrecking ball, that was how. Like a tsunami! The bottomless grief of his tender hostess swamped him. His Army Ranger heart felt hollowed and gutted. Sweat ran in tiny rivulets between his shoulder blades and at his temples. Gran Mere wasn't just Miss Church's relative, she was her only friend and her closest confidant. He stiffened his knees to keep from falling on his face. Keller didn't need a glass of water. He needed to get the hell out of there!

Until Miss Church touched him, he'd been in control. Supreme control. He had! Despite a burgeoning migraine that would've disabled him for days, he'd been in charge. So what if he'd been operating on instinct instead of eyesight. He'd learned long ago to rely on all his senses.

Then with one delicate hand on his muscled forearm, the same arm that had carried men, equipment, and hundred-pound packs of gear without breaking a sweat, she'd swamped him with more comfort than he'd had a right to. With one genteel woman's touch—and it wasn't even skin to skin, just her soft, sweet palm on his sleeved arm—his heart had damned near stopped.

First contact with Savannah was powerful, like brushing against a sizzling, downed power line. In that split second, in that exquisitely sweet, tender caress of a compassionate woman, every last ounce of her heartache had poured into Keller. And he knew heartache. He hadn't needed another dose of it. Not one like this.

Yet he did. This was the cost of empathy. The tradeoff. The balance. With one touch, Miss Church had immersed him in her pain, and he'd shot to the surface of it like a drowning victim. He'd forced himself not to gasp at the crushing weight, the volume and depth.

But then...

But now...

Keller drew in another breath of calm and quiet. His heart calmed to its normal sinus rhythm, as if nothing out of the ordinary had just happened and no one had died. The vise squeezing his brain released its hold. The horrific F10 migraine gathered behind his eyes dissipated like the San Diego marine layer at sunrise. Simply because he was holding Miss Church in his arms, and she was holding him. This had to be the purest energy exchange he'd ever experienced. Hell, he wasn't even grinding his teeth.

Steady now, because for the first time since he could remember, empathy didn't hurt, Keller inhaled another long pull of the fragrance in the ebony locks at the tip of his nose. He closed his eyes as an oddly reassuring sense of wonder lapped over him like the turquoise green waves at Hanauma Bay in Hawaii. She was a luscious armful, his chin barely touching the top of her head. The sweet scent of lilacs drifting up from her worked wonders on his jagged nerves. The crescendo of bright, stabbing pains that had heretofore crested at the raw, pulsating end of every last one of his nerves evaporated. The burden of his gift lifted, leaving him relaxed yet weak at the same time. Emptied of a grief that hadn't been his to carry, he found himself hollowed, yet filled to the brim at the same time.

Breathing deeply, because that's what he did when panic attacks got the better of him, Keller inhaled nothing but the flowery scent caught in every strand of Miss Church's sleek, black hair. Which was telling. Usually, he'd smell blood after an empathetic meltdown, and that blood would've come from his cheek, tongue, or sinuses. Migraines made him bleed. Thankfully, this one hadn't gotten that far. It hadn't unmanned him.

Relieved at the absence of anticipated misery, Keller began to sway. Miss Church's brand of magic he could deal with. It was pleasant and strong, but passive. Nonaggressive. Feminine. "Do you feel better now?" he asked as if he'd never lost control.

Knowing he'd arrived just in time and that he'd helped Miss Church was the only saving grace to this debacle of a mission. Soon he'd have to contact Tucker and explain what had happened. There had to be another way to help Isaiah.

Her head bobbed against his chin as she followed along, her hips moving in sync with his. Like a lover...

"Then it's time we call someone to come get her. Unless you already planned on using the local funeral parlor," he said, still trying to get his head back in the game.

She eased back on her heels. Her palms slipped from his waist, down his arms to his wrists, and there they stopped, her thumbs on the insides of his wrists as if taking his pulse. "She wanted Rudy John to handle everything. He was her doctor. I'll call him."

The moment she'd eased back, Keller missed the exquisite heat from her slender body. The soft press of her cheek against his chest. The way her knee had rested comfortably between his knees. The lilacs...

Her face tilted upward. Her brown eyes were clear again, but so tender. So close. So dark.

He licked his lower lip at the thought of kissing her full, lush mouth. What would she taste like? Honey and spice? Mint? Perhaps a sweet Moscato from far off Napa Valley? Coffee or cinnamon? Not cigarettes. He hadn't caught a whiff of anything on her but temptation.

Out of the blue, an odd little ray of light glimmered into the darkness that was the normal state of his practical, downtrodden soul. A genuine smile cracked his tough FBI mask. His heart kicked into overdrive for different reasons now. This stress he could deal with. It was delightfully tempting. Tantalizing. Enlightening.

Miss Church's bright light had found its way into his impenetrable darker side, and he wanted to bask in her glow a while longer.

She lingered as if she too felt the attraction between them. When she stepped away to make that call, Keller's gaze dropped to the soft swell of her backside and those long legs. Her bare feet. The sensual sway of her body… The hint of lilac in the air around her…

There wasn't a part of her he didn't want to taste, touch, and weigh. But that wasn't about to happen. He was an officer of the law, a man sworn to defend the Constitution against all enemies, foreign and domestic. He was not an oath breaker, nor could he ever be. It wasn't in him. As much as he disliked his current assignment in the Bureau, he was still a respected federal agent, and Miss Church was merely a vulnerable woman who needed his care, not his body. She was not to be taken advantage of nor objectified. Nor anything.

Tugging his tie out of his pocket, Keller put it back where it belonged and deftly tied it under his chin. It was time to remember, humidity or not, he was FBI Special Agent Boniface. The hug they'd just shared would not happen again.

It took Miss Church a minute to dial Doctor John on, of all things, a pink princess wall phone hanging beside the monstrosity of a china cabinet that took up most of the space in this peculiar home. After she made the call, she leaned one hip against the modern, white oak kitchen counter that clashed with the darker French Provincial vibe throughout the rest of the place.

"You must be hungry. There's a Waffle House a few miles back," he offered. "After Dr. John leaves, I'd be happy to take you there for something to eat. My treat."

She shook her head. "No, sir. I know we were just snuggling, but I don't know you well enough to owe you anything. I said I'll make breakfast, and I will."

But sitting down to eggs and bacon had lost its appeal. He gave her an out. "Another day. I have a call to make."

Relief glimmered. "Wouldn't you rather sit in here while we wait? I mean, with Gran Mere out there and all..."

Miss Church gestured to the tiny built-in breakfast nook opposite the china cabinet, which now that Keller looked closer, contained a bizarre mix of voodoo, Christian, and contemporary. Dainty china teacups sat atop hymnals and bibles. Shiny black crow feathers stuck up from a crystal flower vase, while polished rocks, tiny brass goblets, and colored beads littered any unoccupied space. The whitened human skull on the top shelf, the one with a crucifix glued to the center of its bony forehead, intrigued him. But Keller was hard pressed to care who it had once belonged to at that moment, or if the crucifix hid a bullet hole. Those were questions best left for another day.

"Yes, ma'am." Grabbing his suit jacket from where he'd left it, Keller shrugged into it, then straightened his tie to make sure he represented the Bureau's best interests. Only then did he join Miss Church at the small dinette crammed into the galley corner. He took the chair opposite hers. Placing both hands on the table where she could see them, he interlocked his fingers, intent on keeping his hands to himself from now on.

"You've seen Death," she told him, not asked.

"I've seen enough," he answered, surprised she wanted to talk about that with her great grandmother nearby.

"Tell me about her."

That was his first clue. "Her who?"

Miss Church drew in a long breath, then let it out on a whispered, "Your wife, Carol Marie."

*Aww, shit.* Keller closed his eyes as all the hints he'd failed to consider hit him like a brick. The whisper from the shadows that had warned him to leave and never come back. The psychic push to leave. The way he'd felt when this woman touched him. The ease with which she'd transferred her grief for his comfort, then balanced the transfer so neither of them were left unsettled or wanting. Miss Church was not just psychic. She was an empath. A better, stronger empath.

He canted his head, needing to understand how she knew, but not ready to share memories of Carol Marie. "Are you psychic or are you some kind of voodoo priestess?" he asked, still not sure if even that explained everything. The integration of white man's religion with African witchdoctor medicine began with the earliest slaves brought to Louisiana. Compound those ritualistic, and pagan belief systems with a powerful psychic, and you ended up with an entirely different kind of magic.

Miss Church's thick, black lashes fluttered. Those red crystal rosary beads glistened like precious jewels at her neck. "What if I am?"

Because it might explain why Keller was here instead of another agent from the Deuces Wild team. Either this beguiling woman or her great grandmother had drawn him here, or one of them had somehow influenced Tucker's decision to send Keller. Since his empathy had manifested itself when he'd turned eleven, he preferred ignoring it when he could, recovering from it when he couldn't. To him, his psychic talent had always been more curse than gift. Until today...

"Does everyone around here know?"

"I've never hidden my sight. Gran Mere wouldn't have let me if I'd wanted to. What do you know about voodoo priestesses?"

He bowed his head, swallowed hard and revealed, "Enough. I'm from Louisiana."

Her brows narrowed. "Where?"

Keller loosened the tie he'd just tightened because... *Shit*. He needed to breathe. "Turkey Creek."

Miss Church's head tilted, drawing his focus to the dark strands tumbling off her shoulder like ebony silk. "I don't know where that is."

"Up north, off LA-13." Admitting he'd come from that particular two-bit grease spot on the highway was nothing to be proud of, nor anything Keller wanted to share. Even the name declared wrong side of the tracks. Redneck. Loser. He'd spent his time in the

Army blending in, not sticking out. He'd worked hard to lose his Southern accent, too, the twang that labeled everyone this side of the Mason-Dixon Line a rebel. He'd worked just as hard to hide his gift.

But he wouldn't lie. Recalling the prickly sensation of eyes on him while he'd waited for Miss Church to answer the door, he rubbed the back of his neck. Like he did whenever questions about Carol Marie came up, he changed the subject. "That was you telling me to leave and never come back, wasn't it? Out there on your porch?"

"You heard me then. I couldn't tell."

Keller ran a hand over his scalp. "No, but I felt the push. You certainly lifted the hair off my head."

"What hair?" Mischievous sparkles lit up her pretty eyes. "When you kept knocking, I wasn't sure. Most folks back off and run when I warn them the first time, but you—"

"I wasn't leaving until I spoke to your great grandmother." Remembering why he was there—Isaiah—hit Keller. The loss to Tucker's team would be phenomenal, but to Roxy Zaroyin and that babe she was carrying? The son Isaiah would never live to see? Keller couldn't bear the thought. That kind of pain Keller knew all too well. Isaiah and Roxy wanted this little boy. Every time she came into the office to meet him for lunch, she glowed as if she'd swallowed a piece of the sun. But now...

Miss Church reached one hand across the chipped Formica tabletop, and again, the instant her fingertips made contact with the back of his hand, a soothing wave washed over Keller. "Why are you here, Agent Boniface? You didn't come all the way from Washington, DC just to talk to Gran Mere."

"It doesn't matter," he answered truthfully. *I failed.* "She's gone now."

"But why Mariposa Church? What was she to you?" The smooth, sleek waterfall of Miss Church's hair swished over her shoulder as she leaned forward, her dark eyes brimmed with uncommon compassion and intelligence. "How did you know her?"

Keller shook his head. "I didn't. Never heard of her until yesterday." His phone vibrated from his inner jacket pocket. Damn. Had to be Tucker. Just when one migraine ended, another one dialed his number. "Excuse me, but I have to take this."

Miss Church pushed back from the table. Her gaze strayed to the settee beyond the kitchen. "I'll, umm..."

Keller took hold of her hand before she could escape. "Stay. This won't take long." *Because I've got nothing good to tell my boss. My boss, ha.* The title still chafed.

As she settled back into her chair, Keller hit ACCEPT. "Agent Boniface—"

"Why haven't you called? Are you there yet? What's going on?"

"Yes, sir, I arrived, and I've made first contact, but—"

"But what?" Tucker's angst crawled through the connection. "Have you met her yet? What's she like?

What'd she say? Can she help Isaiah or not? How long's it gonna take to fly her back to DC? Do you think she's strong enough to handle the flight or should we plan...? What the hell's going on?"

Keller swallowed hard, then gave it to Tucker straight. "She won't be coming back. Mariposa Church passed away this morning before I had the chance to speak with her. Tell Isaiah I'm so—"

"She's dead?" No one did obvious like Tucker Chase.

"Yes, sir," Keller answered quietly, suddenly aware that the pad of his thumb was drawing tiny circles on the back of Miss Church's hand. Tucker could get under his skin quicker than anyone Keller had ever met, yet as upset as his highly-strung boss was at this unwelcome turn of events—and he had a right to be— Keller was not. The calmest sensations floated up his arm from Miss Church's skin, to his neck muscles where he carried his stress. There was still no sign of a migraine. Not even the slightest inkling. No aura. No urge to kill anything or anyone, either.

He locked eyes with Miss Church. She was nothing like the alleged voodoo queen he'd grown up with. Yes, there most certainly was a human skull in Gran Mere's fancy cabinet. That by itself spoke of black magic and witchcraft, possibly murder. He might not have been able to read Miss Church's mind, but empathy had its own language, and Keller knew the desperate people who practiced voodoo. He'd witnessed the dark side of it up close and personal as a kid. His mother was

Cajun. She'd married a soldier, an alcoholic who'd never pleased her until the night he'd died in his sleep. After Keller's father was gone, she'd turned her only child's life into living hell.

Queen Elaine Boniface. That was how folks addressed her, as if she had anything to do with royalty. Keller knew better, and he knew wicked. His mother derived more pleasure than power from killing the chickens, kittens, lambs, and birds she'd used in her despicable rituals. She'd always made him watch, and he'd never been strong enough to defy her. He'd watched and afterward, he'd cried. Like a blubbering wuss, he'd cried for every one of those helpless creatures. It made him sick remembering. How they'd squealed and screamed. How they'd cried...

At her deepest core, Elaine was never anything more than a mean-spirited woman who'd cursed, hexed, and convinced others to believe that she could and would curse them if they didn't do what she wanted. They had to buy their way off her hit list or risk losing a crop, a herd, or a child. Queen Elaine was cruel, and fear ran deep in both her chicken-shit son and the neighbors.

Hence the double hex Keller had lived under as a kid. Folks in Turkey Creek got back at Elaine by taking their revenge out on him. They spread stories and lies. Their children bullied him until he'd whupped every last one of their asses just so he could walk down the gravel road where he lived without having to run for his life. Fact was that he'd never have gotten out of

Turkey Creek alive without sweet Carol Marie's faith in him.

Back then he'd been a scrawny kid, all legs, no balls. Born dirt poor to the local drunk, he'd been looking for validation and redemption all his worthless life. The Army gave that to him, along with confidence, pride, and an unrelenting dedication to serve decent, law-abiding Americans. But it was Carol Marie who'd given him his first taste of heaven. She was the reason he'd sought out the local Army/Air Force/Navy recruiters. She was the only one who'd believed he'd amount to something better than getting drunk off one-hundred-ninety proof Everclear.

But that was a long time ago, and in the end, Elaine had taken Carol Marie, too. And here Keller was, nearly back home again. Close enough to smell its stink.

"Jesus H. Christ!" Tucker sputtered, jolting him out of his melancholy reverie. "Already? Damn. What'd she die of?"

Like cause of death mattered to Isaiah? "Old age," Keller replied. An unexpected calmness still lingered as he studied Miss Church's delicate, slender fingers. They were pink against his callused, scarred, and rugged skin. Even his palms seemed stained with use, but hers were clean. Dainty. Pure.

And once again, he'd crossed the line between agent and client.

Clearing his throat, Keller settled her palm to the tabletop and patted the back of her hand to signal the end of the touching. All this familiarity growing between them had to stop. She was off limits. Breakfast wasn't going to happen, either. That had been an out of the blue invitation he still couldn't believe he'd extended. She'd seemed so lost and... Yes. Okay. He hadn't wanted to walk away from her just then, either. No child should have to face Death alone, and okay, she wasn't exactly a child, but still. He couldn't do it.

"Roxy admitted him two hours ago," Tucker said, his voice a mere whisper. "He's bad. They're putting him on a ventilator. Possibly inducing a coma until..."

*And so it begins. Another all-night vigil. Another tragic waste of a good man's life. Another viewing. Then onto Arlington...*

Looked like Keller was leaving after all. Breathing a ragged sigh of resignation, he rapped his knuckles on the tabletop and stood, needing to be gone. "I'll catch the first flight home, sir."

"Yeah. Okay. Sure. Whatever."

The line went dead. Tucker had never sounded so deflated.

# Chapter Six

The distress in the air carried the scent of ash and smoke. Of incense. Of Death. This was his way of saying goodbye. Agent Boniface had politely disassociated himself from Savannah the moment he'd released her fingers. Even now, his calculating brain fluttered over a to-do list. *Call the hotel. Cancel reservation. Turn in rental car. Fly back to DC before—*

Something was wrong. Savannah could smell it. "Who's dying?" she asked gently.

The bleak glance Agent Boniface leveled at her did not invite her into his confidence. Where once a meaningful window had opened, shutters were now slammed tight. Locking her out. He seemed especially good at that. "Don't worry. You've got enough on your mind—"

A silent whisper came to her like an unearthly summons. *'Isaiah. Me.'*

Savannah leveled her unique gift of sight on the stone-faced man across the table as she told him, "Your friend is here, Agent Boniface. Isaiah is why you came to see Gran Mere, isn't he? He needed something from her, didn't he? He needed her. Why?"

Agent Boniface didn't answer. The sadness welling in his honey-gold eyes confirmed the worst. "Isaiah's dying. We thought your great grandmother could help, but now…"

"But now there isn't time to waste," Savannah said as she hurried into the other room and pulled the middle drawer of Gran Mere's hutch open. "Please clear the kitchen table for me. I'll be right back."

Isaiah didn't just need *something*. He needed to live, and just possibly, Savannah could help him do that. She had to. She sensed a terrible menace, a fear and a sin riding him, like conjoined twins tormenting him into an early grave.

*'You can help me?'* that same small voice asked. A child's voice, really. A frightened little boy's voice.

*'I will most certainly try,'* she told him honestly.

*'There is no try, only do…'*

*'Then hush and let me do,'* she scolded silently.

While Agent Boniface obediently moved Gran Mere's potted lavender plant from the table to the counter, Savannah chose the items that called to her from her great grandmother's vast collection. A red flannel drawstring bag. A crystalized shard of rose quartz for Isaiah's fragile heart, that even now beat too weakly to sustain him much longer, fell into the bottom of the bag.

Next, she snagged a jagged but not rusty piece of iron the size of a thin dime. Iron invoked raw masculinity, another one of Isaiah's traits. He also needed the talisman of a pure white feather for purity. A single dried rose petal for....

Her fingertips hesitated over the crispy, dark red petal. Gran Mere always kept a small basket of dried rose petals on hand for love potions and spells. She grew the bushes deep in the swamp. Said they needed seclusion and a certain amount of direct sunlight for her spells.

But this was not a love potion Savannah meant to cast. The iron, rose quartz, and white feather were powerful natural magic that would go into the good luck amulet that Agent Boniface would soon take to Isaiah. Whoever Isaiah was, he needed the divine help the universe had to offer, and he needed it now. The reddest roses for the purest love and the brightest passion, so, yes. Into the bag the petal went. Then...

*Oh, where in blazes are they? Whatever did Gran Mere do with her marbles?*

Any other time Savannah would've chuckled at what she'd thought, but the need to *'hurry faster!'* shivered up her spine. Isaiah stood at the edge of a precarious cliff. He was running out of time.

Filled with prickling foreboding, Savannah finally located the small wooden box of marbles behind a stack of antique china saucers. Choosing the clearest glass sphere, she dropped it into the bag. Seemingly innocuous, it would enhance the combined energies of the other items.

*'Please hurry,'* Isaiah urged from far, far away, his psychic voice growing weaker, yet fiercer, as if he were engaged in a great struggle. As if he were already losing, yet fighting to hold on to life with all his might.

*'Hold on,'* Savannah ordered as she tightened the drawstring, then grabbed a white sage smudge stick from its newly opened carton, a squat red candle, and one of Gran Mere's best abalone shells from another drawer.

Once back in the kitchen, she gathered the rest of her supplies: a box of wooden matches, a thick kitchen towel to protect the now cleared table in case the abalone shell grew too hot during the ritual, as well as a few sprigs of fresh rosemary and sweetgrass from Gran Mere's boxed herb garden by the kitchen porthole window. Last, but not least, she scooped up a handful of cedar chips Gran Mere used when she smoked—*used to smoke*—pork ribs.

Once again, the stranger in her mind begged, *'Hurry.'*

"Can you hear him?" she asked Agent Boniface, her heart lodged in her throat at the impending death Isaiah projected. "Are you listening to your friend?"

A bleak shadow shifted over the staunch agent's face, and Savannah's breath caught. He'd turned as pale as a ghost. He hadn't the gift. "Isaiah? He's talking to you?"

She nodded.

Keller groaned. "No. I can't hear him. I'm not that kind of psychic. But I feel his pain. He can't breathe. He's dying. We have to…" At the same instant, he and Isaiah ground out together, *'Hurry!'*

"I am!" she replied. Frightened now that there wasn't enough time in the universe to do what needed to be done, Savannah's fingers trembled as she retrieved her smudge bowl, holy oil, and the tiny, precious bottle of frankincense from the kitchen cabinet. At last it was time.

"Sit," she told Agent Boniface while she quickly organized her altar on the now cleared table and took a seat. The shell went to her right, the smudge bowl to her left. Everything else went in between while her heart pounded that all was already lost. That she was too late.

"No," Agent Boniface said, which told her he knew precisely what she now meant to do.

"Yes," she told him sternly. If he knew what these items meant, then he needed to stay out of her way and let her work. There wasn't time to argue. "This ritual isn't for you. It's for your friend, so sit and do what I tell you. Please," she added, trying not to sound like a shrew.

He made that sound at the back of his throat again.

"Did you just growl at me?"

"No," he declared, then lifted one shoulder. "Yes. I hate this mumbo jumbo stuff. It's useless. A waste of time. It won't help him."

"You say potato, I say po-tah-toe," she told him firmly. "Now either join me in trying to save your friend or take your negative energy out of here and leave me to my work."

"I say bullshit," he grumbled. Yet even as she fluttered her fingers at him to give her his hand, he took hold.

"And I say everything, even the most unlikely cure in the known world, cannot hurt a man who believes he's dying," she replied evenly. "The mind is a powerful thing. Let's us turn Isaiah's away from the path he is on."

Her inner sight had never before been so in tune nor so crystal clear with the universe as it was this morning. Maybe that clarity had to do with Gran Mere's passing, but Agent Boniface needed to face facts. Mankind did not yet know everything there was to know. Like most teenagers in the cosmic universe, the human race just thought they knew everything. "Let us now be the conduit your friend needs to live."

*Hurry!* A wave of despair flooded her with darkness, but Savannah knew better. Of course, Isaiah would project his anguish and hatred at her. That was all he had.

"Please," she pleaded out loud to Isaiah. "Don't let go. We are coming. We are here."

Gran Mere always said the darkest dark always proceeded the brightest bright. Savannah meant to be that brightness. Closing her eyes, she began the purification ritual she knew by heart. The holy oil went from her fingertips to her forehead as she quickly blessed herself and called upon the four elements to join her. Water came in the guise of the abalone shell, Fire in the wooden matches. The feather brought Air, and rosemary was the Earth. So simple yet so powerful in the right hands.

She'd barely started the blessing when shuddering, angry images hit her with a force far stronger than anything she'd encountered before. Intense. Definitely male. Probing. Frantically touching places in her soul she hadn't realized she had. Sensual places. Dark places. Forgotten places.

Opening her eyes, she said, "You think you are stronger than me, but you are not, Isaiah. Step back and stay out of my mind. Give me space that I may pray for you."

Releasing Agent Boniface's hand, she selected a single matchstick, snapped her thumbnail to the end of it, and lit the sage. Into the abalone shell the sage went, sending its lovely fragrant tendrils wafting upward into the air, tickling her nose. Purifying everything within her circle. Her heart. Her mind. Even Agent Boniface. At the same time, it drew Isaiah in to the circle of Earth, Air, Water, and Fire. He was now anchored to life.

Agent Boniface's fingers tightened as she gave him her hand once more, then interlocked fingers. "Hold onto me," she ordered. "Do not let go or we'll lose him."

"I won't," he answered, tightening his grip. For a professed non-believer, he seemed to understand how strong this circle needed to be.

Breathing deeply, Savannah exhaled and projected the aromatic scent in her home out into the universe and onto Isaiah, who felt more like her adversary at the moment. Yet she sensed a vulnerability to this frantic, angry spirit, an out of control innocence that spoke of integrity and honor and an undying, childlike love, nearly lost. She sensed pain and panic. Fear. He didn't want to leave, yet he didn't know how to stay.

"Be at peace. Breathe with me, Isaiah," she commanded him while she again released Agent Boniface's hand to add fragrant evergreen rosemary sprigs, sweetgrass, and cedar to her smudge bowl. Adding a few drops of frankincense, Savannah handed the bowl to Agent Boniface, then told him, "Light this for me with a matchstick. Hurry."

"A lighter would be faster," he grumbled even as he flicked the matchhead with his thumbnail, sparking an instant flame. Why did he argue at a time like this?

"Easier does not mean better," she told him as Gran Mere's brand of magic began to fill her. To Isaiah she said, "Breathe deeply. Rest. I command you to let go. The peace you seek is here. It is ready to fill you up, but first you must let them go."

Agent Boniface canted his head, not yet understanding or not yet willing to believe. Savannah couldn't read which, because his doubts were not important. Not now. Only Isaiah's doubts mattered.

Snapping her fingers, she cast her purification spell to an unclean but sterile place far to the north, to a place she'd never seen nor visited before. A pure white place of glass and chemicals and mankind's pride in his limited, narrow knowledge. An empty, lifeless place, when Isaiah desperately needed the healing powers of the wise, eternal universe.

As she fanned the combined smoke from the smudge pot and the shell upward and outward, Savannah told him, "Let them go, Isaiah. Do it now. Do it fast."

Never before had she encountered so much power within a single person. So much resistance. Yet as strong as Isaiah was, he was weak, too. Like most of humanity, he suffered from the burdensome weight of hubris. His own pride was killing him.

Groaning, Savannah winced at the anguish he'd carried for years because of that misplaced pride. "The weight of the world is not yours to carry. It never was. Let it go. Quickly. Do it now. Let them all go."

A tortured wail came out of nowhere, filling the confined space of Gran Mere's simple home with an ice-cold blast of mental anguish. Isaiah was enraged by her revelation. Her accusation. *I. Am. Not. Proud!*

Agent Boniface clutched her fingers as if he feared she might blow away. It could happen. Isaiah's wrath was that powerful.

Savannah continued to speak out loud, so Agent Boniface could hear her part of the conversation. "We're all proud, Isaiah. Please. Just do as I ask. Let them go."

*'How?'* the wind howled, rattling every dish in the cupboards and anything not nailed down.

*'Teach me!'* it begged, and Savannah was sure the floorboards creaked and the walls groaned. Even Gran Mere's magnificent hutch swayed beneath its assault.

At last relenting, Isaiah cried, *'I'm not strong enough!'* The utter anguish in his voice rocked the houseboat on its foundation. Like a frightened lost boy... He. Cried.

"You *are* strong enough," she told him fiercely. "You are magnificent and powerful, and you are brave. You can do this. There is no try, remember?"

The terror emanating from his poor tortured spirit broke her heart. Isaiah hadn't the strength to do what needed to happen next. He'd fought his demons alone for too long. Worse, he believed himself too far gone, too despicable to come back from the ledge he now balanced precariously over. All he could see was down. Beguiling Death whispered at his back, tantalizing him with its promise of sweet release. Isaiah needed something—someone—to hold onto, and he needed her now.

Savannah had never encountered a spirit so broken nor so lovely. So fraught with compassion that he'd willingly taken on the sins of the many perpetrators of evil whom he'd bested during his years. Isaiah wasn't old enough to have shouldered so much agony that he could barely draw a breath. That's what was killing him. The weight of the world.

She didn't have all the answers. Gathering every last bit of her resolve, she did precisely what Gran Mere had trained her to do for all of her twenty-five years. With a firm hold on Agent Boniface's hands, Savannah mentally reached across the miles for Isaiah and ordered him to, *'Take hold of me and Agent Boniface. Trust us. At the same time, focus your heart and your soul on Roxy. If she is there with you, grab hold of her hand and do not let her go. Above all, hold on to what is most dear to you, Isaiah. Choose. Roxy or them...'*

The fight to save Isaiah from his most intimate demons was on. Bowing her face nearly to the table, Savannah acknowledged the almighty power of her Lord and Master. *'Please help me help him,'* she prayed privately.

The struggle was real. It all came down to the power of light against darkness. Good against evil. Folks thought Gran Mere a sorceress or a witch because they chose to. It was easier to accept magic than truth. Always had been. But the truth here today was that Gran Mere wasn't really a witch or a voodoo priestess. She'd just chosen long ago to believe in the most ancient magic of all magics.

Savannah prayed harder now. "For thine is the kingdom, the power, and the glory," she chanted. "For thine is the kingdom, the power, and the glory. For thine is the kingdom, the power, and the glory."

Isaiah struggled to let go of the souls his exceptionally powerful, and all too compassionate mind had snared and retained—for their own good. Of all the sins known to mankind, his compassion was the saving rope he'd extended to even the depraved and wicked. But at the end of life, every soul had to stand on its own merit, not his. He had to let them go, all of them. There was no other recourse. The lifeline he'd offered to others was now a noose around his neck.

Out of the blue, Agent Boniface's hoarse baritone vibrated along with Savannah's softer alto. "For thine is the kingdom, the power, and the glory," he chanted along with her. "For thine is the kingdom, the power, and the glory."

*Ah, so he does believe.*

"Please, cher, let them go," she crooned to Isaiah, his internal battle manifesting itself in the whirling vortex swirling around her and Agent Boniface, battering them with its fury. "You have to let each of them go, or they will take you down with them. Think with me. Pray with me. Picture the wicked men and women you saved as tiny little fish that you've caught in a net. Lower the net into the river that is the universe and give them back. Let. Them. Go."

Agent Boniface now clasped both her hands within his powerful fists, squeezing her fingers. The scents of nature swirled around them. The wind built to a thunderous roar. It seemed Gran Mere's tiny home had captured a hurricane. The boat would surely break apart soon.

"Please, Isaiah. You can do this, but you must do it quickly," Savannah ordered the stubborn man. "You can do it. I will count with you. On three, okay? One..."

The wind lashed out, lifting her hair into the center of its fury, the ends of it whipping her face as if fighting her for Isaiah's soul. Savannah held onto Agent Boniface as he held onto her. It was them against a force so strong that, for a single moment, she doubted they could save Isaiah. He was so hurt. So angry. And embarrassed. As he should be. It was never easy to admit to one's pride. To be humble. But confessing sin was the first step. If he didn't...

As if he knew precisely what Isaiah was going through, Agent Boniface called out, "Isaiah. Buddy. Come on, you've got to let those creeps go. If anyone can do this, you can. Let 'em all go. They're not important, but Roxy is. They made their beds, let them sleep in them. But I'm telling you, man. Roxy needs you now, she and that baby boy in her belly. Your family deserves you more than anyone else. She loves you most. She's gold, Isaiah. Everyone else is dross and chaff. Give 'em back to God. Let 'em go. Isaiah, let us all go. Save Roxy and your son."

"Two..." Savannah breathed, secretly thrilled Agent Boniface knew how to reach his friend.

To Isaiah she said, *'You're not the savior of this world. That job was taken long ago, and it was never what your power was meant for. Who do you think you are? God? Do you think you are more powerful that He is? Than His Son? Do you think you can save them when He could not? I promise He will catch them if they choose to be caught. Redemption has to be their choice, but you must first let go of your pride, and then—'*

*'I never knew. I didn't realize. I'm... I'm... Not. That. Guy.'*

*'I know, my poor brother,'* she told him mentally. Quietly. Privately. *'I see you. Are you ready now? Can you do it?'*

Isaiah's spirit was bowed down with so much remorse for things he hadn't done and couldn't change. But it was time he let go of the thing that was killing him—his pride.

Before he had time to answer, Savannah breathed one final, "For thine is the kingdom, the power and the glory, forever and ever... On three!"

Just that fast, the struggle ended. The howling stopped. The wind stilled. Dishes settled onto the cupboard shelves with a clatter, as the windowpanes stopped rattling. Savannah's hair fell softly to her shoulders and over her face like a veil. She swallowed hard at the sudden silence ringing in her ears. Holy Mother, she hadn't realized how hard her heart was pounding until then. What a frightening, electrifying, sacred, fulfilling experience.

A whispered, *'I understand now,'* came to her as Isaiah's tortured spirit collapsed in upon itself, trembling from the tremendous battle he'd won.

"You are most welcome," Savannah told him kindly. "Be good to yourself until you are strong again, my friend. I hope to meet you some day."

*'Ssssssooooon...'*

"What'd he say?" Agent Boniface asked, frustration gleaming dark in his eyes.

"He's at peace," Savannah murmured. Man, she was tired. "He's going to live, Agent Boniface. Because of you, he'll live a long and happy life."

Agent Boniface made a face. "Thank God, but it was all you, not me."

"And thank Isaiah for finally letting go and letting God," she scolded. "But understand, this fight took both of us. You'll see."

Satisfied, she blew the messy curtain of hair out of her eyes. Despite, or maybe because of the tragic morning, Savannah felt oddly lighthearted and at peace. Isaiah had just triumphed. He was in a better place. Like Gran Mere.

"Are you gonna be okay, buddy?" Agent Boniface asked his friend, his big hands still squeezing Savannah's fingers, his eyes dark and shimmering as if he might be able to finally mentally communicate with Isaiah.

Isaiah still lingered. *'Yes, Roxy's here. She's really here. She stayed,'* he said tiredly.

Savannah hurried to pass that psychic message onto Agent Boniface. "His wife is with him. Roxy helped him to hold onto us. He needs to rest."

"She'll never leave you, man. She loves you," Agent Boniface whispered to his friend, a definite sheen in his honeyed eyes.

*'You heard your friend, Isaiah. Agent Boniface will never tell you, but he loves you, too.'*

*'I know,'* Isaiah whispered. *'Gotta go-o-o-o-o-o...'*

Savannah smiled as the spirit of a man she'd never met retreated northward like a feather on the wind, back to the loving embrace of his distraught wife.

*'Go in peace,'* she told him privately, wiping the back of her fingers across her bleary eyes. Tears brimmed again, but this time they were happy tears.

Still seated across from her, the tough FBI agent let go of her to brush a big hand over his face. Isaiah's rescue had touched him too. The circle was broken, and that was okay.

"It's over," she said out loud.

Agent Boniface inhaled a cleansing breath, then pushed back in his chair, his legs stretched under the table. "You're not a witch and you're not a voodoo priestess, either. There's more Catholic in you than pagan. What the hell are you?"

"I might ask you the same thing," Savannah replied as a sharp, impatient knock sounded at her front door. "You're not just an FBI agent, are you? You're an empath. Like me."

# Chapter Seven

"I am not just like you," Keller groused as Miss Church answered the door. Exhausted by the psychic battle to save Isaiah from—of all things—himself, Keller wanted to talk to her about what had just happened. He wanted to understand how a bag of rocks and part of an ancient prayer held enough power to change the world. This was magic he didn't understand. This was something pure and holy, but it'd have to wait. Keller now watched her deal with the wiry young man who'd shown up in a wrinkled denim shirt and just as wrinkled gray Dockers.

He'd expected Gran Mere's doctor would be some older guy with gray hair, a seersucker suit, and maybe spectacles. At least someone respectable—like her. But Doctor Rudy John was not that man. The first thing he did once he cleared Gran Mere's doorway was smooth a hand over his already slicked-down hair like some punk on a date instead of a concerned physician attending a tragic death call.

Lurching straight at Miss Church, he grasped both her hands and nearly pulled her against him. "You poor, poor thing. I came as fast as I could. Don't you worry none, I called the mortuary on your behalf, darlin'. They'll be here directly. Musta been terrible being alone with a dead body so long."

Only her stiff-arming the guy prevented closer, more intimate contact. But *'dead body'*? Really? That was his idea of compassion?

"I haven't been alone, Rudy John," she said as she extricated herself from this guy's proprietary and inappropriate grip. "Gran Mere's spirit is still close by. She's lingering. I can feel her."

"Sho you can, cher. Sho you can. That's just the shock of watching somebody you love die. You just keep on thinkin' your granmama's hangin' 'round, and you'll snap out of it real soon. Yes sirree Bob, you'll see, darlin'. You'll be fine."

Keller bit his tongue at the patronizing sweet talk spewing out of this guy's yap.

"No, umm, you're wrong," Miss Church told RJ, her voice clear and strong considering all she'd been through in the last couple hours. "I'm not in shock, and I've never been afraid of being with Gran Mere, not even now. Besides, I'm not alone, RJ. I've had help." She nodded at Keller. "Very good help."

He sent her a subtle chin-lift of appreciation for the show of faith, but when she stepped away from RJ and scrubbed her palms up and down her bare biceps, she confirmed Keller's opinion of the guy. Dr. John wasn't there to take care of Gran Mere. He had designs on Miss Church, and she knew it.

"'*Very good help?*'" the creep she'd called RJ mocked. "But I just got here and—" His gaze followed Miss Church's line of sight right over his shoulder and behind the front door he'd burst through. The doctor could've given himself whiplash the way his neck cranked when he ended at Keller. "'Scuse me, suh, but who are you?" he asked indignantly, his lips twisted.

"I'd ask you the same thing," Keller replied drolly. *Only I'd never call you suh like some backwoods slave, you pretentious oaf.*

Miss Church rolled her eyes behind RJ's back, and for a split second, Keller wondered if she'd heard that last unspoken comment. Damn, was he the only one who couldn't read minds?

"Agent Boniface, this is Doctor Rudy John, the only physician around for miles. We call him RJ," she said by way of introduction. That certainly explained why Gran Mere insisted this guy take care of her remains. Who else was there? "RJ, this is Special Agent Boniface."

"Special Agent of what? Insurance? Immigration?" RJ's brows narrowed and his beady eyes turned black. "You with the almighty Internal Revenue Service, suh? You a revenuer?"

Keller hadn't heard that term except in history books. "Federal Bureau of Investigation.

Headquarters, Washington, DC." He tossed his chin at the cocky charlatan, growing more certain RJ was involved in something illegal. Why else would he have pulled the IRS out of his hat when there were so many federal agencies to choose from? Moonshiners used to battle Revenuers during Prohibition. What exactly was RJ running these days? Guns? Drugs? Women?

RJ's nostrils flared. His upper lip curled as if he'd caught a whiff of noxious fumes. "A federal agent? What's the FBI want with Miss Church here?"

The man reminded Keller of a crow. Everything about him seemed bird-like. His build. His face. Even the long, thin blade of his long nose ended at an arrow-shaped point that could've passed for a beak. The shadowy scruff on his narrow chin looked like he'd once entertained the idea of a goatee. All it did now was emphasize his beak. A haircut wouldn't hurt this guy. He kept running his right hand over his head to keep the straggly, greasy bangs out of his eyes. His hair was glossy black, shiny with a bluish, feather-like sheen. His eyes were just as shiny, just as black. Piercingly black.

"That information's between *Miss Church here*—" Keller couldn't help the condescension that dripped off his tongue with a Southern twist, "—and the United States government, *Dr. John.*"

It gave him a morbid thrill to voice this joker's last name. Would've been better if it'd been Head. He looked like a Dr. Head. Dr. Shithead. Might also do him some good to know Miss Church wasn't the *poor thing* he seemed to want her to think she was. "Fortunately, Miss Church is a capable woman. She had things well in hand when I arrived. She knows what her great grandmother wants. I'd listen to her if I were you."

Miss Church shot Keller a shy smile, and he telegraphed a nod of respect back. She was no idiot. He knew precisely what she was capable of.

RJ's cheeks hollowed. Unshaven and sweaty, he gave off an antsy vibe for a medical practitioner. Most doctors Keller knew exuded calm to keep their patients from panicking. Yeah, something was very off-putting about this joker.

Keller one-upped the cocky ass, nonchalantly leaning against Gran Mere's hutch with his arms folded. Cocking his knee, he crossed one ankle against the other, and gave RJ a chin nod toward the settee that he had yet to glance at. "Might want to check Mariposa Church for a pulse while you're here. She's right over there." *In case you missed her.*

"There's never no need to disturb the body of a loved one," RJ snapped, his double negatives inadvertently declaring that was exactly what he should've done. "You Northerners might stoop so low, but not a true gentleman of the South. Even an idiot can see she's dead."

Not one to let an insult slide, Keller volleyed back with, "Now you're being insensitive. Where's all that Southern charm I've heard so much about?"

"And you, sir, are being an antagonistic, pigheaded republican. State your business!"

*Whoa, just whoa. Pigheaded republican?* RJ was turning this visit into a political debate? Keller had more respect for Gran Mere than that. *Sorry. Not happening.*

He locked onto Miss Church's pretty face. There was no reason to stay, much less bait Dr. Shithead. Now that she'd calmed, his duty was done. She was no longer the frightened, angry great granddaughter who'd just lost her precious Gran Mere and had proudly told him to *'beat it.'* She didn't need Keller hanging around, and he knew it.

Yet her eyes glowed for reasons Keller couldn't fathom. She looked stronger. More confident. He didn't understand why. It had taken him more than a few years to be civil after Carol Marie's sudden death. For too long he'd been hateful and mean, surviving on booze, smokes, and venom. There were still days he couldn't bear to think about all he'd lost when she'd passed. Didn't want to. Her death had taken everything good from him.

Yet Miss Church seemed to have already processed her great grandmother's death. She was sad, but no longer undone. She knew something Keller didn't. Yes, her eyes were rimmed with red, and there was a tender vulnerability to her. But there was also strength and conviction. She had every right to break down, but she hadn't. He couldn't bring himself to leave her alone with RJ. Like Gran Mere's spirit, Keller lingered, wondering if this *Mizz Church* would share her secret.

His inner suit pocket buzzed with an incoming call. Probably Tucker. Keller made a mental note to set his alarm for thirty-minute intervals from now on. Fingering his cell up and out of his pocket, he nodded politely to Miss Church. "Excuse me, ma'am, but I have to take this."

"I'm not going anywhere," she replied.

Turning his back on Dr. John, Keller faced the kitchen altar with all its mystical paraphernalia still on display. There was a time he'd thought all voodoo, magic, and witchcraft was evil like his mother, but Miss Church's half-magic, half-Christian ritual had changed his mind. Maybe there was some good to it after all.

"Boniface."

"He died," Tucker ground out, the pain in his voice raw and overpowering.

*WTF? No!*

But, WTF, yes. The clear image of Tucker Chase breaking down in a bright hospital corridor overwhelmed Keller. Stumbling with a searing dose of empathy for this hard man still miles away, he took a chair before Tucker's angst billowing through the connection dropped him to his knees. "But Boss, I thought... I honestly thought..." *God, what have I done?*

All at once, Keller was a thousand miles north, inside the prestigious George Washington University

Hospital west of DC, hovering over a bed, and watching Isaiah struggle to breathe through the oxygen mask strapped to his face. Isaiah was gray, his lips blue, as Roxy, his adoring wife, clung to him, her face buried in his chest. Dressed in jeans and a light gray hoodie, the bottomless grief that racked her pregnant body overwhelmed Keller. Every shudder and sob was another breath-stealing stiletto stab to his chest.

*Miss Church was wrong? No. She couldn't be...*

Like an angry Navy SEAL, Tucker stood stock-still at the end of that bed with both fists clenched, primed to jump into action. But there was nothing to be done. His rumpled dress slacks and white dress shirt looked like he hadn't slept since yesterday. His jaw flexed forward and back as he ground his teeth, fighting the same emotions as Roxy, but forcing a brave face for her sake. But so damned sick at heart.

For the first time, Keller really saw Tucker. He saw the man under the gutsy bravado. Tucker honestly thought of Isaiah as a kid brother. He adored Isaiah, and losing him hollowed Tucker's heart. This hard, brash man was crying inside like a child, great gulping sobs he'd never let surface.

Fighting the image—*Please let this be Tucker's memory. Please let this be the past, not the present!*—Keller tried again. "But Boss..."

"You did it," Tucker choked. He could barely get the words out. "You... you saved him. It was all you. He flatlined, but all at once... Then you..." His voice turned incredibly tender. "You saved my boy, Kell. I owe you."

*My boy? Kell?*

Keller swallowed hard as Tucker's unvarnished love for Isaiah poured over him like a sweet, warm baptism instead of the wrath he'd expected. Not that the rest of the Deuces Wild team didn't also know that Tucker and Isaiah were close. Whatever battles Tucker and Isaiah had been through, it had welded them into the unlikeliest of brothers—a flaming asshole and a genius, a hard-as-nails SEAL and a genuine guardian angel.

But Keller had also heard what no one had uttered in years, Carol Marie's endearment for a kid who'd never known gentleness or love before she'd come along. He'd been someone back when he'd been hers. Back when he was—*Kell.*

But how the hell could Tucker have known? By then Keller could barely manage a hoarse, "Hey, Boss?"

"Yeah?" Tucker's voice was the same trembling baritone, so low and so deep that only the barest murmur came over the connection.

"I'm taking a couple personal days."

"Take a week."

"Thanks. I might just do that."

Glancing over his shoulder, Keller locked eyes with Savannah. Her eyes glowed with something other than sadness. But it wasn't pity, either. Almost looked like compassion, as if she and Keller shared the same connection Tucker and Isaiah did. Which was true. Savannah and Keller had saved a life today. But they'd lost one, too. At least, she'd lost one. In Keller's mind, the negative canceled the positive, and he was back to zero. Wasn't that Nature's way, to strive for a net sum of nothing? Yet Keller also felt as if he'd found more than that net sum of zero.

He just wasn't sure what.

# Chapter Eight

They ended up at the nearest Waffle House. Savannah wouldn't have accepted Agent Boniface's offer, but she needed a break after watching RJ manhandle her beloved great grandmother's remains into a body bag. But when he'd dusted his hands on his pants when he'd finished as if he'd taken out the trash? She could've cried all over again.

It hadn't taken long for Agent Boniface to catch onto Dr. John. RJ'd always given Savannah the creeps, but today he'd outdone himself. After he'd left and the professional, polite, and sensitive mortuary attendants had taken Gran Mere away, Savannah slipped into a pair of her great grandmother's sandals, locked the houseboat, and forced her thoughts away from all she'd lost.

There was nothing she could do for Gran Mere now, and at some level, Gran Mere had been preparing her for this day for years. A deep sigh eased out of Savannah's heart. She was tired, but rest was better left for another time. There were still things to be done.

She'd been on her feet since before sunrise. Kennels didn't clean themselves, and while she'd hosed and disinfected Sanctuary, the dogs had free run of her portion of Gran Mere's property. Only now it was Savannah's property, all one hundred-plus acres of the swampland Gran Mere had loved. Savannah didn't want to think about that, either.

Agent Boniface was a pleasant diversion. Now that Savannah knew he was an empath, she kept her hands to herself to avoid overloading him with her emotions. Not that he had unraveled at touch alone. He'd also turned gray when he'd gotten the call from his boss. His empathy receptors for others' pain seemed to be running him instead of the other way around. Empathy could be an all-consuming taskmaster. She would know. That was why Sanctuary now needed every bit of its five acres for her rescued dogs, cats, and birds.

Yet when the hostess showed them to their booth, Agent Boniface hadn't started sweating or breathing heavily when he'd put his hand at the small of Savannah's back.

But Savannah did. No man had ever touched her as gently. She'd shivered at the simple gesture that probably meant nothing to this tough-minded, professional FBI agent. He probably did the same thing to female agents he worked with all the time. It was no big deal. Gentlemen did little gracious things like that every day. She'd seen it in movies and on TV. But to Savannah, it felt like the sweetest caress. It meant something.

Agent Boniface wasn't just being cavalier like Dr. John. *Eww.* She cringed recalling the smell of RJ's bad breath in her face and his grasping fingernails digging into her forearms. What had he thought, that she was his girlfriend now that Gran Mere was gone? He'd acted like it.

Agent Boniface's touch felt more sincere, as if everyone watching had better understand that she was in his care and under his protection. Unable to resist the masculine warmth at her back, Savannah leaned into him instead of taking her seat.

His palm curled around her waist. "You're not going to pass out on me, are you?" he asked in that gruff, no-nonsense FBI tone he seemed able to summon on command.

Savannah cast a glance over her shoulder and up at him. Agent Boniface was standing so close, his chest was almost touching her arm. Her bronzed and golden man looked down at her. Time seemed to stop.

That was how she'd always remember this tawny skinned, amber-eyed federal agent who'd come to her aid on the worst day of her life. Something coiled between them, and for one heart-stealing moment, the world of syrup and waffles ceased to exist. It was just them, just Agent Boniface and her standing together— somewhere. His eyes were extra dark, his pupils big and black. The amber around the edges had turned soft, more brown than gold. His breath hitched. He canted his head. Just barely. Just enough to make her think he wanted to kiss her.

She licked her bottom lip, wishing he would and wondering if he'd taste like the melted maple syrup she saw in his eyes. All at once, the manly hold on her waist felt exquisitely intimate, as if he didn't want to let her go any more than she wanted him to release her. As if they really were a couple. As if she had any claim on him.

"Do I, umm, have to call you Special Agent Boniface?" she asked breathlessly as her wayward tongue slid over her bottom lip again. "Don't you have a first name?"

His gaze turned smoky, tracking the innocent movement of her tongue. "Keller," he answered, his voice uncommonly hoarse for a man so refined and proper. The grumpy corners of his mouth turned up the tiniest bit. "Please, call me Keller."

"Keller, huh?" Her heart pounded like a flock of hummingbird wings had suddenly taken flight in her throat. "It fits you. I like it." *Kiss me.*

And just that fast, up-tight, in-control Sergeant Friday was back on duty. Keller stiffened as if he'd suddenly remembered who he was. He took a step back. He dropped his hand. He let her go.

*Darn.* Disappointment was a hard pill to swallow. Savannah masked hers as she stepped away from the man who wasn't really her knight in shining armor.

Why had she thought he was? *He's a stranger, a federal agent on a mission to save his friend, not you. You're the last person he expected to see. Stop acting like a duck.*

Sliding all the way across the smooth burgundy upholstered vinyl seat, she still wished he'd take the hint and sit on the same bench with her. That'd be nice.

He didn't. Instead Keller—*oh, I like that name*—followed common social convention and took the opposite bench. Kissing him was a foolish idea anyway. He wasn't one of the silly boys from town.

Puzzled at the way her mind and body seemed to be working against her today, she nodded, silently agreeing with herself. She'd bet her last two cents Special Agent Boniface had never traveled in a pirogue or trapped a gator. The man was big-city pressed and big-city clean. Professional men didn't waste time gigging frogs or trapping nutria, the big rats chewing their way through the bayou. They were civilized and they held civilized jobs. Clean jobs. They had clean hands, too.

His asking her to breakfast meant nothing. He was just being polite. This wasn't a date, and she was not going to entertain a silly schoolgirl crush by thinking it was. His treating her like a lady was simply what nice city guys did. They graciously took care of business. They were polite and kind. But when their social obligations were met, they went back to their white-collar lives and their high-society wives. End of story.

But Savannah also recognized a troubled animal behind that crisp, clean façade. Smiling did not come easy to Keller, and she wanted to know why. Married or not, this elegant male held his cards too close to his chest. His unwillingness to share might win a hand in poker, but in the game of life, it made him vulnerable. It left him wanting and bereft of things he had a right to. Happiness, for one. Love, for another. Comfort, for sure.

The moment he'd held onto her to keep her from falling back at Gran Mere's told Savannah a lot. He'd expected to receive nothing but pain at the contact, but Savannah had shocked him when she'd offered relief instead. Gran Mere had always said to do unto others like you'd wanted them to do unto you. So Savannah gave Agent Boniface what she gave her dogs. Solace and Sanctuary. Maybe a tiny bit of—

No. This was not love. Dogs were easy to love. Men were different. They were complicated. He wasn't a dog. Like Agent Boniface, she was just being nice.

"Can I get you kids something to drink?" the perky platinum-blonde hostess who'd been waiting for them to take their seats asked. "Coffee, sweet tea, soda?"

"Coffee," Savannah said simultaneously with Keller. A quiet laugh bubbled out of her, a sound she very much needed to hear after the events of the morning.

"Two coffees," Keller said, then asked Savannah, "Cream or sugar?"

"You tell me," she teased, needing to feel normal instead of embarrassed for being such a hick.

*But you are a hick.*

*I know that,* she answered herself, *but he might not know it.*

His eyes narrowed for less than a second before he looked up at the hostess and said, "We'll take a couple flavored creamers. Sugar too."

Savannah could've laughed out loud. He'd just tried to probe her mind. She'd felt his energy, but it evaporated at first contact with her energy. Oh my gosh. She'd suspected as much, but now she knew for sure. Keller wasn't telepathic. At. All.

"You betcha," the hostess replied as she placed two menus on the table and gathered the extra napkins and silverware. "Tyrone's your waiter this morning. He'll be right with you. Y'all have a nice day now, ya hear?"

"What'll it be?" Agent Boniface asked as he flipped quickly through the sticky, plasticized two-page menu. "Waffles or—waffles?"

"Good morning, America!" a tall, slender young man exclaimed when he placed two hearty mugs filled with coffee to a good inch below their brims on the table. Dressed in the corporate uniform of the day, black slacks, WH issued tan shirt, and black apron, the bright yellow name tag on his chest declared Tyrone had arrived. "Whatcha all eatin' this mornin', folks?"

Keller nodded at the mugs. "Thanks for not filling them full."

"I'll bet you're one of them guys who likes a little coffee with his creamer, huh?" Tyrone's chocolate brown eyes sparkled.

"And coffee's easier to stir when it's not sloshing over the edge. Good job."

"You bet. Mama always says make room for all the sugar and cream you can, cuz life's tough enough. Don't need to make it tougher."

Keller's eyes narrowed on Savannah. "Do you know what you want?"

"Oh, my, I umm..." And there she stalled. There were so many choices. So many different versions of pancakes, omelets and breakfast combinations. Whoever heard of peanut butter waffles? "I, umm..." *Hmmm. Cinnamon French toast...*

"We'll need a few more minutes," Keller told Tyrone.

"Sure. I'll check back in a couple."

"I'm sorry," Savannah whispered after Tyrone sauntered away. "I don't get out much." The understatement of the day.

Keller nodded like he understood. Man, was he in for a surprise. "I imagine you've been busy taking care of your great grandmother."

"Not at all. Lately, I've been too busy at Sanctuary to visit Gran Mere..." Instant remorse swamped Savannah. Wasn't that the truth? She'd been so preoccupied with the latest additions to her four-legged family that she'd neglected the one person in her life who'd meant the most.

Keller reached across the table and lifted her fingers from her menu with a gentle squeeze. "I am sorry for your loss, Miss Church. I wish you'd let me do something for you."

She put on her brave face as his body heat once more lapped over hers. For some reason, he seemed able to share his strength as well as his comfort through touch. Pinching his fingertips, she let go of him first this time. "I'm handling things at the moment. But if you're Keller, then I'm just Savannah."

A glittering vein of golden amusement twinkled deep in his eyes. "Of course. So what are you hungry for, Savannah?"

He'd made her name sound as delicious as those peanut butter waffles. "Pancakes," she breathed as she skimmed the menu, hurrying to decide, so he wouldn't think she'd never been to town. She had, just not recently. "Ummmm..." The chocolate chip pancakes looked good, but those pecan waffles... "I'm ready to order."

Keller signaled Tyrone. The moment he trotted back to the table, she told him, "I'd like pecan waffles, please." Gran Mere always said to put on your Sunday morning manners when you went to town. 'Course, she also said to make sure your underwear was clean in case you got into an accident, which Savannah always did.

"Excellent choice. Would you like eggs with that?"

*Oh, that'd be nice.* "Sure."

"One egg or two?"

*Ooo, choices.* "I'll have two," she replied, proud of herself for adding protein to her all-carb order.

Tyrone must know shorthand. He had everything written down on that little tablet of his before she'd finished speaking. "How would you like them cooked?"

She blinked up at him. He was so nice!

"Sunnyside up? Over-easy? Over-medium? Over-hard? Scrambled? Poached or—?"

"Scrambled," she replied before she lost track of her choices. There was a reason she didn't eat out.

Self-conscious now, she looked past Tyrone to the woman and the older gentleman in the booth across the aisle. The woman was upset, and the gentleman stared at his food. Something was wrong, but not with him. The more the woman talked at him, the worse he felt, until the despair rolling off him hit Savannah like a slap in the face. The woman was his daughter and she'd decided he needed an assisted living home. She couldn't handle him leaving the stove on in her house anymore. She'd had enough.

"Cheese?" Tyrone asked.

Savannah nodded to get him to go away. "Please."

"What kind? We've got provolone, swiss, cheddar, American, gouda, and—"

*Oh. My. Gosh!* "Cheddar."

"Grits on the side?" Tyrone's dark eyes really did sparkle, darn him.

"No. That's all I want, just waffles and eggs and..." She waved a hand at him. "...and whatever else I already ordered."

"Excellent." He turned to Keller. "And you, sir?"

"Ham and eggs, over-medium, wheat toast, no hash browns. And please don't forget the creamer."

Savannah sighed, mentally storing Keller's succinct order for the next time she ate out. He made it sound easy.

# Chapter Nine

Savannah Church really was quite lovely. The more she'd sputtered over her menu selections, the more Keller watched, cataloged, and relaxed. In truth, he couldn't take his eyes off her. Her cheeks had long since turned a delicious shade of Georgia peach with embarrassment. She still worried her lush bottom lip with each decision to be made, but when she blinked those expressive chocolate windows to her soul at poor Tyrone... When she batted those thick, long eyelashes...

*Lord help me.* Keller and Tyrone were in trouble. There wasn't so much a mystery to Savannah Church as there was a shockingly sweet innocence inside of her that took a man by storm. What you saw truly was what you got with her, and Keller saw an uncomplicated woman of uncommon worth. A beauty beyond compare. A unique gift in a world gone batshit crazy with decadence, porn, and entitlement.

When at last Tyrone walked away, Keller asked Savannah, "You really don't get out much, do you?"

She made a face that took his breath. Her forehead wrinkled, her nose crinkled, even her moist mauve lips wrinkled, and he was a smitten man. No. He was still poor white trash, but damned if she didn't look like an exotic Egyptian princess sitting there with a solid gold glimmer in her eyes. The urge to kiss the back of her hand like an unworthy, humble servant was compelling.

"I know," she all but growled at him. "Did you hear how many choices there are? I never knew ordering at a restaurant could be so... so complicated."

He cocked his head at her. "You've never eaten out?"

"Sure, but..." There went those delightful wrinkles again, wrinkles no doubt derived from smiles and laughter, things he'd forgotten how to do. Despite how horribly this day had begun, Savannah was somehow still able to smile. In doing so, she spread sunshine over everyone else in the overly-sweet-smelling restaurant. Better yet? She was smiling at him.

"It has been a long time," she admitted. "Gran Mere was a stickler for fixin' her own food at home instead of buying store-bought or eating out. She said what's in most processed grains and meats these days will kill every last one of us. Did you know a lot of dogs can't eat store-bought dog food unless it's grain-free?

What's that tell you about what we're about to put into our bodies, huh?" She tossed that question at Keller like a challenge.

Forget the grain. Keller knew what he wanted to put into her beguiling, sensual body.

When Savannah's fingers curled around her steaming mug, she lifted it to her mouth, blinking. Waiting for him to say something clever. His brain kicked out of gear. He was not a man of many words, but he couldn't help but track her tongue as she licked her lips, then tasted the rim of the cup, tipping it for a sip. She had yet to doctor her coffee with sugar and cream and...

*I'll be damned.* Savannah drank her coffee black while he was still waiting on sugar and creamer. And that simmering smile? She knew he'd tried to read her mind—and failed. His tough FBI façade cracked. At least she was nice enough to not comment on his pathetic psychic skills.

Chagrined, Keller changed the subject of dogs and grains to more urgent matters. "If you need help with your great grandmother's service, anything, I'm here to help. I've got a couple days off."

Her lashes fell like artist's paintbrushes fanned over a palette of blushing mocha latte. "I'll be okay," she replied, a shimmer replacing her earlier confidence as her gaze dropped to the table. "Gran Mere has, umm, *had*..." She cleared her throat, emphasizing that hard, last word. "...everything taken care of. She did that years ago. Her final resting place.

Her headstone. Even her obituary. She said the more she took care of things, the less I'd have to worry when... when..."

"Gran Mere was a rare woman," he murmured, wanting Savannah to look at him again. "If you'd like, I can stay for the service."

The ends of her dark hair trembled at the crest of her shoulders. "That's generous of you, but I'm sure you have a life to get back to."

*I do but... not really.* "Nothing that can't wait. At least let me drive you to where you need to go. Use and abuse me. Might as well. I'm here for the duration either way."

"Here you are, folks," Tyrone interrupted as he set a small bowl of various creamers on their table. "Your order's up. It'll be out in a minute."

"Thanks," Keller replied before the young man all but ran away. He doctored his coffee.

Her cup went down to the table and her hand came up, raking over her head, unsettling those ebony locks that fell like so many strands of black silk, kissing her shoulders again. Shoulders that shouldn't have to deal with the heavy burden of handling funeral arrangements alone. The red beads sparkling at her neckline should have been rubies. *Rubies fit for a true queen.*

She met his gaze, her eyes glistening. "I don't want to talk about it. Can we please—not?"

"No problem. You've got my number. Call when or if you need anything." Keller's nose twitched to catch her delicate scent among the overpowering aromas of sugar and steaming batter. He'd never paid attention to flowers before, but he would from now on. Especially lilacs.

But he knew better. She'd never call, and after this one pathetic morning, Savannah would be out of his life forever. She didn't know him. He didn't know her. They were two strangers who'd shared one helluva bad day. Nothing more.

From this day forward, she would learn how to cope with her Gran Mere's death. She was strong, she was young, and she'd learn quickly. She'd adjust. Time would pass and she'd heal. That was what people did. They got on with their lives. *Time heals all wounds, and all that crap...*

He grunted. He was a great one to talk about healing. He surely hadn't. Didn't know how. Didn't want to learn. Just plain refused to move on. Wasn't sure he could. So he asked her to, "Tell me about Sanctuary."

"It's nothing special, just a home for stray cats and dogs. Some birds." The muscles in her slender neck contracted as she swallowed. "A couple of barns. One of these days, I need to set them both on stilts in case the levee breaks again or if the swamp floods. That's all Sanctuary is. A no-kill shelter."

"Sounds like you manage the local pound."

That got an indelicate grunt out of her. "I guess I do in a way. Some days, seems more like it manages me."

"Is it located in town?" He probed to keep her talking.

"No. That'd be unfair to all my dogs and cats. They need fresh air and room to run."

*So, where then?* Keller waited Savannah out. There was something about the way she moved her tongue over her lush lips as if she relished talking about the work she did. "I could show you," she whispered over the rim of her cup.

Good idea. That might be the diversion she needed. Keller toasted her before he drained his cup and then said, "It's a deal. How about we swing by Sanctuary after we eat?"

"Why do you care? It's out of your way, and I'm sure an FBI agent has better things to do than visit a bunch of smelly, old dogs and cats."

Ah, now she was playing with him. Savannah didn't believe her dogs were smelly, and he doubted many of them were old. Keller lifted both shoulders, not ready to analyze why he'd requested time off or why he felt the need to linger anywhere in Louisiana. He had no vested interest in this state. Only he did. Where once this land held nothing but ghosts, he now smelled lilacs.

"Do you have other family? Does Dr. John live near you?" *Please, say no.*

She met his question with one of her own. "Are you always this attentive to the... the victims you meet in your line of work?"

He shook his head at her assessment. "You're not a victim. You're a survivor."

Tyrone returned with their orders, interrupting as he shuffled plates full of waffles, ham, and eggs onto their respective placemats.

But Keller recognized the talk-to-the-hand in Savannah's reply. Which meant good old RJ was part of her life, and Keller should mind his business. Which was true. It wasn't like he had reason to hang around Gran Mere's great granddaughter. Turkey Creek was a few hours north, and Carol Marie's headstone needed to be tended. That was where he should go. Weeds grew up quickly in the South, kudzu even quicker. He lifted his cup in a mock toast and said with as much cheer as he could muster, "To Sanctuary, then."

Savannah offered a weak smile but met his cup with her own mid-table. "To your safe return home."

*Yeah. That.*

# Chapter Ten

The pecan waffles weren't that tasty after all. They stuck in her throat and they were too sweet. Savannah couldn't seem to summon enough spit to swallow the dough, but worse? She couldn't wait to get away from Agent Boniface. That annoying voice in the back of her mind kept telling her she'd been foolish to think this handsome white man could be attracted to her. He was a professional federal agent, uptight and in strict control of everything he did. He could never want a woman like her. The sooner they visited Sanctuary, and once he realized what she did for a living, he'd be long gone.

But that poor elderly gentleman across the aisle... She couldn't keep from eavesdropping on the turmoil in his mind. *Lyle Goldenrod. Former basketball coach at the local high school. Recent widower. Going on seventy-seven with a heart condition. A has been.*

*Washed up. A burden to his daughter and her two sons. Easily confused. Prone to wander off and forget things. Like his car. Where he lived. Where he left his keys...*

And enough. "Excuse me," Savannah told Keller as she eased out of the booth, calling out, "Mr. Goldenrod? Oh my gosh, is it really you?"

That stopped his daughter cold. Made Keller look, too. But the sweet silver-haired gentleman's sweet blue eyes lit up as if he knew Savannah. "Well, hi there, Miss—"

"Church! Savannah Church!" she interrupted as she crossed the aisle and slid into the booth next to him. "I meant to call earlier to tell you congratulations! You're hired!"

"I'm hired?" he said the same moment his daughter spiked an imperious brow and asked, "He's what?"

It took Savannah mere seconds to retrieve this unsmiling woman's name from her overly organized, calculating, stress-filled head. "Oh, hi, Virginia. Your dad told me what a help you've been. Yes, I put an ad in the paper for a ground's assistant a couple weeks ago, and your father applied. I'm afraid I don't have enough work for a forty-hour week, but I do need someone to help around Sanctuary while I tend to my dogs."

"And just what is Sanctuary?" Virginia asked.

*Whoa. Could she get more condescending?*

"Excuse me, I should've introduced myself better. I'm Savannah Church, the owner and manager of

Sanctuary, the only privately-owned dog shelter east of New Orleans. It's not far from here." She turned to the elder Goldenrod at her side. He'd already made room for her on the bench and had turned his shoulders to face her. "Do you still want the job? Oh, I hope so. If you do, I'll need you to start first thing Monday morning. The job comes with free room and board, meals, plus plenty of fresh air and all the four-legged companionship you can stand."

He took her hand in his, which gave Savannah another chance to instill calming reassurance into him despite her out of the blue announcement. His hand was cold to the touch and frail. But she sensed determination and pride. "I'm afraid it isn't technically challenging work, Coach Goldenrod, but I really need someone I can trust. Someone I won't have to train. Someone like you." And he needed this opportunity to get out from his daughter's domineering plan for the rest of his life. An assisted care center? What a waste of an intelligent man's life. So what if he was a little forgetful? Savannah forgot things all the time. She ended with, "Please?"

"I most humbly accept, Miss Church," he said, a light back in his weary blue eyes. "How about we negotiate wages and benefits Monday morning? I might have a few ideas for Sanctuary."

What a charming fellow! Savannah could have hugged him for catching on so fast and playing along.

"Dad," Virginia said sternly. "I don't think—"

That was the problem. Her stern attitude. She talked down to this delightful father of hers as if he were an errant child instead of her respected elder. Which Savannah understood. Caretakers were the easily forgotten shadows in the waning years of their parents' lives. They suffered in silence as the joy and satisfaction of their lives was slowly sucked into the never-ending health issues of their aged mother and father. But that was the circle of life.

"Ginny," he replied just as sternly. *Go, Lyle! Go!* "I need this, and that's all there is to it."

"But Dad..."

Lyle Goldenrod's left brow lifted.

Ginny rolled her eyes.

He cocked his head.

Reaching across the table, Savannah laid a hand over Ginny's white-knuckled fist to infuse her with a titch more trust in her father. "I've looked up to Coach Goldenrod since the first time I saw him." Which was true. Lyle's projected grief and loss for his wife were what snagged her attention about fifteen minutes ago. How could she not admire a man who'd loved the same woman for more than fifty years? "You're so lucky your father lives with you. I never knew mine."

Ginny's gaze scrolled to her father. "If you're sure..."

The corners of his eyes crinkled as if they'd forgotten how to do that. "I am. I know this comes as a surprise to you. Frankly, I'm surprised, too." He squeezed Savannah's hand. "Let's discuss your plans for my future more after breakfast, Ginny. I'm not ready to be put out to pasture."

Savannah took that as a good sign. Dialogue worked so much better than domination. She plucked Ginny's home phone number from Lyle's mind and said, "It's been so good to meet you Ginny, but I've taken enough of your time. I'll be in touch, Coach. See you Monday!"

"I'm counting on it," he replied as he patted the back of her hand before she got away. "Until Monday."

"Until Monday," Savannah purred, pleased that Lyle Goldenrod had accepted her off-the-cuff offer. Just as pleased she'd thought of it. A groundskeeper was precisely what she needed. She wished she'd thought of it sooner.

Sighing, she eased back into her booth to face the self-controlled federal agent across from her. She had herself convinced Keller was as uptight as an Army general until he stretched that clean, gentlemanly hand across the sea of dirty plates between them, took careful hold of her fingertips, and said, "You're something else, Savannah. Why'd you name your place Sanctuary?"

Her heart nearly leaped out of her throat at the gentle contact. She used the same tactic to instill peace in her outcast cats and dogs. A calming touch worked wonders on frightened creatures, even that possum she'd rescued one time.

Only Savannah wasn't frightened. Suddenly, she was mad at herself all over again for ever thinking a *'woman of color'* like her stood a chance with a strong, handsome white man the likes of Keller Boniface. Holy Mother, he was beautiful. Yet even his title declared their differences. Special agents were highly skilled, intelligent professionals. Men of the world. White collar all the way. No doubt he had a college degree, possibly a masters.

*But you're just an enterprising woman with a high school diploma who cleans kennels and collects unwanted strays for a living. Someone like you has no business lusting after a man like him.*

There was her nagging inner voice again, reminding her what the two of them must look like to the other customers in this restaurant. Him in his elegant business suit and polished leather shoes. She in everyday shorts, dirty denim shorts at that, ratty pink tank top, and wearing Gran Mere's old canvas sandals. Him from the civilized world, dining with a hick from the swamps who barely knew how to order breakfast. She hadn't even combed her hair since that freakish windstorm inside Gran Mere's.

Self-conscious now and aware of every other customer in the place, Savannah raked her free hand across her bangs just in case her hair looked as bad as she thought. Somewhere along the line she'd inherited the straight hair gene. What she wouldn't give for a little curl right then to tuck her hair behind her ears and keep it out of her eyes.

Stretching forward, Keller traced the tip of his index finger over her forehead, then tucked another loose strand behind her ear. Clever man must read body language.

"I called it Sanctuary because animals aren't any different than humans," she told him earnestly. "Every living thing needs safe shelter. That's where we heal best."

Where on earth was Tyrone? She needed another sip of coffee, and she needed it quick. Her throat had gone sandpaper dry, and her poor heart seemed to be climbing up her throat and into her mouth. She could barely think with the warmth whispering off Keller's fingertips.

"Are all your rescues adoptable or do you rescue them to keep them?"

"Every l-l-last one of them's adoptable." And now she was stuttering. *Wait, is he leaning forward? No, I am!* She promptly stiffened her back. Gran Mere always said guys didn't like pushy women. "And, and, and..." *And now I sound like a teenage girl with a crush.*

Pulling out of his tender reach, Savannah cleared her throat to keep from scrambling across the table and into his arms. "I...I advertise. That way people know my dogs are healthy and safe."

Man, this guy had thick, let-me-touch-you eyelashes. She wanted to run her hands all over that intent, sexy face, her thumbs over his brows, not to mention what she wanted to do with that mouth. Those lips. "I run..." *Cough, cough, cough.* "...adopt-a-thons out of the local pet stores when they let me.

Howie's is the best. Mr. Howard even fosters some of my babies to help me find homes for them."

"In N'Orlinz?" Agent Boniface pronounced New Orleans like a local.

"Why? You looking for company?" Why did that sound like a sleazy come-on? Savannah could've stabbed her eye with her sticky, syrupy fork. "I mean, umm, are you l-l-looking for a pet?"

"Maybe. Let's go see what you've got." And why did that sound like he wasn't talking about cats and dogs?

"Umm," Savannah stalled. She'd thought she had him figured out, only now...

He was so cut and pressed. So clean. So proper. She could almost smell the starch on him. "Are you sure you want to do that? There'll be barking and other noises, smells and—"

"Trust me. Those hound dogs of yours won't smell any worse than some of the soldiers I've bunked with over the years." He slapped two twenties to the tabletop as he tugged her over the slippery bench.

Savannah dashed her napkin to her mouth and climbed to her feet. Once again, his hand settled at the small of her back, and she lost track of where she was going. The world narrowed down to the firm outline of his palm and the illicit tactile sensation of each finger and thumb on her body. Even if his deference to her was nothing more than making sure she didn't stumble like some backward hick, Savannah's heart thundered at the sublime sensation of this man's touch. His hand was warm and big, and it felt good. So good.

Agent Boniface seemed able to pass comfort with just a touch. No wonder Gran Mere had smiled after he'd checked her pulse. He wasn't anything like her stoic, emotionless, letter-of-the-law Sergeant Friday after all. Uh uh. Agent Boniface was one tall, manly beacon of tawny eye candy, and Savannah meant to treasure this moment the rest of her life.

Like the pictures she'd taken of Gran Mere over the years, she'd shake the dust off this delicious memory in years to come. She'd recall how once upon a time an authentic gentleman had treated her like a real lady. She'd remember how his eyes simmered when he thought she wasn't looking. Savannah was caught in the same teenage conundrum: *Look. Don't look. Eyes colliding. Oh, my gosh, he's looking at me. Hurry! Look away! Only to glance back to see if he's looking again...*

Ah, the silly struggles of the heart.

When the heat of his palm coiled around her waist, she stopped where she stood, needing to savor the gentle way he held her without really holding her. The way he towered over her, making her feel sheltered and cared for. The all-male sensational way he smelled. Her lungs expanded as they filled with scents unique to this man. Honestly. Most of her days were spent with cats and dogs. She knew stink, and she knew how to disguise most of it. But all the air fresheners in the world couldn't compare with the delectable, provocative scent of the male at her side.

Agent Boniface didn't remove his hand until they were on the sidewalk, and she leaned away from him to climb into his rental, a sleek, silver Camaro. Forcing her mind off feelings she could never reveal, Savannah settled in, fastened her seatbelt, took a deep breath of that new car smell, and directed him to Sanctuary.

"Tell me what mojo you put in the bag," Keller said, nonchalantly steering away from the restaurant. "I assume it's for Isaiah. You want me to take it back to him?"

She dug into her front pants pocket and pulled up the red bag. "I almost forgot. Yes, I'll leave it here in the center console. Tell him to wear it around his neck at all times. The cord's long enough and it's a small bag. It'll tuck under his shirt. It won't show."

"What's in it?"

She kept her eyes on the road. "The usual. Rose quartz to steady his heart. Iron for strength to fight. A single white feather for purity and..." Would Keller understand why she'd chosen the rose petal? Savannah hoped so. He seemed to understand the rest of Gran Mere's ritual that, over the years, had combined her odd brand of Catholicism with the universe. "And one dried rose petal. That's all he needs."

Out of the corner of her eye, Savannah saw Keller's lips purse. "A flower petal, huh? Never would've guessed that one."

"Not just any petal. A red rose petal. It's for love. I wasn't casting a love potion, though." Agent Boniface needed to understand that. "The petal magnifies the power of the feather."

"So you don't..." He coughed. "...you don't kill anything? You don't do the whole blood sacrifice thing?"

"Oh, heavens, no!" Where'd that crazy idea come from? "I know some folks might, but not me and Gran Mere, never. She always said more good came from prayer than ever came from cruelty. You really can catch more flies with honey, you know."

That answer seemed to calm Keller. He nodded, his eyes still on the road.

Savannah pressed on about Isaiah. "Until this morning, your friend thought he was responsible for all the evil in the world. Somewhere during his life, he convinced himself it was his job to save everyone else. The petal will help him remember who he is and who he isn't. Like him, it's one small part of the whole flower. It'll help him focus on what's true, not what everyone else expects of him."

"And what is true?

"What else? His wife and his unborn baby boy. Everything else is less. Don't you think a man's family should be his first love, his first priority?"

"Well, yeah. Sure," Keller said quietly.

Savannah knew she'd said too much to a man who'd lost his wife and still carried a torch for her. But that question about blood sacrifice bothered her. He'd seen things and had possibly done things that still haunted him. She could tell.

He drove in silence while Savannah directed where and when to turn. Past the rice paddies and crawfish ponds. Over the levee. Way out around the edge of the bayou, then over Jefferson bridge, past the turn-off to Gran Mere's place and onto the southern-most corner of Gran Mere's property. With his index finger tapping the steering wheel, he finally asked, "Would you mind explaining the bag?"

"The red pouch I put everything in?"

"No. The magic you believe you put into the gris-gris."

Savannah turned in her seat to look at him then. Keller had unbuttoned his jacket after breakfast. His body was a study in angular, relaxed muscles. With his long legs folded, his knees bumped against the underside of the steering wheel. He'd loosened his slacks at his knees, accentuating his muscled thigh every time his foot worked the accelerator. He kept one hand relaxed on the wheel, the other on the open window, his fingers tapping into the wind.

But mostly, she liked how his shirt wrinkled over his stomach before it tucked into his pants and belt. Keller was so much like a sleek gold puma, long-waisted, relaxed, yet wary. Simmering.

Loosening her seatbelt, she tucked one foot under her other leg. "You say it right, gree-gree instead of griz-griz like grizzly bear, which is how most tourists pronounce it. Yet you don't know what it means? Didn't you learn anything in Turkey Creek?"

Those wide manly shoulders lifted. "I know a little," he admitted. But a dark note had crept into his voice since he'd asked the question, as if simply mentioning his hometown bothered him.

"A gris-gris is just a prayer in a bag," she told him honestly. "It's a collection of natural items that resonate specific energies. Certain vibes, I guess you could call them. Gran Mere taught me to match those energies to the needs of the individual. Even the color of the bag means something."

Keller nodded without taking his eyes off the road. "I get it, red's for love, so in a way, you did make a love potion for him."

"Yes, but not romantic love. Isaiah's problems were not about falling in love. He's already there. His problem was his heart. It was being torn apart by things he'd been told as a child, things he'd long ago accepted as fact. Like his being responsible for everyone else in the world." Savannah cleared her throat. "What happened to make him that way? Do you know?"

"His last name's Zaroyin," Keller replied as if that explained everything.

Savannah ducked her head into her shoulders. "So? My last name's Church. Doesn't mean I hear confessions or say Mass."

"As in he's Abraham Zaroyin's kid."

She resisted the urge to scratch her head at yet another non-answer to a simple question. "Is that supposed to mean something?"

Keller glanced at her out of the corner of his eye. "You really don't know, do you?"

"No, but I wish you'd stop beating around the bush and just tell me." Savannah gave him her sweetest smile. But then she wished she hadn't.

"Isaiah's mother was murdered one night when his father wasn't home," Keller said evenly, "which I imagine was most of the time back then. Doc Zaroyin was a brilliant scientist, but he got mixed up with the wrong people. He might've told Isaiah to take care of his mom, that he was the man of the house, before he'd taken off for the night. Which made Isaiah responsible for what happened. But he wasn't. That sin's on Abe Zaroyin's head. Doc's responsible for her death, for what that death did to his traumatized teenaged son. The son of a bitch is responsible for everything that happened to Isaiah after he lost his mom. For the deaths of hundreds of FBI agents a few years back, too."

Keller drew in a deep breath after that long rant. "His old man's in prison now, which is hard enough on Isaiah. I honestly think he still loves the bastard, but his mom was the only real parent in his life. I know she loved him. He has no other relatives. He was an only child—"

"An exceptional only child..." Savannah breathed.

"Yes, and when she died, this team, this mixed-up—"

"Deuce's Wild Team..."

"...became Isaiah's only family..."

"And Mr. Chase is...?"

"The biggest ass in the world."

"But you respect him as much as you care about Isaiah."

Keller's mouth snapped shut at what Savannah knew was a truth he wasn't ready to admit. She'd strayed too far into personal territory again, but she was right. "You said you knew Isaiah's mother loved him? Did you know her?"

"No."

"Well then, how do you—?"

That earned her another snort. A grunt. Then a terse, "Because I feel Isaiah's loss every Mother's Day. Every Christmas and every time the sun sets, that's why."

Savannah sat back in her seat at all the suffering this man kept to himself because of his unique but torturous gift. Even now, Keller carried the pain for all his friend had lost. He was another one who needed to learn how to let it go. But now was not the time for that lesson.

"Is that why you came all this way to speak with Gran Mere?" she asked quietly. "To save your friend?"

"Yes," Keller answered, his voice gone flat. "He couldn't shut his mind off. He said it was powering him instead of him powering it. And he was dying. Somehow, Tucker knew about your great grandmother, that she had the same problem as Isaiah, but could control it."

Savannah pursed her lips, considering that perspective. She'd never considered that an outside force from the universe might have powered her sweet Gran Mere all these years, but it made sense. The universe did echo back all that a person projected into it. Good did return for good. Evil for evil. But to get back more energy? She'd never thought of that.

"Isaiah's problem was not his gift. Rather, it was his guilt for thinking he wasn't good enough to save everyone," she explained gently.

"See? How do you even know that?" Keller asked, his temper rising. "I get that you're an empath, but why couldn't I help Isaiah? If you could reach into his psyche to help him, why couldn't I? Shit, I've worked alongside the guy for months."

Savannah reached out, projecting quiet energy to the suddenly tense male bicep that felt hard as a rock beside her. Keller wanted to hit something. He was frustrated with his perceived failure, yet he also felt a genuine kinship with Isaiah. He felt closed off and alone, yet he belonged to an amazing team of federal agents. And he was warm. His arm throbbed with energy and remorse for never being good enough.

"Because you also carry remorse for sins you didn't commit." She cleared her throat as the first jackhammer of denial rolled from Keller to her hand and up her arm. Man, this guy's negativity packed a punch. "It's okay," she soothed. "It's a skill learned from childhood. I can help you with that, but first you need to understand that you're already good enough, Keller. You *do* help people, and you're constantly looking for ways to help others. I sensed it in the way you talked to Gran Mere. It's part of who you are. You just don't give yourself credit for it."

He growled, his customary answer when he didn't want to share and needed people to back off. But Savannah kept talking. Just because she'd made him angry didn't mean she didn't like him. "Gran Mere taught at a psychic symposium a couple years ago. That might be where your boss learned about her. Like Isaiah, she also lost her mother when she was quite young. In fact, she witnessed her father murder her mother and her two sisters. I don't know if that experience caused her mind to snap and expand, or if she was born with her gift. But Gran Mere believed her power saved her life that awful night. She was the youngest, only three at the time, but—"

And there Savannah stopped. If Gran Mere had remembered the events of that night accurately, and if she hadn't, as a small child, embellished what had actually occurred, she'd been a powerful three-year-old indeed. Scary powerful.

"She influenced her father to kill himself before he could kill her, didn't she?" Keller asked quietly. "Was that what you were going to say? Is that what you believe happened? That a three-year-old had the power to influence an enraged and drunken adult male to end himself?"

"I believe that some minds are strong at birth and some are not," Savannah admitted softly, mesmerized by the white dashes and lines running down the center of the highway as all Gran Mere had told her flooded back like the bayou reclaiming the land in a storm. Unfortunately, what she believed happened begged more frightening questions. Had Gran Mere known how strong her powers were before her father killed the rest of her family? Had she manipulated her father to kill her mother and sisters? Had she known as a three-year-old that she'd never be held accountable? Had she been that powerful? Those thoughts were too mind-numbingly terrible to entertain. Gran Mere had always been wise and kind. True evil begot evil, not someone as sweet and giving as Gran Mere. The universe just didn't work like that. Like did attract like.

"A good Christian family took her in the next day. The O'Reillys. They loved her as if she were their biological daughter. They adored her, and she adored them. They gave her everything, including what she needed to heal."

"What? No, don't tell me. Let me guess." A deep sigh breathed out of Keller. "They gave her a dog. A puppy. I'm right, huh?"

"Yes, they gave her a Pitbull puppy named Shank, and they gave her love." Savannah nodded as another circle closed. Now Keller knew why she rescued endangered animals. Because of the healing power of that first perfect puppy that saved her Gran Mere's life.

Cats were the aloof familiars who reached out when and if they felt like it. Instead of just anyone who fed them, they claimed only specific people during their spiritual travels. Dogs, on the other hand, claimed everyone, even cruel men and women who beat, starved, and abused them. Like divine messengers sent from above, they freely forgave mankind, over and over again.

The asphalt highway had reduced to red gravel by then. They were halfway to Sanctuary. Tall pine trees rose deep and green alongside the raised roadbed, while cypress trees stood knee deep in the perpetual swamp, water glistening between their gnarled trunks.

Savannah glanced at the man at her side. "You guys call yourselves kings of heart? Really?"

Keller made a funny face like he'd just sucked the pucker off a dill pickle. "Where'd you get that idea?"

"I saw playing cards when your friend contacted me, all hearts. A queen. A joker. An ace. But the king of hearts kept whirling around the other cards like a tornado."

Keller growled low in the back of his throat. "Had to be Tucker Chase, our director. He was beside himself when he thought Isaiah was dying. That and he's got some cockamamie notion each of us is a playing card in his lucky Deuces Wild deck. Which is really stupid. It's not like he's Alice, the Bureau's definitely not Wonderland, and I'm no soldier in the Red Queen's army."

Savannah would've laughed if she hadn't heard what Keller didn't say. He not only resented his superior, but he hadn't *seen.* He had no gift of *sight.* Only gut-wrenching empathy that drowned him in other's pain and anguish.

"You felt him dying, didn't you?" she breathed, understanding the rare type of empathy that ruled Keller now. "When Isaiah reached out to you, you felt exactly what he was feeling. That's why you couldn't breathe. You didn't need a drink of water. You needed to touch him, to take his pain away even though it would've killed you."

"Yeah, umm..." His Adam's apple bobbed when he swallowed, and wasn't that an attractive, masculine feature? Generally hidden from view, this man's neck added a certain caveman appeal to the overall robust male persona. Only it seemed Keller had something stuck in his throat.

Savannah didn't want to take her eyes off him. Long and lean, he'd slouched back in the driver's seat, itself pushed back as far as it could go as he stretched his legs forward. Until then, the man had been driving from a relaxed, prone position. He'd loosened his tie, but taut cords now stretched up the back of his tanned, shaved neck. Keller cut a handsome, albeit troubled profile with the early afternoon sun streaming through the window at his left.

The urge to reach out and cup this tawny jungle cat's jaw or scratch behind his ear compelled Savannah. Instead she rested her palm on his forearm. "Your gift is killing you, isn't it?"

He nodded a short, curt answer. "Sometimes, yeah. You could say that."

Knowing how he'd resisted her cure for Isaiah, she asked, "Will you let me help?"

"No. I'm good." Said every stubborn man ever.

She settled for, "Then tell me about Isaiah and your boss."

His broad chest expanded with a long, slow inhale. "They're both around six foot. Isaiah's a buck forty dripping wet, but Tucker's older. Bigger. Wider. He's a ruggedized Humvee while Isaiah's more like a sleek sports car. Tucker's crass. Isaiah's polished. Suave."

"A buck forty? What's that mean?"

"Sorry. Means Isaiah weighs around a hundred forty pounds. He's a lightweight, but he's dark-haired like Tucker. Honestly, he could pass for Tuck's baby brother. Isaiah's smart as a whip, though. Tucker's the boss, but Isaiah's the real psychic genius on the team. You'd like him."

"I already do, but that's not what I meant. Who are they? Really. To you?"

His chin came up. "They're just guys I work with."

He said that as if Isaiah and Tucker were merely ships he passed in the night, but Savannah knew better. She'd seen Keller nearly collapse when his boss called earlier. This tough FBI agent might not want to work with these particular men, but it was obvious they meant more than—

*BOOM!*

# Chapter Eleven

*Son-of-a-bitch!* Keller slammed both eyes shut as shattered safety glass from Savannah's side window blasted his face.

Savannah jerked into him like a rag doll. She screamed, "Someone hit us!" then gripped the dash with one hand while her other dug into his forearm.

"You hurt?" he asked, fighting to control the rental.

"I don't think so."

"Hold on," Keller ordered as he slammed the Camaro's brakes to keep it from slipping down the opposite bank and into the swamp. This section might not be deep, but he wouldn't risk getting caught in the tire-sucking mud, not with a monster truck climbing onto the road and dead on his ass. Damned thing was outfitted with a snorkel smokestack.

"You sure you're not hurt?" he asked, verifying the panic and anger vibrating off the womanly body at his right. Empathy had its silver linings. Being able to read Savannah's emotions the precise moment she touched him was definitely one of them. And right now, she was as pissed as he was. She wanted to strike back at whoever'd rammed them, too.

"Just scared. Didn't see that truck coming, did you?"

"Sure didn't." *But I sure as hell see it now.*

By then, the Camaro had settled back onto all four wheels on the road, but faced the opposite direction. After crossing the road and charging down the shallow embankment, the truck was in the process of churning a wide half-circle at Keller's left. Rooster tails sprayed high behind both rear tires when it gunned its engines and drifted sideways. The son-of-a-bitch was gunning for a second shot. The damned thing could easily climb over the Camaro like stink on pig shit. One more shove like the last, and the Camaro would be on its side in the swamp with Keller and Savannah trapped inside. Not happening.

Dropping the Camaro into low gear, Keller slammed his foot to the metal. Instant power. The car's rear-end engaged like a beast. Its racing tires dug into gravel and bedrock. *Oh yeah.* All four tires kicked ass while Keller executed a tight U-turn, showed that POS hillbilly truck his backside, then peppered the monster climbing into the center lane with a hefty shot of gravel.

Shifting into neutral, Keller asked Savannah, "Can you drive a stick?"

"You bet."

"Then slide over here and take the wheel. Get to Sanctuary as fast as you can. Wait for me there." He gave her no time to answer, just rolled out the door and onto his feet while he simultaneously unleashed both cannons he packed. Squaring his shoulders, Keller didn't stop until he stood between the truck and Savannah, poised to kill.

If only she'd done what he'd asked.

Pissed at the fools sitting behind the massive cold-rolled carbon steel push bar on the hefty truck ahead of him, Keller straightened his right arm and aimed at that now cracked windshield. Two men. Two targets. Two damned good P226 Sig Sauers packing forty-caliber Smith and Wesson rounds. This wouldn't take long.

"FBI," he shouted. "Put your hands where I can see them and get out of your vehicle."

There was no way to get a clear view of the driver from where Keller stood, not that he cared. Plucky sort though, sitting there with mud all over his ride and revving his engine like he thought he had a dog in this fight. No hands lifted out either driver or passenger windows, but Keller had time. These bastards would either comply or go down resisting arrest, he didn't much care which.

The Camaro had yet to move.

Not wasting time, Keller commenced forward, his pistol on the joker behind the wheel. Firing over the rig, he ordered both suspects again, "I'm FBI and you're under arrest. Put your hands up and step out of your vehicle. Do it now."

That elicited precisely what Keller expected. Gears shifted. The mighty wheels lurched, sewing mud up the rear flaps. Keller found himself looking up at a rig with three-foot high, heavy-duty, mud-terrain tread monster tires. A wicked slash cut through the tread on the left tire, a detail Keller stored for future use when he wasn't about to kill someone.

The truck lurched again. Spinning mud. Taunting him. Not one to let an insult go unchallenged, Keller charged the damned thing. Pissed at what this asshat attempted against Savannah, he fired one round through the windshield to make his point, then three into the radiator behind the fancy GMC emblem. No steam billowed skyward—what the hell? The truck kept coming. Worse, Savannah was now standing at his elbow. *Damn it!*

Fighting for her life now, Keller fired both weapons. But nothing slowed the beast barreling toward him. At the last second, Keller lifted both barrels to the sky, grabbed Savannah against him, and together they rolled down the embankment and straight into the swamp.

Landing on his back, he wrapped both arms around her, then crossed his pistols behind her back, ready to shoot if those bastards came after her. Whimpering, she buried her face in his chest, but Keller had no time to process the protective instincts roaring to life in his soul. They had to move. "We need to get back on the road before they run us over," he said.

That produced the proper response from Savannah. Pushing gingerly away from him, she eased to her knees between his legs, then to her feet. And wasn't she a pretty sight, her face splattered with mud, the rest of her—?

'Drenched' was the word that burst into Keller's all-male mind. Savannah was dirty and drenched and delightfully wet. Possibly aroused. He certainly was. Her nipples surely were, the nubs clearly defined beneath her skimpy shirt.

Since he was already covered with mud and slime, and he couldn't get any dirtier, Keller rolled onto his knees and took a much needed moment to get his body to stand down. This was not the time or place. His suit and shirt were ruined. His go-bag was still on the back seat of the car where he'd tossed it at the airport car rental garage. Which was a good thing. At least he'd have clean clothes to change into once they got to Sanctuary. Hopefully, he could shower there.

Like the thought of being naked in Savannah's shower helped? Instant images sparked Keller back to life. Savannah in the shower with him. Water cascading off her brown sugar skin. She'd melt in his hands. He'd bury himself in her lush, warm body. They'd pound into each other until the water ran cold and then...

Argh! He had the hard-on from hell straining to get out of his pants. He'd never be able to get back on his feet at this rate. Keller glared at the audacious woman who now stood with one foot on the bank, holding a hand out.

"You coming?" she asked.

Keller looked up at Savannah. The juxtaposition felt right somehow, him on his knees in the filth, her looking like an angel with the bright sun at her six, her gentle, helping hand outstretched to deliver him from evil. Not that Savannah was big enough or strong enough to lift him to his feet, but she was there. Damned if those red rosary beads hanging from her neck didn't add to her exotic allure.

Her fingers fluttered for him to take her hand. "Come on, Secret Agent Man, get your butt moving. The truck's gone. I don't have all day."

At last, Keller could stand without embarrassing himself. Grunting, he took her tiny hand, and gripping it gently, he let her think she'd rescued him. Who knew? Maybe she had.

By the time he'd climbed onto the road, the monster truck was long gone. *Bastards.* "Are you okay?" he asked the lady climbing up the embankment with him.

"Just dirty," she replied as she swiped mud away from her nose and mouth only to smear it across her cheek. Talk about plucky. She was one gutsy woman. Disobedient, but courageous.

Blinking to clear the murk out of his eyes, Keller held onto her other hand, hoping to instill comfort as well as dissolve any pain she might have acquired in the fall. At least this part of the swamp was shallow. The dirty water came up to his ears. If he could only get his heart to stop pounding. "I told you to get to Sanctuary," he huffed as waves of contentment flowed from Savannah to him.

She was doing it again, comforting him. "And leave you to face those creeps alone? You know who they are?"

"No," he answered, pulling back to see the truth in her eyes. "Do you?"

Two feminine brows lifted while her forehead filled with those adorable wrinkles. "I don't and I've never seen that truck before, either."

Like a trusting child, she closed in on him until her cheek melted against his chest.

Instinctively, Keller closed his eyes while his body reacted like a hound dog to the shivering, womanly flesh pressed into his arms. Her heart was pounding as hard as his, and for one fleeting moment, he wished it pounded for a better reason than her fear. As much as she pushed comfort at him, she couldn't disguise her adrenaline spike.

As easily as if he'd willed it, a different picture of her riding him imposed itself over his cavalier feelings. Keller wanted to kiss those lush chocolate lips, now pursed with indignation and sass. He wouldn't have minded threading his fingers into all that hair, holding on tight while he... while they...

*Aw, hell.* Now he was fighting to keep his hands from wandering too low. From grabbing two hands full of her backside and scooping her off the road and into his arms. Gran Mere's lovely great granddaughter was fast becoming more temptation than he'd expected.

"We should get going before they come back," he told Savannah, sounding like he'd swallowed a mouthful of that red gravel road.

"Mmm," she murmured huskily, the lovely vibration of her voice soothing and apparently just what Keller needed. With the monster truck long gone and Savannah under his arm, he allowed a deep breath. This road was certainly the one less traveled. Not a car in sight. Only the birds coming back to life in the trees and—

*BOOM!* A thunderous tail smacked the muck and mud behind them. *An alligator? No, two.*

"Get back in the car," Keller told Savannah as the spiny back of a third good-sized reptile wound its way through the shallow water toward them. "Hur—"

Keller could've sworn he'd heard incoming ordnance just as—

*BLAM!* The Camaro lifted off its wheels with a hiss of flames and spitting body parts.

Turning his back on yet another catastrophe, Keller pulled Savannah into his body. He hunkered over her, around her, shielding her from flying shrapnel whistling past. She clung to him even as he kept both eyes on the reptiles now on the road, one at his left, two on his right and all headed his way. Jesus Christ, did everyone want them dead?

Just when he thought things couldn't get worse, they did. Another alligator peered over the edge of the road, its short, stubby legs scrambling for solid purchase on the gravel bank. Only this fourth one to the party was no American native. This one was a gharial, a long-snouted crocodile that normally inhabited rivers in northern India and Nepal. The big fellow looked to be nearly fifteen feet long, and as it climbed onto the road, it dragged a thick heavy tail behind it.

*Shit.* Straightening his arm, Keller fired at the closest alligator. But he missed its eye. The beast halted, annoyed but uninjured. Not even bleeding. It kept coming.

The alligators Keller understood, but gharials weren't known for hunting humans. Their preferred diet was fish. The slender, toothy jaws on this beast were designed to sweep from side-to-side through their primary habitat while they fished. They didn't hunt land animals, and they weren't known to attack humans. What was it doing here?

The thing hadn't slowed since it climbed the bank. Which meant either there were no fish in this part of the swamp and this guy was hungry, or it preferred white meat.

"Get behind me," Keller growled, not giving Savannah the chance to disobey again. With the burning car blocking the road behind them and the alligators in front, they were trapped. Worried now, he steadied his arm and fired again.

Direct hit. The beast's jaws snapped open as its left eye exploded. A roar bellowed out of those cavernous jaws. When the other reptiles stopped advancing, every hair on Keller's body stood up with primordial fear. These four creatures were hungry, man-eating predators. Their species was more than one-hundred and fifty million years old. They'd avoided extinction when much larger dinosaurs had not. He and Savannah were nothing but snacks.

But at least the wounded alligator's roar distracted its buddies. They turned, their stubby, lizard-like legs now advancing on it. Judging the distance, Keller fired again. Another eyeball exploded into bloody goo, and an all-out feeding frenzy ensued. Even the gharial attacked the massive thrashing bodies.

Taking one definite step back, Keller pivoted on Savannah. "How far are we from Sanctuary?" he asked, keeping watch over his shoulder.

"'Bout a half mile," Savannah answered breathily, her eyes frozen on the horrific battle.

The first injured reptile was now fighting for its life, whipping its massive tail at its brothers-in-crime even as they attacked. The gharial held the wounded reptile's leg in its jaw even as the injured beast bit down on the first alligator's snout. It was a scene straight out of *"Jurassic Park,"* dinosaurs fighting dinosaurs.

"Run," Keller told her as he holstered one pistol and grabbed her hand. "Run!"

"But the car," she yelled as the gharial broke rank, its unblinking, round yellow eyes focused on its human prey once more.

"I said run!"

# Chapter Twelve

Never more certain that she was going to die, Savannah ran down the embankment and into the swamp to get past the still burning Camaro. Man, that fire was hot. She could feel it from where she splashed through the swamp. Were other alligators waiting to snap her feet or break her legs as she ran through their domain like a frightened goose? Possibly. But they'd have to be pretty damned quick to catch her as fast as she was treading water. Holy Mother, how she ran. She'd walk on that water if it meant living another day.

Out of the swamp. Down the gravel road that stretched to Sanctuary. Faster than fast. Her heart pounded and her lungs were on fire. Gran Mere's sandals slapped and flapped against the soles of her feet as she flew. A half mile hadn't sounded far away when she'd said it, but now that her life was on the line, she was sure she heard something running behind her...

The danger was real. Those alligators would kill her. They would drag her, kicking and screaming into the deepest part of the swamp. There they'd begin the death roll. She'd seen it in action. The sure knowledge of what happened when an alligator ate its prey added speed to her blistered feet. How it drowned its victim. How a hapless creature suffered from their wicked wounds inflicted by massively strong jaws. How alligators fought each other for the prize of fresh meat. How they ripped chunks off their bloated victims and swallowed them whole.

*Run!*

Yet even as frightened as she was, Savannah had never been more acutely aware that Keller wouldn't let anything happen to her. Damn, he was a good shot. He'd hit those lizards' eyeballs. He'd stood there brave and absolute, sure those gators were going to die. Not him and not her.

*Run! Run! Run!*

At last, Sanctuary's heavy ten-foot-high chain-link gate came into view through the lush shrubbery where the swamp gave way to solid earth. Keller's broad hand was suddenly between her shoulder blades. Thank God! But was he now planning to shove her into Sanctuary while he stayed outside and fought those lizards alone? *Uh uh.*

Dodging to her left, Savannah slapped the switch on the gate's upright to open it and activate lockdown.

"Savannah," Keller growled.

But yes, Secret Agent Man. She nodded at him, panting to draw in enough air and tasting blood from running so hard. He didn't know this switch was her failsafe in case any animals tried to escape. One of several switches located strategically throughout Sanctuary, it activated the gate to automatically close or open. She was no dummy.

This switch kept everyone inside from getting out. Frightened dogs often bolted from their kennels or crates. They ran when they couldn't cope or when they were cornered, and she didn't blame them. She'd run too after some of the things they'd suffered, so she'd installed extra precautions to save everything she rescued. Looked like it was going to rescue her now.

Keller's anger dissipated once they were both inside Sanctuary and the gate swung shut behind them, then locked with a clang and a hiss. "Pneumatic locks?" he asked, his tone surprised and maybe a little—proud? Was that approval she detected in those honey-amber eyes? By heck, it was.

A ripple of pleasure skated up her spine as Savannah drew in her first full breath in a half mile. Dropping both hands to her knees while she sucked more relief, she scrunched her head into her shoulders, thrilled at this FBI agent's off-handed compliment. "Yeah." *Pant. Pant. Pant.* "Cool, huh?"

Keller stood there breathing just as hard, one pistol still in his right hand, the other holstered, and his magnificent chest expanding like a machine. What she wouldn't give to run into those muscled arms and rest against that well-defined chest. To wrap her body around him and let her heart calm while she listened to his heart pound. It seemed such a fair trade, her giving him comfort after he'd saved her life.

Even drenched in sweat with his back still dark from murky swamp water, Keller Boniface cut a magnificent sight. Able. That was the word for him. Refined and courteous, yet able to take on the world and whip its ass. Able to fight with a ferocity like no other, yet gentlemanly and kind to her deceased great grandmother. Savannah's eyes watered at the mere thought of his genuine care. Okay, so tender *and* able. That was Keller Boniface. And remote. He was still so much a mystery.

With an odd ache beneath her breastbone, Savannah forced her eyes off her handsome rescuer. Straightening, she gave him her back. Keller might not have the kind of sight she had, but he was a smart empath. And he was a man. After their near-death experience from which she was still recovering, he might actually want to hold her like he had back at the houseboat. He might want—maybe need—the feel of human touch. Savannah couldn't let that happen. Her heart was already on the line, but he must never know what she was thinking or how foolish she was.

Yet her breath caught when he came up behind her and rested his hands on her shoulders. "You're not hurt, are you?"

She shook her head, still not facing him. "Just..." Confused. Hopeful, yet full of despair. Smart enough to not do something stupid, but wishing she could. "...cold and dirty. Come up to the house. I've got a shower, soap, and towels. Coffee too."

Instead of stepping aside, Keller's wide palms slipped smoothly down her biceps, sending waves of warmth and a tide of comfort throughout her body. He was doing it whether she wanted him to or not. Offering comfort. Absorbing her panic. Sharing his gift.

He didn't pull her against him though, and that was smart. She'd burst into flames if he did. She'd burn, but she wasn't yet sure that he'd burn with her. Above all else, Keller Boniface was a man in control. She just didn't know why. It couldn't be because of the color of her skin, could it? He didn't seem to care one way or the other, and he'd only treated her like a lady.

Closing her eyes at the innocent sensual touch, Savannah longed to be in another place and time where blacks and whites were loved at first sight instead of labeled and segregated and held at arm's length. Where different colored people were seen for who they were and what they contributed to the whole, instead of being judged by the biblically-challenged and condemned to hell because of the tone of their skin. Yes, the laws of the land proclaimed freedom for all, but this was still Louisiana. The Civil War with all its hard feeling, regrets, and unrealized expectations lived on in some of these backwater bayous. Prejudices died hard. She would know.

Holding still, she shivered as Keller's hands slipped from her arms to the tuck of her waist. "Don't ever disobey a direct order from me again," he breathed huskily into her ear. "I told you to drive that car to Sanctuary and I meant it. You should have done what you were told back there."

Striving to not fall apart at his touch, at the sheer power emanating from his much bigger, stronger frame, she whispered, "I couldn't leave you."

"I was armed, damn it. You weren't." Yet even as he hissed, his breath curled warm and sweet past her ear lobe and down her neck.

"But there were four of them, and..." And she could barely talk by then. Magnetic energy crackled around her and Keller, drawing them together like two lost halves of a whole.

"Not the gators, damn it. I meant the assholes in the truck. I told you to leave, but you—"

Savannah turned into Keller's arms then, needing to see the answers to her questions in his golden eyes. "Are you mad at me? Why? I stayed there to help. I stood by you. I—"

"You could've died." His upper lip twisted into a grimace of—fear? Fear of losing her? His grip on her hips had weakened. His fingertips fluttered as if at any moment he'd let go, yet he hadn't. But he had locked his heart and his soul up tight again. He'd morphed back into Sergeant Friday. He was that one-dimensional guy again. The guy in control. It was safer. It was easier. But why?

Savannah planted both palms on his broad, sweaty chest, needing Keller to understand one thing. "I'm not Carol Marie," she told him earnestly. "I'm. Not. Leaving."

Sheer pain flickered like a lightning bolt through the dark amber in his eyes. "She didn't leave. She... she..." And there he stopped. His lips sealed. The light in his eyes went out. Darkness descended like the coming of a moonless, starless night.

But Savannah was not dissuaded. Just convinced this animal required more kindness and tenderness than even Sir Galahad. More time.

Lifting one hand, she curled her palm along Keller's tight jaw, her fingertips under his ear. Scraping the sensitive skin as if he were a dog, she told him, "You think you are stronger than me, but you're not. I see you now, and I like you anyway. Let's go get cleaned up."

Dropping her hand, she let go of him first. He could stay or he could go. There was no doubt in her mind he could get past those alligators and the idiots in that monster truck if he decided to leave. He was smarter and stronger than all of them. But she also knew Keller Boniface wouldn't leave a woman behind. Men like him weren't made that way.

She was right. Just like one of her most faithful dogs, he followed.

# Chapter Thirteen

It wasn't supposed to work this way. Keller was the FBI's only empath. He should be comforting Savannah. That was his job. Yet every time she handled him—and he loved that she did—every single time she looked into his eyes—and he adored those chocolate browns of hers—his curse of a gift worked in reverse. It did!

Instead of being bowled over by a killer migraine that would normally take him days to recover from, touching her made Keller feel good. Not just good, but better. Lighter. Verging on no-kidding happiness. It was as if Savannah possessed some kind of narcotic in every last one of her skin cells. The more she touched him, the more his entire being gravitated toward her. He couldn't get enough of her touch, her scent, or her over-the-top optimism. How could she maintain such an incredibly steady outlook after just losing her great grandmother?

For the first time since he'd found Carol Marie's cold body all those years ago, Keller felt—*Was it possible? Could he really be*—free?

He didn't know, so he followed the pretty lady with the magic touch into Sanctuary. Now that she'd proven to be more than just another animal hoarder, he took in the lay of the land. A one level plantation-style building lay directly ahead. Painted light gold with bright white trim, it was as cheery as its owner. A single, screened front door opened onto a wrap-around porch, itself filled with wrought iron monkey cages, some of them eight feet high.

But none of them housed chimps. All were filled with birds. Big birds. Parrots. Green parrots. Blue parrots. White parrots. Bits and pieces of fruit and vegetables littered cage floors. The cage of umbrella cockatoos caught his eye. One bright white, black-eyed fellow with barely any feathers on its raw-looking breast, clung to the side with one black scaly bird-foot extended, his toes curling and uncurling as if he wanted Savannah to grab hold of his nasty-looking claws. Which she did.

"Hey, Popeye," Savannah cooed as she shook the bird's foot through the bars. "Told you I'd be back as soon as I could. Thanks for not shrieking at me because I'm late, pretty boy."

Popeye reached through the bars with his razor-sharp beak. Even that didn't slow Savannah down.

Reaching her fingers between the bars, she stroked the damned bird's beak like it couldn't lop her finger off with one snap. Sure as hell looked like it could do just that.

"Guys, this is FBI Agent Keller Boniface, and I promise, he won't hurt you. He's one of the good guys." She talked to the birds like they understood, stroking the cockatoo's crest as she nodded at the other cockatoos in the same cage. "Those guys are Aladdin, Pip Squeak, and the pretty pink and gray girl's Rosie. She's a galah, native to Australia. But lucky me, I found her in a bird net a couple months back, and she's been part of my family ever since."

"A bird net?" Definitely illegal.

Savannah nodded, opening the cage door and bumping the side of her hand under Rosie's belly. "Yeah. Somebody's been out here trapping birds and bats. I figured they might've been trying to re-catch her, that she'd gotten out of her cage or something, and they just wanted her back."

The galah stepped onto the proffered perch as if she'd been trained. Which she obviously was. Keller had no doubt that Savannah spent a lot of time with her animals and birds.

By then, Popeye was well on his way out of the cage to freedom, but Savannah gently blocked his escape with her shoulder, then closed the cage door on him. "Too bad for them, I got her first. She'd hurt her wing and she could've died. Poor baby was dehydrated and so weak, I thought I'd lose her. I slept with her under my shirt to keep her extra warm that first night. It was the only thing I could do. Birds die when they're in shock. Not that I slept much."

The fluffy pink and gray cockatoo with the brilliant pink head-crest preened as if she knew Savannah was talking about her. All the while, Savannah stroked the bird from the tip of its head to its tail while she kissed the top of its head and murmured, "I don't care who you belonged to before, I'm not giving you back. Not ever. You're safe with me, baby."

Now hanging off the side of the cage, jealous Popeye stretched one scaly black leg between the bars to Keller. Cautiously, he shook the bird's paw, err, foot. The bird's pure white crest lifted into an impressive headdress, making him look like an Indian chief.

"She's beautiful," Keller admitted, "but so's this guy."

Savannah's eyes lit up. "Wow. That's a first."

Keller cocked his head, not understanding. "How so?"

"He likes you. You have to understand. I got him from a friend of a friend who'd kept him locked in a parakeet cage because he was noisy. Which is why he's a feather-plucker now. He doesn't trust people. Except you. Huh. How about that?"

Her eyes lit with a warm smile. "Honestly, people need to do their research before they buy exotic birds. All birds need to be happy is room to grow and fly. They need to spread their wings, but if you live in an apartment, the last pet you need is a cockatoo. They're messy and noisy. Each day begins and ends with the most ungodly shrieks. Really. Wait until you hear how loud this pretty boy is. Plus, birds need real food, fresh fruit and veggies, not that pellet crap most pet stores sell. But fruits and veggies spoil quickly, another problem. Another chore. Popeye's better now that he's eating right and can socialize, aren't you?" She leaned into Popeye and planted a kiss between the bars to the end of that killer beak.

Unlatching the cage door, Savannah angled Rosie back onto her perch, then shut Popeye in before he could escape. Crossing her arms over her chest, she shook her head, her eyes still aglow as she turned to Keller. "My, my, look at you. Mr. Secret Agent Man is a bird person."

"No, I'm not a..." Keller stopped as Popeye returned and regurgitated something onto the tip of his finger. Gross. Disgusting! Keller flicked the bird vomit off and wiped his hand down the leg of his already filthy pants.

"You should see the look on your face!" Savannah giggled, her grin a ray of pure sunshine despite the mayhem they'd escaped. "Oh, stop. Bird throw-up won't kill you. It just means Popeye trusts you enough to share his food. He likes you and he's feeding you like he'd feed his babies or his mate."

Still not sure that Savannah was completely safe, Keller alternated between listening to her and surveilling the open yard around them. Dogs barked from the rear of the house. Must be where the kennels were. But the rest of the wide lawn was clear and trimmed. Crystal blue water sparkled from the inground swimming pool to the east of the house. A row of lilacs bordered that entire side of the yard, while a simple dirt drive connected the gated road out front to the lawn in back. A riding lawnmower parked alongside the house testified she had help. Or not. Keller wouldn't put it past Savannah if she ran this place by herself.

"Mind if we move inside?" he asked, needing to get her out of plain sight. His Spidey senses were still tingling. They'd just survived an ambush. Those guys in the truck had meant to kill her. They obviously knew where she lived and worked. They knew her schedule. They'd come looking for her as soon as they knew she'd escaped the alligators.

"No can do," she replied as if she were ambushed every day. "I've got dogs and cats to feed. Come, I'll show you."

With the swamp still squishing in his waterlogged dress shoes and his clothes uncomfortably sticky and wet, Keller followed Savannah around the house, past the riding lawn mower, and into a long narrow barn. Barks and yowls escalated when Savannah stepped over the threshold, and he was glad when she shut the door behind them. Finally, she was out of sight. But she was still only semi-safe. Not good enough.

He moved swiftly down the wide lane between the kennels, taking stock of Savannah's rescues as he assessed a strategic exit plan and cover. There were two points of egress he could see, the door they'd just come through and one at the extreme opposite end of the building. A screened channel ran the length of the roof under the eaves, letting light in. Twelve kennels lined each side of the barn, and all were filled. One large breed dog stood behind every gate, barking, whining, or howling. Some stood on their toes, dancing to see their pretty savior.

A firefight inside here could get messy, but that wasn't going to happen. Like Savannah, Sanctuary would be protected.

As he passed the kennels, one pure white Pitbull hit his already concave chain-link gate like a freight train—a whining, drooling freight train. His powerful body wiggled as if he were a baby, and he wanted Savannah to pick him up. Not what Keller expected from that notorious breed.

She had several other Pitbulls, all in separate kennels. A gray muzzled bloodhound that looked like a stack of wrinkles on legs. Three labs, two black, one white. A couple mixed-breeds with telltale Airedale coloring and whiskers. A long-legged Irish Setter. A Saint Bernard. A coon hound. But not a single Chihuahua or poodle in sight.

Savannah left Keller's side to enter the wooden door at the far back of the barn. She hit the light switch, illuminating a storeroom stacked high with what had to be over fifty large bags of pellet dogfood.

He hurried to catch up with her as she uprighted the wheelbarrow leaning against the wall and angled it alongside the stacks of red bags. "Here. Let me do that," he said as she tugged a hundred-pound bag off the stack and slid it into the wheelbarrow. "After we feed your rescues, we're going inside and calling for backup. Understood?"

Savannah dusted her hands together as she retrieved a pair of well-worn gloves from the shelf behind the door. "Darn, I forgot my gloves. You want a pair? I've got plenty." She had a way of ignoring him.

He shook his head, not planning on getting any dirtier than he already was, at the same time wishing he could grab a quick shower and get her the hell out of there. Time was not on their side. Those guys knew her schedule. They'd be back. "Let's just get this done. I don't want you exposed any longer than you have to be. How many bags do you need?"

"One will do for the dogs, one for the cats." She nodded toward the smaller green bags. "Grab one of those, would you? I feed everyone once a day, but I left so quickly when Gran Mere called that I... I..." Her voice trailed off.

Keller busied himself opening the mammoth red bag, curling the lip so Savannah could scoop the kibble, while giving her time to collect her emotions. It was maybe one or two o'clock. She'd had one helluva day, but he grew more anxious by the second.

"I left my cell phone in my car this morning," she whispered, her back still to him. "I forget that she's gone now, you know. Everything happened so fast."

"It's easy to forget," Keller lied. He hadn't forgotten one detail of the nightmare he'd lived through the day he'd lost Carol Marie.

"I broke all speed limits to get to her on time. I parked my car. I ran as hard as I could, but in the end..."

*In the end, you're always too late, and they leave you behind anyway. You can't make them stay, and you can't go with them.*

Keller steeled his heart and his fingers, not going to hug Savannah, comfort her, or lead this young woman where he had no intention of going. He refused to take advantage of her. Not now. Not ever. He didn't seduce women, much less vulnerable victims who were under his protection.

The morning had already dredged up enough tender memories from the deepest pits of his soul. The drive here had been the peaceful reprieve he'd needed. For a moment there, it had been enough to just push back in the Camaro's leather seat and feel the car's power at his fingertips. To know that, with the slightest pressure of his foot, he could accelerate to racing speed and leave his problems behind. He could be free.

Almost.

But he was wrong and that truck crashing into him had proved it. Simply connecting with Savannah, just touching her, was what made him believe the horrors from his past were exorable. Escapable. But they weren't, and he knew better than to lie to himself. Life didn't work that way. It was hard, cruel, and unfair, and he was a fool to think this quiet interlude with Savannah could turn into anything more. Those bastards in that truck, the gators, even this damned state proved life was no picnic. They were what was real.

Keller and Savannah were polar opposites. He operated on structure and discipline. A warrior's code. She believed in magic rocks and voodoo, a practice he'd never accept again. She wore her heart on her sleeve. He wasn't sure he had a heart. They were ships that passed in the night. If it hadn't been for Isaiah, they never would have collided.

Even their losses were light years apart, different. He was a professional federal agent carrying a whole world of hurt and misery that she had no business getting involved in. She'd just lost her great grandmother, a good woman who'd truly cared for and loved Savannah, to old age—not violence. One natural death didn't measure up to what Keller had seen and done and lost in his life. Mariposa's passing was the well-earned rest from a long life well-lived. She hadn't suffered like Carol Marie or any of the killers he'd put down.

Keller swallowed hard, assaulted all over again by the disaster that was his fucking life. Everything shouldn't have to be so hard, but it was, damn it. He'd learned to deal with death before; he could do it again. He'd almost convinced himself that he didn't care what happened to Savannah Church, that she was just a job, when a slender hand circled his wrist, holding onto him in its gentle, feminine way.

"Are you okay?" she asked softly, her big brown eyes dewy with unshed tears. Looking through him. Reading his mind like she seemed so easily to do. Needing comfort. Echoing back the same. But not needing him, and Keller was certain that her idea of comfort wasn't the same comfort his body yearned to give her.

"They're gone, Savannah," he told her brusquely. Harshly. "Your great grandmother and my wife are both gone."

The sooner she dealt with that hard fact of life, the better off they'd both be. Maybe then he wouldn't feel the compulsion to gather her into his arms as if she was a lost little girl. To kiss her and whisper that everything was going to be okay, when it would never be okay again. This wasn't a fairytale. To emphasize his intention, he pulled away from her grasp.

Letting him go, she tipped her head to the side. The beads around her neck mimicked the sway of her long straight hair brushing over one shoulder like an ebony waterfall he didn't dare touch. But oh, how he wanted to.

"No, they're not, Keller," she murmured softly. Sweetly. "The dead don't leave us behind when they die, not if they truly loved us when they were alive. That's not how the universe works. I thought you of all people knew better. They stay close, and they smile, and they laugh with us when we're happy. They cry with us when we're sad, and they stay with us when we're scared. The energy of true love doesn't evaporate into nothingness. It can't because it's the only thing in the universe that's real. Better than any other force God created, He gave us love. And love transcends time, space, and the physical distance between where you are today and where you were when you last saw your wife. You are never alone, Keller. You never have been. That's the point. God never wanted you or me to be alone. That's why Gran Mere lingers, so does Carol Marie. Where do you think she would rather be?"

"Stop saying her name," Keller growled as Savannah's words rocked him to his core. "You never knew her." He wanted so much to believe what Savannah said, yet he was a man. A cold, cynical man who hadn't deserved Carol Marie to begin with, and who didn't deserve Savannah now.

What the hell was up with her? Why did she give herself away freely when the world would only eat her up and spit her out? How could she? Why didn't she hold anything back? That was how he survived. As much as his gift of empathy demanded its due, he was in charge of who, when, and where he shared it. That was his real gift. Control! That was his real power. It had gotten him through combat, and it would get him through this... this... whatever *this* was.

"I rescue dogs, cats, and birds," she said as if that answered his unspoken question. "Every bird in the forest sings, Keller. Not just the brightest or prettiest."

What was that supposed to mean? "What the hell are you?" he snapped. "A psychic or a damned fortune teller?"

Her sad countenance melted into a sincere little smile. "I'm just one of a million different voices in the universe. Come. Help me feed everyone, so we can get back to town."

And that was another thing! No matter how much he cussed, grouched, and snapped at her... as much as he pushed her away... Savannah Church kept coming back for more. She kept smiling and giving. But he was not a dog to be tamed, damn it!

# Chapter Fourteen

There was no way Keller could understand, not given his preconceived mental constructs. To him, everything was either black or white. There was only man's law, man's view of the world—as if mankind knew everything. But really. Psychic or fortune teller? Those were her choices?

Savannah filled the last bowl with kibble, set it down in the corner of Sir Galahad's kennel where he wouldn't spill it, then straightened the kinks out of her lower back while he ate. It'd been a relief when Keller loaded the dogfood and shuttled the wheelbarrow from kennel to kennel. Those bags were heavy. Then he'd volunteered to feed the cats in the next barn over, cutting her immediate chores in half. But the funeral home would need to hear from her soon. They'd have questions, and she needed to get back to Gran Mere's place before night fell.

Running her hand lovingly over the knots and scars on top of sweet Galahad's hard head while he ate, she told her sweet boy, "Will that last you while I go into town to take care of business?"

The happy dog broke from noisily snuffling, slurping, and inhaling the last of his food to give her a slobbery, comical grin of appreciation. Where once he would've snarled at her close proximity to his food, now he smiled.

When he'd been a pup, starvation had been his original owner's cruel brand of discipline, making his daily allotment of dried kibble the prize he now protected at all cost. He'd quickly established that he'd fight—maybe kill—for food. Thankfully, he trusted Savannah.

But he still went after his food like a steam shovel gobbled up derelict buildings. Instead of leisurely enjoying it, he lowered his massive lower jaw into his bowl and didn't stop swallowing and scooping until every last crumb was gone. Poor baby had a definite eating disorder.

Here at Sanctuary, Savannah fed all dogs inside their locked kennels. If any of them thought for one moment he was big enough to fight in the common yard, she simply sent them a stern, mental push that let them know who was boss. Her. End of story.

If only she could do the same for Keller. He'd grown quiet before he'd left for the cat barn. Morose. No doubt worrying about those guys in the truck or those alligators. That odd coming together perplexed

Savannah too, especially the scary, long-snouted creature. That fellow looked like he'd stepped straight out of prehistoric times.

Backing out of Sir Galahad's kennel and making certain his door was securely fastened, Savannah ran smack into her favorite Secret Agent. A hearty *'Oomph!'* wheezed out of him as they collided, her butt to his very nice—zipper.

"Sorry, I didn't hear you come back. You're so quiet." Flustered, she turned and cupped his shoulder to catch her balance, then let go just as quickly, avoiding contact he didn't seem to want.

He stood there looking down at her. Not reaching out. Not offering a hand to steady her. His arms long and lank at his sides. The poor man needed a shower, yet he'd pitched in and fed the three dozen cats she housed, mostly because he hadn't wanted her stepping outside the safety of the barn until he could walk her into the house. Until he could protect her.

Savannah peered up at her knight in shining armor, her hummingbird of a heart high in her throat again, fluttering to get out. It was funny. She'd never needed saving before Keller came along, but she felt that way now.

Peppermint breath drifted into her face as he stood there staring down at her with a definite tick in the muscle of his square and oh, so stubborn jaw. Clean-shaven, his hair trimmed extra-short enough to still look neat and combed despite the brownish stain of swamp water embedded in his scalp, the man was unbelievably handsome in a breathtaking way. Ruggedly sexy, he gave off the lethal aura of a mankiller, yet she knew different. Keller was a protector more than a predator. He was *'that guy.'*

"Ready for a shower?" she asked as perkily as she could. It took all her willpower to not take that last step forward into his arms. To not touch him. He'd hold her if she did, but he'd do it out of duty, and Savannah didn't want that. She'd just lost the only person in her life who'd truly meant something. She didn't need a dutiful placeholder.

But if he were to kiss her...? If he were to reach out and pull her to him...?

His nostrils flared as if he'd heard her thoughts. "When we walk out that door, you will stay glued to my side, understood? We will not run, but we will not dally. If I tell you to hit the dirt, you will not argue or hesitate. You will obey me in all things, at least until I get you inside your house. Do you understand, Savannah?"

*Interesting. He hadn't used a single contraction. He must really mean what he's saying.* She nodded, wondering if this supreme alpha male expected argument and disobedience once they were safely inside the house. *That might be fun.*

But his lips were set in a grim line that brooked no argument. His amber eyes burned with a cruel golden light, all but stabbing her with their intensity. Even the straight blade of his nose seemed sharper. Surer. He meant to keep her safe, and he meant for her to listen.

And he'd ignored her question about showering—not that she'd intended they could shower together, but...

*That too might be interesting.*

Darn. Why was she fixated on getting naked with Agent Boniface? He was just another pretty face. So what if they were standing like nervous teenagers inside each other's comfort zones? That didn't mean anything. So what if she was drooling? That didn't mean anything, either.

Savannah couldn't help but smile. This fierce federal agent meant for her to live. Self-consciously, she brushed the back of her hand over her chin in case she was drooling.

"Ready?" he asked as he unholstered both pistols, plastered her firmly against his side under his arm, and...

She closed her eyes, relishing her fantasy come true as his body heat enveloped her. Together they walked to the front of the barn. My goodness, he was a long, lean drink of sexy warm water. Her hand went automatically around the small of his back, holding onto her own personal Secret Agent Man.

Leaning into the door jamb, Keller opened the door just enough to peer through the crack.

Savannah couldn't see past his broad shoulder or arm. But the way his jacket slipped open, revealing his swamp dampened shirt, and the way that shirt rippled against the taut muscles it encased... *Sweet Mother Mary*. It took every last bit of control not to flatten her other hand to his belly—just to touch him again—to feel those solid abs. Everything about this guy warmed her insides and other places. "Is anyone out there?" she squeaked.

The tick in his jaw jumped as he studied the lawn between here and the deck off the rear of her house. "We won't know until we're outside."

Savannah could've stood there for the rest of her life. No man had ever cared for her like Keller did. So what if he was just doing his job? If this stolen moment of semi-intimacy was all she'd ever have of him, so be it. She'd relish it as long as it lasted, and when it was over, long after he'd left Louisiana and gone back to Washington, DC, it'd be one of those rare memories she'd tell her kids about in years to come. Maybe her grandkids, too, though fat chance of having any of either. A gal needed a social life that included adult men rather than just rescued animals and birds if she wanted to end up with children. A date once in a while would be nice.

So yeah. She swallowed hard and faced her truth. This stolen moment with all her dogs watching was as good as it was going to get.

"Promise you'll do as I asked," Keller growled, still not looking at her. Still wound as tight as the homerun pitch in the last game of World Series playoffs.

*Always.* "Yeah. Sure," she breathed against his neck. "I'm ready whenever you are."

Tucking her tighter against his body, he shoved the door open.

And they ran.

She kept her head down.

He kept her moving.

Just as they reached the steps up to her deck, he grabbed hold of the railing and stopped cold. She felt it too. A strong, hard mental push, this one from Keller, restraining her. Tugging her backward. "Stop!" he ordered as he whirled around, his pistol aimed alongside the right of the barn. "Shit. Get down, Savannah. Don't watch!"

*Watch what?* She crouched, frightened but not sure what she wasn't supposed to watch, him shooting someone or him dying. Either way, she could not obey that order. Until she felt the hundredth-of-a-second inhale at her back. Until her modest, I-built-it-myself house sucked in upon itself and—

*WHOOSH!*

Savannah ducked, her hands over her ears and her eyes closed as the house she'd turned into a home some four years back belched out a thunderous stream of dragon fire over her head.

Keller tackled her to the patio like a linebacker nailing the winning quarterback. His broad, muscular body took the brunt of the debris hurtling over them. Shards of splintered wood and broken glass. Dust of sheetrock. Ragged remnants of the brand-new curtains that had, just seconds before draped the sliders, pummeled her cheek and the backs of her hands, now wrapped around Keller's waist.

He had to be pulverized by now. Yet still he blanketed her, on his belly like a penitent, his thick arms tucked around her head, shielding her face and eyes. His elbows dug into the concrete patio, his fingers interlocked over her hair. Blessing her. Keeping her from harm. Saving her yet again.

"My house," she cried even as she rubbed her nose over his collarbone. "My birds! I have to—"

"Stay down," her very own guardian angel hissed even as he raised his face from the crown of her head to glare at the backyard, now littered with burning debris.

Savannah had no choice but to lie flat, pressed to her back like she was. Closing her eyes, she sought after the soft flutter of worried cockatoo wings and the shrill shriek of panicked parrot voices for reassurance. The birds had been frightened by the noise, but overall, they weren't worried. The explosion had been noisy, but it was confined to the rear of her house, not the entire structure. Which meant someone had planned it to go off when she and Keller entered the rear door. And that someone was still watching.

She found it hard to focus when her cup felt suddenly filled to overflowing instead of empty. But it was true. Ever since she'd met Keller, her life seemed— more. More unpredictable. More dangerous.

There was a reason they kept being thrown into each other's arms. It was as if some cosmic energy was afoot in the universe, and they were destined to spend time together. She was his and he was hers, and she knew it. She could almost see Gran Mere's coy smiling face.

Savannah couldn't have let go of Keller if she'd tried. She found herself presented with the impressive underside of Keller's neck and chin. Her treacherous fingertips curled against the pad of her thumb, fighting her need to stroke the tawny panther hulking over her. Maybe scratch behind his ear. Listen to him purr. Or growl.

Yet even if this were nothing more than a deliciously dangerous wet dream, Savannah was content to lay there, pressed against the hard concrete by this stern, unyielding man. Especially now that she knew her birds were still safe and accounted for.

Everything about Keller declared king of the jungle. He was the epitome of masculine power. Sleek, hard, and lethal. Like a big cat on the hunt, he bristled with deadly intent, ready to pounce. If her burning home were the sun, he was its core, hot and ready to lash out with a flare so powerful it would incinerate whoever had dared destroy her home. But where was his gun? She turned her head enough to see the pistol clutched in his right hand, his index finger curled into the trigger guard.

Lifting one hand, she cupped Keller's jaw to calm the rage shuddering off him. Tantalizingly aware how his hips cradled hers, of the impressively hot and solid steel spike digging into her belly, she breathed into his ear, "Do you see anyone out there?"

"No, but I can sense them. Him. There's just one," Keller growled as he stuck his chin toward the barns.

"Can't you hear the dogs? They're frightened, but they know he's out there, too."

She honestly couldn't hear her dogs, not with the wall of Keller's arms bracing her head. Certainly not after his voice turned into the sexiest baritone she'd ever heard. It rendered her deaf and blind the second it struck her tympanic nerves, right before it cascaded over the rest of her instinctive, feminine receptors. Her nipples stood up like tiny cheerleaders, pressed hard against the flat wall of masculine muscle, giving him a rowdy, *'Rah! Rah! Rah!'*

Adrenaline was indeed a heady aphrodisiac. It not only blinded a woman, but it tempted Savannah to do things she wouldn't ordinarily dream of doing. Like ripping his clothes off. Biting him. Everywhere. Here. Now. Her heart fluttered like a butterfly gone crazy with desire, beating to get out. To climb all over him. Into him. While her house still burned.

Lying there inside the all-encompassing barricade of his arms, pressed beneath his slightly sweaty, testosterone-amped body, with her ear against his thundering heart, Savannah found herself bursting with ten gallons of pure lust. She was that hidden, barren cove on a lonely dark shore. He was the crest of the incoming tide with silvery ribbons of moonlight laced on its crest. Surging over her. Gushing into her. Drowning her in a heady, swirling sensation of—life.

She had to say something before she kissed him. "I should go to them. They're scared."

"You're not going anywhere," he snapped without sparing so much as a quick glance down at her.

Keller Boniface was a magnificent sight to behold, so Savannah beheld. He meant for her to live, and he meant to die to make it so. How could she dismiss love like that? She couldn't. Savannah had never felt safer. More certain. This was how he showed his love. He protected. He fought for the people who meant the most to him. He'd die for her.

Closing her eyes, she let her inner sight seek out whoever had destroyed her home. They hadn't yet accomplished what they'd intended. They were merely watching at this point. She was frightened, but she'd bet they hadn't expected to run up against a federal agent. Bullies weren't that kind of brave.

*Ah, there he is. A male.* Standing in the shadow just under the eaves at the far side of the cat barn. Thinking he was invisible. Tall. Wretchedly thin. Dark-eyed but pale-skinned. Evil incarnate twitchy, like he needed a fix. Or like he'd just realized who and what he was up against, and that he'd made himself a target.

Stretching her neck to see around Keller, Savannah ended up pressing her lips to the soft underside of his taut chin instead. She breathed in the luscious scent of manly sweat and bourbon and tobacco. Of him...

"Do you mind?" he bit out, ever the strait-laced federal agent just doing his job.

Yet there on her concrete patio with the heat of her burning home radiating over her like a gigantic oven, Savannah didn't mind at all. "Look toward the far end of the cat barn," she told him quietly. "See the man in the shadows? He planted the bomb and he set it off. But he's not the one behind everything that happened today. He's just the tool."

Keller's manly jaw slid forward in defiance, exposing more luscious neck. "How the fuck do you know that?"

"I can see," Savannah said as she breathed deeply, oddly aroused when she should be angry or scared or— anything besides romantic. "I have the same sight as Gran Mere."

"Got him." Keller stretched his weapon forward and bellowed, "FBI. Drop your gun and— Oh no, you don't!" His right arm flexed as he fired three deafening shots.

Wincing from the thunderous noise, Savannah cried, "Wait! Was he armed?"

"Ah-huh, twelve gauge. Long barrel."

"A shotgun?" Why hadn't she seen that?

But Savannah knew. She hadn't seen because she'd been distracted by Keller.

# Chapter Fifteen

How was a man supposed to work with a warm, sensual body like Savannah Church's pressed hot and willing against his loins? Concerned she could read his salacious intentions as easily as a book, Keller didn't dare spare her a glance despite, or maybe because, his wayward, all-male mind had moved onto a lovelier scene. One that had everything to do with crisp, clean sheets, bare tangled legs, and her black hair spread like a silken fan on rumpled white pillows. With his body tight inside hers, pumping for home base. The musky scent of her sex in his nose. She'd be smiling. He'd be in heaven and ready to go again.

Damn, he was a pathetic monster to be aroused now, at a time like this. It took all Keller had to not plant his body between her legs and thrust into her. He already lay over her in a compromising enough position, fighting the primal urge to not only protect her, but to claim her and do it now. Right here.

Growling at his sudden lack of restraint in what was a most dangerous situation, he glared at the lanky man hidden in the shadows at the opposite end of the mowed lawn. The idiot thought he was invisible just because he hadn't moved.

That simple mental shift in targets did what Keller needed. His mind snapped off Savannah and onto the bastard who'd meant to kill her, damn him to hell. He'd have to come closer if he intended to use that shotgun. It was probably just loaded with birdshot, and birdshot couldn't kill at this distance. But Keller's Sig could.

"You know that guy?" he asked as he adjusted his weight and finally allowed Savannah enough room to get a better look. Not a good idea. Her taut belly strained against his when she curved her body to see around his arm. Her small breasts mashed soft and melt-in-your-mouth sweet against his chest. He'd already been fighting the urge to bury his face in her hair. Now strands of it lifted into his mouth, and the lovely scent she surrounded herself with was mighty distracting. Keller filled his lungs with mouth-watering temptation as he turned his head to tug her hair off his lips. He blinked and...

*Pffft!* The would-be killer had vanished. "Shit!"

"Let me up," Savannah ordered as her palms hit his chest. "My dogs—"

Like she stood a chance of moving him. "Will you forget about your dogs and birds?" Keller snapped, forcing her flat again—where every nerve and fiber in his being wanted her. Even so, a sudden calm infiltrated his adrenaline flooded body. She was doing it again. Comforting him, this time through the fabric of his shirt. "Stay down. You're more important than—"

"Possibly..." she agreed, but Keller felt outright denial in her vague reply. "It's just that once I set them loose, they'll go after that guy and whoever else is inside Sanctuary. They'll track him and his friends, if he brought any with him. You'll see."

"But won't they get out? Aren't you worried they'll run away?" Now Keller was worried about her dogs.

"No, silly," she chided gently. "I give them the run of the place when I'm here. They know to come when I call. You'll see."

They were trained? Keller hadn't thought about that. Calmer now, he pulled Savannah to her feet along with him, but kept one arm around her shoulder, one weapon holstered, the other still in his hand. The car, the alligators, her house, and now this stranger with a shotgun all added up to someone holding one helluva grudge against Savannah. What was more interesting was all this happening the day Gran Mere died. Coincidence? Not on your life.

"You make anyone mad enough to want you dead lately?"

She shook her head as he steered her back to the barn, his senses on high alert even as the feel of her slender body bumping against his spiked every last protective instinct. "I don't think this is about me. It's got to have something to do with Gran Mere."

"Why do you say that? I thought everyone loved her."

"Every *reasonable* person loved her. But there are always haters."

Keller couldn't shake the image of those alligators and Savannah's house burning behind them. Or that she'd answered as if she were an inconsequential detail in the attempts on her life. They were completely cut off from emergency responders, and someone had tried to kill her. There was no way this was just about Mariposa Church. "But you're the dog rescuer," he argued, his pistols still at the ready. "And that truck meant to run you down. Hell, it hit the passenger side. That guy could've killed you right then and there."

"I doubt it. She was the one people came to when their babies were sick or trouble struck. She was the heart of this parish. I'm just..." Savannah shrugged one shoulder. "To be honest, I'm just the kid no one wanted. Not even my father hung around after I was born. He handed me off to Gran Mere, then went and got himself killed."

The length of her stride increased. "Don't get me wrong. Gran Mere always wanted me. I knew that. I was everything to her, but deep down, I'm just another stray she took in and loved." Another shrug. "Which suits me fine. Really. That way no one pays attention to me, and to be honest, I think that's why I like working with animals so much. We're the same, you know. We're strays. Rejects. We speak the same language."

"Not buying that," Keller grumbled as he stopped her at the door to her rescue barn, which all by itself proved she was more than she gave herself credit for. Humility was all good and fine, but this woman should be proud of what she'd accomplished, with other people's rejects no less. "You're not just another stray. I mean, look at you."

And time ground to an awkward halt. Yet again, he'd moved in too fast and he'd gotten too close. Every cell in his body leaned forward like a vine seeking the sun. Savannah was that sunlight, and he was a troll living under a bridge. In the shadow. Afraid to get burned by the sun, but dying for the light.

Savannah looked up at his unplanned outburst. She blinked those big, beautiful, dark chocolate eyes. Her lashes fluttered like an exotic, ebony butterfly's wings. Long. Enticing. The perfect frames to the windows of her soul. The tip of her pink tongue moistened the lush bottom lip his whole body ached to taste.

Keller looked down at her. At her mouth. It was the smallest glance. He meant nothing by it—honest. Yet in that instant he saw everything. Her instinctive generosity. Her kind heart. Her willingness to share her gift. The glowing love she had for Gran Mere and two barns full of strays. All those birds...

Damn, she'd sought out every last one of those creatures, then built and managed this complex to protect them from a world that hadn't wanted them in the first place. How could she not know how beautiful, sensitive, and charming she was? How appealing that rare quality of kindness made her? How utterly seductive?

But Keller was not a trusting man. Even stuck inside the FBI's one and only psychic team, he'd fought the Deuces Wild welcome, but he'd fought harder against belonging. Settling down wasn't in his blood. A man didn't work his ass off for a Ranger tab only to end up a family man. Life didn't work that way.

Truth was Tucker Chase wasn't that hard of a boss to work for. He was just so damned cock sure of himself. And every last team member had welcomed Keller with open arms. He was the problem. Not Tuck or Isaiah, not Eden or Ky, certainly not Tate Higgins, a man more remote and stoic than Keller.

Yet here it was again, a second chance, life and sun and all good things shining up at him. Enough love to make a man believe he wasn't just another ugly cur in a world that ran over infants, the weak, and animals in its greedy quest for power, wealth, and fame.

His eyes tracked the sultry smile stealing over Savannah's countenance. Man, she was everything he'd avoided since he'd lost Carol Marie. Comfort.

Belonging. Finally, actually, being a man with a pulsing heart in his chest instead of a cold stone.

In the barest fraction of a second, Keller had Savannah inside the barn and the door locked. He holstered his pistols and wrapped her tightly in his arms like a treasure finally found. His heart hammered in his throat as he strived for control.

Federal agents didn't do crap like this, not the honorable ones. Not him. Not ever! He'd never taken advantage of any woman like he was thinking of doing now. Even this hug was more sexual assault than friendly. Surely, unwanted. Certainly, unexpected. Never mind what else he was thinking.

She should shove away. She should tell him, "No!" She should scream at him to quit. Savannah should do anything but what she was busy doing now. Dragging his shirttails out of his pants. Loosening his belt. Making the sexiest frantic sounds of a woman who wanted the same thing he did.

*Mind the gap. Mind the gap. Mind the bloody gap!* his out of control brain sang like the conductor on some London train he hadn't thought of in years.

"We're not safe here," he warned as she lifted her chin and closed the distance between their mouths. Instinctively, he sucked in his gut to help her questing fingers find their way under his shirt, down his belly and into his pants.

"I don't care," she whined as her hand closed gently around him. "I need this. I want you."

It wasn't mere comfort she passed to him then. It was the sweetest feminine need, raw, new, and delightfully rare. Keller was done fighting. The only question was where and how fast he could get there. He wasn't about to nail her against the nearest barn wall. She deserved better.

"I'm not hurting you, am I?" she asked.

"Uh uh. No way," he growled. He hadn't meant *nail*. No, no, no. That was entirely the wrong word choice. This brave woman deserved soft, tender loving while surrounded by decadence and luxury, silk and candlelight, not dogs, kennels, and kibble.

"To hell with the gap," Keller growled when Savannah's other palm flattened under his shirt on his spine, shocking him with a stinging current of lust that felt so damned good. She had to be standing on her toes. He leaned over to accommodate whatever this amazing woman wanted to do next. If she said no, then no it was. He'd stifle and he'd quit, no questions asked.

But suddenly she was in his hands, at least her ass was. He'd had to grab hold where he could. She'd climbed his body like a woman on a mission, dragging her open mouth over every patch of bare skin in her path. Inhaling him. Licking and tasting his neck as if he were her mission. Like a heat-seeking missile, her mouth collided with his chin, her wet tongue sweeping over his lips before he wholeheartedly obliged and let her in.

*God, yes. Yes, yes, yessss!* He knew she'd taste sweet, but her mouth was heaven. Her lips, manna, honey and spice. Ambrosia! *More.*

Keller didn't remember pressing her against the wall beside the barn door. He didn't recall angling his chin for better access to her mouth. The little sounds she made drove him crazy, but there they were. Him standing with his belt undone and clutching her ass in his thrumming fingers. She was still dressed, but he knew her blood had to be on fire for maybe the first time ever. And him with her beguiling scent in his nose.

"Are you sure?" he asked before he stripped her bare. "I mean, your house is burning, and we're not doing a damned thing to put the fire out."

Her nose wrinkled with the cutest petulance. "I've got a brand new fire suppression system, sprinklers and all," she mumbled around his lips. "Let's see if it works."

"How on earth do you have enough money to do all that?"

She lifted one shoulder. "Simple. Gran Mere. I helped her and she helped me."

Who really cared? Keller didn't. By then he'd lost track of where and when, so focused on the exquisite who in his hands. Somehow, she had his zipper down by then. She was still dressed; he was still undecided. He'd never treated a woman like this before, not with his pants slipping over his thighs and her fingers gripping him, steering him toward heaven. Or...

*Holy. Hell. No.*

He ground to a complete stop, sweating like a beast and close to being out of his damned mind with lust. His legs were shaking. Things were moving too fast. He hadn't been with a woman in years, much less one this enticing. His body demanded release, the quicker. the dirtier, the better. Yet he knew the second his hand slipped down her belly to her core, the instant his fingers breached her most intimate secrets. *Aw, shit.* She was too small. Too tight. Was it even possible—?

Knowledge hit him like a bucket of ice water thrown in his face. Quick and dirty wouldn't be good enough. Not for her. Savannah Church was one of the rarest treasures in the world. She was beautiful, yes, but unsophisticated. How could she be untouched?

He gulped back a hearty dose of WTF. "Are you...?" But how could she be—that? Savannah seemed to know precisely how things worked. She certainly hadn't minded touching him. Fondling him. Leading him into temptation. "Have you ever done this before?" he asked the woman who, even now rubbed her nose up his neck and growled like a sexy feline in heat.

"No, have you?" she asked, the innocence in her question the final breaking point.

She *was* a virgin. Damn it. She was pure.

"Ah, yeah," Keller replied, oddly more aroused by her quick, unabashed reply. But ever honorable. Always the perfect gentleman. He couldn't do it, not like this. Not to her. He was everything she wasn't. His ardor shrank in her hand.

Breathing hard, she leaned back far enough to bump his forehead with hers, still fondling his manhood with the gentleness of a saint while panting like a wanton woman. Still as enticing as hell whether she knew what she was doing to him or not. "Don't stop," she whispered. "Please. I've never done this before, but I've wanted to—with you—since the moment you..." She swallowed hard enough he heard it. "...since the moment back at the houseboat when you..."

"When I what?" he asked evenly, peering into the deepest, darkest, sexiest eyes he'd ever been caught by. This was Mother Nature's oldest, truest snare—the heart of a pure and honest woman.

Tilting her chin, she blinked at him, her lashes thick and glistening with tiny teardrops. Drawing him back to the flame. Filling his view with the only thing in the world that mattered. "When you didn't think I was watching you. When you wouldn't."

"When I wouldn't what?"

"Leave me," Savannah whispered, the tips of her fingernails scraping over the top of his head, soothing him. Possibly, enthralling him, too. But you can't enthrall the willing, and Keller was no fool. Since the first moment he'd laid eyes on her, he'd been drawn to her, also. And it wasn't just her long legs and taut backside.

"You were about to explode, remember?" she breathed. "Pain hung over you like an anvil the moment you stepped onto Gran Mere's porch. I knew then. You're an empath with unique, almost otherworldly skills. But you were ready to crash, and you would've suffered for days if I hadn't touched you when I did. I didn't touch you until later, yet still you stayed. You would've suffered for me. Why'd you do that?"

"You needed me," he corrected, uncertain if Savannah knew how desperate he'd been then. He'd only planned to shake her hand for the release he'd needed. But now he needed an entirely different kind of release. "I could see it in your eyes. You were in worse pain than me. You'd just lost the woman who'd raised you. Gran Mere was everything to you."

"Yes, but you didn't know me. I was a stranger. You didn't have to stay. You could've walked away." Her fingertip caressed the curl of his ear, melting the last of his resistance. Keller's hips automatically jutted back toward her heat. "You could've left while the leaving was good. It would've been easy."

"But it wouldn't have been right." Yes, he wanted her. Just one taste. One more kiss. Yet even as he welcomed the thought of spending the night with Savannah, Keller knew one kiss wouldn't be enough to quench the hunger crackling to life inside. He'd never felt more alive, yet still so hollow. Was any of this real or was he simply bewitched?

She traced the tiny star-shaped scar at the corner of his eye, the one Queen Elaine had given him the morning he'd caught her with Carol Marie. The moment he'd nearly killed his mother.

"I'm ready now, Secret Agent Man," Savannah murmured huskily against his lips. Licking him. Tasting him. "My house isn't the only thing on fire."

# Chapter Sixteen

Never did a man look so torn. So conflicted. Broad in the shoulders. Long in the waist. Long where it counted, too. Yet she was still mostly dressed, and Keller had slowed things down as if he carried the weight of the world on those broad, tense shoulders. Savannah could now feel him springing back to life in her hand. Pulsing. Thick and ready. Hard and silky soft at the same time. So hot that her eyes watered. Yet she wouldn't ask again. He had to want this, too.

Instead she whispered coyly, "The supply room locks from the inside. There's a kennel release switch beside that door. Carry me so I can let the dogs out?"

That seemed all he needed to hear. Savannah found herself straddling his hips after he pulled his pants up, then hurried past the kennels to the far side of the barn, his zipper still open. Giggling, because this was the most delightfully daring thing she'd ever done,

Savannah leaned out of his arms and smacked the release pad as he walked into the supply room with one hand while still holding onto his manhood with her other.

Thrilled for the hunt, every last one of her dogs launched out of their kennels.

"There," she sighed at the first baying of her precious, one and only coon hound. "Let's see how smart that guy with the shotgun thinks he is now."

"Aren't you afraid he'll shoot one of them?"

Savannah shook her head. "My dogs are smart, and they know the lay of the land. Lots of swamp and scrub brush to keep them hidden. You'll see."

"If you say so," Keller grumbled as he set her on the nearest stack of grain-free kibble before he locked the door and secured their privacy. Keller turned, his shoulders wide as he shrugged out of his jacket and stripped the tie off his neck. He hung them off to the side on a stack of cat food. His holster went next, but he laid it carefully nearby, within reach.

Savannah's heart melted at the sight of her Secret Agent Man. This was insane. It was foolish. She'd just lost her home and there was a killer on the loose, but were those things stopping her? Uh-uh. Until her sight included what had once been a white shirt, now tinted swamp-water tan and splotched with red streaks. Holy Mother, what was she thinking? Mugging an injured man? This man had sheltered her. He'd taken the brunt of her home exploding. Those wounds needed to be cleaned and dressed before infection set in.

"You're hurt," she cried, tears washing her vision clear as she finally looked closer. Even her fingers were stained with Keller's blood. How selfish was she?

"I'm fine," he answered, running a hand over his head like he'd just realized his condition. "Really, I'm—"

"No, you're not." Savannah slid to her feet. "You're hurt. Sit down. At least let me doctor you before we..." *Before we get carried away again.*

Like a well-trained dog, he sat on the bag she'd just jumped from. Sex would have to wait.

With her heart still fluttering as if a flock of butterflies were caged inside her ribs, she retrieved her first-aid kit from the cupboard beside the supply room door. She'd doctored plenty of animals before, even birds. They'd all lived How much different could doctoring an adult male be?

He'd removed his dress shirt by the time she turned around, but still wore what had once been a white t-shirt. Now dingy brown and wet, it clung to his massive chest, delineating the rigid valley between his pecs and the well-defined six-pack below.

"Holy Mother," hissed out of Savannah. Keller wasn't one of those massive, thickly muscled bodybuilder types. But he was athletically fit and larger than life, and so-o-o-o much better than any animal she'd ever laid eyes on.

Shaking his dress shirt, he spread it on the nearest bag before he looked over at her.

Deep dark amber eyes locked on her.

Her heart zeroed in on Keller Boniface. On the hashmarks up and down his magnificent bicep. On the amber heat in his eyes. On the tiniest quirk of a smile curling his lips. He was a magnificent golden panther, tanned from head to toe, and he was stalking her.

"Savannah," he said with a deep throaty purr.

"Keller," she whispered back, her feet moving toward him. Her heart already his. The hummingbirds in her chest fluttering up her throat for release. This patient wasn't like any she'd ever treated. He was wilder. Hotter.

"You're right."

"I am?" *Wait. What?* She couldn't imagine what he was talking about.

"I need a couple band-aids."

The rest of the world came back into focus. *Oh, that.* "Y-yes, you do. Then take your t-shirt off," she ordered before her brain melted again. "I've got antiseptic wipes, and I've stitched plenty of dogs and cats, and I'll take good care of you, too, if you trust me." *And I'm rambling like an idiot.*

"Yes, ma'am, I do." Dutifully, he reached behind his head and dragged the t-shirt off.

Savannah never realized how hot the supply room could get with one gorgeous, half-dressed male in it. He seemed so much larger now that she could see more of him. "Whew," she muttered as she blew a stray lock of her hair out of her sweaty face, trembling with the knowledge of where on his body her fingers had just been.

"Good," he murmured when she set the kit on the bag beside him.

"Good?" she asked, her voice gone as limp as starched lace on a sultry southern afternoon. "What's good about any of this?"

Keller captured her wrist and pulled her between his spread knees. "It's good that you feel it, too."

She couldn't think when he touched her like this. "But I'm supposed to be helping you," she reminded him though her voice had grown needy and soft. "You're hurt. You need—"

Strong capable hands mapped her forearms to her shoulders, then slid to her waist, pulling her against his belly. "I need you. Stitches can wait. May I kiss you again?"

Her vocabulary narrowed down to, "Yes, please, yes!" before she closed the distance, and with her fingers fluttering on that magnificent abdomen, she gave him her mouth and her tongue. Her heart.

The sexiest sound vibrated through Keller as their tongues tangled. Savannah had kissed a few boys in her life, but this was no inexperienced kid in the backseat at a drive-in. Keller was all male and all man. He knew what he was doing. He was bigger in every way. Definitely in charge.

In seconds she found herself undressed and sitting on his lap, sucking raspberries on that strong neck while his fingers explored her naked body. Every touch of his fingertips sent electricity sparking through her. From the tips of her nipples, now hard and aching for his mouth, to the tingle in her toes, Savannah wanted him. All of him. Every last inch and drop.

He had to get out of his pants, but holding Savannah on his lap like this was more than Keller deserved or expected. She was no little girl, and yet she was. Wearing just those blood red beads and with them dangling between her small, firm breasts like they were, he knew the moment he took his pants off that he'd ravish her before he pleasured her. Not his style. Women like Savannah were treasures, goddesses to be adored and honored, never cheapened, which was how this encounter had started. Yet he couldn't do it.

Oh, he could do *it* all right. Getting *it* up was not his problem. Taking her as if she were some tramp in the back room of a bar was the problem. As fast as this thing between them was happening, Keller was nonetheless a gentleman, and Savannah was something special. Something rare. She was a lady, so much like Carol Marie, yet different. Savannah was strong and defiant. She was sexy and tougher than Carol Marie. And why was he thinking of his wife now? Here? With another woman in his arms and about to come on his lap?

Keller couldn't restrain the way his thumb had zeroed down on that tiny nub between Savannah's legs. He could give her what she wanted. He could make her first time, this first coming—a thing of exquisite beauty for her. Dipping his head, he licked at her nipple before he sucked it into his mouth. And that was all it took.

Savannah arched back. Her body tensed with what he suspected was her first orgasm. In doing so, she filled his mouth with a warm, soft breast. She ground herself into the palm of his hand, then exploded with, "Kellerrrrrrrrrrr..."

The throaty, earthy sounds she made were the best. Aftershocks coursed over her bare buttocks and thighs, her tiny belly, itself a thing of beauty. Her nipples hardened like the rarest rubies. He stroked those nubs until she went limp, then covered her panting mouth with his and breathed the taste and scent of her into his soul. There would never be another first time for this woman. He'd given this to her. Pride in that surged through his veins, pride and a sense of ownership he had no right to claim.

Yet he did. For this singular moment in time, she was his, and he was hers. It could happen. Lightning was known to strike the same tree twice, and this had certainly felt like a lightning strike. Rare. Powerful. Else why was his heart pounding so hard?

Sighing, Savannah melted under his chin, one hand on his chest, her other around his back. Petting him like he was one of her dogs. Comforting him, though why she thought he needed comfort, he didn't know.

Until she said, "Lose the pants, Keller. Your turn."

# Chapter Seventeen

The dogs had stopped barking, howling, and baying. No gun shots. Which meant the trespasser was long gone, and the dogs were now happily exploring Sanctuary. Keller hadn't argued like Savannah thought he would, but he needed to be as bare as she was. He needed to lose control, and she meant to make sure he did.

Sliding off his lap, between his knees to the floor, she knelt, embarrassed at the explicit thoughts running through her head. Suckle him? There? Why not? The notion sent waves of liquid heat coursing through her overheated and still tingling core. She'd just seen fireworks. Here. In her barn, of all crazy places. Keller needed to take that same amazing ride, only this time with her. He'd just given her something precious. Now it was his turn.

"Savannah," he growled as she pulled his pants down to his knees, her eyes wide at the bulge in his briefs. White briefs, now tinted with the same swamp water as his skin and dress shirt. Briefs like she suspected Sergeant Friday had worn. *Oh, my.*

"Yes?" she asked as innocently as she could, while, one by one, she slipped the waterlogged dress shoes off his feet. Argyle socks? Was this guy for real?

She tugged the socks off before she leaned between his legs, reaching for the waistband of those tighty-whities.

But Keller grabbed her hands before she got a good hold. "No. Please. It's not that I don't want to..." Dark amber skated down her neck and the length of her naked body before his gaze crawled up to her face. Even then, a sad smile quirked the corners of his mouth. "Trust me on this, Savannah. I want you more than I've wanted any woman in years, but you deserve better."

"Than what?" she asked coyly. "Than who? You? I know who I want, Keller Boniface, and I choose you. But if you don't choose me—"

Dark eyes glowed back at her. With a growl, he jerked her off the floor and back onto his lap. He covered her mouth, his tongue frantically delving between her lips. "It's not that. It's just that... that..."

He had trouble talking with his mouth full. Well, good, he was human after all. She could work with that. More composed now, and quite possibly in charge for the first time since he'd stepped foot inside

Gran Mere's home, Savannah placed both palms on his chest, loving that he let her handle him. Ah, those muscles were hard and warm. She spread her fingers, soaking in the ripples and ridges of this man's hard body.

While he consumed her tongue and lips, she let her inner sight wander into the vault of secrets this man held locked deep inside. She already knew Keller was a man of darkness and mystery, but now she realized he was also a man of hard-won honor, truth, and more regret than she'd ever encountered. He'd done things in his life he'd never forgiven himself for, but above all, he was noble. He knew his sins. He just didn't know how to forgive himself for them.

He never intended to rob her virtue. That's what he worried about now, not about his boss or the would-be murderers on the prowl. He thought a man like him would defile her. He'd suspected she was a virgin from the start, and he'd wanted to make love to her. But sexual relations meant something to him. They were sacred. In his mind, decent women were angels sent from heaven to bless a man. A good man. That was the problem. Keller didn't think he was a good man. *Oh, my.*

"You're right, we do need a proper bed," she told him between kisses and licks, loving the musky, salty flavor of his mouth and chin as she blessed him in her way.

"Yes." His shaven skin abraded her lips like the finest sandpaper when he spoke. "Room service wouldn't hurt. Champagne."

"But I don't want to wait." Threading her fingers over his head, Savannah crushed herself against him, warming his rugged hard body with her softest places. This panther might be injured, but he needed more than a band-aid. He needed forgiveness and absolution. He needed her brand of comfort.

Savannah spread her knees over his thighs and ended the kiss. But she didn't go far. She couldn't, not with her ass in his capable palms. "Let me love you," she murmured, tipping forward, brushing the tips of her breasts over the crisp hairs on his chest. Relishing how those hairs incited her tender nipples. How her core wept for him. Watching her panther transform into a willing partner.

His eyes had grown big and black, the irises wide open with what she offered. "But I—"

"But nothing," she told him as her hips slid closer to those Sergeant Friday briefs.

Dropping his gaze, he tracked the nest of curls at the apex of her thighs. "Are you sure?" Keller asked, his voice tight as if he were holding his breath.

"About you? I've never been more sure," she whispered as she tipped forward and planted a kiss to the center of his tensely wrinkled forehead. This man was so tightly wound that this simple act of love felt like she was torturing him. Maybe she was. But he needed this and Savannah decided it was now or never. "Lift up," she ordered. "Give them to me."

"I've got it," he replied. Dropping his hands to his waist, he shucked out of his underwear.

She climbed back onto those muscular thighs.

He'd stopped her before she reached his impressive shaft. "Condom."

Which proved what a novice she was. Savannah hadn't thought about protection. Not even once. Not with Keller.

But he was prepared. Tugging his pants up from the floor, he retrieved his wallet and the foil-wrapped condom within it. He gloved himself, and wasn't that an erotic sight? His fingers seemed to know just how to roll the latex over himself. He didn't falter, not once. He knew precisely what he was doing because, well, he was a man. A capable, experienced man of the world.

"You've never done this before," he told her, his voice intimate and quiet. Sincere.

Savannah swallowed hard as she met his eyes. Because of his empathy, Keller knew precisely what a babe in the woods she was. "No, but I'm a fast learner," she bluffed.

Her answer put a twinkle in his eyes. "Sex is the most natural thing between a man and his woman," he said earnestly, his head ducked down so he could peer into her eyes. "But understand that I will stop if you change your mind. Trust me. I'll stop whenever you tell me to, but if you want to continue—"

Her curiosity strayed to that fascinating organ standing at attention between them. Beautifully lined with veins, it made her mouth water thinking about him sliding that magnificent part of himself into her. Yeah. There was no way she was letting him get away.

"Eyes up here, Savannah," he teased, his head tipped sideways.

Flushed with an all-over naked kind of heat, she jerked her chin up, reconnecting with his handsome face. "I'm sorry. It's just that you're so big," she told him honestly, her eyes now opened to the truth. After all the biology in action she'd witnessed here at Sanctuary, this was a first. She'd thought her body would easily accommodate his. It worked with animals. But now she wasn't as sure. Keller was a big man. He was hard and hot. Wide. Thick. She was so much smaller and inexperienced.

But she was no quitter and she wanted this. Savannah stared into the warm depth of Keller's gaze as she lowered herself onto him again.

There was a tenderness in his eyes this time. "Just take it slow," he murmured as his eyes drifted down to where their bodies were about to join.

She licked her lips, knowing this man now knew her more intimately than anyone else in the world. That he'd seen parts of her body no one else had. She centered him at the heat of her core. Liquid fire dripped between them.

"Easy," he whispered, the black in his eyes swallowing the gold. "There's no rush, baby. Take your time."

She pushed harder, consuming the blunt tip of him. Easing her body down. Ouch. That pinched. A lot. And she'd barely begun. "You might be right," she admitted begrudgingly. "I'm not sure I can do this. I'm too small for, umm, you. Darn it."

One big hand now held her there at the cusp of their joining, keeping her from her original plan of charging full steam ahead. Of not holding back. Masterfully, he reached down and took hold, easing himself in and out, centimeter by centimeter.

"No, you're not too small, and tight is a good thing." He licked his lips when he said that. "Your body was made to accommodate mine. You will adjust. But I'm not going to lie to you, the first time might hurt. We can stop if you want."

"Uh uh," she told him, sure that he was the perfect one and this was the perfect place.

"But I don't want to hurt you." His words came out strangled, his breathing ragged.

*And I don't want to lose you,* she thought, but she said, "I know we've just met, but time waits for no one, Keller, and honestly, I'm afraid I might never get the chance to love you again. You might leave."

A tender smile breached the hard line of Keller's firm, I'm-in-control, federal agent lips. If Savannah hadn't known better, she'd think he'd heard her unspoken cry for him to let her inside his heart.

Threading his free hand into her hair, he pulled her mouth to his and he kissed her with the heart-sealing passion of a hungry man about to eat his first meal. So gently. So sweetly.

Savannah got lost in the sublime sensation and heavenly taste of his mouth as...

Slowly.

Carefully.

He arched his back just enough that he eased all the way into her and... *Holy Mother*... Keller was finally tucked inside her body where it felt like he'd always belonged. They were one. It was a tight fit, but the sizzling sensations of this first-time intimate invasion were beyond description. She squeezed her eyes shut, relishing every last tingling quiver. The exquisite pain. The fullness. The heat. This was what she'd wanted—all of him.

Still latched to his mouth, she bucked gently, needing more motion to soothe the delicious inferno raging between her legs.

A rumbly groan breathed out of him as he eased deeper inside, then withdrew just far enough to soothe. Pleasing her with his ridges and warmth. Holding her as if she were fragile and delicate. As if he cared.

"Don't stop now," she mumbled around his lips. *I love you* begged to be spoken out loud, but now was too soon, and Keller was so much like that fierce Pitbull she'd rescued. Still wary. Still not trusting this was real. That it might last. That she wouldn't break his heart.

Smoothing a hand up his spine to the back of his head, Savannah flexed her most intimate muscles around him. Her body clenched, and she thrilled to the rich timbre of another rumbling masculine groan. Happy beyond words that she, a mere woman, held any power over this magnificent beast, she squeezed again. "You like that, don't you?"

"You have no idea," he muttered as he quickened the pace. In and out. Fast, then faster. Pumping. Sweating. Panting.

Savannah tossed her hair out of her eyes as she held onto the man she now knew she could never stop loving. It took less than a minute before a sexy rumble ground out of him. One more thrust, and he gripped her hips. The heat of his coming filled her. Instinctively, she contracted around him. He pushed deeper inside and... and...

She lost her mind and the rest of her heart. "More," she breathed. There was no pain. Only need. Only lust. Only... "More!" she ordered her king of the jungle.

Keller complied. His grip on her hips tightened, holding her in place as he reached deeper. Pushed harder. And—

*Oh. Oh, oh, oh!* This coming far surpassed the first in intensity. It stormed like a sizzling wet firecracker through Savannah. It blossomed deep inside her core like crazy, wild, wonderful fireworks. She couldn't breathe. Couldn't think. Could only hold on for the best ride of her life. Her blood pressure soared along with her heart as she, a mere mortal, flew for the first time ever. She had wings! She was an angel. What a thrill!

The only things holding her to earth were Keller's long fingers on her hips, his breath in her ear, and the steady thrum of his heart pounding. This was perfect. It was wonderful. It was—love. Her gift to him. Her one-time blessing for a man who deserved so much more, that joy sprang to her eyes.

*I do love you, Keller,* she thought. *So much that it hurts. Even if you never love me in return, I'll love you forever. I want you to stay.*

"You okay?" he asked, breathing hard, his lips pressed to the side of her head.

She nodded, afraid to talk. Just as afraid to let go.

# Chapter Eighteen

He couldn't make his arms relax. He couldn't bear to let Savannah go. Keller was no idiot. He knew she was crying, but he didn't know why. Empathy never supplied all the answers. Just more questions. What he'd done was inexcusable. If he'd hurt her, he'd never forgive himself.

What the hell was he thinking? Short answer, he wasn't. Yeah, that about summed it up. Like some horny two-bit asshat from the wrong side of the tracks, he'd been thinking of himself all along, and he knew it now. The quicker he got out of here, the better off she'd be. He'd call the local authorities and let the sheriff take it from here. He'd go back to DC and never step foot in Louisiana again. Hell, he never should've come here in the first place. This was all a mistake and—

"Can we do that again?" Savannah breathed as she licked his lips. Like a soft ray of sunshine, she dropped her head and kissed the center of his chest, then ran her nose up his neck, over his Adam's apple until she ended at his mouth. Only then did she open her eyes. Yes, tears glistened on her lashes, but her bright smile lit the room.

He had to know. "I didn't hurt you?"

Her brows lifted like two gentle arches. "A little at first, but then, wow. I never knew." Creases replaced the furrows. "What's wrong? Did you think—?"

"I just wanted to make it good for you," Keller said as he pulled her flat against him, his palms splayed over her back, silently undone by the glow radiating off this woman. They were both sweaty and plastered to each other, yet he didn't need the cool refreshment that separation would bring. He craved more light from that perfect glow. More contact. More everything.

Why anyone so pure would let him do what he'd just done, Keller truly didn't understand. Yet he did. He knew. He could see the light of her heart sparkling in her eyes. He could feel the energy throbbing between them, transforming them into an entirely new, yet separate entity. Pulsing and warm, weaving them together, but not with threads of eternity. He knew better than that.

She thought she loved him. He could read that easily in her eyes, but this wasn't love. He'd just been in all the right places at all the right times today, and Savannah wasn't sophisticated. This was simply a schoolgirl crush on her part. Hero worship. Infatuation. Nothing more.

But he was no hero, nothing special at all. Yet his hungry heart argued with his hard head. What he'd had with Carol Marie had begun just as quickly. One look. One touch. Fire did that. Light a match and watch how fast an abandoned house burned to the ground. And he'd been abandoned most of his life.

Savannah nuzzled under his neck, bumping his chin with the top of her head in her delightful demanding way. "Umm, did you, umm...? Was it as good for you as, umm... it was for me?"

Keller lifted one hand from the lush comfort of her backside and cupped her jaw, needing to peer into those liquid brown windows to her soul when he answered. He tipped her head up until she met his gaze. "Savannah, you're not just good," he murmured as he planted a kiss to her forehead. "You're..." *You're making me feel everything I've kept bottled up inside for years. You're warm and sweet, and I'll never deserve you. But right now it feels like you're everything, and—what is wrong with me? You're too good.* "You're perfect."

She shrugged even as a peach blush stained her mocha skin. "I've never done this before. I just wanted to make it good for you, too, because, wow..." That smile again. "I think you just rocked my world."

"Trust me, you did good. Real good," he whispered as he drew her back under his chin, content for the first time in how long... Man, he couldn't remember. If this was witchcraft, he was all in. A convert. A true believer.

But he hoped it wasn't. It'd be so much better if this were real.

They'd have to separate soon. He'd have to dispose of that condom. They'd have to get dressed. They'd have to leave. But how he yearned for a better day and enough time to lay in bed, then take his time showering with Savannah. That'd be the perfect way to end this singular encounter. To feel her slippery skin as he washed her back and her front. Her long legs. Her bottom and every last one of her creases and curves. Her hair.

He'd lift her into his arms, press her back to the tiled wall, and he'd start all over again. Kiss her. Play with her. Mark her neck and her breasts with his mouth. Nibble on every delicious part of her. Lick her. Taste her. Make slow, easy love to her under a spray of warm water. He'd do things to her sexy body that she'd never known a man could do with a woman.

He'd watch tiny goosebumps burst all over her mocha skin when the water turned cold. Stay under the cold spray until she shivered and curled into him. Until her teeth chattered and he had to warm her up again. He'd take her back to DC and they'd—

*Whoa! Just whoa. Stop the fairytale. You don't really know this woman. Not like that. There is no love at first sight, you moron. It's a myth, a lie two horny people tell themselves. Just. Stop.*

Yet Keller couldn't bring his hands to let her go. Savannah was sunlight incarnate, and he'd been in the dark for so long. He'd almost forgotten what it felt like to be warmed from the inside out. To be special. To maybe be that one in a million. To be the right guy. The only guy…

Like a fool, Keller closed his eyes, lost in the sensual delight of a woman he barely knew. Was this love? He honestly didn't want to think about it. The only love he'd ever known had ended badly. He didn't want to jinx whatever *this* was. All he knew was he couldn't afford the pain of losing another gift so precious or so freely given.

Which proved he was now in some serious shit. The corners of his mouth curled at the paradox. No man worried about losing something he didn't already have or desperately want. Yeah. No doubt about it. This thing with Savannah could be the real thing, and God knew he wanted it. *Her.* Finally. Lightning just might've struck twice.

"We need to get moving," he whispered, letting Savannah go before he couldn't.

Her arms tightened as she ran her nose up his neck and placed a soft, wet kiss on his chin. "If you say so, Secret Agent Man."

"I say so," he growled, his voice gruffer than he'd intended as the reality of what he'd just done to an innocent woman slapped the romance out of his hard head. There was no bathroom nearby. No way for Savannah to clean up. This was her first time and she might be bleeding. That was on him. What a bastard he was. Taking a young woman's virginity in a barn. Could he have stooped any lower? Any creepier?

"You sound upset," she murmured, still in his arms. Still snuggling and kissing his chin and headed for his mouth.

"You deserved better for your first time," he told her sincerely. Instead of crushing her first afterglow, he sighed and gave her room to process what she'd just done, so she'd come to her senses, too. Yet he still held on tight to what just might be precisely what—and who—he needed.

The dogs hadn't made any noise lately. Which had to be probably, at the most, twenty minutes. Maybe not even that long. Man, he was an ass—

"Will you stop?" Savannah's arms snaked around his neck. "You are not an ass."

He found his head pulled down and his face pressed to her breasts, his mouth at one sweet nipple. Oh, yeah. She was talented like the rest of the Deuces Wild team. She could hear his thoughts. Damn. Distracted now, he licked at the lush pebbled berry within reach. Instant satisfaction melted on his tongue when his lips closed over her breast. Hollowing his cheeks, he sucked her in. *This. Oh hell, yes, this...*

One of her hands cupped the back of his head while the other massaged the spot between his shoulder blades where he'd taken a hit when he'd been on patrol in Slovenia years ago. There was no scar, just a bruise. It still ached like a mother most days, but like the superficial scrapes he'd gotten when her house exploded, he'd live with it. But how had she known? Or was she simply able to zero in on old wounds on old dogs?

"I don't want you to have any regrets," he admitted as he released her nipple with a wet pop, then inhaled the luscious scent between her sweat-slickened breasts. "We could've waited—" Her head tipped back as he breathed her in. Ahh, lilacs and sweet, salty woman. Nothing better in the world.

"Never wait, Keller," she scolded into the top of his sweaty head. "Life doesn't give second chances. I'm happier now than I've ever been. I feel complete. Isn't that enough for you?"

He kissed his way up her neck. "You'd be happier if we'd done this right and, in a hotel, at least with you lying on your back on a soft mattress instead of sitting on me while I'm sitting on kibble."

"Oh, is that what makes me happy? Soft beds? Fancy hotels?" she teased as she tipped her head back, giving him more access. "And here I thought it was you."

"And you," he breathed into her ear.

Savannah wrapped her arms around his neck, pressing her lips to his ear. "Of course. Happiness is a two-way street. Aren't you happy, too?"

Tipping back to see her, Keller fell into two glowing pools of warm, rich fire. The warm rich hues of Savannah's contentment could've dimmed the Northern lights. "I am," he whispered, as if saying it out loud might jinx the mixed feelings of his heart.

Savannah was right. Carol Marie's ghost did linger, and as much as he knew he needed to let his sweet wife go, he wasn't sure how. He was that idiot with one foot in two boats headed in opposite directions. One to his future. One to his past. Him in the middle. Unsure. Undecided. And about to fall into something he hadn't planned on and wasn't ready to deal with. He'd only come to Louisiana to help Isaiah. So why couldn't he make himself leave?

# Chapter Nineteen

Between the extra wipes in her first-aid kit and an extra roll of paper towels, Savannah took care of her business, while Keller did whatever he did with the condom. Embarrassed at her lack of experience as much as her lack of decent clothes, she made quick work of dressing even as she watched him from the corner of her eye. The man's thighs were thick and muscular. They made hers look like skinny twigs. But that chest...

Dusted with crisp, dark blond hairs, she couldn't stop thinking how she'd felt pressed into those pecs when he'd held her tight. She'd never forget what his skin smelled like. How he tasted. Her tongue slid around the inside of her mouth before she licked her lips, still savoring the decadent man she'd just tasted.

She had a one man show all to herself. He'd already pulled his pants up, but his zipper was half down, his fly unbuttoned. He'd left his shirt off while he washed at the utility sink in the corner. After a quick once-over his chest and arms with a handful of sudsy paper towels, he rinsed, then bent over and stuck his head under the gooseneck faucet.

*Note to self: This barn needs a shower stall.* That'd be a sight worth remembering, Keller naked in her shower. All that rugged bare muscle wet and on display, him hard and ready.

Savannah growled as her imagination took a delicious day trip. Fever swept over her. The fire between her legs was scorching hot. One look. One touch. And she'd climb that man's body again.

The wounds on his back needed cleaning, but none were serious. Not another mark marred his tanned body, only that star shaped scar by his eye and those hashtags on his bicep. What on earth were they? Too evenly spaced to be normal workday wounds, she stored her question for another time. But she couldn't make her eyes *not watch* what her body craved.

Sputtering, water in his eyes and running down his chest, Keller tossed his head back. A tiny rooster tail of crystal droplets sailed over him, and Savannah's pulse slowed at the gorgeous man in her barn. Forget the shower. This was a heart-pounding sight she'd never forget.

"Hey, you still with me?" Keller had yet to step away from the sink. He stood there holding paper towels out for her. "You want to wash up? Not that you need to, but we did land in the swamp today. It might feel good." He'd caught her staring.

*Oh. That.* Savannah snapped out of her lust-fueled haze. *Oh, yeah, I'm so with you... All. The. Way.*

She'd forgotten how dirty she was. Most of that slimy swamp goo had probably sweated off on their mad dash to Sanctuary, but a shower wouldn't hurt. She had landed on Keller, but then she'd nearly lost her mind at the scorching heat of his body between her legs and the strength of his arms crossed resolutely behind her back. Like her very own guardian angel. She'd known then she'd have to straddle him again—and soon.

But for the first time, Savannah worried how she must smell. Her hand went automatically to her hair, smoothing, checking for clots of mud, twigs, rats, and just generally ashamed that he looked so good, while she must look like a whore on Bourbon Street.

"Um, yeah, s-s-sure," she stuttered like the total backwoods hick she was.

A no-kidding smile breached the sharp corners of his beautiful face. "Man, you're something," he murmured, shaking his head.

At last by his side, she turned the faucets to warm, and there she stopped. He hadn't moved. Just leaned his hip to the edge of the counter beside the sink. He crossed his arms over that magnificent chest, the towels still in his hand. A small grin tweaked his sexy mouth. Was he just going to stand there and watch? *Apparently so...*

Trembling at the wicked thing she'd just done with this handsome man, Savannah took the towels, held them under the water enough to dampen them, and turned to face him. Keller's crossed arms were no help. Her gaze dropped to the pecs he'd just framed. His biceps bulged tight and round and solid. If he were one of her dogs, she'd reach out and pet him, but her courage flagged. Apparently, lust was like adrenaline. It didn't last long.

He touched her first, one hand cupping her shoulder. "May I?" he asked as he took the towels back.

"I can do it."

"But I want to do it," he murmured, his voice low and gravelly. Sexy.

Despite a sense of trepidation, Savannah's body burst into flames once more. Sizzling. Liquid. Flames. Because she wanted to do *it* again, too.

Keller pulled her toward him, her butt against the counter, and her legs between his knees. Her palms and all five fingers landed on that manly chest. Warm and rough, hard yet smooth, she could barely stand still while he wiped those cool, damp paper towels over her forehead and cheeks. Down her neck. Across her shoulders. Gently. Kindly.

The first hint of his crystal-clear compassion and tenderness hit like an ocean wave. Closing her eyes, Savannah let it wash over and through her as if she were an empty vessel. Keller's empathy was a powerful force, crashing into her, flooding her, filling every nook and crevice, every hidden part of her soul with uncommon comfort for all she'd suffered and lost today.

This man's understanding and genuine kindness knew no bounds. He knew and understood Gran Mere's death at an intimate level most others never could, and he wasn't judging her. He wasn't just picking up on her grief, smoothing it out and pouring in kindness to buoy her up. Somehow, he'd incorporated her loss into his soul, as if it were his to bear. Not only had he been there when she'd passed—although he hadn't known it at the time—he was now shouldering Savannah's grief as if it were his. *Who does something like that?*

Only this golden man who was as fierce and as proud as Isaiah. But like Isaiah, Keller gave his gift away as if there were no rules for anyone but him. As if everyone deserved his compassion, while he did not.

"Lift your hair," he ordered gently.

Opening her eyes, Savannah reached both hands behind her head to tie her hair up into a messy knot. Keller's gaze slid down her neck to her meager cleavage. His top teeth slid over his bottom lip. She'd forgotten the feminine power she held over him. It was such a simple thing to lift her arms, but he wanted her again. And she wanted him.

She took extra care securing every last wayward strand. He needed this private little show, and she could tell by the way his breath hitched that he liked what he saw. A tender darkness enveloped the gold in his eyes. He didn't blink or swallow, just stared like a hungry man standing outside a bakery window, with only the thinnest pane of glass between him and a tray of warm-from-the-oven, powdered sugar frosted beignets.

At last, Savannah cupped his jaw in both hands, her heart opened wide to whatever Keller wanted from her. As freely as he gave to others, she would give to him. "Do I stink?" she asked to draw his gaze back to her face.

"Uh uh," he growled, his tongue darting out to quench his lower lip. Reaching behind her, he grabbed another handful of towels, dampened them, then left the faucet running as he wiped her arms.

Teasing she asked, "Would it be easier if I took my shirt off?"

"God, no," he groaned. "I mean, yes, yes, but not until we're some place where I can worship you like you deserve. I've never done this in a barn before."

"That makes two of us," she said blithely as she took the towels and made quick work of refreshing herself. A shadow stole his smile, and she knew he considered himself a lowlife for what he'd just done to her.

Tossing the crumpled towels into the trash bin beside the counter, she walked into Keller's arms and put both hands on that massive chest. "I wanted this," she breathed. "Don't, please don't let the fact that we made love in a barn ruin it."

He didn't flinch, didn't even blink. Instead he circled her inside his arms, holding her as gently as if she were a child. She snuggled in where she wanted to stay. Could things get more perfect?

"We need to talk," he murmured as he rested his chin on the crown of her head.

"We do?" Now was the moment she'd been waiting for. She nuzzled, rubbing her nose along his collarbone and breathing in every last male epithelial she could. Now she could tell him she loved him. Once he said the word—

"What we just did was fantastic, no doubt about it," he purred, his hands so warm against her back. So big and strong. "A guy could get used to coming home to you. But it can't happen again. We're—"

*Wait. What?* Savannah tipped back in his arms, needing eye contact. "You don't love me?"

Didn't that make her sound high school pathetic? But they had just made love. That was what sex between consenting, caring adults was called, wasn't it? Making love? And if they'd made love, didn't it just naturally follow that he loved her? He certainly cared enough for her. He'd used a condom, and he'd said all the right words. He'd been gentle and kind, possessive and dominant. He'd made her think that he felt the same way she did. How could they have done what they did and he not love her? Was that even possible?

"I do care about you, Savannah," he answered, the sexy glow in his eyes replaced by an earnest light. "What we just did here today rocked my world, too."

Okay, that sounded promising. He had felt the same things she did. She let him explain, certain he was getting to the good part.

"But we're from two different worlds. I work a dangerous career in the District, while you have a steady business and a full life here. It's my fault. I'm a bastard for misleading you. I shouldn't have let this go as far as it did. I'm sorry."

She had no idea what to say to that. The man she'd just given herself and her heart to didn't love her back. Because of his job? "But I, umm…" Her heart fell with a soggy splat at her feet. *I am so dumb.*

"I'm sorry," Keller said even as he cupped her jaw in the same gentle hands she'd fallen in love with back at the boathouse, the same hands that had earlier caressed Gran Mere's pretty face. Savannah knew she loved this guy then. How could he say these untrue things to her now? She knew better. He did love her, he did!

Yet the warmth left her when he dutifully untangled his hands and legs and set her apart. The instant loss of his body heat chilled Savannah to her soul. He didn't love her. He never had. He'd just used her. Yet that didn't make sense, and it didn't feel right either. The righteous words coming out of his mouth didn't match the tender vibes rolling off him. That was his gift, his empathy. But right now, Keller needed to knock it off. Empathy was something he could walk away from. It wasn't love.

Savannah closed her eyes, not ready to face what truth she might read on his handsome face. The instant her eyes shut, her inner sight opened with a rush. Once again all the threads of the universe flowed through her. This was her gift, and she saw the real Keller clearly.

He was a proud man of finely-honed honor that gleamed around him like a halo. That honor was the code he lived by, his pledge of allegiance. He was a combat-hardened warrior more than a sleek federal agent. Yes, he'd killed for his country, and he'd do it again. But while he'd dealt with the personal aftermath of taking those lives, a few of those deaths still clung to him. A woman in the tangled Amazon jungle. A young man—no, a boy—in some far-off desert. Of all things— a dog that ran beneath the wheels of his car while chasing a cat across a busy highway...

He knew the cost of war and loss, yet he'd pledged his whole heart and soul to his country. He'd seen the worst of mankind, but in the camaraderie of the men he'd fought with, he'd also seen the best. She didn't know what a ranger was, but Keller did and he was proud to be one. So proud. Those intangibles were all he'd had left after he'd lost his wife. His black suit and tie were just another disguise.

Despite the gleaming honor, a darkness lingered within him. It breathed. It slithered. And he believed it would eventually consume him. That was why he guarded his heart. He refused to drag anyone down with him. Especially her.

"You're lying, Keller Boniface," she whispered, "and you know it."

# Chapter Twenty

Well, shit. That didn't go like he'd planned. Not at all. Keller took a full step away from Savannah. It was either that or jerk her back into his arms where he wanted to keep her forever. He should've known better than to disguise the truth from this mind-reading wonder. When the hell would he learn?

Yet neither was he ready to declare his love for a woman he'd just met. Not yet, not yet, not yet. Life didn't work that way, and he wasn't a dumb kid anymore. He had responsibilities. Duties! Those things didn't go away just because a guy fell in love.

*Not in love,* his heart screamed. *Can't give away what's already given!*

Savannah's pretty head canted to her right, nearly to her shoulder. As much as he tried to resist, the warmth in her chocolate brown eyes drew him back in. "It's okay," she told him, her voice caressing the mixed-up feelings in his head. Why did it feel like she thought she needed to gentle him? He was no mad dog, damn it. He was a federal agent and a damned good one. He worked hard, damn it, and—

She touched the center of his chest, his breastbone. One sizzle. One tiny fingertip. And he was what he'd been from the start, lost and found and so damned sad. The dam inside felt ready to burst.

Keller took a step back, not ready. Never ready! He refused the magic this woman held over him. No more, damn it! No more voodoo spells or witchcraft or curses or whatever you wanted to call it. Not now! Not ever!

Yet the tender swell of love in her eyes, the pure love she'd just professed, stopped him short. He knew it then. This emotion he felt wasn't magic and she wasn't evil. If anything, Savannah was one of the purest women he'd ever met.

And Keller was tired of the empty life he'd been forced to live. The last time he'd found any comfort had been in Carol Marie's arms. Never thought he'd find another woman equal to her. Not until Savannah Church jerked her door open and told him, *'I. Said. No.'*

Weakened by that sweet enlightenment, Keller dropped to his knees and grabbed Savannah to him, burying his face in her soft, sweet belly like a bastard kid with a gut full of sins to confess. Only these were sins of the heart. Failures. Omission. Shortcomings.

"I killed her," he cried, so damned ashamed and embarrassed and weary. "She wanted to meet my mother, but I never should've taken her home. I should've left town and taken her with me. I should have protected her. Hell, I should have killed Ma first! Carol Marie would still be alive then."

Savannah's fingers captured his sweaty head, pressing him against her body. "Shush, it's okay. Everything is okay."

"No, it's not. You don't understand. Elaine killed my wife. I know she did, but God! I didn't know she was already pregnant." Tipping his chin to the ceiling, Keller roared as the sin he'd never forgive himself for poured out of his soul like a wicked, writhing serpent. Fanged and vicious, it never let him rest, not once since the morning he'd found Elaine bent over the body of his precious wife. In his witch of a mother's own home, for the love of God!

Poor, sweet Carol Marie had a baby in her womb then. She'd meant to tell him that day. It was supposed to have been a surprise. Her doctor told him that sad news at her funeral. Keller'd had a son. A tiny son! *Elaine took everything!*

Full of hatred for his biological witch of a mother, Keller took hold of Savannah's hips to shove away from her. She had no right to think of him with kindness. To think of him at all! He hadn't deserved kindness from his wife, and he didn't deserve it now. She shouldn't have shared the pleasure of her sweet, pure body with him, either. He could never be good enough. Not with the level of hatred in his heart. Any man who wanted to murder his flesh and blood was no saint.

Yet he couldn't summon the strength to make Savannah go, not with her holding onto him as if she were suddenly the stronger one. Which she most certainly was. She'd never killed a thing in her life, and he'd taken so many lives. So damned many... Except the one he should have taken. How he hated his mother. Every day. In every way. If he could do it over again, he'd still have Carol Marie. Not Elaine and not Savannah.

Somehow that didn't sit quite right. He'd never missed Elaine, but Savannah... He wasn't sure he could live another day without the warmth of her all-or-nothing love in it.

"Let me go," he begged as the first of many sobs wrenched out of him. More of the snake. More of the beast. Migraines and hell. Those were his lot in life. Not this gentle woman. Life just wasn't that kind.

Yet Savannah's fingers worked a peculiar kind of magic over his sweating skull. Slow and steady, they massaged and blessed, threading over his skull and through his hair. Until at last, he could breathe again.

Bowing his forehead to her belly and sick of fighting, Keller circled his arms around her slender waist, needing a connection with this woman more than he needed air. There was no keeping anything from Savannah, and for once in his long lonesome life, he didn't want to be alone. He needed this. He needed her.

The lovely fragrance of lilacs enveloped his ragged soul while she continued massaging her gentle kind of magic into the tense muscles that encased his hard Ranger head. Until slowly... Gradually... Comfort seeped into the deepest crevice of Keller's locked-up heart. He began to understand. This woman standing with him now had given him every last piece of herself. She'd given freely because that's who she was. She truly loved him. His denial of that love hurt her. But she was right. She had stood beside him, and even now, she did what she could to soothe the bitter hatred he'd carried for years.

The least he could do was man up and admit that, yes. It might be a betrayal to his dead wife, but he did have powerful feelings for this living woman, this mysterious, mind-reading Savannah Church. It was time she knew, although he was pretty certain she already did. Which meant it was long past time for him to voice those fears—to himself. Savannah didn't need to hear what she already knew, but Keller did.

"I couldn't," he murmured into her warm body. "I couldn't take the chance. You already believe, and once people believe—"

"They fall prey to those who misuse their power, right? Is that what you believe?"

"Yes," he declared raggedly. He'd seen more evil than good during his life. Most people were grubbers, content to exist in poverty while they groomed their version of the truth into something it wasn't. He'd never understood how self-righteous the poor could be, or how entrenched in snobbery the have-nots were.

You'd think only the wealthy were stuck up, but the wicked poor were just as bad. Just as small-minded.

They twisted reality until those who had honestly worked for a living and made something of their lives, had only done so because they'd lied, cheated, or slept their way to the top. Ignorance knew no limits. There were as many poor people as rich who lived to lord their measly sense of self-righteous power over others. Elaine was that grubber. Mean. Poor of spirit. Vicious. But never to people's faces. Only to their backs.

"There are good and bad people, Keller," Savannah said quietly. "Gran Mere taught me that. Even among those we believe are better or smarter than us, maybe wiser, there is still deceit and evil. It's the way of this world we live in. To everything there is a season. A time to..."

He nodded, rubbing his cheek against her hip as he inhaled her unique, feminine scent. "Trust me. I know Ecclesiastes. *'To everything there is a season, and a time for every purpose under heaven: a time to be born and a time to die, a time to plant and a time to uproot, a time to kill...'"*

And there he stopped. The rest of the bible verses were more juxtaposition of goodness balanced against evil, but Keller was spent. Mourning, dying, hating, and war he understood. They were the bedrock of his life. But loving, peace, and heaven? Those concepts were strangers. Damn, he was tired.

Savannah's fingers tapped lightly on his head. "Get up," she commanded.

Reluctantly, he stood, looking for his shirt, needing a barrier—anything—between him and this strange woman. She and her Gran Mere had a way of twisting Catholicism with voodoo to make it appealing, and for sure, Savannah had a gift of sight. She'd had not problem seeing through him. What a joke. For a federal agent, he'd certainly turned into a pussy. If Tucker could see him now... Shit. He'd be on the streets, looking for another job.

"Stay," she ordered softly, her hand circling his wrist before he could get away, drawing him back into her arms. "I'm going to tell you a secret," she whispered, looking to her right, then to her left as if there were anything besides mice in the barn with them. "I love you, Keller Boniface, and I'm not afraid to say it. I believe I fell in love with you when you knelt to pay your respect to Gran Mere. I could see you clearly then, but I see you better now. You weren't who I first thought you were. You are..." She paused as if searching for the right word. "...better. You're better than I'd judged you to be, certainly more than I'd expected from a federal agent. I was wrong when I took you at face value. You have gifts, but you've stifled them until they cause you great pain and consternation. They hurt you, and yet they should bless you. Pray with me."

"No," he told her. "I don't pray and I don't—"

"I know, I know, you don't pray, and yet you swear and curse. But who do you swear and curse at? Is it not

God or Jesus Christ? Is that not how many of your curses begin and end, using the Lord's name in vain?"

*Well, hell, yeah.* He had nothing to say, so he kept his mouth shut.

Savannah breathed a drawn-out sigh, her breasts heaving. "Is not cursing also a most desperate form of sincere prayer? Is not hating the God who created you and Carol Marie an angry man's way of acknowledging there is a relationship between Him and you? That you still believe, even enough to damn Him?"

"No!" he nearly shouted. Cursing was vile and full of hate. Especially cursing God. Blaming God. That was what he'd done. He hurled accusations and condemnation heavenward at a power who could have and should have been there for Carol Marie, but who hadn't bothered to show up! Goddamn it. Cursing was not prayer. It was mean-spirited and vengeful and...

So what if it was communication between an angry, hurt man and an indifferent God? It still wasn't prayer, okay? Prayer was gentle communication of a higher nature. It was communion, trusting and kind. It was a son speaking frankly with his Father, and...

Keller turned away from Savannah at the thought. Could she be right? Were his out of control tirades still communication with a God whom Keller knew to his core was truly there? Did God see it that way? Had Keller been—somehow—praying all these years with every curse?

Keller ran a hand over his sweaty head, dragging his fingernails through the prickly stubs of his cut. It didn't seem right, at least, it surely wasn't proper. Men used the Lord's name in vain all the time. Ask anyone. That was what hard men and soldiers did. They cursed and they swore, they drank like fiends and they sent wicked bastards to Hell. They sure as hell weren't praying then.

Yet deep in his soul, Keller knew he'd only cursed the Lord hardest when nights got too dark and self-pity ran roughshod over him. When he'd missed his wife. Which, until Savannah came along, had been all the time.

She stood patiently waiting, her hair pulled into a messy ponytail that curled at the nape of her neck. Patience. That was her magic, damn it. She'd given him a lifeline, and now she was waiting to see if he hanged himself with it or... what? If he dropped to his knees and said, *'Thank you, Jesus, I'm saved!'*?

Not going to happen. He was no saint and this was no miracle. Cursing was one thing. He refused to pray.

"We really need to move," he reminded her. "Pack what you need. Keep it light."

"But you need the same kind of help Isaiah needed. You need—"

"Not now," he snapped, needing to get this woman to safety if it was the last thing he did today.

"Okay then," she said as if she'd gotten the precise answer she expected. "But know this. You don't have to love me back for me to love you. I offered my heart, but not in exchange for yours. If you never find peace, know I gave freely what was mine to give. I do love you. I always will."

What the hell was a guy supposed to say to that?

Savannah smiled. "I'll let the dogs run until I get back. They'll be okay."

He'd forgotten the dogs. They'd been so quiet. "How about your cats?" he asked like a complete ninny. Savannah had just bared her soul and given him a precious gift in the process, yet he couldn't—wouldn't—give her what she needed. Not yet.

"They'll be fine. You made sure they had water when you fed them, didn't you?" she asked as if she still respected him. As if she still loved him...

"Sure. Water and food." Like the dogs, each cat had an individual indoor kennel as well as its own outside caged run. Answering was better than thinking about the love she'd just professed. How could she do that? Love *him*? Surely there were better men—

"Then I'm ready," she declared as cheerfully as ever. That was another of Savannah's gifts. She gave freely, while he doled out his meager gift of empathy and comfort in the smallest increments and only when he had to. Giving seemed to make her happy. Now that was something to think about.

She crooked her elbow like they were going on a date instead of running for their lives. "Shall we?"

Keller shook his head. If there were a way to deny this woman, he didn't know it. He linked his arm through hers and humbly said, "Let's roll."

# Chapter Twenty-One

Red and Sir Galahad were lounging on the grass outside the barn door when Keller opened it. Savannah chuckled. Her handsome pittie was really her most faithful baby, but the Red Irish Setter sprawled on the ground with him was a surprise. Most other dogs were tail-waggling happy, still chasing each other through the yard, sniffing at the debris from her house, and chasing birds they'd never catch. The fire was out now, but the interior would be a wet mess. She should have been more worried, but hey. It was only a house, and this was Louisiana, aka hurricane central. She'd learned that lesson early. Houses could be rebuilt, but those birds on her front porch...

Keller stooped to pat Galahad's broad forehead. "Do you have another car we could use?"

He was wearing his holster again, both pistols loose in their cups, the leather strap comfortable across his shoulders. He'd left his jacket and dress shirt behind and wore only the swamp stained t-shirt. For some reason, it looked tighter this evening, either that or his biceps were larger. Or maybe it was just that Savannah now knew the width and breadth of the manly body beneath the clothes.

Funny Red had crawled on his belly and inserted himself between Keller and the Pitbull like a jealous child trying to get Keller's attention. She smiled at the glow in that crazy dog's eyes.

Red had come to her in tears and tatters. His now sleek, glassy coat had once been torn away by other dogs, and if Keller took the time to pet the dog, he'd discover a wealth of knots and gnarled ridges beneath the shine. Dear, sweet, happy-go-lucky Red had been used as a bait dog in one of the worst underground dog-fighting rings in the state.

Savannah's fingers curled into fists as she recalled the day she'd faced Dickie Bob Boudreaux, aka Bubba, in front of his so-called friends. *Killer,* that was what she'd called him to his face that day. *Murderer!*

Defiant and as angry as she'd never been, she'd climbed into his bloody fighting ring to rescue Red. When Bubba jumped in after her, screaming "Get the fuck off my property!" she'd stood up to him in front of all his jeering homies. She'd told him, "Go on, then, hit me! That's what big tough guys like you do, isn't it, Bubba? You'd hit a girl the same way you beat these dogs!"

She'd been out of her mind that day. But she'd also been filled with righteous wrath, and determined she wasn't leaving without Red. The poor bloodied dog had curled at her feet by then. She couldn't have left him, not with two vicious pitties skulking around the ring like slathering monsters out of a nightmare, waiting to tear him apart.

Bubba's buddies urged him to, "Slap that bitch, bro! Do it! Show her who's boss, Bubba! Give it to her! Bloody her. Do it! Do it!"

He'd curled back his fist, and Savannah was sure he'd punch her rather than look weak in front of his buddies. But she was way past cowering to the likes of Bubba. She wasn't sure which she'd been that day, stupid or brave, but she'd gotten right in his face, close enough to see his nose hairs. And she'd told him, "Go ahead and hit me, Dickie, but you'd better kill me when you do, because I'm taking this dog with me if you don't. And I'm telling Gran Mere what you're doing out here on the land she gave your mama!"

It might've been because she'd call him by his name. It might have been because she'd invoked his mama and Gran Mere's holy name. But whatever... Dickie dropped his hand and took a full step back before he told her to, "Go to hell and take that shittin' dog with you. Go on. Get outta here before I turn you into one of my bitches! They made rape stands for women like you, ya know."

"And they make prison cells for men like you!" she'd volleyed right back at his squared-off, empty head.

He'd turned on her then, his face red and the pits of his yellow shirt stained with sweat. "I said git!"

Which Savannah did. She'd dragged poor Red out of there, and she'd gotten him inside the back of her car, and she'd driven straight to Doctor John's clinic. There was no vet close by, and she'd been afraid Red wouldn't last if there were. Rudy had been surprised to see her, but he'd come through for her. Between patients, he'd doctored Red, then kept him overnight until he was sure Red was going to make it.

"I think Red likes you," Savannah told Keller. "But no, I don't have another car, and before we leave, I want to check my birds. I'll be right back."

Before she walked three steps, Keller was at her side, his hand at the small of her back. "Not without me, you don't."

"Suit yourself," she replied as Galahad and Red followed along. Together the four of them circled the house. Savannah was right. Her birds were okay. Most of the damage had occurred at the rear of her house and on her deck, but her fire suppressant system had worked. She'd have a watery mess to clean up later, but this was nothing compared to what the last hurricane did.

"You need to feed them?" Keller asked as he escorted Savannah up the porch steps.

"If you don't mind. I'll only take a minute."

While he and the dogs took up post at the top of the steps, Savannah hurriedly washed water bowls and filled food cups. She snuggled each of her nervous feathered babies and told them she'd be gone until morning, but she'd make it up to them as soon as she got back.

At last, she turned around. By then, Keller sat on the top step with a dog at each side. But while Galahad stood like a rock, panting, drooling, and snorting, Red had climbed onto Keller's lap and rolled over on his back. Keller cradled the silly heart like a baby, scratching Red's poor scarred belly. Tears filled Savannah's eyes. Her favorite lost warriors had finally found each other.

"He likes you," she whispered.

Keller looked up. Too late, he tried to mask his heart, but she'd seen. He'd let Red into a place in his heart where he'd blocked her out. Keller cleared his throat, then coughed again. "Someone hurt this guy, didn't they?" he asked. "How'd you...? Where'd you...?"

"I rescued Red from an illegal dog fight. It's closed down now, not that Dickie's not sneaky enough to open another one. But if he does, I'll find out. I always do."

"Red was a bait dog. Shit."

*Exactly.* When he couldn't seem to speak, she said it for him. "I think Galahad and Red should come with us, don't you?"

"Yeah, ahh, sure. That'd work for me."

*Of course, it will, you softhearted, badassed guardian angel of mine.*

By then, Keller wouldn't look at Savannah, and that was okay. Even tough men cried, and she'd cried plenty over the sweet boy now resting with his eyes closed on Keller's lap. Didn't they make a handsome pair of bodyguards, Red with his patchy but silky scarlet hair and Keller with his golden, tan skin? They were a perfect match, familiars who'd recognized each other at first sight.

"Are you guys ready?" she asked as she breezed by them on her way to the cat barn and the garage behind it. Little did Keller know that she'd kinda, sorta not told him the truth. True, she didn't own another car. She owned something better.

"Hey, wait up," Keller grumbled while he, Galahad, and long-legged Red scrambled to keep up.

"You boys are slower than dirt," she teased as she kicked into high gear and ran ahead of them. Red outpaced her easily, but Keller overtook her just as she passed the cat barn.

"Slow up," he growled. "We still don't know if it's safe yet or—"

*Yap. Bark. Woof!*

Keller found himself surrounded by the rest of Savannah's waggling, posturing canines.

"I think we're safe," she told him, grinning at the enlightenment spreading like sunshine over his grumpy countenance. Wow. That smile turned Keller into a completely different man. He was so damned handsome that it hurt to look at him.

Savannah's breath caught. Not only did she stop, but she changed directions and threw herself into him. He caught her as easily as he had every other time today. In his arms. Against his heart. Under his chin. She snuggled in where she wanted to stay, inhaling her favorite masculine scent. "I do love you," she told him sincerely.

# **Chapter Twenty-Two**

He believed her. He did. Keller just couldn't give Savannah what she wanted. Hell, it hadn't even been twenty-four hours since he'd met her, and love just did not—could not—work that way or this fast. Not for him. Could it?

He set her back on her feet and like one of her hound dogs, he followed her to a one-car garage behind the cat barn. Keller stopped short when Savannah flipped the garage door up and revealed, of all things, an airboat. *I'll be damned.* He stifled the urge to swing her back into his arms and shout 'Hallelujah!' This woman and her remarkable gift of independence and self-reliance would be the death of him.

"Surprised?" she asked coyly.

Thrilled was more like it, yet he offered a mere, "It'll work. Is it gassed and ready to go? Does it even run?" The craft was inside dry storage after all, cradled on a trailer that rested on some kind of track. Not docked in water like a respectable boat should've been.

"Oh, ye of little faith," she murmured as—of course—she smacked a pad similar to the one that locked her gates, this one on the wall inside the garage.

Gears moved, simultaneously flattening the garage door up to the ceiling while moving the trailer forward. Out the door. Momentum took over from there, and for the first time, Keller noticed the gentle swell in the land that no doubt led to the bayou. The trailer had four wheels instead of two. No hitch. Over a barely concealed gravel path it moved, straight for the line of brush Keller now understood was most likely just a blind disguising the swamp. Probably a dock. This lady was smart.

"You've thought of everything, haven't you?"

Her shoulders lifted as if she were used to being minimized. "Have to, living out here. No one else to rely on."

Not even him. Chagrined, Keller ran a hand up the back of his stiff neck as the trailer plowed through the thin line of brush. He'd made Savannah sound like an inexperienced fool, when the real fool was him. He should've known better, yet he'd discounted her merely because of her gender. Sure enough, the trailer's wheels jolted to a stop at a strategically placed log in its path. Alongside a wooden dock jutting into the swamp. Just like she'd intended.

The garage door eased shut behind them. With one hand, Savannah released the straps securing her boat to the trailer, while Keller cranked the lever that released the craft into the water. It was a good boat. Flat-bottomed with a caged three-blade propeller aft, one molded plastic bench sat forward and low to the deck, while two captain seats sat behind with the tiller and instrument panel between them. It sat high in the water but it was clean and well-cared for. Very few scrapes or scratches marred its wide aluminum hull.

Savannah's baby had been a fishing boat in a previous life, since the instrument panel boasted a Garmin depth finder. But Keller had to wonder just how often she went to town or if she did. Sanctuary seemed to offer everything she needed to survive, and if it didn't, the swamp did. Yet he'd treated her like a helpless female when she was anything but.

"What horsepower?" he asked to redeem himself.

"Five-fifty," she answered without blinking. "There's bigger boats out there, but I don't need big. Just good."

*Ouch.* He'd been anything but good. Or decent. He'd been patronizing. "Where do you want me?" he asked, not assuming anything from here on out. Savannah was captain of this craft. He was just a knucklehead at her disposal.

"Not with the boys," she answered distantly as she grunted and shifted several gear boxes out of the aisle and under the front bench seat. The boys being Red and Galahad, the other knuckleheads, who were now side by side on the front bench like a couple kids ready for a ride.

Keller boarded, carefully distributing his weight while he took stock of the gear strapped below deck. Spotlights. Oars. Two long-handled nets. A couple cane fishing poles. That made him smile. He hadn't seen bamboo cane poles since he was a kid. A couple empty plastic buckets, the tall kind with wire handles. An ice chest. A rifle and what he hoped was a real ammo box with real ammo in it instead of stored junk.

"You carry?" he asked, still trying to make solid eye contact.

But Captain Savannah had grown remote while she readied her boat for travel.

He tried again. "How do you trailer this little baby of yours when you're done? How do you get it back in storage all by yourself?"

"Elbow grease and willpower." Another shrug like what he thought of her didn't matter. Damn, she must get treated like an idiot all the time, and she'd come to accept it. How sad. Keller had just joined the last group on earth he wanted to be aligned with—the closed-minded male assholes club.

"Will you need to stop for fuel?"

"Nope. I never dock without filling up first. Get in. It'll be dark soon. We've got to get going."

"Are you sure your dogs will be okay?" Red and Galahad had no problem leaving Sanctuary, yet Keller hesitated. The rest of Savannah's dogs now lined the bank, some barking, some already standing in the water like they meant to go with her. She seemed to have taken Gran Mere's dying and the mayhem of the day in stride. Or had she? Was she just finally so numb that she had to get away?

Or was it him? Was she upset that he hadn't returned her endearments or that declaration of love? Keller sat behind the dogs in the right captain seat. That'd put the stick at Savannah's right when she sat with him. It'd work if she were right-handed, but Keller had no idea if she was or wasn't. Which also proved why he couldn't profess emotions he didn't feel. He didn't know Savannah well enough yet, and oh yeah. He was leaving in a couple days, maybe sooner. He had an important life and a job to get back to. Well, a job anyway.

Seemingly preoccupied or at least, ignoring him, she handed him a heavy-duty headset. "Here. Put this on."

Keller promptly snapped the set over his head, adjusting the muffs to protect his hearing. Airplane propellers were one helluva big fan, but they also made an extreme noise. Quickly, she strapped smaller headsets on the dogs, and wasn't that a sight? Two dogs with silly smiles as if they knew they were her favorites. Make that three. Keller felt a smile coming on, too.

At last she called to the other dogs on shore, "Stay. I won't be long. Y'all know what to do while I'm gone."

Keller tapped his headset when her voice came through loud and clear. Which meant she understood

Bluetooth audio technology and there had to be a cell tower nearby. She wasn't uneducated at all, and Sanctuary wasn't as remote as Keller had initially thought. What else didn't he know about Savannah Church?

Proficiently, she backed the airboat away from shore before she turned it around and gradually accelerated. Sir Galahad grinned, long strings of drool streaming into the wind. No wonder they sat forward. All that drool hit the plastic back of his chair, thank heavens.

Meanwhile Red's long ears trailed behind him. For a badly used bait dog, he seemed happy and carefree instead of jumpy and traumatized. Big and gangly, he'd shocked Keller when he'd first brushed against his hand back on Savannah's porch. As usual it had only taken one touch and Keller had felt precisely what Red endured in the dog fighting pit. It'd taken all he had to not break down in front of Savannah and cry like an idiot for the torture Red survived. There were times Keller was ashamed of humankind. They could be such monsters.

Glancing out the corner of his eye, he sneaked a look at the competent and beautiful woman at his side. He knew now that Savannah would've understood if he'd broken down. She'd have cried with him. He just wasn't ready to fall apart again.

Night had fallen and the water way glimmered from the last of the fading sunlight. The boat's soft blue interior LED running lights turned on under the deck, while yellow driving lights along the deck did the same. Keller took a deep breath of the only part of Louisiana that he considered home. The bayou. Here, he finally felt at peace. How could he not? Beauty was everywhere.

Tattered curtains of silvery Spanish moss hung from dark fingered branches high overhead. Humidity hung in foggy patches like a stifling damp blanket over the swamp, filling Keller's nose with the distinct smells of fish, mold, and mud. It'd been a long time since he'd been in the bayou, but it seemed like yesterday. Part of him was still here.

The soundtrack hadn't changed a bit. At his left, the too close swoosh of a gator sliding into the water turned his head. Several pairs of bright, beady eyes glittered starboard. A lazy fin or perhaps a spiny tail stirred the water between those eyes and the boat. Could be an alligator checking them out. Not that Keller was worried. He'd learned years ago that alligators were near-sighted and easily distracted. They were ambush hunters. They survived by sneaking up on unwitting prey, generally along the edge of the swamp.

The rules were simple. If you were close enough to hear an alligator hiss, you were too damned close. But if you were unfortunate enough to encounter one on land, your best bet was to run like the wind in the opposite direction. Rarely did an alligator run its prey down, mostly because its top running speed was shit. The rules changed in the water, though. There they could burst into speeds of twenty plus knots per hour. You were in their domain. All they needed was a good hold on a leg, arm or foot, and the infamous death roll began. Gator one, idiot human zip. Crunch. Crunch. Gurgle. Gurgle. You died. The end.

Even as Keller lifted his fingers out of the water, his soul seemed to unwind and relax. Here there was peace. Even as dark as it was becoming, there were still waterfowl everywhere, bobbing for minnows attracted to the surface or fishing for crawdads. The chorus of the bayou swelled around him. Tree frogs croaked. Bullfrogs bellowed. Owls hooted and the spring's first fox kits yipped in the dark. So much life layered upon life. It was an opera like no other. Though he couldn't see or hear them, Keller knew there were possums, muskrats, raccoons, and snapping turtles along the muddy, marshy shoreline. During the day he might spot a great white egret or a heron. Other shore birds. Thick vegetation lined most of the shoreline. Rats and mice lived in the sawgrass. Snakes. Lizards. Which made him think of the long-snouted crocodile, the gharial that had seemed intent on attacking them. Add that to the mystery of Savannah's rosy red bird from Australia, and Keller came up with an inevitable conclusion. Someone was smuggling rare birds and animals into the bayou. They'd lost track of a shipment.

Instinctively, he reached for Savannah's hand on the stick. She knew this part of the bayou and it showed. The boat had yet to scrape sand or hit any submerged stumps. Pursing his lips, Keller sent her an air kiss. A smile curled her pretty lips and she sent one back to him. She wasn't angry. Just busy. She deserved more, but that would do for now.

They made good time. By the time Savannah cut the motor and pulled her craft into shallow water, Keller had no idea where they were. He hadn't thought to ask. The glide through the swamp had been restful and distracting. Even now fireflies twinkled from the reeds along the murky shoreline. There was a time when the bayou had been home. He'd missed that.

"We're back at Gran Mere's," Savannah announced through his headset. "At least, we're close. My car's parked a mile or two from here."

Here being a secluded sandbar beneath the crowded boughs of a shadowy enclave of bald cypress. The most prolific plant in the bayou, these hardy giants with their unique, submerged buttressed trunks thrived in brackish water all their lives. They stood firm and unmoving. Many of these enclaves shared the same root system for miles of shoreline. Like the grasses of the Everglades, all they needed was water and sunshine, and they could take over the world.

Savannah had chosen well. This tree's mighty branches disappeared into the night sky. Its base measured at least six feet wide, and its needle-like leaves were thick and fragrant overhead. Once he doffed his headset and jumped on shore, Keller put one palm to the tree's trunk. Instant calm filled him. Instant peace. The last of his apprehension melted in the sublime contact with a lifeform older than the United States of America. Another benefit of his unique gift of empathy was that trees communicated with him. Not like they spoke English like the Ents of Middle Earth in Tolkien's *"Lord of the Rings."* But all trees definitely passed a sense of calm and peace to anyone who stopped long enough to listen. It was as if they knew puny mankind needed assurance that life would always find a way.

Patting the tree's stalwart trunk, telling it goodbye in his way, Keller turned to find Savannah staring at him, her eyes wide as if she knew precisely what he was doing.

"You communicate with trees but you can't hear human thoughts?"

"No big deal." He shrugged. "I like trees."

Which made her smile. "And I like you."

What else could he say? "I like you too, Savannah."

# Chapter Twenty-Three

They made quick time to where Savannah had parked her car, but she walked past it in the dark, needing to get to Gran Mere's humble home before her flashlight flickered one more time. It had been one heck of a long, hard day, and she was tired. She had extra clothes at Gran Mere's, and she could sleep. Keller could rest there, too. But something was wrong. There was discord in the threads of the universe tonight. Savannah could sense it.

Keller must've picked up on her unease. "You feel it, too," he said as he fell in step at her side.

"I sense something," she admitted. But not until Red let out a battle cry did Savannah break into a run. Ever faithful Keller jogged beside as she batted branches and shoved low hanging vines out of her way, hoping her toes or flip-flops didn't snag a vine or root as she ran. Sir Galahad plowed through the brush at her side. The way loomed extra dark ahead, and she could feel it. Whatever it was. Something big and black and—empty. A void.

Savannah nearly tripped over Galahad's stalwart body in the dark. He'd stopped in her path. Only then did she understand what she wasn't seeing. Gran Mere's houseboat was gone.

"What the hell?" Keller hissed, his feet spread wide and his hands on his hips. "I didn't think that boat was mobile."

"It isn't," she replied as her flashlight spotlighted the empty space. "It was on concrete blocks, not wheels or a trailer. That's why the skirting."

Deep ruts marked where heavy equipment had dragged the houseboat off its concrete pad and through the brush. The gangplank now lay flat to the ground, and Gran Mere's overgrown flowerbeds were crushed. Her oak tree had been smoothly cut at ground level, the massive hardwood rolled aside to make room for the theft.

She coughed, her heart stuck in her throat. "They...He... S-s-someone took everything."

"This had to have happened right after we left this morning," Keller said.

Savannah combed a hand through her hair, tired of running only to end up empty-handed and bereft. "Whoever did this must've had heavy equipment on standby. They must've been watching me. That tree's been here forever. But who would've known Gran Mere was gone, and that we'd just—?"

"Left? Dr. John," Keller interrupted. "He knew. Where's he live?"

She turned to Keller, shaking her head. "He wouldn't do this. Not RJ. He's been Gran Mere's friend since I can remember. Even as a kid, he used to bring her flowers. He was good to us."

Keller cupped her elbow. "We'll still need to talk to him. Maybe he knows something. Come on. Give me your keys."

She handed her car keys over, and Savannah let Keller usher her away from the barren hole that had once been Gran Mere's magical humble home. Both dogs trotted along, Galahad at her side, Red at Keller's. They hadn't gone far before she couldn't go any farther "No, Keller. Not tonight. Please. I can't. I just can't keep going."

"I'm sorry," he muttered. "You're right. What am I thinking? You're exhausted. I should've picked up on that before now. How about we get a couple rooms instead?"

"Yes, please," she said on a sigh. "A shower'd be nice, too."

"And dinner. We haven't eaten a damned thing since breakfast, and we've both been running our asses off."

The flashlight died, plunging them into darkness, and that was the last straw. The day won. Gran Mere was never coming back, and no matter how hard Savannah tried, she couldn't contain her grief. She stumbled. But before she fell to her hands and knees, which would've been humiliating, Keller caught her and pulled her into his arms. Her head hit his chest and there she stayed.

"I'm sorry," she cried, ashamed for her weakness.

"Shush," he told her as he backtracked to her car. "Even tough guys need to recharge their batteries once in a while, and you're one tough princess."

Hmmm. Princess. She liked the sound of that. Savannah dried her tears as she curled one arm over his shoulder. Peace came to her as she absorbed the strength and power rolling off this man. She listened to the steady beat of his heart. He hadn't faltered. Not once. Not really. Even his perceived weakness—his need to provide comfort at the risk of a killer migraine—had simply been another gift he hadn't known how to properly handle. Psychic talents didn't come with user manuals, and he hadn't had anyone like Gran Mere in his life to teach him.

"You've got me now," she murmured as they cleared the trees. Thank heavens her car was right where she'd left it. Its parking lights winked when Keller hit remote unlock.

"And you've got me," he answered quietly.

*Hmmm.* That was even nicer than being called Princess.

In minutes, they were on the road. Red and Galahad sat obediently in the backseat, and Keller seemed to know precisely where he was going. Savannah closed her eyes, so weary. So sad. She'd been strong long enough. She needed to sleep for five minutes. Ten at the most.

Didn't it figure? The girl drove a Buick. And not just any Buick, but an older model like so many retired people owned. Probably Gran Mere's. Not what Keller expected, yet he should have known. It handled smoothly enough, but the car was a long, gray boat. Something flashy and red would've suited Savannah better, yet this one accommodated the dogs. They'd certainly been on their best behavior tonight.

Keller adjusted the rearview mirror, smiling as he glanced at Galahad and Red. Both sat looking at the scenery flashing by. Activating the rear windows, he gave them some air. Just what they wanted. Both put their snouts to the cracked windows, and damned if they didn't look like they were smiling in the dark. Dogs. Gotta love them.

Keller steered toward the bright lights of New Orleans. Lit against the western night sky, it loomed ahead like Vegas. Carefully so he didn't wake Savannah, he retrieved his cell from his pants pocket and asked Siri for directions to the closest five-star hotel. Why settle for decent when this might be the only night he had with Savannah?

Siri complied promptly, and wasn't that the best reason for these heavier, ruggedized FBI phones? They still worked after a swim in the swamp.

Adeptly, Keller navigated away from the bayou, over the I-10 bridge, and past the Bayou Sauvage National Wildlife Refuge. Finally in the Big Easy, he headed through the winding streets for one of New Orlean's better hotels. He could've stopped at the Windsor on Gravier Street, but the Ritz-Carlton on Canal Street was a mere eight blocks away. He kept going. Savannah didn't wake when he parked the car. This was where a woman like her belonged.

He told the dogs to be quiet, then locked the vehicle and quickly procured a ground-level, pet-friendly suite with two bedrooms and a full kitchen. Keller ordered room service for four before he turned the Buick over to the baby-faced valet attendant, gave the kid a twenty, and then lifted Savannah out of the front seat and into his arms.

That was when things got tricky. Two dogs. One passed out woman. How was he going to get from the car to his room? Leave the dogs in the car in this humid heat? Not going to happen. He couldn't leave the Buick running—

"Y'all need some help?" the attendant asked.

"Actually..." Keller couldn't take a chance on losing Galahad or Red in this city, but neither could he manage getting two dogs and Savannah into their room at the same time. And he sure as hell couldn't risk this young man's life by leaving him alone with these dogs. "Listen. I can't take the dogs with me just now. If you don't mind keeping an eye on my car, I'll make two trips. I have to keep it running." *And hope Savannah has a couple leashes in her trunk.*

"Ya sure I can't walk your dogs up for you? They look plenty friendly—"

Galahad chose that precise moment to hit the window like an Abrams tank, smearing his drooling chops across the glass.

"Holy shit!" the valet hissed as he stumbled backward.

Still holding onto Savannah, Keller managed to snag the young black man's sleeve before he tripped on the curb and broke his face.

"These dogs are dangerous, mister," he said, his eyes wide and white against his dark skin. "You can't be bringing killer dogs into this hotel. No sir, you just can't do that."

"Listen," Keller said evenly. "I'm a federal agent and these dogs are my witnesses. They're under my protection, same as this woman. But I'm in a bind, and I don't have crates to secure them yet. All I need is for you to watch my car until I get back. They'll be fine, I just can't turn the engine off. It's too hot out here. I'll only be a couple minutes, and trust me, these dogs are not killers."

Galahad hit the window again, making Keller look like a liar. Just great. "Will you knock it off?" he ground out, losing his temper. "I get it. You're hungry. Well, so is Savannah and so am I, now sit. You're scaring my new friend here."

Of all things, Galahad sat on his haunches like the good boy he wasn't.

"Your name please?" Keller asked his 'new friend.'

"Roger," the young man supplied as he eyed the dogs. "Roger Tanner."

"Good to meet you, Roger. I'm Special Agent Keller Boniface out of FBI Headquarters, Washington, DC. I'd shake your hand, but I'm a bit busy." As light as Savannah was, he needed to put her down before his right arm fell asleep.

"You sure these dogs are safe?"

Keller nodded. "They are but they've both been used in dog fighting rings. They don't trust just anyone. The setter's Red, the Pitbull is Galahad."

"Aww..." Roger leaned into the window again, his forearm braced against the car roof. "I'd never hurt a dog. You can trust me, boy," he told Galahad through the glass.

The Pitbull stared up at the young man, drooling like a beast.

"We've had a difficult day, and they're both worried... Wait! Don't do that!"

But Roger had already opened the car door. He stood with one hand extended for Galahad to rip off, the other easy on the handle. Both dogs peered up at him like torpedoes primed and ready to launch.

"Stay!" Keller ordered even as Roger told them both to, "Come on down."

Red glanced at Keller before, gingerly, taking one elegant step around Galahad's squat, square body. The

Pitbull still looked like a slobbering, grumpy troll who might eat Roger alive—just because. But Red stepped out of the Buick, and inched toward that extended piece of meat called Roger's hand.

"I wish you hadn't done that," Keller growled, but the deed was done. There was only one thing to do. He projected his empathy for these particular dogs into Roger. What he came up against was... *Whoa*. Roger had the heart of a lion and the memory of...*Zero. Golden Malinois. Smartest, dumbest, bestest K-9 in the world!*

Roger's impressions tumbled into Keller's mind like a handful of Legos. He was no kid. He was a baby-faced USMC vet, a jarhead who'd not only seen combat in Afghanistan, but who'd seen it with an EOD trained K-9 named Zero. Together, Roger and Zero had sniffed out IEDs, suicide bombers, munitions dumps, you name it. They'd saved USMC and Army lives.

That was a weirdly wonderful first, reading memories instead of pain. Damned near took Keller's breath.

"Sit," Roger told Red once the nosey dog took a good sniff of the back of his hand.

Politely, Red dropped his butt to the driveway, and Roger knelt with him. "Good boy," he praised as he fondled Red's pointed head. "As for you..." He turned to Galahad. "I'm not going to hurt you. Come."

Keller held his breath. The Pitbull looked like a cross between a bulldog, a snout-nosed alligator, and a miniature tank. All jaws, chest, muscle, and teeth, he stared at Roger, then looked away and sniffed the air. He snorted, but by hell, he dropped out of that Buick like a bag of cement on four stubby legs, then calmly took his place beside his kennel mate.

"You're good with dogs," Keller said though he already knew the answer.

"We get along. You boys know how to heel?" Roger asked the dogs as, tentatively, he offered the back of his hand to the drooling pittie. Damned if Galahad didn't wrinkle his nose and snort like he might chew on those fingers. But then he sniffed Roger's hand.

Red's tail swished, his eyes now bright instead of distrustful.

And Keller started breathing again.

"Sir, are you ready to move forward?" Roger asked. "I'll handle the dogs for you, no problem, but we need to be quick. I still have to park your ride."

Keller didn't miss how Roger's sharp black eyes skated over Savannah's long legs to her backside to her pretty face. It had been a long and interesting day, but Roger needed to keep his eyes to himself. Keller tucked his sleeping beauty under his chin and led the way.

# Chapter Twenty-Four

The ground level suite included a full kitchen, a living room with a view of the terraced patio, as well as two plush bedrooms. The master bedroom lay to the right of the sitting area, the smaller lay to the left. Keller took Savannah into the master bedroom and put her to bed. He retrieved a dampened washcloth from the lavish en suite master bath and cleaned her face, neck, and arms. Carefully, he extracted the rosary from her neck and hair and put it in his pocket for safe keeping. Poor thing barely stirred when he tugged the blanket up to her chin.

Keller shut the bedroom door just as room service knocked. He waved the waiter and his rolling cart inside, while Galahad and Red barked their heads off from the other bedroom. That got Keller a raised brow from the waitstaff. At this rate, Savannah would soon be awake, and they'd all be back on the street with two loud-mouth dogs.

"Allow me," Roger said as he let himself back into the spare room.

Keller had no idea what Roger would do with Galahad and Red, but he'd no more closed himself in with the dogs when the ruckus ceased. No yelling. No swearing. Just silence.

"Shall I serve?" the young waiter asked. Red-headed, stern-faced, and dressed in a short-jacketed tux-like uniform, he stood with a white towel over one forearm, gesturing toward the spread under several silver domed plates.

Keller extracted his wallet, dug out two slightly damp twenties, and handed them over. "No thanks. I've got this."

"As you wish." The prim waiter pocketed the bills without looking at them and exited stage left, no doubt on his way to alert management they had a pest problem on the ground floor, and it wasn't bedbugs.

Closing the spare bedroom door behind him, Roger stuck a thumb at the exit. "I'd better get back to parking cars."

Retrieving another twenty from his pocket, Keller offered his hand. "Thanks for your help. Before you go, tell me what you said to keep them quiet."

"Thank you, sir," Roger said as he stashed the bill in his pocket. "I take it those dogs belong to your lady friend, not you."

"Yes, she runs Sanctuary, a dog rescue east of here. Savannah Church. You ever heard of her?"

"No, but she trained those boys well, I can tell. What'd you call that Pitbull? Galahad?"

"Yes, the other's Red."

Roger cringed. "Aw, he needs a better name than Red, but yeah. Those boys know all the basic commands, like quiet, stay, heel, and sit. If you need them to settle down after I leave, just tell 'em 'quiet.' They're good boys. They'll listen."

"That's all?" He just might have to keep Roger around. "Good to know. Thanks again. I owe you, man."

"No problem," Roger said as he let himself out. At the open door he paused. "I'll be back to walk them at oh-six-hundred hours if that works for you."

"You don't have to do that," Keller protested, "but it would sure help. I don't have any leashes, though. First thing in the morning, I've got to contact a pet store, see if they'll deliver a couple dog crates and—" Shit, this night just kept going from bad to worse.

"Hey, Mr. FBI. Dude!" Roger snapped his fingers. "Cool your jets. I've got a couple crates and sturdy leashes I'm not using at the moment. I'll bring them with me in the morning. Until then...." He offered a quick salute. "You've got a midnight snack waiting, and I've got work to do. Later."

Four plates of steak and potatoes were not Keller's idea of a midnight snack, but he dug in and finished off one serving before he fed the dogs two of the others.

Remembering how Savannah kept them separated, he put one plate in the kitchen for Galahad. Once the pittie was noisily slurping his treat, Keller took the second plate into the bedroom. He ducked inside to see what damage the dogs had done. Surprisingly, none. Red gave Keller a regal look from where he'd stretched out on the bed like a prince who owned the place.

"Get down," Keller groused at the smart-aleck setter while he set the food on the floor. "You're getting steak tonight. Don't get used to it. Tomorrow you'll be in a crate and back to kibble."

Slinking to the floor, Red ignored the food and rubbed against Keller's leg, his tail wagging, and his snout raised. Keller stroked the setter's long neck and scratched his ears. "You're a good boy, you know that, fella? Damn those men for hurting you."

The dog's face, ears, neck, and well, most of his skin was knotted and scarred. One long ear bore a ragged notch where it had been bitten. But when Red closed his eyes and groaned at Keller's touch, Keller kept petting. He could relate to this sleek beast. He knew what it felt like to be unloved and untouchable, ragged on, chewed on, and mistreated. Affection hadn't been a staple in his childhood, either. Not until Carol Marie came along had Keller known any kind words.

So he poured a heaping dose of empathy into everything he did with this pretty red dog. Overall Red's coat had come in long enough to cover his scars. Most weren't visible. You wouldn't know he'd been badly used until your fingertips encountered the real dog beneath the silky hair. Savannah had worked nothing short of a miracle saving this fellow's life.

Keller knelt, pulling Red into his arms for a hug. The crazy dog had a way of sliding his muzzle over Keller's shoulder like he was hugging back. Lifting to his feet, Keller brushed his tears away. They never solved anything.

Once Red settled down to eat, Keller closed him in the bedroom and checked on Galahad one last time. The pittie had finished eating and was now stretched alongside the sofa. He looked comfortable and tired. Maybe a little smug.

"Stay, and for hell's sake, be quiet," Keller told him as he walked by on his way to the master bedroom.

Galahad snorted but didn't budge. If Keller was lucky, the food would make both dogs sleepy, and he'd have a quiet night. Closing the bedroom door behind him, he paused until his pupils adjusted to the dark. The slightest sound of steady breathing confirmed Savannah was still out cold. She hadn't moved since he'd laid her down.

Stepping into the bathroom, he doffed his dirty clothes and took a quick, hot shower. If he'd thought of it sooner, he would've called the front desk and had them order new clothes for him and Savannah. He couldn't bear the thought of climbing back into his rumpled, smelly shirt and pants. But that was what he did, sans day old underwear. Come first light, he'd hit the nearest department store and make things right.

Finally showered and semi-fresh, Keller pulled the padded chair from the corner of the bedroom over to the bed, where he could see better. Resting on her back with her head turned toward him, Savannah held one hand to her chest, the other hidden under the blanket. The light from the bathroom barely reached through the cracked door, but it allowed him to see enough.

She was by far the most beautiful woman in his world. With his elbows on his knees, he leaned toward Savannah, content to watch her sleep and listen to her breathe. If there were anything better in the world, he didn't know it. This woman had changed his life in less than a day. Who would've thought someone so delicate could be that powerful?

In her sleep, she pursed her lips. With every rise and fall of her chest, a warm glow of satisfaction suffused Keller. It'd been a long time since he'd been privileged to stand guard over a treasure. Yet here he was, the man Savannah Church had accepted as her first lover. The beast she'd allowed to ravage the sweet fruit of her body. Yet he hadn't felt like a beast when they'd made love. Even then, she'd comforted him in ways he still couldn't explain. It was as if she'd reached into his psyche and made him a better man. She'd made him feel like he'd finally come home. On what had to be the worst day of her life, she'd done everything she could to soothe a hard, worthless man like him.

Pushing back into the chair, Keller stretched his legs alongside the bed and crossed his ankles. Hell, she'd gentled him just like she gentled her dogs. And that was okay. Keller didn't mind being lumped into the same category as Galahad and Red. They weren't so bad once you got to know them.

But about those would-be killers in the monster truck, those uncanny alligators that seemed to show up at the same time the Camaro blew, the explosion at Sanctuary, and the fact that Gran Mere's houseboat was missing? That four-pronged attack was nothing less than a diversion and he knew it.

Whoever was behind it had money. The bastard meant to keep Savannah too busy fighting to survive to interfere with his moving Gran Mere's home. He'd had a good-sized crew and heavy equipment on standby, too. He'd had this move planned for days, maybe months. Which meant he'd had someone watching Gran Mere and Savannah for a while now. He'd known precisely when Gran Mere died, also known when Savannah left the houseboat with Keller.

All clues led to Doctor Rudy John, and that made Keller uneasy. Not only had he stalked her, the sweetest woman on earth, but John knew Keller was in town. But precisely who else was RJ working with, and where was the houseboat now? Who was the money man behind this coordinated attack? It sure wasn't Doctor John. Keller meant to find out.

Easing out of his chair, he leaned over Savannah to tell her goodbye, that he had work to do. Breathing in, he drew in the lovely scent unique to this diminutive bundle of extraordinary fire. Closing his eyes, he brushed his lips over the satiny expanse of her forehead. How sweet. How rare.

Unable to resist, Keller toed out of his dress shoes and knelt on the bed. Peeling half the covers away, he slid one arm beneath her shoulders and settled alongside Savannah. Rolling her to her side, he tucked his knees into the back of hers and reached his free arm around her shoulders. Aroused at the contact of her soft breasts against the inside of his bicep, he basked in the contentment seeping into his soul. It only took one touch of this woman. Didn't even have to be skin on skin. Just holding Savannah melted away every last one of the psychic barriers he'd erected to keep his heart safe.

Keller's best gift hadn't always been empathy. Used to be solitude and distance. Ever since he could remember, he'd been pushing people away, fighting for personal space and a comfort zone that excluded Elaine and her treachery. But lying here with Savannah...

Breathing her in...

Fighting the urge to make love to her...

Unabashed happiness washed over Keller. For the first time in years, he released the death grip on his inner control. He allowed himself to remember.

Shane Boniface. His father. The town drunk. The waste of skin. The do-nothing bastard and ne'er do-well husband. All Elaine's harsh edicts. He'd died when Keller was six. For whatever reason, the forgotten memories of quiet times with Shane surfaced like a rush of effervescent bubbles to the silvery surface of a glass of 7-UP.

Yeah. 7-UP. Keller remembered now. Shane always had a glass or a can of 7-UP in his hand, laced with whatever rotgut was handy. Vodka or whiskey, the poison didn't matter. Only the endgame. After tossing back enough of those doctored 7-UPs, Shane developed a cute sense of humor. He took Keller fishing for catfish or carp, crawdads or frogs, not that little boy Keller knew then why his dad was more fun with a can of 7-UP in his fist. All Keller knew was that Shane took him away from home and Elaine. Besides, poor white folks ate what they caught, didn't matter if it was trash fish. Trash begot trash, least that was what Elaine always said.

*I remember now... Dad let me steer the outboard. We were fishing and he trusted me. He called me Killer Keller. He said I had guts... He called me Buddy, and he gave me his baseball cap.*

Keller scrubbed his free hand over his bristly head, wondering what happened to that ratty old Army cap. Where was it now? Was his dad really in the Army? Was he a vet or was that just the cheapest cap at the five-and-dime? Keller honestly didn't know.

Yet the persistent memory of a real, no-kidding father and son connection lingered. Tall, gangly, and quiet, Shane had never once been mean, snarky, or abusive. Keller couldn't remember him yelling or cursing, never hitting or kicking, either, which Elaine was prone to do. It didn't take much to push her over the edge on a good day. Keller had often thought his breathing set her off some mornings.

More often than not, Shane was the buffer between him and his mother, the peacemaker and the quiet man who'd suffered Elaine's worst temper, vilest outbursts, and sharp tongue. Her belt. Her fists. Her lies.

# **Chapter Twenty-Five**

But for the life of him, Keller couldn't recall Shane's face. The color of his eyes. His nose. Any defining freckles, moles, or scars. Lying there with Savannah snug, warm and soft in his arms, the frightened little boy he once was came back to Keller like a shivering, puny ghost who'd never had the guts to stand up for himself. He couldn't, not back then. Kids weren't born tough or hard. They didn't instinctively know how to hit back or hit first, especially when the one doing the hitting was a parent. It took a lot to pummel a child's innocence and trust away. But Elaine finally did it. She broke him. Damn her.

Shame for the weakling he'd been suffused Keller. He used to stare down at the table between his dirty fingers whenever she came unglued—which was most of the time—afraid to make eye contact in case it made her angrier. Not like that was hard to do. But he'd never fought back once the vicious name-calling started. *Puny pig. Lying thief. Rat bastard. Crybaby!* So many others. But never 'son'. Rarely even Keller.

What he wouldn't give to confront her now. For what she'd done to his father alone, Keller'd knock her on her ass. He'd set her straight.

The only time Keller stood a chance was when Shane was sober enough to intervene. If he was, he always stepped up and took the blame for whatever his skinny son stood accused of. Which meant Shane couldn't win any more than Keller. Elaine seemed to hate the entire male gender, and she focused that hatred like a demented surgeon's scalpel on the two males who were stuck in her life.

It was the Army that saved Keller. The discipline, structure, and rock-solid brotherhood he found there changed that scrawny, wimpy, snot-nosed crybaby into a man. The Army recruiter promised him the world, but it was Keller who'd grabbed onto that promise and made it come true. There wasn't a rucksack, mortar, or fellow soldier he couldn't carry, a mission he wouldn't accept and complete, or a target he couldn't nail.

After Carol Marie passed, he'd poured every fiber of his broken heart into the Army's *'Be all you can be'* bullshit. He became more focused, more lethal, and more controlled. He became the deadliest marksman. He became Death and Destruction. For a while that was enough. But the day finally came when it wasn't.

His few friends had either died in action or left the service. So Keller moved on.

But what kind of bastard forgot his father? Oh yeah. The angry, beat-up kind who needed someone to blame when Shane up and died and left his only kid behind.

"She was bigger than you," Keller remembered out loud. But Elaine couldn't have been. He might not remember his face, but Keller knew his dad was a tall man. Maybe that was just how a raging, belligerent mother in a full-blown tirade appeared to a little kid. For whatever reason, Shane never knocked her on her ass. Not even once. But when he died...

Keller closed his eyes to kill the relentless slideshow playing in his head. He'd been defenseless then, and Elaine took a peculiar, sadistic joy in tormenting her son. She insisted he be there for her gruesome rituals. If he cried, she'd beat him. Whipped him. Kicked the shit out of him. She never left any scars though, only the hash marks on his arm for trumped-up infractions he'd never committed and lies he'd never told. Elaine relished pain—other people's pain.

But that was a long time ago, and Keller was a man now, a trained professional who had ended more despicable men and women than Elaine. He had no regrets for what he'd done. Those kills weren't sadistic nor joyful. They were simply taking out the trash.

The more Keller remembered, the more he wanted to know if his dad had been Army. If so, where had he served, abroad or stateside? What rank was he when he retired? What had he seen and done? Was PTSD the reason he drank himself to death? Or was marriage? Was he honorably discharged or kicked out? Hero or coward?

And that Army ball cap. Was it Shane's or just junk? Keller recalled soldiers at the cemetery the day they buried his dad. A twenty-one-gun salute. A folded flag. Respect. The soldiers were immaculately dressed, clean and sharp, their weapons polished, their gloves pure white. Medals and ribbons decorated their chests. Their caps were clean and neat. One of those men gave Keller a spent brass shell after the salute. Like a treasure, he'd stuck it deep in his pants pocket to make extra sure he didn't lose it. No one had ever given him anything so cool. It was all he had to remember his dad.

But when he got home, Elaine beat the shit out of him, screaming how poor they were now that Shane was gone, that anything and everything was hers. *Give it to me!* Even that measly shell. She'd thought that kindly soldier had given Keller a silver dollar. When she found out it was just a spent cartridge and as worthless as her son, Elaine ripped Keller's last memory of his dad out of his grubby hand and slapped him so hard, she'd knocked him down and out. When he came to moments later, she made him stand in the kitchen corner the rest of the day. So he did. Crying for the father who would never save him again and wishing he could leave too. Just die. It couldn't have hurt worse than living.

"I hated her that day," Keller told the Man Upstairs, his Heavenly Father, the one he usually cursed. Funny. He might curse, but he'd always known God listened. Guess that saying about there being no atheists in foxholes was right. "I truly did. I still do. She's one of the cruelest people in the world. Never should've had a kid."

He'd blamed Shane for leaving him, that was why Keller forgot his dad. Remembering only made him soft and weak. It made him cry, and Elaine never tolerated weakness. She was one of those her-way-or-the-highway alpha bitches. Only the house Elaine built was as full of shit as she was.

Back then, Keller didn't know better. He was a defenseless kid with no one at his back but a shrieking, hounding shrew who wore him out. In the end, he'd shut down. He'd schooled his thoughts and hardened his heart until every good memory of the man who'd once loved him turned to dust and blew away. A kid will do anything to survive. Even lie to himself.

But now those memories emerged from the locked-up vault of his child's heart, and Keller grieved for what could've been. He remembered the good times, but he wondered. What exactly was in the tea Elaine gave Carol Marie? Better question: could a decent ME, with the current advances in forensic technology, now isolate the poison Keller believed Elaine used to kill Carol Marie?

Elaine had sent Keller on an errand to fetch one of her crows for the doctor down the road. Elaine kept cages of various animals for her curses. By the time he returned from those cages, Carol Marie was dead. Elaine said she'd choked to death. He'd been so shocked and grief-stricken, he'd just gathered Carol Marie's limp body into his arms and ran to the nearest doctor, Doctor Scratch, another backwoods 'professional' like Doctor John. Also one of Elaine's voodoo buddies.

In the end it didn't matter. The crow he'd fetched had been for the liar, Dr. Scratch, Elaine's friend and cohort. Scratch had verified what Elaine said. Carol Marie just choked and died.

And Keller went berserk. If not for his wife's limp body lying there on Dr. Scratch's gurney, Keller would've ripped the charlatan apart. But he couldn't let that man touch his wife again. After a brief, violent confrontation with Elaine, during which he'd earned the scar near his eye, Keller gathered Carol Marie into his arms and drove to the city and a real hospital emergency room. By then, a deputy waited at the hospital entrance to arrest him.

The witch had outright lied. Elaine told the sheriff he'd killed his wife, that he'd strangled Carol Marie. But the ER doctor was smarter. He let Keller stay with her body until the Medical Examiner arrived, then conferred with the ME. They both agreed. There were no ligature marks on his wife's neck. No petechial hemorrhaging.

But because of Elaine's lies, he spent a night in county lock-up, sick at heart and accused of murder. In the end, COD could not be precisely determined. The ME declared Carol Marie died of hypoxia, but was unable to say how it had occurred. He did say there was no validity behind Elaine's outrageous charge, no signs of strangulation. But Carol Marie *could've* choked to death.

Keller was in the Army at that time. Next morning, the sheriff released Keller, the MPs came for him, and Elaine walked away scot-free. He hadn't seen her since. He'd only returned to Turkey Creek long enough to bury his wife and console her parents, then he'd scraped that sad excuse of a hometown off his boots, and he signed on for one deployment after another. The Army became home, family, and all he needed.

But now it was important to reach out, to finally know what Shane and Carol Marie had died of and to request two exhumations. It was time to know precisely what had gone on in the murky backwaters of Turkey Creek.

Whispers from Ecclesiastes surfaced from the deep dark shadows of Keller's soul.

*A time to cast away stones, and a time to gather stones again...*

*A time to keep silence. And a time to speak...*

*So, speak.* That was the key. Shane and Carol Marie could no longer speak for themselves, but Keller could. And speak he would. He'd get warrants for two exhumations, but first...

The lady in question stirred in his arms, ending the deluge of tender memories when she pushed her soft, warm backside into him. Still fully clothed, Keller's body flamed to life at the intimate contact. It had only been hours, but he couldn't seem to stop touching her. He found himself stronger and surer when he was with Savannah. More masculine, more powerful, and yes, even more calm. For the first time in years, Keller was at peace. And all because Savannah told him she loved him.

How ironic. An innocent creature not afraid to reach out to a war-hardened man without guile or hidden agendas. Her innocence was her gift. Savannah took chances he'd never take. She led with her heart instead of her chin, and she gave her love away to everyone she met. Dogs, cats, birds, recalcitrant federal agents, didn't matter. She wasn't afraid to reach out to slathering, unpredictable beasts like Galahad. She wasn't afraid to get bit. Yet he, the big brave soldier, hadn't thought of petting a dog in years, not until Savannah dumped Sanctuary into his life. Keller wasn't so sure if Sanctuary was a place—or if Sanctuary was Savannah.

What he wouldn't give to slide in behind her, naked and ready. But one more time inside her sweet body would never be enough. He knew that now. No matter how many times he reminded himself he was an honorable arm of the federal government, that men of authority like him should maintain a strict boundary with women like Savannah, he couldn't make himself ease away from her. Even honorable special agents had lives and lovers. Wives...

But she needed rest more than sex, and her needs would forever come first, and...

*Aw hell.* He pressed his nose into the warm crook of her neck, wishing she'd wake up just enough to be friendly.

# Chapter Twenty-Six

"Hmmm," Savannah mumbled as a warm wave breathed into her neck, lighting every last nerve with sweet fire. She twisted around to the man she would love forever.

"Sorry, I didn't mean to wake you," Keller whispered into her hair, his hand cupping the back of her head, holding her as carefully as he would a newborn baby. "Go back to sleep."

As if she could. In the blink of a day, he'd become part of her, and she had no idea how that happened. She'd only met Keller yesterday. There was so much she didn't know about him, so much mystery, buried sorrow, and anger. So much torment. And kindness and gentleness.

Her heart hurt for the death of his young wife. He still carried the pain, worried at it like a dog with a bone, and guarded it as if his life depended on it. He was the metaphorical dog in the manger, unable to swallow his grief, yet just as unwilling to let anyone near enough to help him deal with it. More than anything else in his life, that loss devastated Keller in ways his team would never understand—because they didn't know he'd married. He'd never trusted them enough to tell them about Carol Marie or how she'd died. Keller was not a sharing man, and Savannah understood why. A child learned by example, and if his mother killed his wife, why would he share that sordid heartache? How could he? What proud man would?

Yet from the moment she'd met him, Savannah had also sensed the inner strength of a natural defender and a courageous warrior—a real man. He was one of those paltry few who didn't know how to quit, truly a *'the only easy day was yesterday'* kind of man. He knew what he believed in, and he fought for those beliefs. He'd willingly become an instrument of death for his country, leading the charge and taking the brunt of war and chaos, so weaker Americans, men, women, and children, didn't have to. He took the fight to America's enemies. He met those armies head-on, with guns blazing, probably cursing a blue streak while he'd charged into combat. The unsmiling laugh lines at the corners of his eyes testified of sacrifice, though he'd never admit it. But Savannah knew. She could easily read the grief in those glistening pools of amber.

She and Keller were two sides of the same coin, him reluctant to share and needing to be in control; her unable to hold back her boundless enthusiasm for life.

He, the damaged son of a ruthless, coldhearted woman; she, the precocious great granddaughter of a woman wiser than her years. Combined, they were the ultimate paradox of attraction, complete opposites who couldn't resist each other.

Like now. Her fingers sought the coiled pectoral muscles under his shirt. Her nose twitched. He'd showered, but there was no mistaking his delicious scent. With one touch, he'd ignited the desire banked within her quivering body. It was no longer a matter of if, only when. She licked her bottom lip, her body weeping with anticipation.

Blinking the sleep out of her eyes, she opened her mouth on his throat, licking and savoring the musky, salty flavor of his skin. Falling for him all over again. When he groaned as she ran her tongue up the scruffy underside of his chin, the vibration against her lips and questing tongue urged her on. Hungry now and wide awake, she eased her fingers around his neck, using him to pull herself up the length of him. The crazy man was still dressed. That had to change.

"Let's get you into something more comfortable," she mumbled into his open mouth, loving the sleek heat and taste of him.

"I have things to do. I really shouldn't stay," he mumbled back, his mouth as full, his tongue making love with hers.

"Oh, but you should," she breathed, her fingers tugging at his zipper.

Smoothly, he slipped her panties and shorts off and tossed them to the floor. "But I have work to do."

"Uh uh," she murmured, her voice gone raspy. "You have me to do."

He growled again, and she was beginning to love that sound. But he didn't stop her frantic fingers or hands. Undressing this man turned Savannah on. Taking his t-shirt off. Sliding his pants over his hips and thighs, down his legs. He trusted her with his personal power, and she loved that he did. Tantalizingly wicked suggestions tap-danced across the stage of her aroused mind at all the things she could do with this magnificent naked man. To him.

She adored the heavy muscles at her fingertips, at the tip of her tongue. Opening her mouth wider, she suckled his neck, marking him until his growl turned into a rumbling purr. He liked her mark on him. He trusted her. That single thought sent arousal cascading through her body straight to her groin. Her orgasm came hard and deliriously delicious, a spike of red-hot pleasure percolating up from her toes, over her belly, and peaking at her breasts. And up to the stars.

Savannah flung her head back at the blinding sensations taking her by storm. Her entire body clamped onto the concept of this man's startling faith in her. When she growled her release, he added the seductive suction of his hot mouth to her breast, his long probing fingers to her core.

Which only pushed her higher. Slick and needy now, she opened her body to him, her love for this man a feverish pitch. She needed this, but Keller needed her heart more.

Gently now and breathing hard, her Secret Agent Man poised over her like a dark guardian angel, his elbows at her sides, his breath in her face, and a warrior's heart glowing in his eyes. "I need to be inside you," he muttered, his voice a sexy command that made everything on her body stand up.

"You already are," she whispered as she clamped onto his thick shoulders and urged him down and in and... "Man oh man oh man oh man..." she growled as his body pistoned, driving deeper into the wellspring of her lust and their need.

He groaned, buried to the hilt but holding back, the last thing she wanted him to do. Not now. This was their time. They needed to come together.

"Come for me, Savannah. Come for me."

"I will if you will," she bargained.

That must've been what he needed to hear. Keller's back arched. His hips thrust forward, sharp and hard and hot until he stiffened and came into her. With her. Projecting her like a rocket, past the moon and into forever.

Tears squeezed out of her heart. "I love you, Keller," she cried as she held on through the fury. "So, so much."

He groaned so loudly that Galahad and Red barked from the next room, but Savannah held on until she got every last drop of the best of her man. Slick with sweat, she ran her mouth up the side of his neck to his ear. "Did you hear me, Secret Agent Man?" she whispered, loving the salty taste of him on her tongue as aftershocks continued their squeeze play. "I said I love you and I always will."

This time he didn't pull back. Instead, he buried his face in the crook of her neck, nuzzling in deeper, his belly expanding as he inhaled and said, "I heard you, Savannah." Another deep breath and he murmured, "I really heard you. I did."

Which might just mean he finally believed, and that was enough. Savannah let her body go boneless as the man she adored pressed her into the mattress. This weight she could handle. Keller wasn't heavy. He was everything.

"Sleep tight," he whispered into her hair as he eased his sweaty body off Savannah. Sated and exhausted, she'd fallen back to sleep instead of talking like other women did after sex. Leaning over her and totally smitten, Keller pressed his lips to her temple one last time. "Galahad and Red will take care of you while I'm gone. I've got business with a friend of yours that can't wait. I won't be long."

She didn't stir, didn't even twitch, and that was okay. After all they'd just done to each other, she might sleep until noon. He'd be back by then.

But what she'd said…? Keller hadn't realized how powerful those words were until they dropped off

Savannah's sweet lips. *'I love you and I always will.'*
He remembered now. His dad used to tell Keller he
loved him. Carol Marie said it all the time. But the
words were different. Back then, he'd taken them for
granted. At some level, Shane's and Carol Marie's love
was a given. Fathers loved their children. Wives loved
their husbands. Keller accepted it as if it were his
natural due.

But now...

After living so long without love...

Without hope...

He felt like a hibernating bear when it first breaks
free of its cave in Spring. Savannah had no idea what
she'd given Keller. It'd been years since he'd felt this
tall or so strong. So manly. As if he could take on the
world. So—right. That was it, that was what Savannah
had given him, the kind of balance that made
everything right again. Even him.

The urge to beat his chest and roar like some
primitive caveman swarmed Keller. He wasn't just the
son of a backwoods self-proclaimed voodoo witch.
Neither was he the worthless bastard of the town
drunk. Elaine was wrong about Shane, and Keller
meant to prove it to the world. Then he was going to
find out who or what killed Carol Marie. He'd give her
a proper headstone. Not that flat, cheap marker on her
grave now, the only thing he'd been able to afford back
then. It was time to man up and face the worst demon
in his life—Queen Fucking Elaine.

A smile curled the corners of his mouth at the thought of confronting her. Hell, it even tweaked the corners of his eyes until the damned thing spread over his entire face. Wouldn't she be surprised. He was no longer a little kid to be bullied. She wouldn't stand a chance. But first...

He had a lying son of a bitch to confront before noon.

Keller cleaned the dishes and stored the leftovers in the refrigerator. He rolled the serving cart into the hall, then released Red from the spare bedroom to join Galahad on the couch. There wasn't time for even a fifteen-minute combat nap. Keller needed answers. Now.

But before he dashed off, Keller wrote a quick note to Savannah. *Roger Tanner will be here early to walk the dogs. You can trust him. He's a former Marine, one of the best. There's a cold steak dinner in the fridge, but feel free to call room service or go to the restaurant downstairs if you want something else. Just tell them to put it on our room tab, and please, don't leave the hotel. Wait for me. I'll be back by noon.*

He put the note on the kitchen counter where she'd be sure to see it. RJ was in for one helluva surprise.

# Chapter Twenty-Seven

Savannah stretched lazily beneath a cozy warm blanket, her body sore in the most delicious places. Relaxed and at peace, she listened to soft snoring from the pillow behind her. Keller. How sweet of him to sleep with her. Her heart fluttered. That was Keller to his core, always looking out for her. Rolling over, she reached for that handsome chest, intending to wake him with a long, wet kiss, then jump his bones until—

Her fingers landed on a furry hound instead. "Red? What are you doing in here?"

Pushing all four legs straight, the handsome setter yawned, while of all things, Galahad climbed up from the foot of the bed where he'd been sleeping. Wide awake now, Savannah sat up and pointed at the floor. "Off the bed, boys. Right this instant. Move it." So much for a leisurely morning of steamy sex with her favorite Secret Agent Man. Where was he?

Guiltily, Red melted over the edge in a scarlet ooze. Galahad, still on the bed, now faced the door. His stubby, scarred ears twitched as a menacing growl rumbled from his throat. What could he hear that she hadn't?

Anxiously, Savannah shoved back the covers. She wasn't ready for company, and if the maid had come into the room—yikes! She wasn't even dressed!

"Coming!" she called out just in case some unlucky maid was out there to change the linens. Switching to her sternest voice, she told the dogs, "Stay." The last thing she needed was them to charge after some helpless woman.

Hurrying now, Savannah scooped her dirty duds from beside the bed, then ran for the bathroom. With her heart pounding, she took care of her business, finger-combed the bedhead out of her hair, then used the guest toothbrush and paste to freshen her mouth. She desperately needed fresh clothes, but figured she'd shower after she knew why Keller hadn't been in bed with her, and why Galahad and Red were now both growling at her bedroom door.

Yikes again! Every hair on Red's back was lifted. Not a good sign.

Because of the dogs, she cracked the door open just enough to see a guy dragging two large portable dog crates through the door. A pair of sturdy nylon leashes draped his neck, but who the heck was he and where was Keller? If not for the hotel logo on this guy's trim black jacket, she would've locked herself in her room.

Instead she called out, "Excuse me. Are you room service and is this a special delivery or something?"

"Oh, hi," the guy replied easily as he toed the door closed behind him and let the dismantled plastic crates drop to the carpet. He snagged a couple shopping bags off the outside doorknob and set them inside. "Looks like these are for you, ma'am. I'm Roger Tanner. I told your friend last night I'd walk your dogs this morning." His gaze drifted to the other bedroom door. "I didn't wake you, did I? Is Agent Boniface around?"

Roger stood around six feet with a smile as wide as the sky over the Gulf of Mexico at daybreak. More brown than black, he cut an impressive sight in that hotel uniform. Straight spine. Lean as a whip. Square shouldered. Clean-cut and clean-shaven. What was more, both Red and Galahad were now wriggling with excitement to get at him. And he'd brought kibble!

"I think my dogs like you."

Roger grinned. "'Course they do. Hey, Red! Hey, Galahad! How's my good boys?"

Savannah pulled up her gumption and stepped into the light. "You loaned Keller these crates for my dogs?" she asked as Galahad and Red charged around her, tails wagging. Quickly, she closed her bedroom door behind her.

Roger tugged the leashes off his neck. "Yes, ma'am. I could see he was in a bind last night, so I told him I'd be by this morning to walk your dogs. But I've got to tell you..." He nodded at the handsome setter wagging his tail like a flag. "You've got to come up with a better name for that fella. He ain't no Crayola." Roger said that with enough Southern twang to make Savannah smile. "And don't you go calling him Scarlet. He ain't no Southern belle, neither."

This friendly guy was too much. "What would you suggest?" she asked, thoroughly at ease now that her dogs had obviously accepted Roger into their pack.

"Anything's got to be better than Red," Roger said as he stroked the happy boy from the tip of his pointed head to his fluffy rump. "Hey there. How ya doing, big fellow? You guys been quiet all night like I told ya?"

By then Savannah had seen the note. Her heart clamored at the three little words Keller had written. *'Wait for me.'* Could he have said anything better?

"Keller will be back soon," she told Roger. "Now about that walk…"

Dr. John wasn't hard to find. He lived where he worked, in a small, but tidy white clapboard home on a country road, east of New Orleans and not far from Savannah's great grandmother's place. Patients entered through the front door of the house, where a simple sign marked 'Patients' had been nailed, while the rear exit was clearly marked 'Private Residence'. Another sign staked in the front lawn declared: Dr. Rudy John, MD.

Okay then. Keller scrunched as low as he could in the rental he'd acquired after he'd left the hotel. He'd wanted to rent a nondescript, four-door sedan, but the only vehicle left on the lot until noon was this truck. So here he sat, sweating the morning away in a brand new, bright shiny and white step-side GMC pickup. Talk about ostentatious. Which was probably just as well. No one in their right mind would suspect a guy in this kind of a truck.

He'd taken time and stopped at the nearest big box store for a change of clothes. Now wearing jeans, a faded-blue, sleeveless t-shirt tucked into his pants with a loose, long-sleeved cotton shirt to cover his holster on top, he fit right in instead of standing out. Black Converse running shoes finished his hometown boy look.

The smallest smile breached his lips. He'd also shopped for Savannah, and that made him uncharacteristically happy. He'd only bought a few simple things. A couple pairs of jeans in different sizes. A couple colorful tees that would complement her exotic skin tone. A travel cosmetic bag of basic feminine cosmetics. Purple running shoes. A few sets of delicate intimates...

Keller took a slow breath at the deep-down contentment spreading through his soul like a sultry Louisiana breeze sifts over the rippling surface of the bayou. Sex did that to a man, especially one who'd practiced abstinence like a cloistered monk for years. But this calm was different than simple after-sex glow. He could tell. This was more of a saturating kind of calm that filled him with inner clarity, and all because it came from doing something so ordinary as shopping for a woman. Of selecting comfortable clothes for her that would breathe in Southern humidity. Of estimating her size and shape. Of imagining pleasing her, of making her smile when she saw what he'd had delivered to her room. Of wanting nothing more than to make her happy, especially when he took those same new clothes off her.

It came from wondering if she needed a moisturizer for that cocoa-cream complexion of hers or one for her silky straight hair. Because she liked lilacs, he'd selected purple running shoes. Would she notice? Would she read anything into it, like maybe that he was a man of detail, a guy who paid attention? That he'd thought about her and what she liked? Would she understand how much it meant to provide even the most humdrum items that most people took for granted? And there it was. Keller had spent time on Savannah as if she were his and as if he had a right to shop for her.

But it also came from thinking of Carol Marie with every selection he'd made for Savannah. This morning, the hollow pain in his chest where he used to carry Carol Marie's death like a buried, hoarded treasure, didn't hurt. There didn't seem as big a void in the chambers of his heart. Everything had changed, as if a bone-deep abscess had been lanced and the poison was at last released. Colors were brighter. Sparrows in the trees chirped louder. Even the mockingbird's trill sounded cheerier. The world was a kinder place today, and all because of Savannah.

Until she came along, he'd been that perfectly constructed, masted ship in a dusty bottle on some forgotten shelf, its glue cracked and dry, its mainsail untested, its rudder a poor excuse for a decent captain's grip. Sure, he'd been to war, and he knew the bloody, awful cost of it. Keller had enough glitter, ribbons and awards in a junk drawer back home to show for it. But he'd lost—or run from—his personal battles, and he knew that now. All those things he hadn't allowed himself to think of in years, like dealing with Elaine, tending to Carol Marie's grave, and moving on, he thought of now.

Bottom line, Savannah wasn't Carol Marie. At all. She was ordinary plastic dishes, the kind families used every day, not fancy china or crystal. She knew how to take care of herself as well as anyone else who got in her way: abused dogs, cats, and closed-off, stodgy warriors.

She wasn't afraid to stand for what or who she believed in, either. Her animal refuge proved her dedication to rescuing the downtrodden. And take that guy at the restaurant yesterday morning. Lyle Goldenrod. Savannah had outright taken one helluva chance and offered him a job Keller knew she didn't need done. Not really. She simply couldn't help herself. She was one of those rare individuals in the world who couldn't help but stand for right. She should have been a Ranger.

Not that Carol Marie had been less of a woman. Not at all, she was just different. Always worried what others thought. Always trying to please. Ever self-deprecating. Never one to take charge. Never adventurous or daring. She hadn't a brave bone in her timid little body. Frail and shy, she was antique china with a gold rim, too good for everyday use. Too thin. Too fragile.

Yet Carol Marie's heart was as big as Savannah's. She'd never been anything but kind to Keller. There was a time he thought his world began and ended with her, but here he was, still breathing, still keeping on. And thinking about his wife and a new woman in his life.

He couldn't help but wonder how Savannah would deal with Elaine. But enough of that.

Tired from too little sleep, Keller forced his mind back to RJ's setup. The house was your average, every day starter home. No big deal and no potential. The one level ranch was set back a good half-acre from the road with all the basics: faded green shingles, central air, three concrete steps to the center front door. Venetian blinds covered the picture window on the left as you entered, most likely the patient waiting room. Gray curtains draped the ordinary double-hung sash window to the right. The place needed paint, and Keller wasn't certain the shadows under each line of clapboard weren't mold or moss. Looked like mold.

Unlike Sanctuary, the front lawn was sparse and brown. No hedges, bushes, or trees either. Guess that saved on landscaping fees.

A gravel parking lot ran the length of the yard to the right, ending at a barn similar to Savannah's barns. Just as large. Just as long. Interesting. Two points of ingress that Keller could see, one extra tall garage door at the front. One regular-sized door to the left of that. No windows. Looked like RJ needed someplace to store one of those monster RVs—or something just as large.

Keller watched as the first patients arrived. An elderly couple. After they parked, they struggled getting up those three concrete steps until finally, they pulled each other up and in through not only an annoying screen door, but through a second wooden door as well.

Tsk, tsk, tsk. No handicapped parking and no wheelchair ramp. The Americans with Disabilities Act people would not be pleased. RJ's clinic wasn't even close to being ADA compliant. Strike one. But if he disregarded rules that so specifically targeted some of his patients, what else did he ignore?

Not wanting to draw attention to his ride, Keller changed locations. RJ's home sat opposite an empty corner lot, now overrun with invasive elm, creeping kudzu, and a forest of weeds as tall as a man. Keller pulled out, circled the block, then parked on the adjacent street facing the clinic.

GMC got some things right. This truck was more comfortable than the Camaro. Lots more legroom. Darker tinted windows too. Keller relaxed into the buttery soft leather seat. But the longer he waited and watched, the more he got to thinking. RJ's clinic was a dive as far as professional clinics went. By the unkept appearance of the yard and office/home, Doctor John wasn't wealthy enough to cover his own costs, much less to have financed the speedy removal of Gran Mere's houseboat from her jungle of a forgotten lot. Not that it couldn't have been done, but the trees between her home and the road had been cut down, removed or set aside. That took heavy-duty equipment, chain saws, and a crew who knew what they were doing. At the least, it would've taken a semi-tractor to pull the boat out, not to mention a crane to lift it onto a semi-trailer once it was roadside.

So yeah... Keller had questions. Doctor John was salacious enough when it came to Savannah, but was he smart enough to pull off a grand theft of this magnitude? In one afternoon? No way. RJ was jonesing after something all right, and it might be Savannah, but he wasn't the brains behind this operation. That took money.

Yesterday's event took on a different slant now that Keller suspected the monster truck and the bomb were more diversionary than lethal. Which made sense. Once the truck slammed into the Camaro, it could've kept on pushing and crushing until Keller and Savannah were both underwater. It could've walked all over that sports car and made sure everyone in it was dead. But it hadn't.

What's more, that driver and truck had come prepared. The windows had only spider-webbed when Keller shot into them. They weren't your normal, everyday automotive safety glass, and he'd bet a month's pay someone had installed a heavy metal plate behind that fancy GMC grill. No steam billowed or hissed when he'd shot the radiator, and there should've been. He'd hit the truck, solid. He just hadn't had time to process or remember what went down until now.

Relaxed in the early morning sun, he scratched his fingers over his bristly head, enjoying the smallest of bodily comforts even as he knew he'd been set up. The crash, the Camaro exploding, and the bomb at Savannah's—all were parts of an elaborate smokescreen. Hell, as mellow as Savannah had been when her home exploded, she could've been part of it, but...

Yeah, no. He'd felt her panic when she'd dropped onto him in the swamp. She'd been scared of dying, and that pretty woman's fear had damned near choked him when he'd pulled her into his body after the Camaro blew.

But emotion could lead an empath astray, and once again, Keller's mind drifted back to the lovely lady he'd left in his bed. It had been hard leaving her this morning, all soft, warm, and deliciously snuggled under the covers like she'd been. So sweet.

With that one thought, Keller shifted gears yet again. His impromptu visit would soon be over. He had a job back in DC, a good job. After what he'd sensed in Tucker's heart yesterday, Keller now knew even though Tuck was former Navy, he was a damned good boss.

But what to do about Savannah. That was a tough one. Keller was not the marrying kind of guy. Been there. Done that. Got the t-shirt. Long distance relationships didn't last, and he didn't want to lead her on. Savannah deserved better. She had a life and a future here. One look at Sanctuary and anyone would see that. She might not be college educated, but she was a born business woman. Savvy. Intelligent. So damned pretty to look at, it hurt his heart thinking of a day without her in it.

Another smile warmed his face. Keller stretched his arms over his head, then tucked both hands behind his neck. Man, that woman had the ferocity of a mother Pitbull when faced with bullies. Her heart seemed unstoppable. Dogs. Cats. Birds. What wouldn't she risk her life to rescue? Hell, she'd even rescued him. Could he live without her?

He honestly didn't know.

# Chapter Twenty-Eight

Keller didn't have to wait long. Just before noon, a black limo with darkly tinted windows pulled into RJ's, blocking the few cars parked in the narrow lot. The driver jumped out of the pretentious vehicle and ran to open the rear door just as a tall, lean, white-haired gentleman unfolded his body and stepped out and into the sun. Wearing a straw Panama hat and dressed in an off-white business suit that looked like linen from this distance, he spoke to the driver before he headed across the unkept lawn and walked into RJ's clinic.

Keller knew the guy. Bruce Fontenette, owner of the prestigious Champion Acres, stable of the most talked about racehorse in the country at the moment: Sand Dollar. The one thing Keller had taken with him when he'd turned his back on the South was his love of horseracing. He'd seen Sand Dollar run in the Kentucky Derby two weeks earlier. A spirited chestnut stallion with a white slash between his eyes that extended down his high strung, aristocratic nose, Sand Dollar had roared past the other contenders. He'd made them look like they were tired old nags and standing still. Mighty Sand Dollar was currently favored to win the Preakness, the second gem in the Triple Crown.

That race was just a day away. Once he won the Preakness, he was a sure shot for Belmont Stakes, the final gem in the Crown. His name would go down in horseracing history, one of only thirteen other champions that had mastered all three races since Sir Barton's record-setting run in 1919. The South was alive with the rumor that Sand Dollar had the heart of Secretariat and the stamina of American Pharaoh, that he could and would do it.

The winnings from the Derby alone had to have been in the millions. But the stud fees Sand Dollar would earn the split second that horse set one polished hoof over the finish line at Belmont would set Fontenette up for life. Already wealthy, he'd recently hinted he might run for the governorship of Florida, his home state, possibly the Senate. Maybe the White House. So why the hell was he down here in backwater nowhere Louisiana?

Keller hunched over his steering wheel, watching. Since he'd switched locations, he had no eyes on the side door to the house or the barn. That needed to change. Easing out of the truck, he walked briskly away from his ride to the corner opposite the road from the clinic. Keeping it cool. Looking like he knew where he was going. People tended to ignore folks walking away from them. If RJ were on the lookout for trouble, that was precisely what Keller wanted him to see. No one important. Just some guy.

Backtracking, he made his way back to RJ's barn in minutes, then broke and entered his way inside as quick as the latest 007. The air in the barn was stifling, thick with musty, mucky animal smells. Unlike Savannah's barn, this one sported no overhead channel along the roof to allow any outdoor light or air inside. He located no light switches on the wall. Keller couldn't see a thing, but the place was full. He sensed that much.

Keller dug into his jeans pocket for the tactical LED flashlight he never left home without. Sliding his right hand inside his shirt, he also extracted a pistol. Better safe than sorry.

The tiny hairs on the back of his neck stood up. Something was off in this crowded, dark space. Snapping the light on revealed a semi-trailer backed into the barn, its landing gear down, fifth-wheel coupling facing the barn door. Creeping around to the rear of the trailer, he found the rolling door up, so he climbed in.

Inside the trailer were row after row of stacked wooden crates loaded two per pallet, four pallets wide and maybe ten, make that twelve, deep. Interesting. Several crates had been opened, their wooden lids standing on end between them. This wouldn't take long.

Tucking the flashlight under his chin, Keller dug into the first crate to get a better look. Contents seemed harmless. Nothing but painted clay pots packed and stuffed with brown, shredded paper, no big deal. Grabbing hold of the first pot, he turned it over. No stamp or label indicated price or country of origin, not like that mattered. But why so many, and why pottery? Was RJ in the import business?

He dug through more pots and more shredded paper. But wait. A silvery blue glint sparkled from inside one of those pots. Keller had no more than upended it when a tiny fluff rolled out.

*Oh, my hell.* He found himself holding the prettiest, deadest-looking hummingbird. Green and bronze feathers covered its two-inch long body. Its needle shaped beak was black, but this little thing was unlike any hummingbird Keller had ever seen. Two long tail feathers hung limp over the edge of his palm. A feathered crest of brilliant, turquoise blue topped the little guy's head. A crest on a hummingbird? Who'd ever heard of that? Keller ran his light over the tiny creature, worried he was holding a corpse. Where could it have come from?

"Hey," he whispered into the bird's cheek feathers, holding it as gently as his big hands were capable of doing. "Are you still alive?"

Man, it was hard to tell. The little guy's head lolled, but its body wasn't stiff. That much was good.

Savannah said she'd saved that pink and gray cockatoo's life by sleeping with it inside her shirt, so Keller cupped his new best buddy against his chest to keep it warm. Worried what else he'd find now, he double checked the crates he'd already investigated. Damn. Each paper-stuffed pottery also held one comatose—or dead—hummingbird. Some ruby breasted. Some with that same turquoise crest. All limp as hell.

Keller knew what RJ was into now. Illegal wildlife trafficking. But if all these crates contained exotic birds like this one... If RJ was the reason Rosie and that long-snouted gharial had gotten into the country...

*Holy hell.* Keller ran a hand over his head. This trailer was stacked to the rafters, five crates high. That totaled nine hundred sixty crates in all, and every last bird or animal in them could be breathing its last. Holstering his weapon, Keller did the only thing he could. He snapped a picture of the tiny jewel in his hand and texted it, along with his current location, to his Deuces Wild team.

*The* Deuces Wild team, not *his* team. Damn it. *The* team. Then he facetimed home. Damn it, not *home.* He facetimed the pic to his *office.* Just his *office.* What the hell was going on in his head? He'd never called his office home before. That shit had to stop.

Tucker answered with an even, "Mornin', Kell. How's the vacation going?"

But not even his nickname rolling out of his boss's big mouth irked Keller like he thought it would. He let the vacation comment slide, too. "You know anyone over at Fish and Wildlife?"

"I have a few friends in FWS Law Enforcement. Whatzup?"

"Not absolutely sure, but I just sent a picture to you of a bird I found smuggled inside crates of pottery at Doctor Rudy John's property. Also sent the coordinates. RJ's smuggling animals and birds into the country. I'm looking at close to a thousand crates. I can't tell for sure, but I think this little bird's heart's still beating. But it's been drugged. Also..." Keller rotated his cell, scanning the length and breadth of the container to relay the size of what could be a huge smuggling operation. "Take a look at this."

"Son of a bitch," Tucker murmured. "Where are you?"

"I'm a mile or so from Mariposa Church's place, only her houseboat's not there anymore. You wouldn't believe what's happened the last two days."

"Enlighten me, damn it."

Keller explained how Mariposa Church had been deceased when he'd arrived, and how that led him to Savannah, then to her saving Isaiah. Which led to a quick summary of breakfast, the drive to Sanctuary, the ambush, the alligators, the theft of Mariposa's houseboat, and...

Keller ran a hand over his shaved skull, shocked at all that had happened since yesterday. It didn't seem humanly possible, but so much of it went down quick and dirty, and... There Keller stopped, not letting himself even think about the sweet time he'd spent making love with Savannah. No, just no. Tucker did not need to know everything.

"You're just not good at taking vacations, are you?" Tucker asked drolly.

Keller could've laughed out loud, and that all by itself—spontaneous laughter—was an impulse he hadn't experienced in years.

"Let me make a call," Tucker said. "Sit tight."

Concerned for what could be hundreds, maybe thousands of exotic creatures on the verge of suffocating, Keller ended the call and tucked his tiny charge into his shirt pocket. He was busy popping the cover off another crate, trying to provide ventilation to as many creatures as he could, when he heard men arguing. RJ and another male. Could be Bruce Fontenette.

Hurriedly, he replaced that cover, then watched from the rear of the trailer, holding his breath as he listened.

"But you never said you wanted her place gone that fast," RJ sputtered as the side door opened inward, casting just enough light that Keller could see him as he gestured for the other guy to enter. Dressed in gray hospital scrubs, he almost looked professional. "You shoulda told me. I coulda helped. She had stuff in that old boat I coulda used."

"Don't take it personal, John," the man said as he ducked his head and stepped inside. Bruce Fontenette didn't look happy. "This is just a business transaction, and that's the way these things go. I provide the goods, and you keep them breathing and quiet until my people arrive to transport them north. But the next time I say now, I really mean yesterday, understood?"

"Yes, suh, but that guy with her yesterday mornin'..." Keller could almost hear RJ groveling. "He's FBI, and he was there when the old lady died, too. I seen him with my own eyes, and Miss Savannah went with him when he left yesterday, too."

"And you're just telling me he's FBI now?" Fontenette bellowed as both men approached the rear of the trailer. "Damn you, John, I never would've sent my guys after her if I'd known she was traveling with a Fed!"

Glaring to his left, he'd crossed both arms over his chest, his fingers tapping. His lips pursed into a scowl. Reaching inside his jacket, he palmed a cell, stabbed in a number and told whoever was on the other side of that call, "Plans have changed. I need you here now." A heartbeat passed. "Then find a way to do it, I pay you enough. Yes, a refrigeration unit will work. I don't care, I only need fifty percent of this shit to survive. Okay, okay, yeah, understood. You'll get that ten percent bonus, but only if you're here in the next sixty. No, damn it, you're already late. The FBI's involved. I need this shit out of here. The clock's ticking!"

Keller stepped farther into the trailer, wedging himself between two towers of stacked crates to keep an eye on the men if they decided to board the trailer. Yes, the FBI was involved, yet he didn't dare make himself known, not without understanding precisely what RJ and Fontenette were into. Powerful men didn't just sell exotic birds for the fun of it. But damn, a fifty percent survival rate meant certain death for half these creatures. Keller patted his hummingbird buddy again as RJ and his boss came to the open end of the trailer. What a tragic waste.

"At least show me what you're so damned proud of," Fontenette groused. "I don't have all day."

"Yes, suh." RJ pulled a remote from his pocket. Instantly, a fine vapor drifted down from a latticework of PVC pipes overhead. "This is why I needed all these trailers modified. With one button, I can now put everything in it to sleep."

*Oh shit!* Keller ducked his nose and mouth into his shirt collar.

"It's my own special blend," RJ explained while a bored Mr. Fontenette looked on. "It'll keep this shipment quiet until they gets to where they're going. Yes, suh, quiet and undetected by even the smartest cops on the road, even that bitch, Brinkman. You'll see. It'll be smooth sailing now."

"Except for that FBI agent," Fontenette growled.

"Don't you worry none about him," RJ purred. "I got friends in low places who gonna take care of him."

*I'll just bet you do,* Keller thought. Like some rednecks in a monster truck and another who likes to play with bombs and remote detonators.

The vapor drifting over the cargo had to be some kind of anesthetic. Keller took a deep breath before it settled over him. He had to get out of there. Once RJ closed and locked the door, he'd be as useless as Junior.

Palming his phone, he hit redial and turned the screen to capture a view of the two men. But he was too late. Keller sagged into the narrow space he'd wedged himself into. The gas was getting the best of him. As darkness closed in, he could only hope Tucker was half as smart as Tucker thought he was.

# **Chapter Twenty-Nine**

Savannah had one of her feelings. Something was wrong, but something else was also right. She cocked her head, puzzling out the odd sensation swelling inside her mind. Familiar yet different. Manly, yet oddly detached. Then nothing at all.

After lingering in a relaxing warm shower earlier, during which she'd used up the body wash and most of the fantastic smelling shampoo the hotel provided, she'd toweled dry, then dressed in a pastel orange bra and bikini panties, one of the several matching sets of intimates Keller bought for her. It warmed her down to her toes thinking of him handling these silky, sexy underwear. She'd studied her gorgeous self in the bathroom mirror, modeling various angles, thrilled at the way her new bra bolstered her breasts, making them look higher and plumper than they really were. How'd he know about stuff like that?

Feeling especially feminine, even a little pretty, she selected the coral tie-dyed tee-shirt to go with the jeans he'd also bought. Man, he wasn't half bad at guesstimating her sizes. But those purple running shoes and those ankle socks... too much! By the time she'd dried her hair and left the steamy bathroom, she was jonesing for that man. She couldn't wait to see the glint in those amber eyes when she modeled for him. Would he stalk her like one of the few bayou panthers? She hoped so!

Red whined at her feet, interrupting her reverie, his brown eyes filled with worry. Until then, he'd been sound asleep. Now he rubbed his muzzle up her leg, pushing as if he needed her to move.

"You feel it too, don't you?" she asked as her fingers sifted over the scars beneath the soft, silky fur at the top of his pointed head.

Roger Tanner had finished walking the dogs hours ago. Galahad had instantly taken to his crate, while Red stayed with Savannah. Keller wasn't back yet. Something had changed, but she had no cell phone and no way to reach him. She didn't even know his number. Or did she?

Tipping back against the comfy deck chair on her private ground level lanai, she projected her mind northward to a city of monumental ego, searching for the one person she knew would help.

*'Good afternoon, Savannah,'* Isaiah said easily. *'What can I do for you?'*

*'I'm sorry to bother you, but I'm worried, Isaiah. Keller left this morning, and he said he'd be back soon, only I can't sense him anymore. Can you?'* Until now, she'd maintained only a light 'sense' of Keller's whereabouts. She hadn't read his mind. That wasn't fair or right. Gran Mere had taught her early on that people's thoughts were private, not to be trifled with or manipulated. Yet until now Savannah had always been able to sense him. She hadn't even had to work hard at it to smell the addictive scent of his skin and breath. Which was why she now sensed only a void. Everything Keller was missing. She couldn't get so much as a hint of his angry vibe from the universe.

*'Hold that thought,'* Isaiah murmured as a tiny infant's sigh came through their psychic connection.

*'Is that your son? You had a baby since yesterday?'*

*'Yes, ma'am. Yesterday's excitement proved too much for him, so he showed up early this morning, as in the wee, wee hours. Roxy's here, too.'*

*'How wonderful! Is Roxy okay? No problems? He's not too early, is he?'*

*'No, he's perfect. His mama's perfect, too. But... did you actually hear him sigh?'*

*'I did. He's definitely your son.'*

Another more masculine sigh flooded Savannah's mind. She could clearly see Isaiah stroking the shoulder and arm of the dark-haired Hispanic woman tucked into his side. In his other arm, the tiniest little dark-haired boy slept soundly. What a sweet picture.

*'Aw, you're right. He is perfect,'* Savannah cooed, her throat thick with tenderness and a titch of jealousy. Isaiah had everything she'd just lost—a family. *'I shouldn't have bothered you, I'm sorry. You're still recovering, and here I am disturbing a new father who's lucky to be alive and—'*

*'Nonsense. I just need a second. Hmmm. You're right. Keller is unresponsive. His heart's barely beating. That's why you can't sense him.'*

A phone rang on Isaiah's end, and Savannah listened while he whispered, "Yes, Boss, I'm already in contact with Miss Church. No, we can't reach Keller, either." A pause. "Excuse me? He's what?"

Closing her eyes to concentrate on the other end of Isaiah's conversation, Savannah eavesdropped as a tense-sounding man snarled, *'You heard me. He's been gassed. That rat bastard Fontenette has Kell. Lucky for us, he was smart enough to leave his cell on. I saw the whole fucking thing go down. Don't know the idiot Fontenette's working with, but U.S. Fish and Wildlife's onto him now. Word is Fontenette thinks he's untouchable.'*

Fontenette, as in Mr. Bruce Fontenette, the owner of the famous racehorse Sand Dollar? Savannah hadn't realized she'd leaned so far forward until she fell back into the deck chair, gasping at that startling information. She'd always wanted to meet Bruce Fontenette, his horses too. The man owned a stable of brilliant racers. But now?

"Man, your powers are growing stronger," Isaiah told his boss.

*'Hell, I wish, but no. This one's all Kell. Damn, he's one helluva operator. Smart man. He facetimed before he passed out, showed me near to a thousand crates of illegally imported birds and what not. We were tracking his GPS, but we lost him. Thought maybe you could do your magic thing and locate him.'*

*'What magic thing?'* Savannah asked.

"Boss, before we go any further, you need to know that Miss Church is listening into our conversation from somewhere near New Orleans, right?" Isaiah asked out loud since he was on the phone with his boss.

*'I didn't mean to put you on the spot, but yes,'* she told him mentally. *'I'm at the New Orleans Ritz Carlton hotel at the moment. Keller got us a room last night. It was a long day and I... I was exhausted and... and...'* And there was no way she'd reveal that she and Keller had slept together, though a psychic as strong as Isaiah probably already knew. Darn, this conversation was growing more complicated by the minute. *'Is Keller okay?'*

*'Can she hear me?'* Isaiah's boss asked.

"Yes, Tuck, she can hear you, but you probably can't link into a three-way mental conference call yet, can you?"

*'Damn it, no,'* came the man's surly reply.

"Listen, Roxy's still asleep and so's my son. Let me call you right back." Isaiah disconnected before his boss could say another word. *'Savannah, are you still with me?'*

'Yes,' she whispered mentally. *'What do you want me to do?'*

*'Hang tight for a minute. Let me get more details from Tuck, and I'll be right back with you.'*

*'Your boss is Tuck, as in Friar Tuck?'*

Isaiah chuckled quietly. *'Ha, that's a new one, but no. Tuck as in Tucker Chase, Supervisory Special Agent and Director of the FBI's one and only Psychic Team. We're headquartered in Washington, DC, but because of the psychic business we're in, we're pretty much able to work all over the world. What level are you?'*

Savannah had no idea what he was asking. *'I, umm... What?'*

*'You've never been tested,'* he said, a note of awe in his voice. *'Incredible. You're a strong psychic. I'll bet you're another Level Ten or close to it. Once this is over, I'd love to sit with you. We need to talk.'*

*'Please tell Mr. Chase I'm sorry I eavesdropped. That was rude of me. I don't usually intrude on other's thoughts. I was just worried.'*

*'Don't sweat it. Tucker's used to us. Sit tight. I'll be right back.'* And with that, her psychic connection stopped. Isaiah had hung up on her. Like Keller, she couldn't get a sense of him in the universe, not even the glowing trace of an aura trail. That was enlightening. No one had done that to Savannah

before, not even Gran Mere. She needed to learn that skill.

"Keller's in trouble," she told Red who still sat at her knee, his big brown eyes soulful. "And Isaiah says I'm a Level Ten. Sounds mighty uppity, doesn't it? Imagine me, someone important." She stretched a hand in front of her, admiring her work-worn fingernails as if she'd had one of those fancy French manicures.

With a growly whine, Red put a fluffy paw on her knee.

Cupping his floppy ears, Savannah leaned into his forehead and kissed the top of his long snout. "I don't know what a Level Ten is, either, but Isaiah thinks it's good. We've got to trust Isaiah and his boss. They're FBI. They know things." She hoped.

Red whined again, his way of telling her he knew things, too. The longer she sat there, the more Savannah knew she had to do something. Keller being in a convoy meant he was on the road. Well, she had a Buick, and she knew how to use it.

"Talk to me, Keller," she whispered across the unknown miles. "If you talk to me, I will find you."

# Chapter Thirty

Keller woke to the harsh dig of splinters in his cheek, one helluva cramp in his lower back, and a mouth full of cotton. Groggy and unsure where he was, he stayed upright, apparently caught between two roughhewn slabs of lumber that hummed. He scrunched his eyes, then blinked to clear the fog in his head, not sure where he was or how he'd gotten here—wherever *here* was. It most certainly wasn't the Ritz.

*The Ritz. Savannah!* Clarity slammed him. Shit. He'd left her sleeping at the Ritz this morning. He'd gone after RJ and... Fumbling for his shirt pocket, he located Junior's tiny warm body, still protected. Not flat. Keller's cheeks ballooned as he blew out an honest to heaven sigh of relief. He still couldn't tell if the bird was going to make it or not, but knowing he hadn't squished the tiny body while he'd been passed out, and that Junior was still warm, was relief enough.

Savannah would never forgive him if he'd accidentally killed this little guy.

Carefully, Keller tucked Junior back into his pocket as more of what happened came back to him. RJ. Fontenette. Being gassed. Damn, he was still in the trailer. He'd been drugged along with every animal and bird in this illegal cargo, which told him plenty. Whatever cocktail RJ used could take down an adult male as well as a bird the size of a teaspoon. Interesting.

Disengaging his sore as shit body from between the crates, Keller stretched to get his blood flowing again. Man, people who reduced living, breathing creatures into commodities were greedy sons of bitches. Yet that was what all mankind did to survive. If he couldn't tame it, he hunted, ate, or hounded it into extinction. Survival of the fittest at its most intelligent and its most lethal. It all came back to Mother Nature's brutal yet ingenious circle of life. But fifty percent? What a waste.

Feeling for his flashlight, Keller backtracked to locate his cell. He found it face up between the crates. And still turned on. Damn. All this time his cell had transmitted nothing but noise and darkness.

He turned it off, then on again and... it was mid-afternoon! He'd been passed out for five hours. What the hell was in that gas? And his cell was down to one measly bar. Unsure when he'd need that bar, Keller flicked his cell and flashlight off as he sank to the floor, his back against the container wall. He wasn't so sure he was traveling by truck anymore. The drone inside this container felt different, as if he were airborne. Fontenette wouldn't have airmailed this container, would he?

Not like it mattered. Without a way to reach Tucker, Keller was trapped like Junior and his friends. But Keller wasn't worried. He'd be plenty capable by the time this trip ended. Besides, all FBI cells were ruggedized and contained tracking chips—GPS locators with internal lithium batteries. Whether lost in shallow water or buried six feet under, his phone would track him, and the Deuces Wild team would eventually locate him. They might be on their way now. He wouldn't have to fight Fontenette and his greedy goons alone. There was comfort in that.

But Savannah? By now, Roger Tanner would've come and gone. The dogs would be fed and walked, but eventually, they'd need more exercise. When Keller didn't return like he'd said he would, she'd worry. She'd think he deserted her, that she wasn't good enough. Which was so untrue.

The misconceived notion that she was somehow less than him tugged at the hollow spot in Keller's chest. If anything, it was the other way around. She was the one who was happy with her life, even as meager as it seemed. But him? That was just another sad story not worth the telling.

Until Carol Marie came into his life, he never knew how much he craved feminine concern, care, and gentle affection. Or how badly he missed it after he lost her. Nor how much Savannah's eternal optimism had buoyed him, lifted him... inspired him. Even now. It was as if she'd always been his missing half, more so because she seemed to have accepted that possibility easier and quicker than he had.

He could still recall the soft blue light in Carol Marie's eyes. Blonde curly hair fluffed around her head like a halo. Keller was pretty sure she glowed from the inside out that day in high school. He'd noticed her plenty before he'd ever spoken with her. Even then, she'd started the conversation.

It was early fall. He'd never forget the unexpected cheerfulness of her first words to him, the place or the time. They were in the school library. He needed to return all the books he'd checked out before he left school that day. Despite being nineteen, he'd still been in eleventh grade. Held back for missing too much school, he was an underclassman, a pitiful junior. She was a rah-rah-rah senior, ahead of the game because of her AP classes and already accepted by some bigtime college out west.

Carol Marie was going places, while he was on his way out that day, never to return. He'd missed too much school. He would've been lucky to graduate with his class, but he couldn't bear being held back. Not again.

Summer school wasn't in the cards either. Elaine's antics made regular attendance impossible, but school had always been Keller's one safe place. He didn't have to like the teachers who looked down their noses at him, but he'd always adored math and science. A kid could get lost in Algebra as quickly as American Lit. Or Robert Frost. Or Carol Marie's pretty blue eyes.

*'Excuse me, sir, but could you reach that book for me, the one on the high shelf. See it? The one with a green spine. It's my book of Robert Frost poetry. Jamie Whitaker thinks it's funny to put my things where I can't reach them.'*

*She'd called him sir. The irony of anyone addressing him respectfully took his breath. By the time he'd stretched one arm way over her head and dragged her book off the top bookshelf, his lungs had closed off and his throat had gone sandpaper dry.*

*Jamie Whitaker was the class jerk, but Keller suspected he had a crush on Carol Marie like every other guy in high school, didn't matter if they were freshman, seniors, or about to drop-out—like him. She was the prettiest girl, the one to be seen with.*

*But Keller was a loser, dressed in rags and hand-me-down pants, doing a favor for the school sweetheart, and having a heart attack while he did it. 'Here you go,' he'd told Carol Marie, making sure she had a good grip on her book before he let it go.*

*She had a good grip on him by then, too. Her tiny fingers fluttered light and soft on his callused, much larger hands. 'You don't say much, do you?' she'd asked, her head cocked to one side like she was trying to figure him out.*

*He'd already figured her out. She was hands-off beautiful, but in a kind and gracious way. 'Guess I don't have much to say.'*

*'Would you help me study?'*

*He'd nearly laughed out loud at her needing anything from a bastard son of a bitch like him, but he didn't. He couldn't. Those gentle fingers on his hand seemed to pour something warm and shiny and good into his usually bleak existence. For the first time Keller could remember, he didn't feel like the biggest dolt in school. He wasn't just the voodoo priestess's worthless son. Carol Marie made him feel like he was—more.*

*'Um, sure. Yeah, I guess.' Man, he'd sounded like an idiot back then. 'What subject you need help studying?'*

*'Robert Frost. I'm writing my term paper on his understanding of rural American life. Did you know he was published in England before America?'*

*'Did you know I don't read poetry too good?'*

*'Did you know I'm not really asking?' she asked, blinking those big blue eyes at him and sucking him into the tenderest trap of his life at that point.*

*Well, okay then. Instead of packing up his locker and moving on like he'd planned, Keller walked her home. The next day they put their heads together in study hall. They whispered, giggled, studied together, and he was a goner. The next day she took him shopping for clothes. He paid for everything they bought. It depleted his meager savings, but she told him he looked manly, and he believed her. The next day she asked him to take her to the homecoming dance. The next thing he knew, he'd graduated ahead of schedule—with her class.*

*Little did either of them know that was the beginning of the end. Elaine never wanted happiness for her son. She'd hated Carol Marie on sight. Yet Keller wasn't yet man enough to know how to walk away from the best thing in his life, not when his pretty wife owned him, heart, body, and soul. Not when she was the one saving grace in life.*

*Yet that was exactly what he should've done. He should've told Carol Marie 'no' that first day in the library, that she shouldn't be seen with lowlifes like him. She might still be alive then.*

*Ever his strongest ally, she was the only one who'd encouraged his need to enlist in the Army after they'd married. She knew the cost, but she loved him. She ran with him, swam with him, even drilled with him on the range preparing his endurance for the physical and marksmanship challenges ahead. Carol Marie was the one standing at his side the day he graduated basic training, not Elaine. After that he was headed for Camp Rogers in the Harmony Church area of Fort Benning, GA, for Ranger Assessment. Carol Marie and he had a bright future. Until he took leave two days later. Until Elaine finally relented to meet the new Mrs. Boniface. Until Carol Marie died...*

"I let both of you down," he told his dead wife and their unborn son. "I don't even know where that graduation picture of us is any more." Remorse crept over him like a sickness. "I'm sorry," he whispered. "You have to know how much I love you. I always will. Both of you."

Bumping the back of his head against the trailer wall behind him, Keller closed his eyes and wished for a bottled water and a way out of the dilemma with Savannah. That wasn't love, and he damned well knew it. It couldn't be. There was no sense fooling himself or her. They'd only met yesterday. Okay, so they were sexually compatible, and they seemed to like each other. So what? Rome wasn't built in a day and neither was love. Lust maybe. There'd been plenty of that.

Yet even as he denied the notion, voracious need for Savannah's tender sweetness warmed Keller's body. He could be in bed with her luxuriously soft body draped over him right now. His nose could be buried in her hair, his hands full of her small, succulent breasts. Or her ass. He could be listening to her expound on some wise thing Gran Mere had said. He could be... *Home.*

But no. There was no home for him. Not anymore. He gave that up the day he buried his wife and child. This thing with Savannah had to stop before she ended up dead too.

A tiny wiggle in his pocket roused Keller from his dark thoughts. The hummingbird was alive—and kicking.

"If I let you go, I'll never see you again," he told the stiletto-nosed creature poking its way up and out of his pocket. For some reason, it sounded like he was really speaking to Savannah.

Carefully, he cupped his fingers, caging the determined explorer where it wouldn't get away and get hurt. "Trust me, you'll get lost in this big, dark container. When the door finally opens, out you'll go, like a shot." *And I'll miss you like I'll miss Savannah.*

The little guy squeaked. It buzzed and stretched its wings, using them to balance on the double-folded cuff of his pocket. Junior was stronger now. He was capable. He wanted out.

Yet Keller couldn't—wouldn't—let Junior go, even though the little guy's stiletto beak poked out between his thumb and index finger. *Just being protective,* he told himself. Maybe it was time to let this tiny jewel do what it was made to do—fly away. Live. Maybe it was time he let Savannah go, too. But the second Junior zipped away, he'd be in unfamiliar territory. He'd get lost. The little thing didn't belong in America. Junior needed to be returned home, where hummingbirds like him sparkled in the breeze as they zipped by. He wouldn't last long in America, and Keller couldn't let anything happen to his new buddy.

Carefully, he tucked Junior into the deepest part of his pocket, then buttoned it so the bird would be quiet and safe. Somehow that simple action assured him that Savannah was where she belonged too. She was safe. Away from him, but safe. Keller settled against the humming wall. Which struck him as ironic. *Humming wall. Humming bird. Har dee, har, har.*

Man, he was tapped, so tired he was getting rummy. He didn't want to fall asleep again, yet the contraption RJ had rigged up would soon switch on and douse everything in this container with another batch of sleepy-time mist. Keller couldn't let that happen.

The risk was real. Stay here on his butt—which his body ached to do—and be unprepared when that rolling door opened. Or get off his lazy ass, break the door open, breathe in a gut full of fresh air, then locate whatever gizmo activated RJ's special recipe. Dismantle or activate it, Keller still wasn't sure. On the one hand, the living things in this container with him deserved to breathe. On the other hand, waking them before he could set them free would conclude in mass death. They couldn't breathe if they were awake while still wrapped in stifling paper, could they? They might panic and hurt themselves trying to get free. He couldn't have that. Keller opted to err on the side of caution. There was no way he could open all these crates to free everything anyway, and there wasn't sufficient room inside the container if he did. It would be kinder to keep the birds and animals, if there were any, drugged.

Keller's head throbbed with a monstrous migraine, but he shook it off. He had work to do and soldiering on was what Rangers did. They didn't whine and cry like a bunch of pansy-assed snowflakes. Hell, no. They fought back and they won. Every. Time.

Okay then. Keller squared his shoulders, ready for a fight. Knowing RJ, the activation switch that released the gas wouldn't be complex. Probably just a simple toggle switch attached to a receiver, running off a double A battery. Whatever. Keller knew he could easily jury rig something to activate from ground level. That way he could keep the birds and other creatures safely anesthetized until help arrived to transport them to safety. But first...

He needed a breath of fresh air.

# Chapter Thirty-One

*'I wish you'd waited until I got back to you,'* Isaiah told Savannah mentally as she sped along the interstate across Lake Pontchartrain. Her inner sense of Keller had turned back on in her head. He'd gone to speak with RJ this morning, but he wasn't at RJ's clinic now. He was somewhere ahead of her. East of her. That much she knew, so she'd packed up her dogs, and she'd gone after him. Waiting was not an option.

*'I couldn't. I can sense him now. He's moving farther away from me.'*

*'But he's in the air, Savannah. Keller was trapped in a convoy of four trucks the last time we spoke, but those trucks stopped at an airfield in Hattiesburg, Mississippi, hours ago. The containers are now on a cargo jet. He's been in the air over an hour.'*

Well, darn. Savannah ran a hand over her face, flustered that she'd wasted time going nowhere, just as flustered she'd wasted time waiting for Keller to come back when he was so far gone. *'When your boss said convoy, I thought I could just... Never mind. You're right. My fault. I should've waited.'*

Still in his Georgetown hospital bed with Roxy by his side nursing their son, Isaiah was acting as Savannah's go-between with his boss, Special Agent Tucker Chase and another FBI agent, Eden Winchester. But it was no wonder Keller disliked working with them. They were all mind-reading psychics, all capable of mentally contacting and communicating with each other, while he didn't have a telepathic bone in his body. Apparently, neither did Savannah. Chagrined, she aimed for the nearest exit to turn around.

*'I'm sorry. My fault. I should've talked with you before now. Keller's heart rate is still quite low,'* Isaiah said. *'That must be why you weren't able to hone in on him before.'*

*'I can only see things through his mind.'* Darn it. *'Wherever he is, it's dark, but he's not in pain, and he's not uncomfortable. I get the feeling he's not alone, either. Someone or something is with him, only I keep losing the connection. It's like he's drifting in and out of consciousness.'*

*'Which he probably is. Sorry, Savannah. Keller was in touch with my boss when he became trapped in the container. Fortunately, he was transmitting video when he blacked out. Tuck saw it. Mr. John used some kind of sleeping gas on those crates.'*

'*Dr. John,*' Savannah corrected. '*Rudy John. He's a general practitioner. He was Gran Mere's doctor.*' But he was most definitely not her friend. '*What's in the crates?*'

Isaiah took a measured breath before he told her, '*According to Keller, exotic hummingbirds, possibly other smuggled animals, too. There are nearly a thousand crates in that one container, and there were four trucks in the convoy. This is a huge illegal shipment. Tuck checked out the photo Keller sent. The bird is called a Marvelous Spatuletail, it's one of the rarest hummingbird species in the world. It only lives in the Rio Utcubamba Valley, high in the Andes of northern Peru. Apparently, there's a huge conservation effort to save these birds. Because of Keller's good detective work, the Bureau's now working with the Division of Fish and Wildlife to seize the shipment. We've been after Fontenette for years on other charges, but Keller might just have found the way to finally bring him down.*'

'*He is dedicated,*' Savannah said. That much she knew for certain. Keller lived to serve.

'*That he is. Let me know what else is going on with him.*'

'*I will.*'

But Savannah felt worse now that she'd connected with Keller. After the way he'd held her last night, she'd been so sure he loved her, that he just didn't know how to say it. Guess not. Because now she also sensed she was fighting a losing battle by loving a man who wanted her, yet was convinced he wasn't good enough. Even as groggy as Keller was, he still transmitted strong undercurrents of honorable doubt that included him leaving her. Foolish man, thinking he knew better than she did.

Yet he'd been so deeply hurt when Carol Marie passed away that something inside him was broken. Savannah got that, but for the first time since she'd fallen for him, she wasn't certain she could save this damaged beast. *You can't make someone love you.*

She'd never been in a relationship with a man like him before, and teenage romances didn't count. This was a fiercely different thing, loving an adult male who'd survived a nightmare childhood, then created an entirely new nightmare by joining the Army and running headlong into war. Burying himself in protective, macho layers of military armor, pride, and male ego that distanced himself from everyone not in that raw, wild brotherhood who'd sworn to die for each other. What civilian—what woman—could compete with a bond built on lives freely given? On blood spilled for love of the warrior at your side?

She honestly didn't know. Maybe Keller was right. Maybe it was time to admit they really were worlds apart. It made sense. War was all he'd ever known. He'd developed a keen sense of survival since he was a baby. How could he not? He knew how to fight with his entire soul—just not how to love.

It was that sense of internal anguish she'd zeroed on the moment she'd opened Gran Mere's door. Just as his empathy had reached out to comfort her, Savannah's aptitude for comforting those around her snagged him at first sight. Like *did* attract like. That much *was* true. That much she knew.

Okay then. *Where there's a will, there's a way, right?* She just had to persuade Keller to let down his defenses and try a little harder, to let her love him a little longer. A little better. That was what this badassed, scarred, banged-up warrior needed. That was who could rescue him from himself, someone strong enough to always be there for him at the end of the day. And that someone was her.

He'd never quit fighting the good fight, and Savannah didn't want him to change, not for her. They were strong empaths. They could be good together. But every warrior needed a safe place to hide when his daily battle was over. Some place safe and dark where he could lick his wounds and know for certain that someone would be waiting there just for him. To feed him and wash away the grime and blood from his handsome body. To listen. To hold him when he cried. To love him with all her heart.

*'I'm worried,'* she confided to Isaiah. *'I'm not sure Keller knows how to let down his defenses long enough for anyone to speak psychically with him. He's blocking me even though he's passed out.'*

*'Which proves he's a stronger psychic than he realizes. This is why he needs you. One day at a time, Savannah. Isn't that what your great grandmother used to say?'*

That made her smile. *'I think you know me too well, my friend.'*

*'It happens. Listen, when this is over, I want you to visit me at FBI Headquarters and undergo a few tests. Meet my boss. Tuck's always looking for new talent.'*

*'No. Strong trees need each other's shade, but they also need to stand in their own sunlight to grow. I'd never intrude on Keller's workplace unless he asked me.'*

Isaiah chuckled. *'Another one of your great grandmother's pearls of wisdom?'*

*'Actually, that one's all mine,'* Savannah answered with a titch of pride. *'Remember, I'm from the bayou where clinging vines kill even the hardiest trees. That's not what Keller needs. Did you know he can't read your mind? Do you know how hard that was for him to sit with me and not know what you and I were talking about that day?'*

*'You mean the day you saved my life?'* Isaiah whispered psychically—as if anyone else could hear him. *'I still can't thank you enough. You'll never know what you did for me and Roxy. My son.'*

*'It was my pleasure,'* she replied. *'You'd do the same.'*

*'I would. But yes, I know Keller's not happy. The adjustment's been hard on him.'*

*'Because the rest of you can psychically check in with each other anytime you want. You talk to each other like it's no big deal, just like we're doing now.

*But Keller can't. Think about it. He was used to being the man in charge when he was in the Army, but now he's the odd man out. The wannabe, always looking in, but never quite belonging to the mean kids' club.'*

*'Hey, whoa, I object. We're not intentionally mean to anyone, and—'*

*'Yeah, I get it, you don't mean to exclude anyone, and if anyone was the odd man out as a kid, it was certainly you. But honestly, Isaiah, each time you Deuces Wild guys converse psychically behind his back, that's precisely what you're doing. All of you. Even your boss. How would you feel?'*

That shut Isaiah up. Because of their shared mental link, Savannah now knew precisely what a misfit he'd been as a kid, even as a young adult, right up until the day he'd met Eden Winchester, the FBI agent now tracking Keller. How could they both not understand Keller when they'd been the exact same type of misfit?

*'I never thought of it like that,'* Isaiah finally murmured. *'You're absolutely right.'*

*'It's simple pack mentality. Dogs do it all the time, and human beings aren't much different. They tend to forget what it's like being the outsider the second they belong to a family, a society, a church, or whatever. They clan up, close up, and they draw a line to fence everyone else out.'*

*'Man, we could really use another Level Ten, someone with your unique insight on our team.'*

There was that term again. *'What on earth is a Level Ten?'*

'Someone like me. Like you and probably your Gran Mere, too. Someone with multiple psychic skills.'

'Like...?'

'There are many different talents, Savannah. Telepaths read minds and Clairsensitives sense other psychic energies. You and Keller are Intuitives, commonly called Empaths. By the way, Keller is the strongest Empath I've ever met.'

'I know. He just needs to learn to balance how much of himself he gives away. He wouldn't have those killer migraines then.'

'Keller has killer migraines?'

Ooops. She'd just told on Keller, not good. But Savannah could also sense Isaiah's I-told-you-so grin all the way from the East Coast. 'I never knew he suffered with his gift until now. See how strong you are?'

'Well, um, yes, but I shouldn't have told you. That's for Keller to share.'

'Understood, Savannah. I won't break your confidence. But as far as other psychic talents, I have yet to come across a true Telekinesist, someone who can actually move physical objects with their mind. Most I've met were fakes who relied on sleight of hand, magnets, or other tricks. I haven't met a Psychic Surgeon yet either, but the Russians claim they've got one. If they're telling the truth, that person would be able to psychically heal damage done to a person's psychic consciousness.'

'Psychic consciousness?' Savannah felt like a sponge.

Isaiah's excitement was growing. 'Amazing concept, right? The belief among scholars studying psychic phenomenon is that all babies are born psychics, to one degree or another. Isn't that wild? Unfortunately, we've come into a world where those gifts are ignored or rejected at birth, even treated as black magic and witchcraft. Psychic babies didn't live long in the Stone Ages. Imagine what happened during the Middle Ages or the Inquisition. Then along came the Renaissance, and the few babies strong enough to have survived, were at last able to contribute to society in phenomenal ways.'

'You believe psychics fueled the Renaissance?' That actually made sense. Psychics did see things differently. How could they not?

'No, I believe all people are psychics, Savannah. Every man, woman, and child walking the earth today is gifted. Some gifts are just stronger than others. Some are encouraged to grow while others are stamped out. Some gifts are scary, like yours and mine.'

She held her breath. Scary?

'Precognition,' Isaiah answered quietly. 'Can you influence people to change their minds without them knowing it? Can you bend their will to suit your agenda? Could you make someone not step on a bus in Israel because you know there's a bomb on that bus?'

'*No,*' she breathed, her heart suddenly beating up high in her throat at all Isaiah had implied. Holy Mother, a person like that could destroy the world if they were evil enough. She had to ask, '*Can you?*'

'*Yes. I'm a Level Ten. I believe you are, too. Think about it. Have you ever compelled someone to, oh, I don't know, leave and never come back?*'

'*Me? Why, umm…*' She didn't know what else to say. That was precisely what she'd done to Keller. Isaiah was right. She was scary, too.

'*The point is that none of the rest of us come from the strong psychic upbringing that you do. You had your great grandmother to guide you. But the rest of us had to figure things out as we went. It's hard for a kid to wake up one day and realize he's different, that he's hearing things no one else can. No teenager likes being labeled 'the weirdo'. We all wanted to fit in, and… shit. I am so dumb. That's it! I should've recognized what Keller needed from the start.*'

'*Why, because you're God?*' Savannah teased. She couldn't help herself. She needed a break from this all-too-serious discussion. Isaiah was doing it again, thinking he was responsible for saving the world. '*Do all men have a hero complex, or is it just you?*'

That bought her a genuine laugh. '*All right, all right, I get the picture—*'

'*Excuse me, Isaiah,*' a woman's mental voice interrupted. '*We've re-located Keller's GPS signal.*'

'*Re-located?*' Savannah asked.

*'Hey, Eden, I'm speaking with Savannah Church. Savannah, my friend and Special Agent Eden Winchester. Yes, Savannah, sometimes we lose GPS signals during air travel. Where is Keller now, Eden?'*

*'Hey, Savannah. I can't wait to meet you,'* Eden called out. *'He just entered Florida airspace. We believe he's being taken to Bruce Fontenette's stables west of Jacksonville, but Champion Acres sits on a large piece of land near Hollybrook Park. It's heavily wooded. I can pinpoint Keller's phone once he lands, just not him. Fontenette's got multiple stables, outbuildings, and plenty of acreage. I was hoping Miss Church could help.'*

*'You can't read him either,'* Isaiah muttered. *'That's interesting. I've never been able to clearly read Keller, but you can, right, Savannah?'*

*'Yes,'* she replied timidly. *'I connected with him before I knew his name. It was easy. Only now, he's so far away. I'm not sure I'll be able to reach him much longer.'*

*'Try,'* both Isaiah and Eden said.

Adeptly, Savannah pulled her Buick to the side of the road. She couldn't concentrate on driving and locating Keller at the same time. She and the dogs had passed Lake Pontchartrain by then, and she'd just hooked onto Interstate 59, headed North. She needed an overpass that would take her back to New Orleans, but she hadn't come to one yet. *'Hello, Agent Winchester, I—'*

*'Eden, please. May I call you Savannah?'*

*'Sure, umm, Eden.'* As quickly as Savannah touched Eden's mind, she could plainly see the confident petite woman with spiraling blonde curls cascading over her shoulders. Dressed professionally in a dark black dress shirt, slacks, and low heels, Eden was armed, a pistol holstered on her hip and a badge on her chest. Her eyes were a vivid, intelligent green that seemed to be looking straight through Savannah.

The images came faster then. Not too long ago, Eden Winchester had been the Bureau's only psychic. This morning, she'd left a toddler, a cute little guy named Kyler at home with her nanny. Ky Winchester, her husband, the strapping, handsome man she adored with her whole heart, stood over her shoulder, dressed in black, an FBI badge clipped to his belt.

Another man Eden respected, her boss, Tucker Chase, hovered nearby. Dark-haired, intense dark brown eyes that sparked with ego, pride and—something else. Had to be love the way that man glowed. Love for an equally strong woman and a teenage son whom he adored—Melissa and Devlin. But Tucker called him Deuce.

The images came faster. Savannah could barely keep up with the information pouring out of Eden's brilliant mind and into hers. Vivid splashes of someone's time spent in Vietnam roared over Savannah. On its heels, vivid, wild blues of frozen Alaska burst like a dynamic Northern light. Next came another mountain of a man, also with dark hair, Special Agent Tate Higgins. His pixie-sized wife,

Winslow Arizona. The freedom loving state of Texas. Longhorns. American flags snapping in a stiff breeze. A desert in far off Sierra Leone, and...

*'Stop, Eden. Stop. You're swamping me,'* Savannah whispered, her inexperienced mind fluttering much like that flag she'd seen. *'Too much. You're sending too much. I can't absorb it as fast as you're sending. Tamp it down. Please. Slow the flow.'*

*'I can do that?'* Eden asked even as Isaiah inserted, *'Come on, Eden, compartmentalize. We talked about this. You just need to practice. Think order. Think calm. Think structure.'*

It took another minute before Savannah could sort out what she needed from everything that could wait for another day. By then she'd pressed her forehead against her steering wheel and her eyes were closed to help her focus. Red whined anxiously from the back seat, while Galahad still snored. Silly boy. He'd been sleeping since they'd left the hotel.

*'Who's traveling with you?'* she asked, needing to understand which of the men she'd just been shown could actually help find Keller now. She'd never met psychics like Isaiah or Eden before. These two were powerful. Even Gran Mere had communicated more with feelings than actual words. Psychic conversation would take time getting used to.

*'Just our boss, Special Agent Tucker Chase. I'm sorry, Savannah. I'm used to talking with the guys, and we're all—'*

'*You're all in sync, I get that, but trust me, Eden, not everyone speaks the same language as well as you do.*' Savannah couldn't help her sharp tone. The deluge of intel she'd just received from Eden had actually hurt her head, and she was more worried for Keller. '*In the future, stick with one idea or one subject at a time until you know who you're dealing with. Then just parse out a thought at a time until you're sure you're not coming on too strong. Have you ever heard that less is more?*'

'*As I've just been properly schooled,*' Isaiah piped in. '*Thanks, Savannah. We do tend to forget we're the different ones in the world. Which is why we could use a psychic teacher and a training program for our newest recruits, instead of them learning the hard way. Think about what I asked. Personally, I struggled for years before Tate taught me how to block the deluge of voices crying out for help in the world. It'd sure be nice to be able to mentor new agents like Keller instead of baptizing them by fire.*'

'*Keller has needs?*' Eden asked.

'*Never mind,*' Isaiah answered. '*But admit it, Eden. A psychic mentor to guide us through those first turbulent years would've saved a lot of headaches.*'

'*I had my mother, but yeah. An expert would've been more helpful.*'

Savannah sniffed. '*I'm no expert, but right now I'm still in Louisiana. Where are you, Eden?*'

'*In the air, East Coast, closing on Jacksonville, Florida.*'

Savannah's heart sank. All this time she'd thought it was just a matter of catching up to some truck on the road. That she could somehow stop that truck and rescue Keller, that she alone could save him. She should've known better. Fontenette was made of money. He only had to snap his fingers, and Keller would be gone forever. A tear slipped from her eye and down her cheek. Pitiful much?

*'A wise woman once told me it wasn't my job to save the world,'* Isaiah whispered. *'Find a safer place to park, Savannah. Get off the freeway. Get where you can concentrate and not be worried about traffic. Eden and I can't reach Keller like you can.'*

Well, okay then. Tracking traffic in the rearview mirror, she pulled carefully back onto the busy interstate. *'Give me a minute. I'll be in touch as soon as I can.'*

*'Thank you,'* Eden said. *'We need you, Savannah. I need you.'*

*'You already know how much I need you,'* Isaiah murmured, *'but Keller needs you most. Don't be long.'*

Savannah stepped on the gas, shielding her thoughts from her intriguing new friends. Keller might need her help right now, but was he willing to risk his heart again? She wasn't so sure. Could he let Carol Marie go and move on with his life? That was the real question.

# Chapter Thirty-Two

Savannah pulled into a shady parking stall at the nearest rest stop. After quickly walking and watering the dogs, she ushered them back into the Buick. Red took up his place in the front passenger seat while Galahad lay on his side in the back. Opening all the Buick's windows brought the barest hint of a breeze. With it came all the luscious fragrances of spring in Louisiana. Magnolia and boxwood. Swamp and humidity. New growth and sunshine on the bayou. Savannah drew in a deep breath to restore her inner sight, then released it slowly as she told Isaiah, *'Okay. I'm ready now.'*

*'Me too,'* he answered. *'My buddy Ky was just here. He took Roxy out for lunch. I've got a couple hours to get this done before they get back.'*

*'Aw, and they didn't take you with them?'*

'Doctor's orders,' he grumbled. 'I'm still under observation. They can't figure out how I recovered so fast. They're running more tests to be on the safe side.'

'Just tell them some voodoo witch from down South commanded you to rise and shine,' she teased.

'You bet. Then they'll lock me up and throw away the key. No thanks. I'm okay hanging around while Roxy's here, but the minute my son's released, I'm going home with them.'

'You haven't picked a name yet?'

'She wants to name him Abraham...'

Savannah didn't understand why Isaiah growled. 'Like Abraham Lincoln? That's a great name.'

'No, like Abraham Zaroyin.'

*Oh. Him.* Savannah snapped her big mouth shut. She'd forgotten what Keller told her about Isaiah's father.

'Don't get me wrong, I love my father...'

'Just not enough to name your son after him. I get it.'

'Why should I? He's the reason the Bicks went after my mom. All he wanted was his almighty three Gs: gain, glory, and greed. He didn't care about Mom. He got her killed.'

*And like you, he has to live with that knowledge every single day,* Savannah thought. Tragedy never destroyed just one person when it crash landed. It always took out the whole family, their home, and sometimes the entire village, whether by first strike or the ripple effect of grief and loss. Instead she said, *'You're still working on forgiving him.'*

*'No, I'm working on forgetting him.'*

How sad. *'How old were you when he... left?'* She couldn't bear to say, *'when your mother was murdered.'*

*'I was a kid, Savannah. A freakin' twelve-year-old kid.'*

Bitterness Savannah understood. It'd be hard to look at the child you adored knowing he bore the name you hated. *'At least you knew your dad,'* she said quietly. *'Mine took one look at me and dumped me at Gran Mere's. Intellectually, I know he did that because my mother bled to death when I was born. Gran Mere said she was Japanese and had some rare enzyme in her blood. My father didn't know what to do with a baby, but then he went and got himself killed. I can't even decide if I hate him or like him because I never knew him. He's nothing to me, just a blank face where a father should've been.'*

*'I'm sorry.'* Isaiah sighed. *'Man, we really know how to get off track, don't we?'*

*'Yes, but it's understandable. Fathers are supposed to be our first heroes, our steady role models, our gentlest teachers, and our constant advocates. When they fail us, we lose a huge part of our identity, and it's harder to understand the world of men. Anyway... I'm sorry, too. Now let me reach out to Keller and see how he's doing before we derail again.'*

'*I really do like working with you,*' Isaiah murmured. '*You're like my sister, Eden Winchester. We're not really related, but she's always been there for me.*' Was that a note of longing in his tone?

'*You do know I'm in the same zone as you guys,*' Eden drawled.

'*I do now,*' Isaiah answered cheerily. '*Hush, woman. Savannah's working.*'

Closing her eyes, Savannah took a deep breath and relaxed into her seat. This was her gift, her ability to search the innumerable threads cast out into the universe. To sense the unique vibration, in this case, caused by Keller's singular sense of honor, pride, and finely-honed rage. Until now, she'd only used her gift of sight to locate endangered dogs, cats, and other animals. Searching out a man—this particularly fierce man—was uniquely stimulating.

The image came slowly. Savannah could almost smell the silk of black ties and starch peculiar to her Secret Agent Man. '*I see him now. He's on his feet, but he's not moving. He isn't breathing, either. He's tense. Poised...*"That was the best word for the aura radiating off Keller. '*He's inside a trailer, holding his breath as if... Oh dear, he's got both pistols up and... He's going to kill someone,*' Savannah breathed. '*Keller's been shot, Isaiah, and now he's.... he's defending someone, something. I can't get a clear reading on—*'

'*Do you have his location?*' Isaiah asked.

'*He's outside a long green barn, no, it's a garage. Fontenette's antique car collection is stored there.*'

'*Narrow it down, Savannah,*' Eden snapped. '*I need more than that before we go in. I need a landmark. Fontenette's spread is littered with green barns and—*' Her tone changed. '*No, Boss. I'm talking to Savannah Church, not you. Hold up a second.*'

The images in Savannah's mind expanded to include Special Agent Tucker Chase as well as several other officers, all armed, all seated inside a large black FBI van idling on the paved road near the mansion. Four other FBI vans were parked near them while an army of SWAT and special agents executed the warrant. Several more agents patrolled all the exits. The entire group moved like precision clockwork, as if this were simply a drill they were practicing.

Just as quickly as the picture expanded, Savannah narrowed it down on Keller. '*I'm seeing a dirt road,*' she told Eden. '*It's just ahead of you behind the mansion. In a mile or so, it branches off the paved road. There's a long green garage behind the cluster of sand pine trees along the road. The garage is hidden behind those trees, so it'll be easy to miss. Once you clear the trees, turn right, then take another sharp right.*'

'*How many men, Savannah? I need to know who and what we're facing.*'

She got the impression of Eden snapping her fingers. '*Three big guys, all armed and wearing overalls. They don't look American, though. They're wearing Carhartts. Seven, no, eight other guys, not so big, not in overalls, sneaking around and under the trailer. I count four semi-trucks with trailers attached, but Eden, these eleven guys are armed.'*

'And Keller is in...?' Again with the snapping fingers.

*'The open trailer on the end, nearest the garage,'* Savannah nearly shouted back at her.

*'What kind of weapons? ARs, pistols, shoulder cannons, or—'*

Savannah cut her off. She wasn't some prissy little girl from charm school. *'Yes, automatic rifles, and a shoulder cannon if that's what you want to call it. Personally, I call it a portable one-shot 66mm unguided Light Anti-tank Weapon, also known as a LAW. Folks, I think the guys in Carhartts are Russian. I'm seeing lots of tats on their bald skulls, some Russian lettering.'*

*'Good job, Savannah. Okay boys, we're going in hot,'* Eden purred as she relayed the intel to the agents with her. *'Let's do this and do it right. Yeah, Tuck. I know. The warrant includes all outbuildings. We're covered. Go! Go! Go!'*

Eden and Tucker's van roared past the house to the dirt road. Executing a sharp right turn, then another, they kicked up a cloud of red dust on their way to the rescue. Shots rang out. All the way from Louisiana, Savannah heard the round that struck Keller's chest. She felt him grunt at the impact. She smelled the rage in his sweat. She watched him go down.

*No, no, no!*

Flustered now, Savannah shut Eden out of her mind and cast her most fervent spell to Keller. Out loud. "For thine is the kingdom." *Deep breath.* "The power." *Then let it go....* "And the glory." She spoke sharper now, her heart pounding with zeal and enough fear to power The Big Easy during Mardi Gras. "I command you, Keller. Listen up and talk to me!"

# Chapter Thirty-Three

*Son of a bitch, that fucking hurt!* Keller damned near slapped both hands over his ears as Savannah's voice exploded inside his head. He didn't know what hurt worse, the bullet that had just ripped through his chest just short of his collarbone, or the angry woman suddenly shrieking inside his head. That was new. But out of the blue, he now had Savannah's fear coiled inside his mind like a living, breathing snake, filled with worry and rattling with love for him. WTF?

"I hear you, baby," he said out loud, not exactly sure where she was or if he were hearing things. He shook his head. This might be that singular moment when a man's life passed before his eyes, and he got to revisit all the wicked things he'd done, right before he dropped dead. That scenario actually made more sense.

Until she breathed a tremulous, *'Thank heavens, Keller. Honey, I saw you go down. How bad are you hurt? Can you breathe? Are you going to die? What can I do?'*

Yup, that was Savannah all right, scared and worried for him. But man, was any of this real? It couldn't be. He'd built strong psychic barriers. They hadn't been breached before.

"Where are you?" he asked, looking around and mad as hell she might've put herself in danger by coming after him. How'd she expect him to protect both her and the birds from all these guys with guns? "Speak to me, damn it." *Tell me you're not going to jump up and run to me and get shot and die, too.*

*'No, honey, I'm not going to get shot and die. I'm still in Louisiana, and for the first time in your life, you're speaking psychically. Do you understand what that means? You're telepathic, you'd just built so many walls, no one's been able to get through to you until now. Until me. But listen—'*

*Bullshit.* "No, you listen! Wherever you are, stay down!" This nonsense had to be the gas talking. Couldn't be Savannah. "These guys will kill you if they catch you, and they won't be nice about it."

*'I know but Keller—'*

"Stay down! Damnit, keep that pretty ass of yours down on the ground, and—where are you?"

*'KELLER! Knock it off. It's true, honey. You are telepathic, so stop arguing and talk to Tucker and*

*Eden. Isaiah would be here too, but he's home with Roxy and his baby son.'*

"What? You're really in Louisiana? I really am telepathic? But..."

*'Let your boss and Eden in,'* she demanded, her voice drill sergeant stern. *'Do it now. Hurry!'*

For the first time in his life, Keller closed his mouth and asked psychically, *'They're here? Tuck and Eden are really here?'* Like he had any idea where 'here' was. All he knew was he'd been stuck inside RJ's container with hundreds of crates of smuggled birds and maybe animals. He was sure part of that trip had been via truck, part by air, yet here he was, on land again, and not sure which time zone he was in.

*'Yes, honey. FBI agents are already inside Fontenette's mansion executing a warrant. He's already under arrest, but he's got hired guns. Talk to Eden and Tucker. Let them know how to help you take these bad dudes down. There's three Russians, eight other guys, who I'm thinking are Fontenette's local security.'*

Dudes? Russians? None of this made sense. Fontenette lived in Florida. Savannah was in Louisiana. What were Russians doing here? Keller had to know. *'Where the hell am I, Savannah? Which state?'* he asked as he sent a warning shot over the head of the seven-foot bald giant coming at him. That bastard had gotten off the lucky shot that hit Keller. He squinted past the numbing pain clouding his vision. Was that a LAW on the guy's right shoulder?

'*You're in one of four containers Bruce Fontenette shipped air freight from Louisiana to Florida earlier today. You were gassed, remember? You were on the phone with your boss when it happened. Now you're on Fontenette's estate near Jacksonville, but you need to work with Mr. Chase and Eden. Communicate with them. Let your guard down. Please, for once let someone help you. I know you can do it. I have faith in you, honey.*'

She did have faith in him. She had from the first moment he'd seen her, and... she'd called him 'honey'. Keller swallowed hard. It'd been years since any woman wasted endearments on him. It shouldn't mean so much, and it sure as hell shouldn't feel so good—but it did. If Savannah trusted him, then so be it. Which was the only reason Keller put a tentative feeler into the universe and asked, '*B-Boss? Eden? Can you guys really hear me?*'

'*Keller!*' Eden's squeal rang his bell as hard as Savannah's first words had. *My hell, that woman had a pair of lungs.* '*I hear you! Finally! Did Savannah reach you? Are you hurt? Can you hear me? Do it again, talk to me.*'

Before he could respond, some rowdy former Navy SEAL with a big mouth picked that moment to stand and deliver a burst of rat-a-tat-a-tat-a-tat-a-rat automatic rifle fire from the open side door of the FBI van. While he did, Tucker yelled, '*Damned straight I can hear you, Kell. Good to have you back.*'

Just like Savannah's sweet voice and Eden's before him, Tucker's rough and ready psychic conviction reverberated inside Keller's pounding head like the unholy bells of Notre Dame. Loud. Deafening. But so damned—good—not sweet.

*'It's about Goddamned time. We're coming for you, buddy. Hang tight. We'll save you.'*

*Like hell.* No SEAL ever—EVER—saved a Ranger. Keller slouched out of his bloody shirt, keeping an eye on the fool with the LAW. Junior needed a safe place to weather the storm. With the pocket folded gently inside his shirt, Keller draped it over the nearest crate and told Savannah, *'I gotta go.'*

*'You saved a bird,'* Savannah whispered in his head, *'for me.'*

*'Yeah, sorta,'* Keller said as he patted the little guy once more. *'I knew you'd save him if you'd been here, but mostly I saved Junior for himself. He doesn't belong here.'*

*'And neither do you. I love you, Keller.'*

But that's where she was wrong. Keller did belong on this Florida battlefield with his team. No place else he'd rather be.

Wounded or not, he dropped off the rear of the trailer without another word, flexing his knees to cushion his fall, while both pistols came up on reflex. He'd taken a shot to his chest, but it was a through and through. He was bleeding, but pumped full of adrenaline. Okay, so his chest hurt. He was a Ranger. He had a job to do. Dying could wait.

Acting on instinct, he fired both pistols at the bastard aiming that POS Russian-made shoulder cannon. It took four center mass shots before the big guy fell, but when Nikita hit the dirt, he was stone-cold dead.

By then Keller knew he was a sitting duck, out in the open like he was. But he was so damned mad at the greedy world of rich, entitled sons of bitches who hired mercenaries to do their dirty work. It didn't hurt that, for the first time since he'd been dragged into Deuces Wild, Keller respected the team around him. Some FBI. Some FWS. All felt like brothers and sisters in arms.

He caught Eden's eye, and it happened just like it used to happen in Iraq and Afghanistan. He, Eden, and Tucker became one. They moved in sync, covering each other's backs as if they'd worked a lifetime together and knew each other's moves and strategies. Damned straight. This was what soldiers did. As if he needed to prove his point, Keller mowed down the other two bald guys who thought they could shoot Eden in the back. *Cowards.*

*'Thanks, Keller. Watch your left,'* she reported as she smoothly took out one, two, then three of the armed men scrambling out from beneath the trailer.

Keller slid to one knee in the gravel, crouching like an Old West gunslinger, and, with the pistol in his right hand, he gut-shot the assassin beneath the trailer who'd taken aim at Tucker, while at the same time,

Keller leveled the pistol in his left and nailed the target Eden called out. Two more down. *Hoo-rah!*

Man, he'd missed this type of teamwork, the coordinated professional takedown of creeps out to ambush federal agents. He loved the smell of gunpowder in the air. Even the coppery scent of spilled blood. Cordite. Ozone!

The whump-whump-whump of an FBI chopper overhead drowned out the final shot Tucker got in. Another asshole on his way to meet his Maker, Keller didn't care if he was Russian or local talent. Tucker fired again and again. By the time the smoke cleared, all mercs were down. Fontenette, eleven dead or wounded assholes. Deuces Wild, zip. It didn't get any better than this.

Still holding both smoking hot firearms, still poised for attack and edgy as hell, Keller listened for Savannah's sweet voice in his head. She'd grown silent, not that he could hear much over the rush of battle and the blood thrumming in his ears. Or with his heart hammering a mile a minute. Silence was always the first casualty in war.

*'We clear?'* he asked his psychic teammates as he quartered the kill zone, alert for just one twitch, one gasp, or one gurgle out of these paid assassins. Fontenette had his nerve, hiring Russian mafia. That boy was going down.

*'Clear,'* Eden called out as she too made the rounds, ensuring all assailants were down and unarmed, but prepared to offer aid to survivors if needed. Which felt

like a bigtime foul to Keller. There was no need to waste first-aid on murderers, terrorists, or these guys. They knew the risk when they'd started this fight, and they'd drawn first blood. A kill was a kill was a kill. Keller never unsheathed his weapon unless he intended to kill someone, and when he fired, he rarely missed. A Ranger practiced at the gun range or in the live-fire house until he could hit a gnat's eye out at a thousand feet—or more. Anything less meant he'd missed. That just plain wasn't acceptable.

*'We've got a talker over here,'* Tucker told his team from where he crouched over a bloody body.

By then, the chopper had landed, its rotor wash kicking up dust and debris over the kill zone. Keller beelined to his boss, while Eden rendezvoused with the newly arrived team. More FBI agents dropped off the chopper's skids, boots on the ground and zeroing in on the bodies.

*'Who is he?'* Keller looked down at the man dying on his belly like a coward. *'Who is he?'* he asked, enjoying the fact that he now knew how to carry on psychic dialogue.

*'Says his name's Anatoly Orlov.'* Tucker nudged the guy's bloody bicep just as the man choked out a bloody clot and expired.

*'What'd he tell you, Boss?'*

Tucker looked up at Keller, a funny twinkle in his eye. There it was again, time stopping in its tracks. Keller looked down at Tucker, fully aware that was the first time he'd respected Tucker enough to call him Boss.

Tucker closed one eye, zeroing in on Keller with his other, his dominant eye. His shooting eye. *'He said we're too late. You know what he's talking about?'*

*'I sure don't, but three of these guys were Russian mafia. What's that about?'*

*'Fontenette's into more than just smuggling wildlife. We need to see what's in the rest of those crates.'*

*'I'm on it,'* Keller replied easily.

*'Like hell you are. You're bleeding, dumbass. Sit down before you fall down.'*

There was that. Wearily, Keller folded his long legs and sat beside the dead guy but facing his boss. *'Know this sounds stupid, but it's easy to forget you're shot. Adrenaline, you know.'*

Tucker nodded. *'Trust me, I know. You done good today, but I've got a feeling we're just skating over the top of whatever this is.'* He nodded his big square chin at the trailer Keller had been holed up in all day, the one four FWS agents were now climbing into.

Night had fallen. FBI spotlights were everywhere, along with EZ-ups set up over the crime scene. Medical examiners, too. More vans and trucks as the usual FBI logistics tail arrived. Agents were everywhere, protecting evidence and battening down the scene. Taking names. Videotaping from every angle. Doing their FBI thing.

Tucker waved one of the few medics over even as he told Keller to, *'Do me a favor and go easy.'*

Keller looked sideways at his boss. *'You're all right for a SEAL,'* he said on their private channel.

Grunting to his feet, Tucker grinned. *'Don't go spreading that crap around. Some of my guys don't think I can hear what they're saying behind my back. I'd like to keep that between you and me as long as I can.'* He winked. The cocky bastard winked. But then he said, *'You know the drill. Hand 'em over, Kell.'*

*'You sure this place is secure?'* Keller asked before he relinquished his firearms.

*'Don't matter. Where you're going, guns aren't allowed.'* Tucker held out a hand.

Keller turned both pistols over. He still had the knife in his boot sheath, but it'd been a long time since he'd been unarmed. Tucker was right, though. Keller was officially off duty until after action reports were filed and he completed the prerequisite after-incident psych profile and counseling. Waste of time as far as he was concerned, but those were the rules.

"Before I go," he said out loud, pointing at the truck that had delivered him to Fontenette's. "I left a shirt in that container. There's a hummingbird in the chest pocket. He's a feisty little guy. Would you make sure he stays alive?"

"You bet. Anything else?"

"Now that you asked, would you also mind contacting Savannah? For some reason, I can't reach her. Tell her where I'm going. Tell her to call me. Where am I going by the way?"

"Memorial Hospital Jacksonville," the medic muttered through his surgical mask.

"You got it," Tucker replied. "We'll catch up with you later."

Exhausted now, Keller let the medic help him onto a nearby gurney where he all but collapsed. It felt good to get off his feet. There was no use arguing with Tuck. Keller did need a few stitches, maybe surgery. Despite the fiery wound in his chest that was all at once screaming at him, it'd been a good day. A rare day. One of those days when a tired old Ranger was damned glad to have been in the right place at the right time.

Turning his still aching head to the side, he watched Eden talk with one of the FWS agents. Man, she was a pretty woman, full of life and enthusiasm for her job. Ky Winchester had a regular spitfire on his hands. Good on him. It wasn't often married FBI agents ended up assigned to the same team, but the Winchesters seemed to be making it work. Probably because of their elite psychic status.

Looked like everything was under control, just the way it should be. Eden turned and stuck her tongue out at him. She was smiling, her big green emerald eyes alight with whatever the FWS agent was telling her. Tucker was out there walking the walk and talking the talk, making nice with the FWS people, letting them think they were in charge.

But where the hell was Savannah? She hadn't piped up, not once since the battle ended. Which was really odd after she'd encouraged Keller to reach out to his team. He'd expected she'd be worried since he'd been wounded. Not that he couldn't take care of himself, but knowing that she cared enough to reach out to him mattered.

A slow ache blossomed in the pit of Keller's stomach. He tried again, *'Savannah? You with me?'*

But no answer came back to him.

Just as quickly as his gut hurt, the pain went away. Had to be the IV the medic had swiftly initiated. Too soon waves of contentment drifted through Keller's veins, making him warm. Sleepy. Forgetful.

He blinked, trying to stay awake as long as he could. He needed to hear from Savannah before he let himself sleep. For hell's sake, where was she? The shadows seemed extra-long tonight. Extra dark. He blinked again. Something had to be wrong if Savannah couldn't reach him. He latched onto the medic's arm. "Wait. Get this IV out of me. I've got work—"

"Shut the fuck up, Boner Boniface," the medic growled as he stabbed a hypo into Keller's thigh, twisting it like a bastard. "You ain't going nowhere but to your own funeral. I've just given you my special elixir. Now lie down and die, you son of a bitch."

Keller had no choice. A thundercloud of forgetfulness swelled up and around him. Dragging him down, down, down...

# Chapter Thirty-Four

Savannah sat staring as the first cloud of fireflies lifted from the edge of the nearly deserted rest stop. It had been another long day, and she'd seen enough. It was true. Keller was right. They were from two different worlds. He belonged in Washington, DC, the heartbeat of America. He was not only good at fighting crime, he excelled at it. But her? She belonged in the bayou with her dogs, cats, and birds. With all her broken dreams.

For hours, she'd been sitting with faithful Red lounging shotgun while lazy Galahad snored from the back seat. She'd watched the gunfight on Fontenette's land unfold. She'd seen Keller turn from a closed-off, angry man into a fierce and lethal federal agent who knew precisely what he was doing. It'd been like watching a dance the way he'd transformed into a skilled warrior, the way he, Eden, and Tucker had fought with perfect synchronicity to overcome those bad guys. The three of them acted on pure instinct, advising each other who was where, covering each other's backs, not even aiming when they fired their weapons. It was as if they'd practiced for this fight. Even wounded and bleeding, Keller had morphed into the hero he was all along.

*Told you so.*

Yeah, yeah, Savannah brushed her annoying inner voice away.

Yet even it was right. There was no sense lying to herself, not when the truth stared her in the face. Like Carol Marie's ghost, Savannah realized it was time to let Keller go. His was a greater mission in life, hers the lesser. He actually saved people, and in her heart, she knew saving people mattered more than rescuing dogs. Yet here she was, the crazy dog lady of the bayou. All by herself. Totally alone. Well, except for the dogs, cats, and birds back at Sanctuary. There was a day, as in only two days ago, when loving those cast-off pets was enough. But Savannah wasn't naïve anymore. Her innocence was gone. She'd given it to Keller. Like the animals she rescued, she was now—less.

"It's time to go home," she told Red on a sigh. "I'm tired. How about you?"

When Red bumped her with the flat end of his wet nose, whining softly as if he knew she needed that kiss, Savannah swallowed past the lump in her throat. Mr. Lyle Goldenrod was due at Sanctuary bright and early in the morning. She still needed to call her insurance to get repairs going on her burned house, then the funeral home to finalize Gran Mere's celebration of life. Then...?

Who knew what she'd do next? There was still Gran Mere's crazy rambling before she'd passed to puzzle out, that something about a warlock. But Savannah was too tired to care. Keller was happier back in his element. He didn't need her. Swallowing hard, she closed her mental channel to him and the rest of his psychic FBI team. He needed to rely on them now, not her. They were his future. She was just a short-lived past.

There was no sense crying over spilled milk. Gran Mere always said that. So Savannah closed her heart as well. It was time to face facts. She didn't cry when she started the Buick.

Sliding the gear shifter into reverse, she swung her right arm over the seat and hooked a quick K-turn, backing out of the parking stall. Shifting into drive, she left the rest stop and the second hardest day of her life behind. Gran Mere always said the darkest dark was always before the brightest bright. Then there ought to be a solar flare come morning.

"I'll walk you again at the hotel," she promised Red. She'd also collect her clothes, her dirty who-she-really-was clothes and the flip-flops she'd left behind. It was time to get back to her reality. Gran Mere was gone. The houseboat too. It was as if Hurricane Katrina had come back and scrubbed everything out of Savannah's life that mattered. Even Keller.

Smoothing her palm over her thigh and the new jeans Keller had bought her, she blinked, fighting tears. The fancy underwear had to go, too. She didn't want it. Them. No mementos. No souvenirs. Just get back to work and make life a little better for some of the lowliest, yet still best of God's creatures.

Red dropped to his belly on the seat, whining.

"Again?"

One red paw landed on her wrist.

"Can't you wait? We'll be there in half an hour. I promise, we'll take a long walk then, maybe head over to the river, watch the barges. Eat a box of beignets. Cry in my beer…"

She ran a finger under her leakiest eye, not needing the reminder, but yeah. Heartbreak hurt.

Or maybe it was that mental push at the corner of her mind that she kept fighting. Might be Isaiah. Might be Eden. But then again, it might be Keller, the last person she wanted to talk to.

Gran Mere always said disappointment took time to get over. Savannah hoped she'd feel different in the morning. Maybe then she could face the man she'd given her heart to without making a fool of herself. *Yeah, and maybe pigs will fly to the moon and back, too.* Savannah tried to chuckle at that funny picture. *Pigs flying. Ha.*

But all she did was sob.

Dazed, Keller peeled his full-of-grit eyeballs open, not remembering much of where he was or how he'd gotten here. Feeling like shit. Breathing fire, and alfalfa dust, polished old wood and horseshit. Oats. Fresh cut hay. The place was dark, a dim light glowing from beyond. He couldn't make his eyes see far enough. Even the ceiling looked dark and fuzzy. His chest hurt damned bad, but his gut hurt worse.

A horse neighed from somewhere a little too close and personal, then a velvet soft lip fluttered over his face, tasting his nose and cheeks. Prickly, short, stiff whiskers scraped his forehead. The animal nudged his head like it was trying to wake him. He forced his eyes wider, but all they seemed capable of seeing was a blurry dark shape hovering over him.

"Where am I?" he asked, batting at the worrisome gnats gathering near his mouth. Pressing his lips together, Keller swiped the drool. Flies. Open mouth. Yuck. Not a good combination.

More neighing. More hooves clomping. The muted jingle of halters nearby. Gradually, a long equine snout came into clearer view.

"Hey, bee-you-ti-ful," Keller said to the horse, his tongue too thick to sound intelligent.

Beautiful stared down at him. The animal's eyes were soft and liquid as she, he, or it nuzzled him like he might be edible. The horse had long eyelashes that made it look as sleepy and dopey as Keller felt.

"G'wan," he mumbled, forcing himself up, his elbows digging into the board he was on. Shit. He really was in a barn, bleeding and all.

The horse nudged him again.

"Yer buggin' me," Keller told his persistent new friend. Dizzy and disoriented, he took his time swinging both feet off the board and down to the floor. The blood gushing down his chest worried him, but he sure as hell was not going to fall. He might never get back up again.

But if he kept bleeding, he wouldn't get far once he was on his feet. He'd bleed to death. Damn, it was hard to think. Summoning his inner Ranger, Keller swallowed hard, took a deep breath—that hurt like a son of a bitch—then shoved off the plank. Whoever'd done this to him was sure to come back. He didn't intend to be here.

"Bye, horse," he muttered as he angled around the big horse's glossy chestnut butt.

*Chestnut.* That rang a bell. Keller backed up to face the animal. Sure enough. It was Sand Dollar, Fontenette's winning racehorse. "Aren't you s'posed to be in Bal-ti-more, Mar-y-lynnnn..." Keller shook his head and tried again. "Mary-land-d-d? At the Preak-Preak-Preak-ness-s-s-s-s-s?" Damn it was hard to spit that word out, harder to make his brain function.

Sand Dollar lowered his forehead into Keller's sore chest and huffed out a snort. Tired of standing, Keller looped both hands over Sand Dollar's neck and hugged the magnificent animal. Chest throbbing or not, he needed something to hold onto.

"I'm tired, Sandy," he whispered, "but I gotta get moving or someone's gonna be back soon and…" He forgot what he was going to say. "Whatever. Whatcha think? You coming with me? You game?"

Damned if Sand Dollar didn't nicker like he agreed. Either that or he'd complained because he smelled blood. Keller certainly could. He was losing enough of it. He had to move. No, *they* had to move. Soon.

Fighting a druglike lethargy that turned his brain, feet, legs, and arms into lead weights, Keller twisted one hand into the thick roots at the base of Sandy's long silky mane. At the same time, he hung his arm over the stall gate and fumbled to open it. Ordinarily, it would've been easy. The lock that kept the horse secure was a simple wooden two-part hasp.

But damned if the narrow pin that slid into the wooden arm wasn't as heavy as Keller's head. His fingers were just as thick and twice as heavy. He couldn't make his digits flexible enough to hold the board. By the time he finagled it out of its arm, he wasn't sure he'd live long enough to escape. Too many shadows danced around him. Everything was just too much.

Patient Sandy—and that was weird all by itself. High strung racehorses weren't known for patience. Yet this guy stood as meek as a lamb the whole time Keller dragged his sorry ass over and finessed himself into a half-vertical, half-falling-off sitting position on the horse's back. It took long enough, and a stirrup and saddle would've been nice. Reins. A rope would've been better. Keller could've tied himself to Sandy's neck then. But time was running out, and he didn't have time or a rope and... Shit. They had to *move it, move it, move it!*

"Giddy up," Keller breathed, his voice so weak he could barely hear himself. Thumping the horse's ribs with legs that felt more like rigid two-by-fours, he whispered, "Hurry. We gotta get outta here."

Sandy took the hint. As soon as he cleared the wide-open door at the darker end of the stable, Keller leaned to the left, toward darker shadows and less yard light. Sandy seemed to understand and headed left. Good enough. It was strange looking down on everything, though. Keller was a good six feet seven, and Sandy was all legs. The height added to Keller's sickening sense of vertigo. Holding onto that silken handful of mane, he tilted forward, content to hug the horse if that kept him in the saddle.

The fresh air helped clear his head. A little. But a wounded man would only get so far, and Keller knew it. He sucked in a belly full of night time, needing a dark place to hide and rest a while. Thinking he could handle more speed, he kicked Sand Dollar into a trot, then a canter.

Too soon the going got rough, and the wicked hole in his chest got the best of Keller. He could barely breathe. Something in his gut twisted. Already leaning to the left, he felt himself slipping.

"Take me to Savannah," he told his mighty beast. "Quick. She'll know what to do."

Sandy kept moving. The night got darker. The wind got cooler. Colder.

Keller never felt a thing. He was already unconscious when he fell.

# Chapter Thirty-Five

Savannah had retrieved her few things from the bedroom at the Ritz earlier tonight. That was harder than she'd expected. Just seeing the mussed bed sheets where she and Keller had made the sweetest, tenderest love shredded her already aching heart. But dutifully and resolutely, she'd changed into her old clothes, then neatly folded the items Keller had bought for her and left them in the shopping bag they'd come in. She didn't need those fancy underwear either, so she left them behind. Plain cotton panties were more her style. Nothing special, like her.

She left a thank you note and a tip for Roger Tanner on the counter for all he'd done for her dogs. But she left no note of goodbye for Keller. Just took her dogs and left. He'd understand. This was what he'd wanted all along. They didn't belong together. It was easier this way. He wouldn't have to face her now. She wouldn't have to face him. The end. Roll credits. Goodbye.

Yet something nagged at the back of her mind, knock, knock, knocking at the mental barrier she'd locked up tight and thrown away the key to. That barrier. The only thing that stood between her and Keller. Try as hard as she might, Savannah couldn't sleep once she'd gone home to Sanctuary.

The entire house stunk of smoke. She wished she'd at least called someone in to clean it while she'd foolishly taken off with Keller. That would've been smart, but apparently, Savannah was not very bright.

Yet she knew the pervasive, pungent odor of smoke wasn't keeping her awake. It was more of a feeling, a sense of something wrong in the universe. It was a presence. Holy Mother, it was him. The warlock! That was who'd crept into the back of her mind. He was the naysayer she'd been unconsciously listening to since... since... She had to stop and think. The whispers had all started the day Gran Mere passed.

Savannah struck out at her unwanted psychic visitor. *'What do you want?'*

*'Is Keller with you?'* Isaiah asked, his tone unexpectedly sharp.

Savannah sat straight up in bed. *'Ooops. I thought you were someone else. No. Wasn't he with you guys?'*

*'Who'd you think I was?'*

*'Umm, no one, I mean...'* She stalled, suddenly embarrassed for running off like she had. *'It's just that I'm pretty sure someone's been stalking me, as in*

*psychically stalking me, and Gran Mere warned me about a warlock, only... never mind. Shouldn't Keller be at a hospital?'*

*'We thought he was, but he never arrived, and no one there knows the medic who drove away with Keller.'*

*'But he's shot. Surely he's at another local clinic or—'*

*'He's not, Savannah.'* That stern voice was Eden. *'And he's not responding to our attempts to reach him, either. I was sure he'd contact you when we were finished back at the stables. Why haven't you heard from him?'*

Savannah couldn't reply. Worry for Keller had closed her throat.

*'What happened with you?'* Isaiah asked, accusation in his tone. *'One minute you were with us, the next you checked out. You stopped talking to everyone. You vanished.'*

*Well, yeah...*

*'Was it something I said?'* Eden asked. *'Because I know I get direct and bossy when I'm—"*

*'No, it wasn't that. It was...'* Savannah tried again. *'It was watching you guys in action. I finally saw the real Keller. He truly loves what he does for a living, doesn't he? He is who he is, and I don't want to stand in his way. I'm just—'*

*'The woman he loves,'* Isaiah said gently. *'Savannah, yes Keller is the best of the best. He can't help but throw his soul into his job, but you're his*

*heart. He needs you in his life, and we need you to find him. Reach out. Don't let him go, not like this.'*

'Okay,' she said quietly. She'd never felt so small nor so foolish before in her life. Where had her self-confidence gone? Her positivity? She, with all her special *inner sight,* hadn't seen the real Keller after all. Yet, she'd thought she had during that fight. Who was messing with her head? Was there really such a thing as a warlock or had she simply felt sorry for herself?

Closing her eyes, Savannah forced her fluttering heart to calm, and then opened her mind back up to the universe. *'Keller,'* she called out. *'Answer me, honey. Talk to me. Everyone's worried about you. Tell me where you are.'*

A muffled *'Can't'* came back to her instantly. *'Where... where you been, baby?'*

What could she say? *'I've been wrong, Keller. I thought you'd be better off without me, but now I know better. We belong together. Where exactly are you?'*

*'Shhhh. Too tired. Too sick. Gotta sssssleep now.'*

*'But you're supposed to sleep with me,'* she scolded gently. Lovingly. *'I need you to come home, Keller. Tell me where you are and I'll send someone to help you.'*

*'With S-S-Sandy,'* he whispered. *'Gotta be quiet. They might hear us.'*

*'Keep him talking,'* Isaiah murmured. *'I've almost located his position.'*

'*I love you, Keller,*' Savannah declared, tears glimmering at what distancing herself had done to him.

'*Know you do, baby. Never doubted… you… one in a million.*'

Yet she had doubted him.

'*Hard men don't know how to express their feelings, Savannah,*' Eden murmured. '*They aren't in touch with their feminine side. Trust me. It took Ky a long time before he let it slip. Now he says it all the time. Keller loves you. I can tell. He'll get around to it.*'

'*Shhhh. Someone's comin'.*' The mental link evaporated and he was gone.

'*Keller! Keller! Don't leave me!*' Savannah cried. She'd never felt so desperate, nor so foolish for letting him go. For leaving him when he'd needed her.

'*He didn't leave you, Savannah. He's been drugged again,*' Eden said. '*I'm sensing cocaine. Ketamine. Something else, only not narcotic. I can't get a decent feel for it. Not even sure which is in him, and which is in the horse.*'

But Savannah knew better. '*He's bleeding. I could smell it. Whoever's got him is letting him bleed to death. He's weak. If we can't get to him in time—*'

'*Got him,*' Isaiah growled. '*Hang in there, Savannah. Tucker, can you hear me?*' Silence reigned while Isaiah listened to his boss. Then, '*Good to know. Listen, he's about twenty miles south of Fontenette's stables on a neighboring horse farm, McGinty's Rainbow. That's why we couldn't locate Sand Dollar at Champion Stables when we served the warrant. Fontenette moved him to McGinty's because—'*

'Sand Dollar's been doped, too,' Eden said. 'They're giving him ketamine to keep him quiet.'

Which didn't make sense. Why anesthetize an animal you needed to win a race?

'Exactly,' Isaiah replied. 'Go, Tuck. Go get Keller. He's passed out, but Sand Dollar's with him. If that horse keels over...'

'Hold on, I'll guide you there, Boss,' Eden said, her voice rapping higher. 'Tell me when you see McGinty's gate sign over his driveway. Are you there yet?' A beat of silence, then, 'Damn it, Boss, can't you drive any faster?'

Savannah could hear Eden's fingernails tapping impatiently all the way from Florida while they waited for Tucker to travel from Champion Stables to McGinty's.

'You're going to need QuikClot and pressure bandages when you get there,' Isaiah advised. 'He's in bad shape. Chest wound. But something else is going on with him. I can hear it in his gut and in his lungs. Okay, yeah, I get it. Yes, I know. You're no pansy-assed civilian. Just the same, I'm sending real medics to your location to transport this time. They're on their way. ETA in fifteen, can you be there by then?'

Savannah couldn't find the words to express her gratitude to these people she didn't really know. These same three professionals were working in tandem to rescue Keller. If it were one of their lives on the line, he'd be doing the same. He'd be just as cool, calm, and steady, ready to charge into battle and do all he could.

The same wicked self-doubt that assailed her before crept back into her mind asking, *'What could Keller possibly see in you? Get out of his way. Let him be all he can be. You're not fit for Washington, DC, girl. That's where he belongs. Not you. You're nothing but poor Southern trash.'*

*Girl?* For the first time, Savannah listened to the unique intonation behind those nasty words. She'd heard it before, at the Waffle House and earlier today when she'd blocked Keller and his team during the shootout. She'd been raised by her beloved Gran Mere to be positive and kind and cheerful, yet today she'd succumbed to an uncharacteristic bout of self-pity that she would not stand for.

*'Who are you,'* she asked the demon who'd been sneaking around in her head, lying to her, making her think she was less of a human being for loving Keller. *'RJ? Is that you?'*

She sensed immediate withdrawal as if someone had slammed a door. Aware and forearmed now, she told Eden, *'I need your help.'*

*'You got it, sister. What's up?'*

*Sister.* That special word brought a rush of tears to Savannah's eyes. She'd always wanted to be more than just a cast-off child, but to be someone's sister? It was more than she'd expected. *'I... I've been shadowed.'*

*'You've got a troll,'* Isaiah stated. *'Sorry, but I sort of scanned your mental synapsis while we were*

*talking. You're right. I'm not sure who the guy inside your head is, but he's not nice. Could he be the warlock your Gran Mere told you about?'*

Of course, Isiah would've seen that. He also had uncommon sight.

Gran Mere's final words flowed back into Savannah's mind like molasses in summertime, warming her as only her great grandmother's gentle kindness could. It felt as if she were actually there in the bedroom with her, whispering again, *'Let me go, Savannah. Look for the wild rose that grow best deep in the bayou. Watch for the warlock. He holds a black magic in his heart that only you can overcome. You hold the key to bring him down, my dearest. Whatever happens, be fearless and strong. Be the blessing the world needs more than it ever needed me. Hold fast to the rose.'*

*'I'm fairly certain RJ is the troll who's been shadowing me. That's his style, whisper lies when you're most vulnerable. But he's no warlock. Gran Mere used to say he was more of a pipsqueak than a man. He's smart, but he lacks sight.'*

*'And you're already the blessing the world needs, but who's the rose?'* Eden asked.

*'I think we all know who,'* Isaiah whispered.

Savannah understood then. *'Keller. He's the rose, because...'* That night in her boat. He'd been relaxed. Calm. Laid-back but possessed with an other-worldly type of calm. Out of the corner of her eye, she'd watched how his chest had swelled with every deep breath he'd taken. How languid his muscles had become. He'd relaxed. For that singular moment in his hectic FBI world, he'd been utterly at peace and serene and—home. Keller not only enjoyed the unique tranquility of life in the bayou, he drew power from it. It was his safe place.

And her Secret Agent Man talked with trees. The clues had been there all this time. Keller Boniface was the wild rose that grew best deep in the bayou. She couldn't speak it. Yet her heart screamed it. *Keller. I love Keller and I'll die for him, too.*

*'Well, okay then,'* Eden said brightly. *'Now, let's focus on Tuck getting to Keller in time, then, you bet, Isaiah and I will hunt this troll down for you and we'll nail his ass.'*

Obviously, she and Isaiah had heard everything, even her memories, but Savannah didn't care. Keller already knew she loved him. A sob choked out of her throat. It hurt knowing she'd done nothing to deserve these federal agents care and understanding, yet here they were, Keller's friends, ready to die for—

*'Your friends,'* Isaiah corrected.

*'You don't have to deserve love to receive it,'* Eden murmured confidentially. *'I think you already know that.'*

*'I do.'* Because I love Keller despite the wall he's built to keep me out.

*'Come on now,'* Isaiah soothed. *'Be fearless and strong like your Gran Mere said you—'*

*'Will you guys knock it off?'* Tucker bellowed. *'I've got him, Savannah. I've got Kell. He's cold and he's weak, but this man's too damned proud and too tough to die, so stop whining. He's Army for God's sake. He's been through worse crap than this little shitty hole in his chest.'*

Savannah winced. She hadn't been able to tune in on Tucker but she saw him clearly now. The man was an imposing sight, sitting on the ground like an angry giant, his legs straight out, and Keller's top half prone across his lap. Tucker's hands and fingers moved by rote over the wound in his chest as if he'd doctored other men before.

*'Something else is going on with him, Boss,'* Isaiah cut in. *'It's in his gut and lungs. I can hear it.'*

*'Copy that,'* Tucker answered. *'He's not breathing right.'*

Tucker's face glistened with sweat, and his heartbeat thumped loud in his chest. He and several other FBI agents had run all the way from his SWAT vehicle to where Sand Dollar still stood swaying on unsteady feet. Keller lay unconscious, his head to the side, his eyes closed and oblivious to his rescue.

*'He's going to make it,'* Eden whispered encouragingly. *'Have faith in that man of yours.'*

*'I do,'* Savannah replied even as she bit her lip. He was so gray, and there was so much sticky, wet blood on his chest and arm. And that thing Isaiah detected in his chest. She heard it too. Was she too late?

Tucker's lips were pressed thin with determination. His coal black eyes glistened while the other agents cornered Sand Dollar. Savannah never felt more certain that this brash man whom Keller hadn't liked from the get-go, would die before he let Keller die. Which only made her sob more. Keller wasn't the kind of man to love her, only to leave her behind. It just wasn't in him. She knew that now. Eden was right. He would come around. It was Savannah's job to love him until he did.

*'I got you, buddy,'* Tucker kept saying as real medics wheeled a gurney and a large medical case on wheels over the lumpy Florida grass to where he sat. *'Trust me, Kell. You belong here. The team needs you. I need you, and I got you.'*

'And *I need you,'* Savannah breathed to the man she loved with her whole heart. *'I need you so much, Keller. Please don't leave me.'*

*'He ain't going nowhere,'* Tucker growled deep in his throat as both young medics knelt at his side, instantly triaging Keller's condition, talking into the two-way radios pinned to their shoulders. Barking orders. Initiating IVs. Saline solution. An antibiotic. The FBI SWAT helicopter hovered overhead, spotlighting the scene. Poor tranquilized Sand Dollar moved closer to where Tucker still held onto Keller. The goofy horse seemed just as out of it as Keller.

"Sir, excuse me," one medic said to Tucker, "but we've got him now. You can let go."

"You'd better take damned good care of my agent," Tucker growled, his dark eyes lethal, "or so help me—"

*'Tuck, let him go,'* Isaiah interjected. *'These guys are the real deal. They're honest medics. You're in their way, Boss. Let them do their job.'*

Swallowing hard, his rigid throat muscles contracting, Tucker muttered to Keller, "I'll be right behind you, Kell. All the way. Don't do anything stupid."

*'I have got to get to Florida,'* Savannah murmured as the medics wheeled Keller to the waiting ambulance.

*'Count on it,'* Isaiah said easily. *'There's a jet on standby at Louis Armstrong National Airport. Call a cab. It can leave as soon as you arrive.'*

*'But I have no money.'*

*'But I do. Stop worrying. It's my jet. Tell the cabbie to call me,'* Isaiah rattled off a phone number, *'and I'll make it worth his trouble.'*

*'But I have two dogs with me, and appointments I have to keep tomorrow, and—'*

*'Savannah, stop with the buts,'* Eden murmured. *'It's Isaiah's private plane. Bring the dogs. And all those appointments can wait. Keller can't. People will understand. We've got your six, sister. Now call a cab, tell them you'll be transporting two well-behaved dogs with you, and get your butt on that plane.'*

*'Okay, I will.'* Savannah nodded though she knew no one could see her. It felt profoundly different having this team of psychic warriors at her back.

Maybe that job offer Isaiah wanted to talk to her about wasn't such a far-fetched idea. *'Director Chase, can you hear me?'*

A curt *'What now?'* came back to her.

*'When you get to the hospital, please tell Keller that I... I love him, and I don't care if me and all my dogs have to move to Washington, DC, I'll do anything to be with him.'*

The ornery man growled, *'Tell him yourself. He's not going anywhere.'*

She was beginning to love this crazy psychic Deuces Wild team. Even Tucker Chase.

# **Chapter Thirty-Six**

Keller stretched his back gingerly as the lovely scent of lilacs floated over him. Had to be a dream. In that dream, Savannah came to him softly, her gentle fingers a soothing balm smoothing over his blistering forehead. He reached for her. She reached for him, intertwining her fingers with his. Kissing his fingertips. Nuzzling his cheek. Loving him like she always did.

Keller wasn't sure which dream was real, this one with Savannah in it or the one with the horse.

"I'm real, my silly Secret Agent Man," she whispered in his ear, her breath the sweetest scent a man could ask for. Beg for. Die for.

But his eyelids were too thick and too heavy to lift. He couldn't make his mouth speak, and his mind was already drifting away from him. From Savannah.

Complex thinking was impossible. All he could tell her was, *'Stay. Please. Stay.'*

*'I'm here, honey, and I'm never leaving you again. Not ever.'*

The fire in his chest roared to life. *'Stay,'* he told her as his fingers slipped out of hers.

*'Always,'* she breathed into his mind even while she gathered his limp hand between her beautiful breasts and pressed a kiss to his forehead. *'I'm calling your doctor. Something's not right.'*

*'Yeah. Sure.'* Whatever. Keller drifted then. Fevered. Angry. Sore and thirsty...

Back in Louisiana, Doctor Rudy John had a plan. The Preakness had come and gone, as had the mighty Bruce Fontenette and that waste of time and money, Sand Dollar. Stupid horse. If it hadn't been for the wiles of Doctor Rudy John and the elixirs he manufactured out of his plain-looking little country clinic, that horse never would've won the Derby. Never would've made Fontenette the hot shit he'd thought he was, either.

Fontenette's scheme to flood the markets with rare, exotic birds had been harebrained at best. Wealthy, grasping men who fancied themselves presidential material should stick to what they knew best, instead of thinking they knew it all. Especially when it came to dabbling in black markets. Bruce had money all right, just not enough brains to understand the intricacies of gentle, but firm mental manipulation in the underworld business. It wasn't the stock market. It was a thousand times worse. Meaner. Bloodier.

The underworld was where men like Doctor Rudy John thrived. He smiled at how quickly he'd reduced Fontenette to an outlaw, while distracting him from the true power broker behind the scenes. RJ never planned for all those pretty little sparkly birds to live.

Too well he knew the secret underbelly of illegal smuggling. He also knew how to act dumb while sniffing out a wealthy client's weakness, how to exact the best bargains while cheating your suppliers and your buyers.

That was where Fontenette fell short. He thought his fame and wealth translated into street cred. Dumb ass. All it did was make him an easy mark. Rudy John pegged him right from the start. The fancy Southern gentleman considered himself above the law and out of the reach of moral accountability. His greed and thirst for power, to be better than all other elite millionaires, made him easy to manipulate.

He'd wanted an idiot to lick his boots, say *'yes, suh'* and *'no, suh.'* So, RJ had stepped on up and acted the part. Why not? He'd been acting since he was nuthin' but a wet behind the ears youngster up in Turkey Creek. It paid well then, and it was going to pay handsomely now. Just not how Fontenette expected.

Smiling to himself and as smug as a bloodsucking tick stuck to a mama coonhound's dripping wet teat,

RJ snapped shut the wide mouth of his restocked and newly filled-to-the-brim medical bag. The race wasn't always to the fastest. No sirree Bob.

Doctor Rudy John was not the dummy folks thought he was, either. All those greedy rich folks who thought they could own birds so endangered that they only lived in limited populations in the rarified altitudes and valleys of the Andes, would've gotten quite the surprise. They'd ordered those birds sight unseen, but that wasn't what they would've got. It wasn't what those FBI agents back in Florida thought they had now, either. Almost made a man shiver with glee. Yes sirree Bob.

Doctor Rudy John was nothing short of a genius. A mastermind. Hell, he actually might rule the world at the end of the day—this day! For once, people would cringe when they heard his name. He couldn't wait.

Because he knew what they didn't. The special gas he'd concocted to keep those smuggled birds quiet was also alive with a rare strain of avian flu that came with a two-week incubation period. Once inhaled, it promised slow and bloody disintegration of an animal's lungs. And those pretty birds had been inhaling it for days. Better yet, it only took one breath to pass the contagion from bird to beast to human. There was no cure, no antidote, because he hadn't made one. Why spoil perfection? This was a dream come true. A chance to purge the earth and start again, only this time Doctor Rudy John would be king. Or God.

The original plan had been for Fontenette to transfer ownership of those hummingbirds to his elitist, millionaire friends and their snobbish wives. Once they fell ill, they'd contact their doctors to come save them and their friends to come cry over them. They contact their families. It'd be impossible to trace the point of origin of the virus by then. The contagion would spread, killing the rich and powerful first, then filtering down to the working classes. Their maids. Their pool boys. Their waitstaff.

But plan B would work just as well. Maybe faster now that Fish and Wildlife had quarantined Fontenette's inventory. If even one of those tiny, germ enhanced birds escaped...

Doctor Rudy John couldn't suppress the smile that crinkled his amazing, but itchy goatee. It was officially too late. There was no way to contain the virus now. He stroked his chin, petting himself and thinking, *'Look out, America. You folks are about to witness some real magic now.'* And he didn't even have to be there to make it happen.

Hefting the medical bag in his right hand, RJ hung the CLOSED sign in his clinic window for the last time. The sun didn't set until well after seven these days. It was spring, and he had a plane to catch. He couldn't be late. He was going... somewhere. Oh yeah. He was going back to Florida. Though precisely where and why...? Well, he couldn't exactly remember. He had a lot on his mind, but he did have business back in Bruce

Fontenette's kingdom. Important business. Yes sirree Bob.

The only fly in the ointment was that he didn't own old lady Church's land. No matter how hard he'd tried, he'd never gotten close enough to Savannah Church to ask for a date much less her hand in marriage.

*That's too bad...*

Yup, damned shame the way things worked out sometimes, but that was the risk of playing. You only won if you risked losing, and RJ didn't plan to lose again.

That Fed, that FBI agent, that self-righteous prick, Special Agent Keller Boniface? It'd taken Doctor Rudy John a couple hours dwelling on that guy, worrying and ruminating on where he'd known Boniface from. But it'd finally come to him outta the clear blue sky, yes sir, just like a bolt of hundred-proof moonshine. The guy's last name should've been his first clue.

*Yes, it should have been...*

But RJ'd been so preoccupied plying Savannah with his best, most sincere compassion at her Gran Mere's passing that he'd missed the connection. Damned if that snotty Northerner was none other than Queen Elaine's bastard offspring without the twang. Pretty boy had gone and got hisself a haircut and an education. Probably had a real college degree in a golden frame on his wall and everything. That was why RJ hadn't recognized Boniface.

'Course, Queen Elaine always claimed she'd been legally married to the drunk when she birthed the boy, but RJ was past believing that lying bitch. Queen Elaine was as uppity as her son, just not as smart. She ought to stick to what she knew best, her needles and her voodoo dolls, her setting folks against each other. That was what she was good at, stabbing folks in the back while kissing their asses and making them think someone else had it out for them instead of her. That nothing was her fault when everything that went bad in Turkey Creek eventually led back to Queen Elaine. She really was a witch, just not a magical one.

Damn! Where'd that come from? RJ smoothed his hand over his head at the sudden sting. Must've been a hornet. Sure felt like a big one.

Locking the front door of his practice behind him, RJ strolled to his late model Ford, tossed the bag in through the open window to the back seat, and climbed behind the wheel. Damned shame about Miss Church, though. He hadn't done a thing to her, well, other than whisper his dark black magic into her empty head long enough to make her believe she weren't no better than other folks. He hadn't even gotten to the good stuff when he'd lost his connection with her, and she'd slipped away. Which had to mean she was dead by now. That was the only thing that made sense. Well, good. Savannah deserved what she got.

Doctor Rudy John always kept his ability to get inside other people's heads a secret. Why share? Seemed what folks didn't know, *would* hurt them. Ha!

But the possibility of Savannah dropping dead made a smart man wonder. What if Queen Elaine's bullshit black magic really worked? RJ knew Queen Elaine murdered Carol Marie all them years ago. 'Course, he knew. Doctor Scratch, the quack who'd given Queen Elaine the poison, was RJ's old man. And RJ'd been there that day. He'd seen Elaine slap Keller square across his smug I'm-in-the-Army-now, you-can't-touch-me face when he'd accused her of murdering his wife. RJ'd seen Keller pull back, his arm cocked and his eyes hard like he wanted to murder his ma. By then, blood poured down Keller's cheek from one of his ma's gaudy rings.

The only thing that stopped him that day was poor dead Carol Marie. One glance back at her, and he'd gathered her up and took off running for big-city help.

Now that he thought about it, RJ wouldn't put it past Queen Elaine to have put a hex on Savannah, too. That actually made sense. Elaine might've already stabbed one of her ugly handmade voodoo dolls full of pins, all the while whispering her spells and her lies, cursing and killing Savannah with black magic.

RJ snorted. *What the hell am I thinking?* Her highness Queen Elaine Boniface was nothing but a big fat fake. If Savannah had dropped dead, it only meant that true love had once again struck Boniface—in the face. Bastard had to be dead by now, didn't he?

*Yes, he should be, but just in case...*

Doctor John patted the medical bag at his side lovingly. Yup, no way Boniface could've survived what

RJ had personally pumped into his chest. Damned straight. He'd been more than pleased to drag Boniface by one leg out of the ambulance and into that stall. Made RJ the bigger, better man for a change, and that alone was priceless. Boniface was bleeding plenty by then. Too bad Sand Dollar hadn't stepped on him. That would've been a helluva great way to die, stomped to death by another old nag. Ha!

But no matter. Bleeding to death by an incurable flu bug would work just as well.

*Jacksonville...*

Oh yeah, RJ remembered now. He was going to Jacksonville. Yes sirree Bob.

Pulling away from his parking place, RJ stepped on the gas and headed west toward the airport. Man, them folks at the Center for Disease Control were running out of time—if the Fish and Wildlife folks had even called them yet. Who knew? Maybe his clever little virus worked faster than he thought. Maybe all them birds and them do-gooder folks who wanted to save the world were already dead. A man could hope.

The miles passed and the sun dipped low in the west. It was one of those rare, perfect Louisiana days when everything had gone right for a change. Traffic was reasonably light. The sky overhead was darn near blue instead of smoggy or hazy gray. There weren't a cloud in the sky. Even the humidity hovered at a decent, breathable level. If only he owned Gran Mere's property. That was what he'd wanted out of her crappy little houseboat—the title to her land.

Sanctuary would've made the perfect location for another clinic, maybe a laboratory, butted up against the Pearl River Wildlife Management Area like it was. No one would've bothered him while he worked on his elixirs and spells there. It was secluded. Private. He could've lived like a hermit while he manufactured more special combinations. More viruses. More death.

That was what RJ craved, to see humankind brought to its knees for a change. All them dogs, cats, and birds Savannah left behind would've made perfect lab rats. They were already trapped in cages and kennels. She'd kept them healthy, clean, and fed. In just months, he could've been rich, and no one would've been wiser. Hell, he might even mix up another batch. Only he'd sell this one. It'd be the antidote. Folks would have to pay if they wanted to live.

If they couldn't, well, he weren't any different than most pharmaceutical companies in the world now, was he? They over-charged for life-saving drugs all the time, and, boo hoo, people who couldn't afford to pay, died. Who cared? Not the rich bastard CEOs of those multi-billion-dollar enterprises. Not elected officials or law enforcement neither. Not even the bully machine out of Hollywood cared unless one of them got infected. *Hmmm. Infect Hollywood.* That idea actually felt—perrrrrr-fect. Yup. Everyone would know his name then.

But RJ needed to get his hands on Sanctuary first. The area was desolate enough, which had made it ideal for Savannah's stinking dog pound. She thought she'd rehabilitated feral dogs and cats? That'd be the day. All she'd done was stick her uppity nose in other folk's business, then act all high and mighty cuz she'd gotten her way and took their property from 'em. But RJ knew she'd only gotten what she'd wanted cuz of who Gran Mere really was. Scary, that was what. Scary powerful.

*No, she wasn't!*

RJ rubbed a quick hand over his chest at the sudden twinge that always came with the thought of Gran Mere's powerful name. He'd only messed with her the one time she'd caught him with a crack pipe. He'd blubbered like a stuck pig that day, trying to convince her it was his first time, that he'd never do it again. 'Course, she fell for it, even gave him the benefit of the doubt. But then she cursed him was what she did. Every time he even thought of lighting up and melting some rocks, his chest hurt like he was having a heart attack, only he knew better. He was a bonafide physician, after all. He had science on his side. It weren't no heart attack. It was Gran Mere's curse.

With the sun glaring through his windshield, RJ made his way across Jefferson bridge, over the levee and past the rice paddies. Cranking the wheel, he passed the chewed-up plot where Gran Mere's houseboat used to stand. Good riddance to that garbage scow.

Yet she'd been another surprise, maybe even what you could call a damned rude awakening. RJ had no idea the old bag owned as much land as she had when she'd passed. Who knew she'd lived like a pauper while she squirreled away hundreds of thousands of dollars? Right under his nose, too. Must've been why Savannah always seemed to have whatever she wanted. The best part of Gran Mere's property. All them gadgets to keep her precious Sanctuary secure. That boat—

*Damn them both to hell!*

Yup, damn them women both to hell, and damn Fontenette, too. The houseboat should've been RJ's. That was the deal, his ketamine in exchange for the boat and Savannah. But Fontenette went and got hisself raided by the FBI. Must've shot his big mouth off to the wrong folks. How else would the FBI have known what Bruce was up to?

RJ still hadn't figured that one out. Those birds were Fontenette's first foray into illegal smuggling. It usually took years of backdoor sales and a shit load of investigative work before Fish and Wildlife had enough evidence to press charges. But this time, instead of FWS raiding Fontenette's place, the FBI showed up and pulled a magic act of their own. They were the ones who'd executed the warrant. They were the ones who had Fontenette now.

They'd almost snagged RJ in that raid, too. Made him sweat just thinking about how close he'd come to getting caught. Whew. He'd been toasting his success with Fontenette in the man's elegant den, when he'd gotten one of his premonitions. If not for stealing that ambulance and kidnapping Boniface, RJ knew he'd be in jail alongside Bruce.

Life just wasn't fair sometimes, but things were about to change. Yes sirree, Bob. Things were about to change.

*Yessssss. They are......*

# Chapter Thirty-Seven

Savannah listened in, psychically watching Director Chase's conversation with FWS from Keller's Intensive Care Room. She'd had to board Red and Galahad at a nearby kennel, promising her dogs she'd be back as soon as she could. At the moment Tucker was leaned against his FBI SWAT van alongside the highway between Jacksonville and the National Guard Base in Northeast Florida. He was trying to play good cop, but he was mad. Dressed down in black jeans and a black FBI polo, he'd connected with two FWS agents, Senior Agents Collins and his assistant agent, Camilla Brinkman, while on his way to Camp Blanding. Brinkman was a hard one for Tucker to work with. Always a pain in his ass.

Savannah now knew the Deuces Wild team was an FBI unit in its infancy. The team totaled four agents, five counting Tucker. Eden and her husband Ky were out looking for Doctor Rudy John. An agent she hadn't yet met, Tate Higgins, was flying in from California to assist them. Until today, he'd been involved with U.S. Customs and Border Protection, San Diego Sector. Eden said Tate was originally a big game hunter from Alaska. His specialty was tracking wild animals. If he couldn't find RJ, nobody could.

Isaiah was right. Keller's condition had deteriorated overnight. A ventilator kept him breathing while several IVs kept him hydrated and medicated. But he was seriously sick, and Savannah was worried. She'd said all her prayers and cast only threads of positivity into the universe, yet he seemed beyond her reach. Even time seemed to be working against him.

"Then we check the birds," Tucker growled at Agent Camilla Brinkman. "Every last one of them."

Since FWS didn't have sufficient on-site space to accommodate an illegal shipment the size of Fontenette's, they'd moved Fontenette's four containers to an empty warehouse at Camp Blanding, some fifty miles southwest of Jacksonville. Savannah knew now those wooden crates in the containers had only hidden a dozen birds each instead of the thousands Keller had originally estimated. Which was good.

But because these hummingbirds were exotic and those containers comprised several of the rarest species on Earth, the world was now focused on Florida. That was bad. Yet every available hand at the

North Florida Ecological Services Office had been called in to assist. Not to be outdone, the commander at Camp Blanding Joint Training Center had volunteered as many off-duty reservists as needed to help save the birds.

Which meant any military member stationed or training there, whether from the Florida Army National Guard, the Florida Air National Guard, visiting ROTC units, as well as Civil Air Patrol, was now handling, nurturing, and otherwise working to save the birds. Assorted college students, interested civilians, even Green Peace advocates had also volunteered.

Word was People for the Ethical Treatment of Animals were sending a group of trained volunteers to provide what they called 'overwatch' to ensure no hummingbirds were injured in the course of saving them. Director Chase called it 'interference'. PETA had already threatened volunteers en masse should a single hummingbird die while under FWS care. It seemed simply saving those birds' lives wasn't enough.

Yet the problem was *those birds*. While Keller lay struggling to breathe with some kind of rare toxin in his system, they were very much alive. Seemingly healthy. Fluttering throughout the industrial-sized warehouse. Establishing territorial dominance. Mating. Some had been dehydrated when the crates were unpacked, but each bird had been handled with tender care from the start, and they'd all survived.

Cadets from Civil Air Patrol hung hundreds of wires between ceiling joists in the warehouse, then hung enough plastic feeders on those wires to provide the right mixture of sugar water and nutrients to keep the hummingbirds thriving. As luck would have it, the packing paper and pots used to smuggle them had also protected them from the full effect of whatever gas RJ and Fontenette used.

At the mere thought of what RJ did, Savannah reached for Keller. His hand was cold. He was so very ill. If something didn't change his prognosis soon, she could lose him.

"But Director Chase," Agent Brinkman replied with her usual lofty tone. "Those containers are safely quarantined. We follow strict protocol to protect endangered species. Surely you know that."

Savannah liked Agent Collins. He was young, but he seemed eager to help. Blond and blue-eyed, he'd pulled over as soon as he'd spotted Tucker signaling them. But he'd gone around the FWS truck to take a call, leaving Tucker to deal with Brinkman.

Of Puerto Rican descent and slight of stature, the twenty-something agent seemed to think she was in charge, that the Bureau had merely been called in to "assist" her. Born of immigrant parents from Puerto Rico, she was a newlywed, having married the son of a prominent DC lobbyist. Which most likely explained her entitled attitude.

Her features were model perfect. She wore her long black hair combed back and pulled into a tight bun.

She would've been beautiful except for the condescending sneer perpetually painted on her smug face.

With everything Tucker said, she either huffed or rolled her eyes like she had better things to do than waste time on the FBI. Agent Brinkman exemplified the worst traits of the millennial generation. Ignorant of rank. Condescending of standard operating procedures. Self-absorbed. Put an iPhone in her hand, and the picture would've been complete.

"Let me explain again," Tucker said patiently. He'd already gone over this information. If only she'd listen. "The night we raided Fontenette's, one of the Russians said something to me before he died. I distinctly heard Anatoly Orlov say, *'we're too late,'* meaning us, the FBI and FWS, we were too late. The bastard thought he'd won. Don't you get it?"

"Won what? You ever consider he might've been out of his mind by then? You shot him, didn't you? In my experience, pain like that'll make a guy say just about any—"

"What experience do you have with pain like that?" Tucker bit out, the veins in his neck as taut as his temper. "Have you shot a lot of people I don't know about? Orlov was gloating, damn it. So hear me out. What if those birds are contaminated, say with some kind of bug?"

Brinkman grunted, "Yeah, right. Have you seen them? They're healthy. All of them."

Tucker Chase's fingers curled into fists. Would he really hit a woman? Savannah wanted to.

Yet he continued struggling for patience. And patience was not his strong suit. "Wait. Hear me out, Agent Brinkman. This is just theory at this point, but what if those birds are infected with a bug that's contagious? We already know Fontenette only sold those birds to his personal list of highest bidders. Some of those elitists forked over millions to own their exclusive aviary of endangered hummingbirds. You understand what I'm saying? He hand-selected every single buyer. What if he somehow planted a virus—?"

Tucker shoved away from the van. "Son of a bitch! That's it! Blood tests. We need to draw blood samples from each and every bird and—"

*'Mr. Chase?'* Savannah whispered. *'What about the men and women handling those birds? If the birds are contaminated, those people could take that bug home to their families?'*

*'Good thinking, Savannah. Thanks.'* Tucker turned on the FWS agents. "Please tell me you guys are protecting the men and women handling all those birds."

"What do you think we are, stupid?" Again with the attitude. "They've all got gloves. Scrubs if they want them. Boots so they don't get their shoes dirty."

"What about full-face masks and protective clothing? What about aspirators? Oxygen so they don't breathe the same air? Scrubs only cover part of a body. Those young people should all be in hazmat suits, buttoned up from head to toe. And who's disposing of the waste coming out of the warehouse? Are your people even treating it as hazardous material until we know for certain—"

"My hell, what are you smoking? You FBI types really do think you run the world, don't you? But until there is actual physical evidence—"

*BOOM!* Tucker's fist bashed the rear quarter panel of his van, denting it. "Goddamn it, Brinkman! Enough of your bullshit! I've got a man dying on my watch! Don't tell me there's no evidence. Keller Boniface is all the proof I need. And don't brag about your son of a bitchin' protocol until you know for damned sure those birds aren't carrying any contagions. That they haven't brought something deadly into our country! Have you guys tested the anesthetic gas in those containers? That's the first damned thing you should have done!"

"Lethal hummingbirds, ha," she drawled. "What do you think this is, '*Avatar*'?"

Tucker stepped into Brinkman's face, and Savannah worried he might hit the insolent agent. "What if I'm right? What if those birds are infected with Ebola or something just as deadly? Are you good with our young military members dying just because you *think* you know every Goddamned thing? You gonna sleep nights once you've got a hundred or so deaths on your conscience? And what if, just what the fuck if..."

*BOOM!* He punched the van again. "...there is a contagion and it sweeps across America killing millions? You okay with that, too? What if this is just ground zero, and this little problem turns into a pandemic?"

Brinkman smoothed a hand over her sleek, empty head. "Tuck, chill why don'tcha?"

Oh. My. Goodness. Savannah's breath caught. Brinkman had just disrespected Tucker Chase as if he were her equal or worse, an underling, instead of the other way around. She'd talked down to him, stepped on his authority as an FBI director, and dismissed his experience as a Navy SEAL operator.

Tucker Chase was no longer mad, he was nuclear. Glowing. Everything about his rigid stance told Savannah he was primed to smack the shit out of this ill-mannered FWS agent. Until Agent Collins took his life in his hands and stepped inside Tucker's comfort zone.

The young man stuck out a quick hand and contritely said, "Sorry, Director Chase, but that was my director on the phone. I had to take it. I speak for my director when I say thank you for all you and your people have done to assist the Division of Fish and Wildlife."

But Tucker was done talking. Down came his aviators. Instead of shaking hands, he folded both thickly muscled arms over his chest.

Dropping his hand, Agent Collins tried again. "Sir, let me assure you that FWS's mission is to eagerly work with others to conserve, protect, and enhance fish, wildlife, plants and their habitats for the continuing benefit of the American people. We do take an oath to do no harm, and some of us live and die by that oath, sir." He cast a sideways glance at Brinkman when he said that.

Savannah couldn't help but smile at what sounded like answers to the FWS entrance exam.

Collins' cell was still in his hand. "As of two minutes ago, FWS quarantined every worker at the Camp Blanding site, sir, right now. They'll be housed in a nearby warehouse but kept separate from the birds until we can clear military, civilians, and birds of disease. I've personally requested assistance from the Center for Disease Control in Atlanta. They're sending their best scientists from their Division of High-Consequence Pathogens and Pathology to handle what we now believe to be a serious threat. Homeland Security is engaged. The National Terrorism Advisory System just now posted an imminent threat warning to all media channels. Is there anything else I can do for you? We really are here to help."

*'How's my boy?'* Tucker asked Savannah even as he leveled an evil eye at Agent Brinkman. *'Is Kell really dying like this guy said?'*

Savannah shook her head even though she knew Director Chase couldn't see her. *'No, sir. He's breathing steadier now, and the last time his doctor suctioned his lungs, the fluid was clear. No blood.'*

*'What about you? How are you feeling? You need to be tested, too.'*

*'Yes, sir, Keller's attending physician did draw my blood. I'm quarantined with Keller, but I'm not sick. The entire hospital's prepared to react quickly if anyone so much as sneezes.'*

*'Good,'* Tucker said before he turned back to Collins. "I want your director's name and number."

"Sure thing, Director Chase." Collins never batted an eye as he handed over a business card. "I answer to Director Carl Simmons, sir. He's a former SEAL. Like you."

By then, Savannah couldn't help but smile. Brinkman had turned gray. She'd stopped rolling her eyes and huffing like a spoiled teenager.

Tucker stabbed the business card into his rear pocket, then snarled at Brinkman. "Get the hell out of my way."

She stepped aside, but her deference to a Bureau director had come too late. Tucker hadn't risen to where he was because of political aspirations. He'd earned his title through more blood, sweat, and tears than she'd ever know. Now he meant to ruin her, and he could do it. Savannah just wanted to be there when he did.

# Chapter Thirty-Eight

A soft knock at Keller's door roused Savannah from a worrisome dream of Gran Mere racing after horned warlocks through a hundred thousand rose bushes, all decked with blood-red blossoms. After Tucker's altercation with Collins and Brinkman, she'd fallen asleep in the chair at Keller's bedside, her arm stretched alongside his body, her hand on top of his on his chest. But her arm had fallen asleep. It tingled when she peeled her cheek off her bicep.

Her doctor had notified her that her tests came back clear. She didn't have the virus that had nearly killed Keller. He wasn't contagious anymore, either.

"Come in," she called out quietly, swiping her other hand over her mouth to banish any drool along with the dream. Man, she'd been out of it. She sat back in the chair as the door opened.

Tate Higgins filled the entrance like a linebacker. Wearing what she now recognized as typical FBI uniform, namely black everything, he came in and closed the door quietly behind him. From his boots to his head, the shaggy-haired man was a mountain of squared-off angles. Thick, black brows shadowed intense brown eyes that shifted from Keller, the ventilator tubes and mask taped to his face, the machines helping him breathe, then back to Savannah, sizing her up, assessing, and deciding. His tanned face sported a trim beard and mustache. He'd pushed his dark glasses under his chin like a strap instead of on top his head. His neck was clean-shaven but his black shirt was too tight over his chest.

He doffed the black ball cap with FBI stenciled in bright gold caps above the brim and said, "Don't get up. I can't stay long. Nurse said to make it quick. I'm Tate Higgins, and you're Savannah Church, Keller's girl."

By then, she was on her feet. "Yes, I'm Savannah," she admitted that much. "Eden thinks a great deal of you."

"Yeah, well, that's her problem. Eden likes everybody. How's my boy?"

"Better today. He's no longer contagious, and his doctors started him on an experimental antibiotic early this morning."

Tate went to the other side of the bed, worrying the cap in his hands. "Seem like it's working?"

"It's too early to tell," she said as a yawn got away from her, "but he is resting more comfortably. Last night he seemed anxious, but that may be because of the ventilator."

"But he's still unreachable?" Tate tapped his temple. "Up here?"

Savannah made eye contact with Agent Higgins. "Yes and no. I keep a thread cast out in the universe feeling for him, but the drugs they've got him on must be too strong. He's not answering, but he's still alive."

"Keller's stubborn. Don't worry, he'll come around when he's ready."

Which told Savannah that Keller was fighting his own internal battles. He wasn't ready.

Tate nodded at the chair behind her. "Sure wish you'd sit down, ma'am. You're tired. Try to rest while you can."

"I am tired," she murmured, sinking into the chair. But sleep wasn't her friend right now. She was afraid of it, afraid of those dreams and that Keller would leave forever if she relaxed too much. If she let him go.

Tate cocked his head. "You use threads? Like spiders? You build webs?"

"More like fishing line. I'm not a spider, I'm fly fishing. I cast threads into the universe, hoping for an answering vibration."

Tate's brows leaned into each other as if he were considering what she'd said. "What kind of vibration?"

Savannah shrugged. "A sigh. A cry. A whisper."

"What do you use for bait?"

That made her smile. "It's not like I'm trying to hook anyone, Agent Higgins. And I don't use bait, I use prayers."

"Tate, please. Just call me Tate. But go on." He made a hurry up sign with his hand. "I fish and hunt, just never considered using psychic fishing line or prayers, though. That works for you?"

"Yes, it does." Her cheeks billowed as she blew out a breath. The last two days had been impossibly long and worrisome. She was tired to her soul. "Gran Mere taught me to pray when I cast, that's all. Think of me as a catch-and-release fisherman, only some fish are already looking for me. Like Isaiah. Casting for him was easy. All I had to do was open my mind to the possibility of saving him and—"

"He reeled you in," Tate said as if that was precisely what happened.

Which it was. Isaiah had been dying then, and dying men were desperate to live. It was only natural that Isaiah grabbed hold and hung on as fervently as he had when she'd offered hope.

"I guess you can say that."

"You ever thought of casting for Doctor Rudy John?"

An instant chill shivered up Savannah's spine. "No," she said, certain she would never go looking for the despicable man who'd tried to kill Keller. "It would take my focus off Keller. I can't."

Tate made a sound at the back of his throat like Keller used to. "You can't? Or you won't?"

Savannah laughed. "Oh, my gosh, did you just growl at me?"

There went those brows again, but this time Agent Higgins' eyes sparkled. He was a bear of a man. Fierce-looking and most likely as lethal as the rest of the Deuces Wild team, but so much like Keller. Tough on the outside, but a marshmallow at his core.

"Did you just call me a marshmallow?" There went that twinkle again.

Savannah relaxed, letting down her psychic defenses. "I'm glad you heard that. You have no idea how much I needed to connect with another person like me. For a moment there, you sounded just like Keller. He growls, too."

Tate cocked his head. "A person like you? And just what and who would that be?"

Savannah analyzed what she'd been told all her life against what she knew now. "You see," she began on a murmur. "All my life people avoided me and Gran Mere, and that was okay. I was different, so was she. I always knew that. And the less I had to deal with people, the easier it was to not belong. But it was hard."

"And people label folks who don't fit in," Tate said. "The Inuit people called me *Qimmiq* when I was younger. Means dog. But after I lost my folks..." His fist came up and thumped his chest. "They called me *Aklaq,* and they stayed the hell out of my way."

"They called you black bear," she said. Tate was easy to read. "I can see why. You understand animals. You know how they think."

He nodded, a twinkle in the corner of his eye. "I like you. You just read me, didn't you?"

Her shoulders came up. "It's a gift. I'm sorry. I try not to, it just happens when I tune in."

"What'd people call you?"

Oh, that. Savannah didn't want to think about it, but she felt safe with Tate. He'd understand. "Most of the time, witch. Voodoo queen. Priestess. Other things…" Her brows lifted at that last one. "But I'm just a woman with a psychic gift who would rather spend her time helping animals than arguing with people. Animals communicate purely, but people—"

"People lie," Tate said. "Yeah. I'd rather spend all day with my dog than one minute with most people, present company excluded. Yet here you are with Keller, one of the baddest guys I've ever met."

Savannah had to smile at that. Tate was pretty badassed himself. "What Inuit name would you give Keller?"

There was that growl again. "*Tarkik*. Means moon."

Savannah hadn't seen that coming. "Moon?"

"Yes. Moon. Fits him. He's got a dark side like me. Are you afraid of that rat bastard John?"

*Maybe.* "I'm not sure. I've been too worried about Keller to think about RJ."

Tate folded both arms over his chest, making himself larger than life. How did men do that? Savannah was a Lilliputian in a room of two giants. "I'm gonna tell you something, *Nuka*."

Aw, he'd just called her little sister. This big bad bear knew just how to touch her heart.

"Isaiah's one of a handful of Level Tens in the entire world. You understand what I'm saying? He's a rare gift in a world gone bat shit crazy, and you..." Tate stuck his index finger at her. "Isaiah says you're strong, maybe stronger than he is. That's something to be proud of. And you pray, which is another rare damned thing in today's world, even for a psychic. I think that's your secret. You believe in a higher power. You're humble. You're kind. But you're also smarter than any swamp rat who thinks he's some kind of magical warlock." Tate's index finger stabbed toward the ceiling. "You don't invoke Satan. You call on the real power. You call on God."

Wow. Just wow. Savannah hadn't thought of her gift that way. She didn't know what to say. Tate had read her like a book, yet she was no high priestess or conjurer of heaven's almighty wrath, either. All she could come up with was, "Umm..."

"Listen, I can't stay," he growled, "but I'll be back. Think about what I said. You've got this, *Nuka*."

"I think I l-l-love you," she stuttered. "I mean, like a brother. No one's ever called me Little Sister before and..."

Tate was around the bed before she knew it. Darn, he could move fast. "That's what makes Deuces Wild work," he said. "We're just brothers and sisters trying to make a difference out there. Stay strong. Believe in yourself. When Keller wakes up, tell him I was here." And Tate was gone.

Savannah stood by Keller's bedside long after Tate left, holding his hand and thinking about what Tate said. He thought she was strong, humble, and kind. He thought she was smart, too. It felt right. It felt true. She'd never doubted herself until Rudy John got inside her head, poisoning her self-esteem like he'd poisoned the birds and Keller. But she'd never tracked a man to hurt him before, and locating RJ would surely end in violence. How could she pray for that?

Violence was not her way. It never had been. Savannah's world had been relatively peaceful all her life. She'd lived with Gran Mere most of that time, then by herself at Sanctuary. She'd been safe and protected. Even confronting Bubba to save Red had cost her nothing but courage and nerve. He might have punched her that day, but she'd never thought to strike first.

Yet the world she'd known was gone. Now she felt exposed and worse, orphaned. No Gran Mere to run to. No houseboat to hide in. Even Sanctuary had undergone a vicious assault. Savannah was twenty-five, yet still very much a babe in the—bayou.

Yet Tate thought she could track Rudy John? It seemed impossible.

Keller's fingers twitched ever so slightly, startling Savannah. She wanted to call for the nurse and shout, "He moved! He moved his fingers! Hurry, come see!"

Yet she didn't. Smoothing her hand over his prickly scalp, she leaned into him and pressed her mouth to his forehead. "You think I can do what Tate said, don't you?"

Another tiny tremor twitched his fingers, imperceptibly small as to be nothing more than her imagination. But Savannah sensed Keller's desperation. With all his soul, he wanted to get back to her. And that was enough.

"I'm going after Rudy John, Keller. Because you and Tate believe in me, I believe. Never forget how much I love you. Rest easy, my handsome Secret Agent Man. I won't be long."

An alarm from his monitors rang out then. By the time the ICU nurse arrived to reset the machine, Savannah was gone.

# Chapter Thirty-Nine

Savannah withdrew to the hospital chapel. Here in the soft glow pouring through the amber-tinted windows was the place of power and solitude she needed to confront Rudy John. An older man knelt far to her left and another knelt just ahead and at her right, almost like two sentinels who had expected her arrival. That alone comforted her on a purely spiritual level. They weren't true sentinels and were most likely there for their own reasons, not hers. But it seemed the universe always provided who and what she needed with clocklike precision. Whoever these men were didn't matter. That they were here and praying was all Savannah needed to begin her quest.

Settling at the end of the row nearest the chapel door, she drew in a deep breath. Most chapels were consecrated places devoted to worship, heartfelt prayer, and divine intercession. They offered calm energy, silence, and reverence. This one was no different.

Blessing herself, she cast the first handful of what would be many threads into the eternal river of the universe. Relying on her inner sight, she let the music of forever and everywhere and everyone flow through those threads to her. With each pure note, the colors of the rainbow coalesced along those threads, washing through her like tiny drops of rain on spidery filaments, filling her soul with peace and contentment.

The threads she looked for first bound her to Keller. They were a vivid, vibrant green this morning. A smile blossomed over her face, lighting her up from inside. When she'd first met him, the threads between them had been brittle and dry. Unexplored and unknown. Now they pulsed with energy. His soul had come back to life again. She'd known their attraction was mutual, now she was blessed to see that attraction in beautiful color. He loved her. He no longer needed to say the words. She believed.

The threads between her and the other members of his team each vibrated with a red hue, like blood coursing through veins. It was fierce, the perfect definition of Mr. Chase, Isaiah, Eden, and Tate. Each of them were proud. Resolute. They stood fast against a world that feared them, and they considered Keller as their brother. Better yet, he'd finally realized that.

Turning away from the comrades she'd grown to love in just days, she cast another prayer to locate Rudy John. A searching prayer.

Oddly, it bounced back, the thread snapping past her spirit as if it had been stretched too tight and had broken. An ugly shadow whipped out at her, stinging her with a snake-like tentacle. A raspy voice hissed, *'You dare challenge me?'*

*'I did not challenge. I only seek answers.'* Savannah paused, for the first time in her life, her instincts on fire, telling her to run, that this might not be who she thought it was. The voice was ragged and laced with pride, yes, but not the one that had attacked her spirit—and lost. Still she asked, *'Doctor John?'*

*'Come to Sanctuary if you're so brave, little one. Come, Savannah, or they die. They all die!'* There was a definite psychic push behind every word, every letter. This was someone of power. But *little one*? Really?

*'Who will die? My animals?'* she asked politely. She'd never encountered such ugly feelings in a single entity before. This was definitely not RJ.

Instead of replying, the voice spewed a whirling cloud of sparks and chaos at her. But Gran Mere always said only bullies resorted to light shows to frighten their prey, and light shows only worked on weak-minded people. Savannah held her ground. *'I ask again. Who will die?'*

*'All of them! Come to Sanctuary alone! If you don't, I kill all of them!'*

*'That is hardly an answer.'*

*'Enough!'* A murky, black cloud boiled out from the now shadowy universe, turning each of Savannah's carefully cast threads to ash. First, Keller's lovely green

drifted into the cosmic wind, then each of the brilliant reds of the Deuces Wild team followed suit. Even Isaiah's purplish-blue thread fell to the rage within the voice.

But those threads were not those people, and Savannah had enough. *'Are you the warlock Gran Mere warned of?'* she asked, needing to know once and for all.

A cackle perforated the silence of the chapel, stealing Savannah's breath like a slap across her face. *'I am more,'* the voice spat, *'so much more than that dimwitted old fool. Now come, damn you!'*

*So, you knew Gran Mere...*

The compulsion in the voice was strong, certainly enough to intimidate. But Gran Mere had neither been dimwitted nor foolish. She'd always said to stand up for what you knew was right. If you didn't, if you let yourself be cowed, and if you ran away from your battles, you only delayed the inevitable. The day would come when you faced that bully again, only then, he'd believe you were weak. Because you had given your power away. *So, don't be weak to begin with. Be fearless and strong and spit in that bully's eye the first time around. Make him remember you for courage, never cowardice.*

Savannah lifted to her feet, shaken but not diminished. Forewarned, not intimidated. This voice belonged to the real warlock, but that person was not RJ nor anyone else she knew. None of that mattered.

She would fight this entity head on. Only then would Keller be safe.

She was going to Sanctuary.

Keller woke wound as tight as a drum and ready to fight. He was choking. Suffocating. Two shadows loomed over him, talking to each other. Giving orders. The larger shadow held a thick heavy arm across his chest, fastening him to the bed. The other, a woman, had her elbow stuck in his pillow. Telling him to lie still, that this wouldn't take long. *Like hell.*

"Get the fuck off me," he meant to yell, but it was hard to breathe. He couldn't think. He needed to vomit. Reaching between his clenched teeth, the woman pulled a fuckin' snake out of his throat! They were killing him! *What the hell?*

"There, that wasn't so bad," she soothed as she stepped back to dispose of the writhing reptile. The big guy eased his weight off Keller's chest. Blinking sleep as thick as glue out of his eyes, Keller saw the snake then. Okay. Not a snake. Just tracheal intubation tubing. These people weren't killing him. They were nurses. Just nurses. He was in a real hospital, and it was just another day in fucking paradise.

Keller tried to growl, but a weak man couldn't manage much intimidation. Damn, his body felt like he'd been run over by both tracks of an Abrams tank. He couldn't move his left hand where his shoulder had been hit, and with two IVs taped to his right hand, he didn't want to move that one. For once, he settled back and just breathed. There were times in a man's life when that was the best he could do. This was one of those moments. Keller was alive and that was good enough. So he breathed and he panted and he reoriented himself to his new reality.

The lights overhead were too bright. They hurt his already pounding headache. He was whipped and he knew it. He was injured. That much he remembered. He'd survived getting shot, then hijacked by that bastard Doctor John who'd faked being a first responder. Keller remembered Savannah hovering over him like an angel, blessing him just by being there. Wherever there was. Faint recollections of riding Sand Dollar, of waking up in a barn, no, make that a stable, drifted to mind. But what happened afterward was a muddled mess Keller couldn't make heads or tails of.

The orderly offered him the straw of a bright pink plastic water mug and said, "Take it slow. Baby sips until we're sure your stomach can handle it."

Keller accepted the straw between his dry lips, so damned thirsty. But the cool water burned like fire going down. He was forced to sip less, even slower. Baby steps were not his favorite speed, but he was too parched to stop. "Where is she?" he rasped once he'd swallowed what little he could.

"There you go, Mr. Boniface. That should help you feel better," the nurse said instead of answering his question. "We'll be moving you out of ICU and into a regular patient room in a few minutes. Is there anything I can get you while we wait for that room to be ready?"

She leaned over him, wiped a cool damp cloth over his face, then over his entire scalp. Instant relief. Blonde and competent, she seemed to think she was in charge, but she was also gentle around his mouth and nose, and... *Ahh, that feels good.*

Closing his eyes, Keller retracted his opinion of hospital help. "Savannah," he whispered as his tougher-than-most, FBI persona grew weaker by the minute.

"Who? That pretty little thing who's been by your side for two days now, waiting for you to wake up? I'm not sure where she went, perhaps to the cafeteria or maybe home. She hasn't left your side until now, so I don't imagine she's gone far."

What the nurse said before finally registered. "I'm in ICU?" That sounded serious.

"Yes, sir, ever since your lungs filled with blood, and we thought we lost you that first night. Which is why you've been on a ventilator until now. I know it was painful having that tube removed, but you were a regular health risk when you first arrived. Where on earth have you been, China?"

"Huh? Me?" What the hell was this woman talking about? Him a health risk? Must be a mistake. He hadn't been out of the country in months.

Her head bobbed as she straightened his blankets. "Oh yes, sir. You arrived here with one of the rarest strains of avian flu in the world, and China's on the top of our avian flu watch list. Let me tell you," she said through a chuckle, "you had every scientist and pulmonary specialist from here to Georgia jumping. I've never seen so many CDC doctors and investigators descend on our hospital at one time. But they sure did, and they all came to see you." She said that with pride in her voice. "Only you showed them."

Keller held his breath. Avian flu? CDC, as in the Center for Disease Control? Holy Christ, what happened while he'd been sleeping? When one of the many machines at his bedside beeped an alarm, his talkative nurse turned her attention to that. He had to ask, "I showed them?"

"Yes, Mr. Boniface, you certainly did," she said softly as she quieted the alarm and turned her sharp gray eyes back on him. "It took all those doctors the entire first morning just to agree which super antibiotic to give you. But by then, the antibodies in your system were already fighting the infection. Your doctor decided which antibiotic to use, and then he intubated you to help you breathe. You'd lost a lot of blood by then, and you were nearly on your deathbed. I dare say he'll be in to see you by and by. Doctor Singh's from India. You'll like him."

Keller's nurse looked up as the door opened. "Ah, here she is. The pretty woman of your dreams. I'll leave you to get reacquainted then." On her way out, she stage-whispered to Savannah, "He's all yours."

How Keller wished. But Savannah stayed at the closed door dressed in jeans and a pale-yellow button up blouse. Her exotic complexion was somehow pale, and her slender fingers trembled. She was frightened? Of who? He opened his arm to her, needing her body next to him.

She came to him easily, out of breath as she took hold of his hand instead of letting him wrap his arm around her. Probably just as well with all the wires and tubes in his way. "You're shaking," he murmured, his voice more wimpy whisper than manly baritone.

"They're moving you," she said, her eyes not yet settled on him.

Keller resorted to their private channel. *'Talk to me, Savannah. What's going on?'*

She shook her head, still not making eye contact. *'Later, okay?'*

*'No. You're scared now. Tell me.'*

She looked around as if someone might be hiding in the corner. *'I'm not scared. Just worried. I thought I could locate Rudy John. I thought I could help your team track him. I said all the prayers. I blessed myself, b-b-but...'* Her throat convulsed as if she couldn't swallow. It took a full minute before she said, *'I have to go to Sanctuary.'*

*'No,'* he declared with certainty.

*'Yes, I have to. Only—'*

Keller wanted to scream. Instead he growled, *'I'll kill him! He's not worth saving. Did he touch you?'*

She shook her head again. *'This is not about RJ. You have to trust me.'*

Another orderly interrupted with a cheery, "Time to move," as he began piling the throwaway patient supplies onto the bed.

But Keller wasn't about to let Savannah go. *'How long have I been out?'*

*'The longest two and a half days of my life. Tate Higgins came by earlier. Your boss sent him to help track RJ, but he stopped by to see you first.'* Savannah stepped out in the hall, trailing the bed.

*'Tate was here?'* Keller couldn't see her, but for once, his gift kept them securely linked.

Man, he'd been a fool, refusing to explore what that unique mental ability offered. Like telepathic communication. Like camaraderie and finally belonging. Like working with, instead of against, an arrogant, egotistical boss who wasn't afraid to man the helm of the brilliant Deuces Wild team, even though it most likely meant political suicide for Tucker. Like feeling Savannah's love when she was out of sight.

That he'd called Tate proved Tucker's innate ability to lead. Tate Higgins was one hell of a tracker. Yet except for his obvious Marine swagger and his innate ability with animals, Keller didn't know much else about his fellow agent. Tate wasn't usually in the DC office. For whatever reason, Tucker kept him embedded inside California's beleaguered border patrol.

To Keller's shame, he didn't know much about Tate because he'd never asked. Not once. All this time, he'd been a stuck-up pain in the ass, keeping himself removed and remote from coworkers and second chances. It was time to man up. Still mainlining those two IVs, he waved Savannah back to his side. *How'd I get here? I know I'm in intensive care, but where? Which state? Which hospital?'*

She gave his free hand a squeeze. *'You're still in Florida, at Memorial Hospital in Jacksonville. Mr. Chase and an ambulance brought you here the night he found you near a barn south of Fontenette's stables. We don't know for sure, but your boss thinks RJ stashed you where Fontenette was already keeping Sand Dollar. RJ's the one behind the avian flu you contracted. He was going to let you bleed out. Then when someone eventually discovered your body, they'd contract the flu and it would spread. Don't worry, Sand Dollar and the rest of Fontenette's horses are in FBI custody. They're safe and under the care of a team of veterinarians. They aren't sick and Fontenette's in jail.'*

*'And John?'*

By then the orderly had wheeled them onto an elevator and pressed the button for the fourth floor. Keller squeezed Savannah's slender hand, so damned thankful he had this particular woman at his side. *I love her,* he admitted to himself. *But I don't deserve her. I never will. But I'm still going to spend the rest of my life trying to measure up to whatever she sees in me. I can do that. I will do that.*

She stared at the floor indicator over the elevator door, her lower lip quivering. Damn that rat bastard RJ for hurting her. *I'll kill him. I will!*

It wasn't until Keller was settled in a private room and after the orderly left, that Savannah let her guard down. Finally, she settled at his side, her hand in his, and the love shining in her sad, chocolate eyes killing him softly. How had he ever gotten this kind of lucky that she cared enough to stay? He honestly didn't know.

"Talk to me, baby," he breathed out loud.

She gulped, then said, "I heard a voice, but it wasn't RJ. He's not the warlock."

"Then who is?"

"I'm not sure. This voice was... peculiar. Not male or female. Just—old."

Was she holding something back? "Then who?"

"Keller, I don't know. The only thing I'm certain is I need to go to Sanctuary or this person will kill my animals."

"Bullshit!" Keller hissed, immediately regretting forceful verbal communication. It hurt! He switched back to telepathy. *That isn't going to happen, baby. I can't let you go alone to Sanctuary.*

A sad smile tugged the corners of her mouth. *And how are you going to stop me? I have to go. It's the only way. Only—*

'*Only what?*' She needed to spit it out.

'*RJ always considered himself better than everyone else. He's one of those people who demeans or minimizes others to make themselves look smarter and better.*'

Keller nodded. He knew people like RJ. A certain witch in Turkey Creek sprang to mind.

Savannah paused as if searching for what to say next. '*But he's smart, not wise. He might think he's clever, but he isn't. Not really. Gran Mere told me to watch out for the warlock, but I think she might've been wrong. I know who the rose is, but I believe the warlock is really a witch.*'

'*What's the difference?*'

'*A warlock is male, a witch, female.*'

'*Who's the rose?*'

'*It's you,*' she said with a tender smile. '*I saw you in the bayou that night. You were at home there, weren't you?*'

He shrugged. '*Well, yeah. Life's simple there. It's easy. Uncomplicated. That doesn't make me a flower.*'

'*But you wouldn't mind getting lost there, living off catfish and gators.*' That same smile reeled him in.

'*I could, yes.*'

'*Which makes you as rare as those roses only Gran Mere knew about. Don't you see? She knew you were coming. She meant for me to look for you, not some flower.*'

That... Keller was going to have to think about. Rangers were not roses or pansies or—Jesus. His team had better not catch wind of this. He'd never hear the end of it.

'*I don't know for certain,*' Savannah whispered, as if she thought someone were listening, '*but I believe this witch is behind whatever RJ's doing or plans to do. I saw your team's threads turn to ash. She means to kill all of you. She is evil.*'

Could it be? '*You think this witch is... Elaine?*' That seemed a stretch. What did she have to do with Gran Mere?

Savannah nodded. '*Yes. I believe your mother is the entity who commanded me to go to Sanctuary. I might be wrong, but I sense RJ's already there. I think she's using him. He'll kill my animals if I don't at least go talk to him.*'

'*And I said no, damn it. Boss!*' Keller all but bellowed for the man he'd tried to ignore since he'd been swallowed up by the Deuces Wild team. '*Damn it, Boss, can you hear me? I—*' Shit, This was hard to admit. '*—I need you!*'

'*Copy that,*' Tucker's deep throaty affirmative came back instantaneously. '*Whatzup, Kell?*'

'*RJ. Is he at Sanctuary?*'

'*Yes. Tate's already there with Eden. They've got eyes on John. What's the problem?*'

'*Savannah just got a call... I mean, a psychic message from some witch.*' Who just might be my mother. Could he sound more hysterical? Closing his eyes, Keller summoned his inner Ranger and said,

'Savannah believes RJ means to destroy her animals unless she shows. You have to stop him.'

'What do you think we're doing? Right now, that smug son of a bitch is about to run into a brick wall. Tate and Eden are already boots on the ground inside Sanctuary. You kids are good to listen in, watch if you can.'

Keller blinked at what was happening without him. He hadn't told Tucker the ugly part about his mother, and he wasn't there with Tate and Eden. If RJ refused to stand down, Keller wouldn't get the chance to end him. Shit. That didn't sit well with him. This was *his* kill, his chance to end the bastard who'd nearly ended him, who'd lusted after and threatened Savannah. Who'd hurt all those birds. But what the hell did Tucker mean about listening in or watching? Keller didn't have those skills. Hell, he could barely communicate with his team.

'Your boss wants you to project your mind to Tate or Eden, Keller, and watch RJ through their eyes. But is that what you want to do? Wouldn't it be better if we both let RJ go and concentrated on your mother?' Savannah whispered psychically, her fingers warm on the back of his IV needle-perforated hand. 'You're part of the best team on the planet. You know that, and my place is here with you. You're not strong enough to travel, but ending RJ's reign of terror can't wait for you to get better. He has to be stopped before he hurts anyone else. Let's trust Tate and Eden, Keller. Let *them handle Doctor John while we handle your mother.'*

He stared up at her. Savannah trusted Tate and Eden, but could he? Yet he already had back at the gunfight, hadn't he? And it was Tucker who waited on him now. Damn. *Deuces Wild, huh?*

*'Yup, Deuces Wild,'* Tucker purred like the smug Navy SEAL son of a bitch he was and would always be. *'Trust me, Kell. John'll never see our guys coming. He already ran into some old duffer with a shotgun. You know a Lyle Goldenrod, Savannah?'*

She clapped a hand over her mouth. *'Oh, no! I forgot Coach. Yes, Lyle Goldenrod! He's my hired hand. Is he hurt?'*

*'Relax,'* Tucker murmured. *'Your buddy Lyle's in charge at the moment, not that pipsqueak moron with a medical license he got out of a box of* Cracker Jacks. *You should see old man Goldenrod; you'd be proud. Why don't you two watch or listen in, whatever you can handle? Looks like RJ's decided to blow Sanctuary off the map. Lyle's got his shotgun on him, but RJ's holding a detonator. Says he planted charges all over the place. That it's too late. You think it's too late, Kell?'*

For some reason, a funny feeling caught in Keller's throat. He coughed, damn it, then he coughed again. Tucker needed to stop calling him—that. *'It's never too late, Boss,'* he finally ground out. *'Light him up. With extreme prejudice.'*

*'My pleasure.'*

Keller drew in a deep cleansing breath, and he simply, finally, let go. He'd heard it said once that there was no 'I' in team. Well, he no longer had to be an army of one, either. Those days and those ghosts were behind him. He didn't need to watch the drama unfold at Sanctuary. RJ would die. That was what small-minded men like him did. They grabbed their fifteen minutes of fame at the expense of others, then went out in a fiery ball of what they called glory. But Keller called it chicken shit, the typical coward's way out. Goodbye and good riddance.

*'Tell Tate and Eden I'm buying drinks next time we get together.'*

*'You bet your ass you are.'*

Keller could honestly feel Tucker's shit-eating grin all the way from wherever he was watching his infamous but incredibly skilled Deuces Wild team.

*'Get some sleep, Kell. See you kids soon.'*

*'Sounds like a plan. Night, Boss.'* Keller felt Tucker disconnect from his mind. It was very much like a door closing. Even came with the click of a doorknob. Interesting. *'You're right. I don't need to watch Tate and Eden do their job,'* he told Savannah. *'Do you?'*

*'No. I'm good.'*

*'But about my mother… We'll deal with her together.'*

*'Yes, we will. She's quite frightening, isn't she?'*

*'She thinks she is.'* The bitch. *'I'm sorry you had to deal with her alone, but yeah. Elaine is evil.'* Even as weak as he was, Keller still wanted Savannah closer.

*'Now forget about her. Climb under the blankets with me?'*

No sooner asked than answered. Toes first, sweet, beautiful Savannah eased the length of her delicious warm body onto the bed, between the tubes and wires, and next to him. From her smooth bare legs to her silky black hair, she poured herself over him like the maple syrup she'd poured on those fluffy pecan waffles only days before.

*'You've got me, Keller,'* she whispered psychically. *'You've always had me.'*

*'I know that now.'* And he did. With the scent of lilacs in his nose, Keller let his need to control all things slip through his fingers in exchange for the softness of her ebony locks. Today, he was just Keller, not a hero. Not even much of a federal agent. Just a man in love with his woman.

He closed his eyes and inhaled another breath of his future. He wasn't going to confront What's-Her-Name today, maybe not tomorrow, either. He didn't need to. Queen Elaine wasn't a witch, and she wasn't worth the wasted drive to Turkey Creek. She was every bit as toxic as Doctor John's avian flu, only now Keller held the antidote for Elaine's brand of poison in his arms. Even Carol Marie's grave could wait. She wasn't really there anyway. But Savannah was here and she was now. She was Keller's tomorrow and his happily-ever-after.

*'Marry me,'* he told the woman he loved. *'Marry me as soon as I can stand on my feet again. I don't want to wait. I want to make you an honest woman.'*

*'I'm already honest,'* she said as her entire body wiggled against him. Oh yeah, Savannah was honest and she was happy. The world wasn't such a bad place after all.

*'Is that a yes?'*

She leaned into his face and kissed him then, her lips warm and juicy sweet. *'Yes, my love,'* she whispered against his open mouth. *'That's most definitely, yes.'*

Keller closed his eyes as she kissed him again. He didn't need to fight every battle or win each war. He was pretty sure he had what he wanted. He had everything.

# Chapter Forty

Tucker stretched both hands over his head to work the cramp out of his back. He'd been sitting outside his newest agent's hospital room for a while now. Kell didn't need to know he was there. Neither did Savannah. Those kids needed privacy, and Tucker didn't mind standing guard, making sure they got it. He had no doubt Kell was finally out of danger, but after losing him to Doctor John, then finding him very nearly at death's door, well, Tucker wasn't taking any chances. He was here to stay.

But he had inadvertently listened in on Kell's marriage proposal. That sly dog. Kell was a smart man who knew what he wanted and wasn't afraid to go after it. That he'd relinquished control of this operation spoke volumes. Kell had finally let himself belong.

Tucker smiled at something Isaiah'd let slip a few months back, that Tucker's powers were growing. Not the case at all. Tucker was simply listening harder and better. Understanding more. Seeking to understand first instead of jumping into arguments and situations before he knew all the facts. He was learning how to let his agents take the lead. They were all capable psychics. They didn't need him treating them like kindergarteners. Hell no.

His wife Melissa had even said she was proud of him. But Tucker knew he owed this enhanced power of his to her. She was after all his better half, and if not for her gentle influence in his life, he'd still be the closed-minded bombastic Navy SEAL he'd once been. Those were the days, but those days were also behind him. He had a team now, the best damned team in America.

Tucker was proud of them. Even now, two of his best were handling the homegrown terrorist who'd intended to kill millions through a new strain of avian bird flu. Dumb ass. The last time Tucker checked, Eden had RJ on his back and her boot on his windpipe. Even now, Tucker had to control his urge to order her to break the guy's thorax. Bust him up. End him!

But once again, he restrained himself and let Eden handle things her way. She and Tate were a dynamic duo unto themselves. Two good agents. Two solid friends who'd helped each other through some harrowing times. Also Tucker's friends. He'd die for them. They'd do the same for him.

Tucker hadn't wanted the directorship when he'd been volunteered to manage Deuces Wild. Hell, he barely wanted to be an FBI agent back then. He'd just gotten his son out of Vietnam. He was a newlywed and a new man. For the first time in his life, he'd wanted to settle down, let someone else fight the good fight. Heroes shouldn't have to step up time and time again to defend their country. That should be every American's job, elitists and commoners alike. There ought to be a better way to balance the dirty job of civil defense across the spectrum of America's entire population.

But there wasn't. Even if there were, the wealthy and powerful would find a way to dodge their most basic duty, that of defending the United States against aggression, internal or external. Which was why good men like Kell would always be there. They didn't know how to shirk or turn aside when their country called. If he weren't injured, Tucker knew damned well Kell would be the one with his boot on RJ's scrawny neck.

*'Hey, Boss,'* Tate drawled extra slow and casual. *'Sorry to report, but this little bastard just offed himself.'*

That perked up Tucker's ears, not Tate being sorry, but the news that RJ was dead. *'How'd he do that?'*

*'Had a derringer in his pants pocket. The minute Eden let him up, he screamed, 'Now you'll get yours.' Then he ate a bullet.'*

*'Hmmpf,'* Tucker muttered. *'Thought doctors were supposed to be smart?'*

*'Maybe in his own mind,'* Eden cut in. *'Nothing scary about a worm like Rudy John. Tate's got the*

*detonator, and Mr. Goldenrod intercepted RJ before he planted any bombs. It was all talk, but we'll double check before we wrap up here. I'm not sensing any explosives or incendiary devices anywhere on the premises, though.'*

'Good work,' Tucker said. *'Swing by Jacksonville on your way home. Kell's awake. He'd love to see you guys.'*

'Will do,' Tate replied. *'Tell Savannah that Mr. Goldenrod volunteered to stay here until she gets back. He'll watch her animals for her.'*

*'Will do.'*

*'Count us in, too,'* Isaiah interjected from his penthouse in Crystal City, Virginia. *'Roxy's dying to show off the squid.'*

*'The squid! Haven't you named that little boy yet?"* Eden scolded.

*'We're down to one name we both like. Thought we'd run it by you guys first.'*

*'Oh, yeah? What?'* Tucker asked.

Isaiah hesitated, but finally admitted, *'We're naming him after you, Boss. All the way. We're calling him Tucker Chase Zaroyin.'*

*'Well, err, ahh..."* That unexpected gesture stole the bluster from Tucker's sails. What Isaiah and Roxy did cut straight to his heart. He never knew his mom and he'd left home early to escape his old man's fists. Then along came Isaiah, a bright young man who'd survived a crap load of tragedy, but who still had stars in his eyes. He'd always been more like a little brother.

Sometimes annoying, but always inside Tucker's head, and, damn. Inside his heart, too.

*'I love it!'* Eden squealed. *'It's perfect!'*

*'Sounds good,'* Tate offered stoically.

*'It's... it's a mistake is what it is,'* Tucker sputtered. *'You can't saddle your son with a handle like that. I mean, think about it. There's a couple things that rhyme with Tucker he's not gonna want to hear, and kids can be mean little bastards. He's gonna have to stand up for himself. He's gonna get in fist fights.'*

*'He's going to be fine, Boss,'* Isaiah replied easily. *'Roxy wants me to ask if you'll be his godfather. She's planning Little Tuck's baptism for a month from today. Will you be there with us?'*

*'Me? A godfather? Well, err, sure. Yeah, I'll be there. That'd be an honor.'* Tucker ran a hand over his head, ruffling his hair and wondering what the hell happened. Damned if Alex Stewart wasn't right. A long-time frenemy of the Bureau, he'd always said the company he'd built had somehow turned into family. Exactly what Deuces Wild had become. A family. Tucker's family. Almost brought a tear to his eye.

A wiry-thin doctor in scrubs, his face appropriately masked, ducked into Kell's room.

*'You're all invited,'* Isaiah said. *'Be sure to bring Kyler, Eden. Little Tuck wants to meet his cousin.'*

*'Do not keep calling him Little Tuck,'* Tucker growled. *'How about just Chase? That's a good name, and it'll go down easier on the playground.'*

*'Hmmm. Let me run that by the boss.'* Isaiah was quiet for the space of a heartbeat. *'Roxy!'*

Tucker listened to Isaiah and Roxy, but something felt out of place. Off balance. He could feel it. The hairs on the back of his neck were on end. The air in the hall didn't smell right. An unseen cloud hovered over his shoulder, like a ghoul...

Urgency whispered, *'Check on Kell. Hurry. Do it now.'*

Tucker didn't need to be told twice. Both weapons sprang automatically from his holster to his hands. He shoved Kell's door aside, half listening to his agents in Louisiana when Eden cried out, *'We were wrong! This guy isn't Rudy John!'*

*'Because he's here,'* Tucker replied evenly, staring at the skinny weasel in scrubs who'd passed him in the hall. The real RJ had Savannah's back pulled tight against him, one arm around her waist, a scalpel at her neck. The mask he'd hid behind dangled under his chin. Should've pulled it over his ugly face.

"Drop the knife, asshole," Tucker ordered, not even aiming. Muscle memory had never failed him. It wouldn't today.

But RJ didn't answer. Just stared at Kell. Which gave Tucker pause the way Kell was staring back at Savannah. The way she wasn't crying. Didn't look worried. Just kept her gaze fixed on Kell.

Tucker asked her psychically, *'What's going on? Did he hurt you?'*

She offered the barest shake of her head. *'Not yet, but that guy at Sanctuary was his brother. Bernie's the one who blew up Keller's car and my house. He was a simple man, probably the only one in the world who idolized his brother enough to do what RJ wanted.'*

Kell was still in bed, but up on his elbows, breathing heavy and pale as shit. The back of his hand bled where he'd torn out the IVs. But the look in his eyes, the strange light emanating from his pupils... It was black, if that were even possible.

Tucker sent a call to his team. *'Eden. Tate. Isaiah. Are you seeing this?'*

*'Be very careful how you end RJ, Boss. That scalpel's coated with poison,'* Isaiah murmured. *'Let me see if I can get RJ to change his mind.'*

*'Wait, Isaiah. Keller's already in his head,'* Eden said. *'He's got this. Give him a second.'*

*'I see that, Eden,'* Isaiah replied, *'but Keller isn't physically strong enough to fight right now.'*

Tucker took it all in. Kell's intense concentration. Savannah's calm acceptance. The sweat beading on RJ's forehead. *'Stand down. There's something else going on we're not seeing. Stand down. For now.'*

*'She's here,'* Savannah breathed across the group consciousness.

Isaiah's breath caught. *'She who?'*

*'The witch behind the warlock.'*

It hit Tucker like a wrecking ball. *'Kell's mother? That bitch is here? Now?'*

*'Yessssss...'* Savannah hissed as her eyes rolled back in her head.

# Chapter Forty-One

RJ thought he had a dog in this fight? That he could waltz into this room and take Savannah without a fight? *Guess again, dumbass.* Keller had never zeroed down as quickly nor been as focused on so much evil in his life. If Queen Elaine was a voodoo priestess, Rudy John was her lap dog. Like that scene in *'Ghostbusters,'* he was a supporting actor, one of those stone temple dogs, a brain-dead zombie, just playing a part. But Keller was in the fight of his life.

He'd recognized Elaine's unique stink the second RJ cleared the door. How could he forget the putrid odor of rotted garbage and fish guts, the lingering scent of death? And blood. Always blood. She was here in spirit as surely as her zombie puppet was here in the flesh. But today she would die.

Savannah had collapsed, but Keller couldn't see any blood on her neck. She hadn't been cut. RJ still had a tight grip on her neck, that might've caused her to faint. The guy was quick, but Keller suspected RJ had only caught Savannah because of his witch of a mother working behind the scenes. Queen Elaine needed Savannah alive for now. Quick and merciful she was not. Not if this was all about making her son suffer.

Still upright in his arm, Savannah's head lolled against RJ's bony shoulder. He ran his nose up her cheek, then licked her, staring at Keller while he did it, the sick fuck.

And Keller wanted to tear him apart.

*'Guys,'* he said to the people he trusted, his Deuces Wild team. *'Meet my bitch of a mother, the God damned—and I mean that in every sense of the curse—queen of the damned, her fucking highness, Queen Elaine Boniface.'*

A cackle filled the room. *'You're no son of mine.'*

*'Halle-fuckin'-lujah,'* Keller returned with the malice of a lifetime. *'You have no idea how I wish that were true, Ma.'* He spat that last twisted word for the cold-hearted female who'd given him life. There was no love for her. No pleasure at hearing her dried up smoker's rasp. No reason to let her live. It was no wonder Gran Mere mistook Elaine for a man. She sounded like one.

But the anger he'd held onto all these years wasn't enough to fight the kind of evil Elaine had honed into a fine art. And Keller was no idiot. In the last few days, he'd witnessed true magic in action. It didn't come from murdering kittens and squeezing the guts out of tiny, yellow ducklings. It didn't come from chanting spells, painting blood on your ugly wicked face, or cursing evil on your neighbors.

It came from the simple purity beating in Savannah's chest. It came from prayers and believing in the goodness of others. It came from reaching out with love instead of hate. And yes, it came from the Man Upstairs, who even now, Keller realized, he had always believed in.

At the most fundamental level of existence, Elaine wasn't as strong as she thought she was. But Keller was. Because he now knew to his tattered soul that, yes, he loved Savannah with all his heart. She and Carol Marie had been true and honest points of light along the dark path he'd been forced to travel. He'd never deserved them, but that hadn't stopped either of them from reaching out to him and blessing him with their unconditional love. Because love was the most powerful psychic talent in the world. Not hate. Not prejudice. Not rumor or slander. Love *could* work wonders. He just hadn't realized it until now.

Like Savannah would have done if she'd been awake, Keller opened his heart, and cast his first thread into the universe. He called upon his friends for their allegiance and their God-given psychic talents. He called upon their friendship and their loyalty to him. He called the four elements to stand with him.

Air came to his mind on a rush, in the guise of the gentle wisdom of the young genius, Isaiah. A bolt of lightning from stoic Tate crackled through the distance. Keller caught the burning lance with his heart and held on tight to a friendship forged in heavenly fire. Eden, the epitome of Mother Earth's fertile goddess, arrived with a psychic soul hug and the scent of lilacs. Lilacs! The lovely fragrance brought tears to Keller's eyes.

'*Savannah sends her love,*' she whispered. '*She'd be here if she could, but someone's blocking her. She's not worried, though. Knock 'em dead, Kell.*'

And his boss? The bonafide Navy SEAL? True to his larger than life ego, Tucker Chase was suddenly standing inside Keller's room, roaring like one pissed off hurricane, "For thine is the kingdom and the power and the glory! Let it fuckin' rain! Hoo-rah!"

Keller nodded, his heart stuck in his throat and completely overcome by the mists of unconditional love swelling around him like a thick security blanket. That's what his team was. His cushion and his safety net. His buddies to the end. Like the humble servant he was, Keller closed his eyes and called upon the one and only Creator of gifts. "For thine is the kingdom and the power and the glory."

Keller sensed Eden standing in Sanctuary, her head bowed and her hands clasped over her heart, whispering devoutly, '*For thine is the kingdom and the power and the glory.*'

Tate's reverent, '*Only the kingdom, the power and glory. Forever and ever,*' reverberated across the miles.

Isaiah too prayed, *'The kingdom. The power. The glory.'*

Again. The chant swelled around Keller from the four corners of the universe.

And again. Filling him. Crowding the darkness out. Lighting his way. It all came down to this one truth. Darkness could not stand in the grace of one pure light. It wasn't fundamentally, scientifically, or spiritually possible. Savannah had shown Keller the way of grace, and he believed. He finally believed.

But he was injured and growing weaker. Elaine was not. If anything, she'd gathered strength from crushing the weak. *'Nice show, chicken shit, but someone still has to die.'* She summoned her slave. *'Kill her, Rudy John. Cut her throat. Now. While he's watching!'*

*'No!'* Keller knew it then. Elaine wouldn't be satisfied until she had her blood sacrifice. *'Take me,'* he begged on what he hoped was their private channel. *'Order RJ to let Savannah go and take me. I'm the one you've hated all these years.'*

An eerie silence filled his ears even as the Deuces Wild team continued their chant.

Elaine cackled, *'Still so much like your worthless father. Still so weak. I should've killed you when I killed him. Would've been easy. I've always hated you and Hell's been coming for you all your life.'*

With every word she uttered, Keller could feel the icy chill of Death's breath on his soul. Just like with Carol Marie, Elaine had never intended to let Savannah live. *'Why? What'd I ever do to you?'*

*'Because you lived! Because the drunken bastard wouldn't let me kill you when you was born! Then you run off to school and you learned things!'*

Mommy Dearest never could control her temper. But to finally hear her verbalize her hatred, to know she had tried to kill him, her only child, when he was an infant, was still a hard kick in the gut. But Keller had also heard something else in her psychotic rant. Elaine wasn't just hateful. She also ascribed to the horrific practice of infant sacrifice. The only reason Keller was alive today came back to Shane. His father had interfered in whatever ritual Elaine had conjured to murder her baby. The man Keller had forgotten had not forgotten Keller.

By then, sweat ran down his face and stung his eyes. Weary to his soul, Keller focused on Savannah. Nothing else mattered. Elaine was only there in spirit, and RJ was just an unwitting puppet. When she released her control on his mind, RJ would either drop dead or wake up. Keller didn't much care which. The man still held a scalpel to Savannah's throat. He deserved to die. All he had to do was tremble and nick an artery and Savannah...

*'Why Rudy John?'*

Her grunt of indifference came through loud and clear. *'Still don't recognize him, huh? That's Scratch's kid. Another bastard. Another disappointment. Like you.'*

Keller almost felt sorry for RJ. For a second, they were brothers. They'd both come from the same shithole town, the same dirt poor beginnings. They'd both had the same idea, to get as far from home as possible. Yet look where they were today. Staring each other down. On opposite sides. One still striving to be good. One goddamned evil.

'Let Savannah go,' Keller told his wicked witch of a mother. *I'll go with you quietly. Willingly. Hell, I'll kill myself for you if it'll save Savannah. You can watch. You know you want to.'*

'It is tempting,' she cackled, *'but where's the fun in that?'*

Keller knew he'd been wrong then. There was no compromising with evil. She had to die. Risking all, he shot a quick glance at his boss and ordered, "Now!"

Tucker engaged without hesitation. Both hands came up. Both pistols roared with fire. RJ never stood a chance. He crumpled behind Savannah. Two to the head. One center mass. The blade fell to the floor.

Queen Elaine wailed as if she'd been sucked out of the room by an unseen vacuum. Which she had. Her curse was broken. Her slave ripped from her poisonous grasp.

Against all odds, Keller tumbled out of his hospital bed in time to catch Savannah before she sagged into the bloody mess that had been Elaine's puppet. With her safe in his arms, he crab-walked backward to the foot of the bed, his chest on fire and screaming, but not screaming as loudly as his heart. Savannah was safe. That was all that mattered.

Tucker was on RJ, checking his pulse, emptying his pockets. "One down. One to go," he said as he produced a cylindrical glass vial filled with golden fluid. "Want to bet this is another dose of poison?"

'*Boss, I distinctly heard you fire four rounds,*' Isaiah interjected quietly. '*You hit RJ three times. Where's the fourth round? Can you see it? Did you miss? Is it in the wall?*'

Keller looked up at his boss, daring to hope. "Did you—is it possible you—Boss, did you shoot Elaine?" he asked out loud, in case Tucker was too rattled to hear psychically. 'Is that even possible?'

Tucker's brows lifted. The whites flashed bright around his dark pupils. "Well, I wasn't about to let her kill you," he growled out loud. "I heard that bitch. She meant for RJ to torture Savannah while you watched. Didn't matter what you promised, he was going to kill her. When you said '*now,*' I must've... I might have... I could have..." He holstered a pistol, then scraped a quick hand over his hair. "By God, I hope I didn't send that round into thin air. Did I? Isaiah!"

'*You think you killed a woman in Louisiana all the way from Florida?*' Isaiah asked, the awe in his tone palpable.

"I honestly don't know, damn it. I'm not the psychic expert here. You are." Tucker's shoulders lifted as he cleared his pistol and checked his magazine. "You're right, I fired four rounds. Tell me where that last one went."

Eden was unusually quiet, as was Tate. Like Keller, they were probably watching their boss come undone at what he might've unwittingly done. Gun safety was paramount in this business. Backstops were a hard and fast rule. A shooter never unholstered his piece unless he meant to kill someone, and by hell, he never unleashed a round unless he knew precisely who his target was, and what was behind that target. But man, if Tucker did what Keller hoped he'd done... If he'd actually, psychically ended Queen Elaine in Louisiana when he'd fired at RJ...

Keller didn't know what psychically transferring a smoking hot bullet through the universe all the way to Turkey Creek was called, but he wanted in on that psychic talent. That was a gift worth a thousand F10 migraines.

*'Holy fuck,"* Isaiah murmured. *'Ah, Boss. Sorry, but, umm, sorry to have to tell you, Keller, but yeah. I reached out to Queen Elaine Boniface, and she's, umm—'*

*'She's dead, Keller,'* Eden cut in pragmatically. *'I checked on her sorry ass, too. First ever psychic headshot in history. Longest sniper kill ever. Not that it'll ever be recorded but yeah. Congratulations, Boss. You ended Queen Elaine Boniface, thank you very much.'*

*'Six hundred forty-two miles, straight as the crows flies,'* Tate added dryly. *'Not bad shooting. Not bad at all.'*

'*You made that bullet travel through space and time with the energy of your mind,*' Isaiah declared like it was something to be proud of. '*You're a no-kidding telekinesist. I've never met one before. You can move physical objects with your mind.*'

"Oh, bullshit," Tucker cussed as he was prone to do when confronted with the unbelievable and bizarre. "You don't really believe that crap, do you?"

'*Yes, I do. It's true,*' Isaiah replied, '*and I can prove it.*'

'*And I know where the missing round is,*' Eden added. '*I'm sorry that your mom's dead, Keller. No, not really. She earned that bullet in her brain. That's where the round is, guys. She won't be bothering us anymore.*'

'*She was never my mom. Not really.*' Keller wasn't sorry. He didn't feel bad, not for one millionth of a nanosecond. If anything, he felt lighter. Queen Elaine's brutal, conniving reign had ended and he was free. She'd only ever been evil and cruel. By her own mouth, she'd admitted murdering her husband, and she would've killed Savannah. She'd murdered Carol Marie and who knew how many others. Good riddance.

Overcome with an odd rush of giddiness, Keller tipped his head back and laughed. Out loud. The most extraordinary miracle had just taken place. Sure, no one would ever believe that a bullet could travel from Jacksonville, Florida, to Turkey Creek, Louisiana. Just as surely, Tucker would never deny or confirm such an outlandish charge. But these fellow agents, these friends, this crazy Deuces Wild team was Keller's most fervent dream come true. They were his family.

Tucker was the first to join in with a big manly belly laugh. Then Tate chuckled. Finally, Eden busted out in giggles. Even Isaiah laughed along. By then, Savannah was awake and smiling. "It's over," she murmured, her fingers splayed on his chest, tapping out her Secret Agent I love yous.

He covered her hand with his. "I love you, too," he declared for all the world to hear.

"I hope so," she answered demurely. "You asked me to marry you."

"I did," he agreed, his cheeks hurting from grinning. "Hey guys, we're getting married!"

# Chapter Forty-Two

It didn't get any better than this. The rented moving van was filled, the dog crates packed and the single bag of kibble stored on board. The rest of Savannah's dogs had been adopted out to loving families, or were down at Mr. Howard's Pet Store. For a while there, it hadn't seemed possible that everything would come together. But it had, and come sunup tomorrow morning, Savannah was headed north with her husband.

"My husband. Did you hear that?" she asked the Red Setter, to be known now and forever more as Prince Harry. Okay so it wasn't Irish, but the handsome fellow deserved a royal title, especially since his drooling, slobbering buddy had been tagged Sir Galahad. "I'm a married woman and I have a handsome husband. Have you seen him lately?"

Prince Harry barked from his post inside the big truck's cab. Like that told Savannah anything, other than he was making sure he wouldn't get left behind. Poor baby still had anxiety attacks.

Keller had to be around here somewhere. Sanctuary was large, and Savannah was leaving most of her belongings behind. Lyle Goldenrod had bought the five acres of swampland, and he'd adopted all Savannah's birds and cats. Said they made him feel like he was home again. Even now, he was fast at work with a team of high school football players, rebuilding the deck and the portion of her home that had been ruined in the explosion and fire. Coach looked happy. He had his life back.

Glancing to her left, then to her right, Savannah brushed her hands together before resting them on her hips. Where was that man? They had things to discuss. Keller wasn't manning the table saw for Coach, and there was nothing left in the house worth packing or boxing, so he couldn't be in there.

To keep things simple, he'd moved in with her at Sanctuary after a justice of the peace married them in New Orleans. His Deuces Wild team was with them that afternoon, and the evening celebration, unexpectedly sponsored by Mr. Chase, was one of a kind.

Unbeknownst to Keller, Tucker rented a private room at a restaurant off Bourbon Street, complete with a blues singer and all the food and alcohol you could want. Outlandish toasts, all at Keller's expense, were offered. Savannah had never eaten or danced so much in her life. But the truly eye-popping moment happened when Keller swept Savannah onto the dance floor, tap dancing to *"Boogie Woogie Bugle Boy of Company B."* Holy Mother! Her Secret Agent Man could dance!

Mr. Chase had just declared there wasn't enough alcohol in the entire world to get him on the floor. At the sight of Keller dancing with enthusiasm no one knew he had, Mr. Chase spit beer all over his table. Tate Higgins laughed so hard his eyes watered. Truly a night Savannah would never forget. She and Keller hadn't been able to keep their hands off each other since then. So yeah. He had to be close by.

Savannah circled her house, told her birds goodbye, and made sure they had clean water one last time. She walked the perimeter, a knot in her throat at the departure looming in the morning. But she'd be okay. Gran Mere always said when one door closes, a window opens.

With Prince Harry now trotting at her side, Savannah inspected her dog kennels and made sure the gates were closed in case a strong wind came up. The overhead lights in the barn were on. Interesting. She could've sworn she'd turned them off.

A noise from the supply room caught her ear. It better not be one of those pesky raccoon twins that had been hanging around, those adorable little bandits. It was hard to be angry with the cute little guys for upending her garbage cans, but they made such a mess.

Striding with full intent, she shoved the supply room door open and— "Oh," squeaked out of her throat.

"Come on in," Keller said, motioning to the blanket laid out in the middle of that small room. He sat there cross-legged, his jeans tight at his knees. His chest was bare and an OD Army t-shirt had been tossed beside a bottle of champagne in an ice bucket. A plate of powdered sugared beignets rested in the center of the blanket. A plate of crispy brown bacon, too. Like a lure...

Savannah's fingers came up to her lips at the sight. There was a hard, hard day not too long past that she'd lured Keller with an offer of bacon. He'd remembered, and he was luring her in now. Which made sense. After all, her dogs couldn't refuse it. Why should she?

Savannah shooed faithful Prince Harry out of the supply room before he made himself comfortable, then closed the door and locked it. Smiling, she knelt on the blanket opposite Keller, the offering between them. He never looked more handsome. His amber eyes were soft and golden. His skin as tan and rich as ever. Keller was so much her heart's fondest treasure. Her most sincere desire.

"I thought you might need a break," he said. Deftly he tore the foil from the bottle and untwisted the wire cage, his biceps taut, his elbows out, and the veins on the backs of his hands on display. He had magic fingers. Just watching them work sent a rush of heat to her core. "You've been at this since the sun came up. You must be hungry. I know I am. Bacon?"

It was hard to speak. This incredible man had only ever offered sustenance and salvation. He was a warrior and her best friend. He already knew her body and her heart.

Fortunately, the cork blasted skyward, breaking the sexual tension. Savannah laughed at the smile in Keller's wide eyes. But enough was enough. She didn't want beignets or bacon. With champagne foaming out of the bottle, she forced him onto his back, licking up his neck to settle her real craving while he kept the bottle from spilling. This man's body had quickly become her favorite addiction, not that she had many others. But she wanted this particular one now.

Keller eased down onto the blanket with a husky groan that lasted until she covered his mouth with hers. Breathing his breath. Tasting Keller. Part sugary coffee, part starched black tie and the whiskey he ended most days with. Now that they were married, she knew he suffered shades of post-traumatic stress. Nothing serious but enough that he'd never admit it. The single glass of whiskey just helped him sleep. She also knew that even when he was hurt, like when he'd smashed his thumb with the hammer while helping Coach build a sawhorse, he was more inclined to tell her he was 'good' when he most certainly was not. She'd married a badass. A tough man's man who still had a lot of secrets to share. And she loved him more every day.

He still held one hand on the bottle, the other on her backside as she mugged him. Her tongue made love to his, her hands now on his chest, soaking in all those tantalizing alpha hormones through her fingerprints. Instant heat spiked when her fingertips grazed his nipples. Already hard as diamonds, her sensitive nipples turned needy against the inside of her tank top. These clothes had to go.

Reaching behind her back, she jerked her top off and sent it flying. That got his attention. "I love a woman who knows what she wants," he mumbled around her lips.

"I want you," she growled. "Lose the bottle and the pants. Food can wait."

"But baby..."

"But baby, nothing." She loved it when he called her baby. With other guys, it might have been a sleazy put down, but when Keller said it, all she heard was love. Her hand shifted from his chest to his zipper. "You want me to help you with this?"

She could feel him smiling through her French kisses. Easing his head back, he shoved the dripping bottle between them and into her chest. Between her breasts. It was c-c-cold. It was wet. His eyes turned more black than amber, the pupils wide, taking in the goosebumps on her skin.

"We should've had a drink first," he growled. "Newlyweds, remember?"

The second she moved, he had her on her back, the bottle poised over her bare belly and mischief in his eyes. "Take your pants off. Quickly, Savannah. Chop, chop. Or else—"

"Or else what?" Her core clenched at the teasing threat.

"Shhhhh. No talking. Just action. Get that ass out of your jeans. You're killing me."

Lowering her hands to her waistband, she unsnapped and unzipped, then waited until he tugged them down her legs and threw them aside.

"There now, it's your turn—" she started to say.

"Uh uh. That wasn't fast enough. Now you pay."

"I pay? But... Oooooo..." He'd poured champagne in her navel. Cold champagne. With effervescent bubbles that were now streaming over her belly. Down her sides. Fizzling and tickling and...

"Ooops, that can't be good. Let me help," he muttered and then dipped his face into her tummy and suckled, making cute little pig noises as he slurped and licked and...

Sweet Mother, he could do that to her forever. She'd never get enough of the wet, warm suction of his mouth and tongue. The soft whisper of his breath on her skin. The scrape of yesterday's five o'clock shadow, now grown thicker. Rougher. Turning her on.

"Do that again," she ordered, her body melting under his noisy, tender care. But she needed more than just play. He needed to get serious before she went up in flames. "Hurry."

"Is my baby greedy?" he teased, the bottle gone somewhere and his hands on her wrists as his tongue journeyed between her ribs to her breasts. He made a meal of her, sucking first one nipple, then the other into the heat of his mouth. Nibbling. Blowing on her wet skin. Leaving her quivering while his knees settled between her thighs. "I'm taste testing. Don't distract me."

Another drizzle of chilling alcohol drenched her chest. His cheeks puffed out before he blew on her breasts. Savannah squirmed. "Now you've done it," she squealed as another chilling blast wafted over her bare body.

"I've just begun." He blew on her again.

"I'm freezing."

"Then we'll just have to warm you up."

She was shivering by then. "Yes, please. I'm turning into a snowman."

His fingers were already doing a fine job. Make that an excellent job. He kept looking and watching where his fingers wandered instead of kissing and snuggling to get her warm. By then she didn't care. She felt the burn down low in her belly. The wave of pleasure quickly turned into a tsunami. It pulled her along with it. Into Keller. Cresting high. So high. Higher. There was only Keller. His mouth. His tongue. Her heart.

She closed her eyes and rode the wave. She meant to tell him he was a terrible tease, but the orgasm smashed over her, pushing her until she could only hold onto him and cry, "Keller! Yesssss, Keller. Yes! You... You..."

Like every time with him, Savannah couldn't think, couldn't form a coherent sentence. Just let the most incredible man in her life hold her tight while sweat poured off her like a sweat hog.

"I knew it," he growled, nuzzling her ear and nipping her earlobe. "I don't even have to take my pants off to make you come. I like that. You're so sweet. So fucking responsive."

Her heart still pounded like a hammer in her chest. "That's what this was all about? My sexual response-o-meter?" she asked weakly, her lips dry but her body drenched and a smile on her face. That smile felt like it stretched over her entire body. And oh, she was still the only one naked on this blanket.

Reaching for the champagne, Keller took a big mouthful, then planted his lips on hers and trickled the foaming drink into her open mouth. "Kind of. Sort of," he said as he licked her lips and the streams of champagne that had gotten away. "I do like to fill you up."

"I like when you do."

"See, that's the thing. You're so open to anything I want to do."

"I love you and you love me. Makes it easy to play games, especially these kinds of games."

"How many kids do you see us having?"

Savannah opened her tired eyeballs at that out of the blue question. "I'm open to suggestions."

By then he'd balanced his weight on one elbow and shoved out of his pants and boxers. "I figure two's a good place to start," he said as he settled back between her legs. "One really is a lonely number, you know. I don't want to do that to a kid. Maybe we could have a couple sets of twins."

"Twins?!" She cupped his handsome rugged face between her hands, her thumbs caressing his cheekbones as she tipped forward and kissed his mouth. The kiss turned feverish and so darned hot she forgot about those twins and found herself on the edge of another orgasm. "You're doing it to me again. Hurry."

"Again?" he mumbled, a huge dose of male pride in that single word. "Was it talking about lots of kids?"

"Keller..."

"Well, let's get serious about making us some babies then." With one slippery rush, Keller slipped into her body, branding her with his thick heat. His passion.

"Yes," she cried into his shoulder, completely undone at the depth of love for him. For this man, she'd do anything. Everything. "Yes, yes. Ah, yessss."

"I love you, Savannah," he purred against her cheek. "You are my world. My sun and my moon. My shiny Christmas star."

There were no words, not as strong as this second orgasm was. She couldn't have answered if she'd tried. Breathing hard, the sensational sexual storm dissipated too quickly, leaving tidal surges that clenched Keller's manhood, still tugging him into her heat.

She lost all control, all sense of composure. He did that to her, his eyes lit amber in sunlight. "I stink," she told him. "I need a shower."

Ducking his head, he licked between her breasts, her neck and up to her chin. "Uh uh," he growled before he ended with a sloppy, wet kiss on her mouth. "I love the way you smell. The way you taste. I love everything about you. Ready for more?"

She was still panting. "More?"

His smile couldn't have been wider. Keller was adorable now that he'd realized he was in love. How could she refuse? "Always," she told him. "Always and always."

# Chapter Forty-Three

Keller stood ramrod straight beside Savannah on the steps of the historic Saint Mary's Basilica in Old Town Alexandria, Virginia. Sandwiched between Wolf Street and Duke Street, a mere four blocks from the Potomac, the old church boasted a reverence he'd only witnessed during Savannah's prayers.

But it'd been years since he'd dared defile a sacred building with his presence, the last and only time when he'd married. That had been an Army wedding, complete with a couple rowdy guys from his unit. Carol Marie had cried, she'd been so happy. He'd teared up, too. But today? Here and now? He ducked when he entered the heavy wooden doorway, just in case God really kept track of sinners who darkened His holy places.

But there he was—in church—dressed in a new suit, one Savannah insisted he purchase for Isaiah's son's baptism. One constructed of one hundred percent *Mélange-weave Italian linen*, as if Keller knew or cared what that was. He didn't care it was a light gray called *'heather myst'* either. One of his reliable black work suits would've been good enough.

He had opted for a simple cotton polo to go with the blazer, but no, no, no. Savannah shushed that notion right off his lips. Like any man being railroaded by a pretty woman, he would've argued, and he might've won. But then she kissed him because she'd thought she'd hurt his feelings. And damn. Because of that steaming hot, sultry Southern kiss, and the fact that whenever Savannah kissed him, he lost his ever-loving mind, Keller bought the damned suit and a white cotton button-down shirt to go with it. Then he bought socks to match the suit and new underwear, which were *not* gray, just to make her happy. And there he was, dressed for fashion in a House of God where lightning could still strike and turn him to a charred corpse any second now. But she'd said he looked handsome...

*'I'm a sucker for this woman,'* he admitted to the Man on the Cross. *'Thank you for bringing her into my life, sir. Thank you very much. And for Dad, too.'*

It hadn't been hard to track down Shane Boniface. Tucker had the report of Shane's military service on Keller's desk the morning he made it into the office. Sgt. 1st Class Shane Joseph Boniface, 39, of Lawrence, Kansas, assigned to the 1st Battalion, 3rd Special Forces Group, Fort Bragg, North Carolina.

How about that? Keller's dad had been Army special forces. He'd been one of three operators sent into eastern Afghanistan, province of Ghazni, to rescue a female reporter who'd thought she could hide behind a veil to get a story. Shane and the reporter were the only ones who'd survived. An IED took the other two. Which made Shane's death at Queen Elaine's hands all the worse. She'd murdered an American hero with a case of severe PTSD who'd simply self-medicated with alcohol. He wasn't the first and he surely wouldn't be the last.

With all his heart, Keller wanted to dig her sorry ass up and kill her again. But he kept it together, even thanked his boss that day.

Tucker had shrugged and told him, "No problem. That's my job." But it wasn't. Not really. Tucker just did what good bosses everywhere did. He looked out for his men and women. He meant what he said and he said what he meant.

Keller meant to pay that kindness forward. He'd already begun the process. At long last, Sgt. 1st Class Shane Boniface was coming home. In less than a month, his body would be exhumed and put to its eternal rest in Section 60, Arlington National Cemetery, where other American heroes lay. It was the least Keller could do for the father who saved his life.

But Isaiah said the baptism was a private affair? *Yeah right.* Keller didn't recognize everyone in attendance, but he knew all the main players. Tucker and Melissa sat in the front row with their son, Deuce, as well as Isaiah, Roxy, their baby son, and Hayden Thurston, Roxy's father. A heavy-duty, camouflage-colored baby carrier that looked tough enough to withstand Armageddon rested next to Hayden. Had to be a gift from Tucker.

Tate and his wife Winslow sat alongside Eden and Ky in the second row. Their son Kyler bounced on his daddy's thighs, drooling, one hand stuffed in his mouth. Next to Ky sat Eden's uncle, the famous and more often than not discredited by both press and president alike, FBI Director Zachary Strong, his pretty wife Helen at his side. Married for more than thirty years, they made a striking couple. When Helen tipped around her husband and smiled at Kyler, the little tyke all but dropped into her waiting hands. Director Strong grinned as Kyler was passed from his father to a great aunt who obviously adored him.

Intermingled among those friends was a large group of contractors, Alex Stewart, his former military men and women. Mr. Stewart and his wife Kelsey were seated in the front pew of the side section, him looking relaxed in a silvery business suit and pink tie, his gorgeous wife in a matching pink dress. Their little girl Lexie Rose, a brown-eyed, curly-haired clone of her mother, sat with Mark Houston and his family. The little girl holding Lexie had to be their oldest, but darn. Keller couldn't remember all Mark's kids' names. But he'd never forget Mark's wife.

It was Libby's sister who'd died during that bungled FBI operation in Wisconsin a couple years back. Faith. He'd never forget that name, either. The operation had been a POS from the beginning. Keller hadn't been part of the Bureau then, but he knew that, if not for Stewart charging in and taking over like the ass he could be, Libby would've lost her entire family. The Bureau had failed to protect and serve—miserably. In that failure alone, they'd also lost nearly a dozen agents.

Only later was the betrayer inside the Bureau discovered. Once again, it was one of Stewart's men who'd charged to the rescue. Only Libby's husband, Mark Houston, hadn't realized he'd ended Faith's killer with a single shot to his smug face the day Mark and Ky Winchester rescued Eden, Isaiah, and his father. The whole convoluted story didn't come out until weeks later, after the Justice Department completed their investigation into the FBI's handling of the case.

But it was true. In the end, conniving Karma had come through with one helluva royal bitch slap. In her roundabout, *I've-got-all-the-time-in-the-universe-to give-you-precisely-what-you-deserve* way, she'd sent Faith Clifton's USMC brother-in-law, Mark Houston, to end FBI Special Agent Matt Hartigen, the lying bastard behind the bungled operation. And like most greedy bastards out to rule the world, Hartigen never saw Karma coming. Guess you just had to have— *Faith*—that the universe would provide. Faith and a company of snipers.

Harley and Judy Mortimer sat behind the Stewarts, along with their twin boys, both smaller versions of their father. Blond, blue-eyed Connor Maher, his wife Izza and their kids completed the second row. Interestingly, Connor sported a black eye this morning. What was that about?

Laid back Zach was present, along with Mei and their daughters. Keller couldn't remember the girls' names, but they were a cute handful. With Zach's massive build, his mocha coloring, and Mei's lovely Chinese glow, they made a gorgeous couple. Zach gave Keller one of those knowing chin nods. Keller returned the greeting.

More of Alex's other agents and their families filled the following rows. Rory and Ember Dennison were there along with Taylor and Gracie Armstrong, Maverick and China Carson, Adam and Shannon Torrey, to name a few. *Well hello,* even Alex's former senior agent, Roy Hudson was there with an elegant black woman seated at his side. Was that his ex-wife? They sure looked chummy.

And how about that? Murphy Finnegan sat in the same pew with Roy. Man, this baptism was like old home week. Keller hadn't seen Roy since he'd retired a few years back after getting shot on that wild operation in Utah. The same with Murphy. He hadn't been in the District much since he'd taken over The TEAM's Seattle office. Looked like the Pacific Northwest agreed with the old fart.

Beau Villanueva! Now that was a surprise. But there he was with his wife McKenna. Keller's hand came up without thinking. Beau waved back. The older Hispanic couple sitting with them must be his parents. Keller waved at them, too. Now there was a story worth the telling. Keller hadn't worked with Beau, but he knew the tough guy's pain. Their childhoods weren't so different.

Dodging more covert waves and whispered hellos from old friends as they made their way forward, Keller and Savannah joined his team on the front row.

The service was fairly quick and informal. After a few introductions, Father McCallion urged the godparents to come forward. The entire Deuces Wild team stood, Keller included. That was Roxy's idea. Once she'd invited Tucker, she'd decided Little Chase might as well have his daddy's entire family at his back.

After the Deuces Wild team made their way to the white marble font, the priest bowed his head and offered a couple prayers. For a few minutes he expounded on faith and charity, on supporting the church, and on being a good Christian. At last he lifted a small silver bowl from the edge of the font, dipped it into the water, and with Isaiah holding his sleeping son over the font, Father declared, "I baptize you, Tucker Chase Zaroyin in the name of the Father—" He poured the first of what would be three streams over the crest of Chase's forehead. "—and the Son—" Another stream anointed the now fussing baby. "—and the Holy Spirit." The last of the water spilled out, and newly baptized Tucker Chase Zaroyin bellowed for his mommy.

Roxy leaned in to wipe his head while Isaiah lifted the infant to his shoulder and soothed him. Keller couldn't help but swipe the moisture gathered in the corner of his eyes. He'd never been baptized, didn't want to be now. What he wanted was the sensational feelings coalesced inside this church today. This was family. Pure and simple. There was no pain. No agony. Only reverence and a tapestry of red, white, and blue devotion binding them to each other and to God.

The empathy binding them together was—wow. Unbelievable. Keller had experienced team cohesiveness in his life before. That was what the Army did to recruits. They tore young men and women apart, then built them back up and turned them into disciplined, honorable fighting machines. But nothing the Army ever did was as powerful as what was happening between these men and women, these families gathered here today. For one little baby. They'd each made time in their busy lives to stand by a child. By the world's standards, this was a non-event. It'd never make the tabloids, certainly not the propaganda laced diatribes that modern media called news. But it hit Keller hard. He needed to sit down before he fell down.

"I've got you, Secret Agent Man," Savannah whispered as her arm circled his waist.

Damned if Tucker didn't clap a big hand to Keller's shoulder with a hoarse, "On your six, Kell."

Shit. Yeah. Now for sure Keller needed to get out of there. His heart was so full it hurt.

Until sweet, understanding Savannah broke the spell. Lifting her hands over her head, she clapped and surprised the hell out of him when she broke into a gospel spiritual he loved, *"Oh, Happy Day!"* by Philip Doddridge.

"Come on folks, you all know the chorus," she encouraged, dancing now and turning this quiet little Catholic service into something bigger and bolder. Wilder. "Put your hands in the air. Praise God. There you go. That's it, sisters!"

Savannah's eyes lit when her grinning choir chimed in with gusto. She'd sing a line. They'd answer as if they'd practiced. All the children danced along with her. Even Father McCallion gave it a spin. The music swelled and took on a life of its own as if angels had joined the party.

Isaiah and Roxy had Baby Chase sandwiched between them while they sang together. Yet Keller couldn't take his eyes off Savannah. She'd brought this quaint Catholic ritual to life, infused it with her brand of joy and enthusiasm, exactly what she'd done with him.

She caught him watching. Dancing her way through the singing joyful crowd to Keller, she got sidetracked by Maverick who grabbed her waist and belted out, *"He taught me how..."*

Savannah danced along, shimmying to his shimmy and answering in her lovely soprano. When Maverick dipped his head to her and bellowed the next line, she nodded back and sang along. But day-um… Keller's throat went bone dry. Everywhere Savannah went people fell in love with her. Even Maverick. Those two looked good together, him with his tall, lean physique, dressed in western wear like he was. She in her simple white, sleeveless dress. The bastard was definitely enjoying himself. Too much. This shit had to stop.

Especially when the man others called Cowboy spun Savannah in a full circle, then busted out with some pretty good moves of his own. Uh uh, not happening. Keller cut in. By then Savannah was sweating and Maverick was grinning.

Okay, enough. Keller cut in, grabbing his woman's hand. Without hesitation, Maverick bowed at the waist and turned her loose. Finally pressed against his chest where she belonged, Savannah's eyes glowed. That was her gift and Keller's eternal consternation. His woman simply burned with a love so rich, it splashed over everyone around her, dogs, cats, birds, and people alike. Even him.

There was no reason to be angry at Maverick. He was just another guy caught up in her orbit. Keller understood. He'd been the same when Carol Marie had taught him to dance. Yet instinctively, his eyes roamed the crowd, checking for the guy who'd dared fall in love with his wife. But Maverick was over by the baptismal font now, mooning over China and swaying to the emotion of the day. Okay then.

Possessively, Keller pulled Savannah in closer. There was no way to explain it. The universe poured light and energy down upon her pretty head, seemingly without her trying. And that was her secret. The more she gave away, the more blessings she received, until like that proverbial cup, she simply brimmed over and spilled it on everyone around her. Like here. Like now. She had everyone dancing, singing, and praising the Lord.

Across the sanctuary, Tucker swayed cheek to cheek with Melissa, while Alex had both his girls, spinning them each in circles, laughing when they crashed back into him. Until that moment, Keller hadn't known Alex smiled. But he surely did, at least with his wife and little girl.

Even stoic Tate was locked in Winslow's arms, her head pressed under his chin as they followed along with the song Savannah had started. These people didn't seem to want to leave, and Keller didn't blame them. The women's voices truly were voices of angels, but those deep, resounding male voices... Holy Jesus, they vibrated the church walls with the energy of thunder and lightning. Of all things male and dominant. So low. So powerful. So damned strong. Shivers raced up Keller's spine at the joyful menace behind every word. Every two-step. Every prayer. It was like watching God's army in action. *Watch and pray, indeed.*

"I have something for you," he whispered as he tugged her red beads up from his fancy new suit pocket.

"My rosary! I wondered where it went. Thanks." She slid the sparkles over her head, and she was his queen again. They belonged there like he belonged around her little finger.

"I took them the night at the Ritz. Didn't want you to strangle in your sleep."

"Dance with me," Savannah answered as if she'd never once worried where her beads were.

He grinned down at her. She knew he could dance, but here? In front of all these people?

Her bright eyes smiled up at him, sparkling as much as those red crystals. And Keller said what he intended to say for the rest of his life. "Yes, ma'am."

# Epilogue

Tucker Chase tipped his wide body back in his chair, far enough to plant both spit-polished boots on his desk and cross his ankles. Life wasn't fair, not that he was complaining. He wasn't. But complainers seemed to show up whenever two or more people put their pointed little heads together. Didn't matter if they were special operators or civilians, popes or convicted criminals, someone in the crowd was always moaning and pissing. They whined when it rained, then whined when the sun came out. The day was too hot or too bright. They whined when they were hungry, and they whined after they'd eaten a twelve-course meal. Nothing was warm enough, cold enough, salted enough, bland enough, quiet or dark enough. Wah, wah, wah.

Some folks were just born to suck the joy out of life. Fun suckers. That's what they were. They were glass half-empty types. Pain in the ass pansies who only offered negative energy to every operation. They were road blockers, contributing argument after argument as to why nothing smart could work or why every proposal was flawed. They tore people down. The Navy was full of fun suckers. Hell, so was Congress.

But not Deuces Wild. Now there was a team to be proud of, and by hell, Tucker was. They might be only a handful in number, but they were mighty. Of course, the concept behind Deuces Wild still spooked the straights, what he called anyone not psychically endowed, but it was what it was. All through history, superior intelligence had confounded simple folks. Not that he was a genius or anything. Tucker knew most certainly that he was not. But Isaiah was. Eden might be too. Even Kell. Tucker wouldn't be surprised. Kell had proven himself to be so much more than just a tortured empath. Once he'd let loose of his past, he'd changed overnight. Might have something to do with marrying Savannah Church. She'd finally met with Isaiah, and yes, she was another Level Ten. But unlike Isaiah, she came without emotional baggage. She'd been raised with nothing but love, and it had made one helluva difference.

Maybe all those sappy songs were right. Maybe love really could change the world.

But *what to do. What to do...*

Any minute now, Eden would advise Tucker that he had a visitor. Fish and Wildlife Agent Camilla Brinkman. Yeah, her. Tucker intended to keep his boots right where they were. He wouldn't usually do that when he had visitors, but she didn't deserve respect. Not yet. She hadn't earned it. The woman needed to learn her place, and it was not on the top rung. She wasn't director material, not even decent unskilled labor as far as Tucker could tell. She might have political backing up her ass, but Brinkman had no experience working in the real world. No talent either.

College degrees didn't mean shit to Tucker. He'd worked with men and women all over the world who hadn't finished school, yet knew more than Brinkman. And he'd gone over Brinkman's personnel file. She'd been bounced all over Division of Fish and Wildlife since the day her connected husband got the job for her. For as smart as Tucker knew she was, her ratings were less than stellar. She rubbed people the wrong way. No one wanted to work with her.

Neither did he.

*'She's here...'* Eden sing-songed in his head.

*'Send her in.'*

The door swung wide and in marched FWS Agent Camilla Brinkman like she had a broomstick stuck up her ass. Dressed in a dark purple business suit, matching slacks and pinpoint stilettos with six-inch heels, she did cut an impressive figure. Out of uniform, yes, but sleek and polished 'looking.' Arrogant as all get out, but fierce. Without offering a civil greeting, she tossed her chin at him and said, "I'm here. What do you want?"

That cued Tucker's disgust all over again. A smart person who really wanted to advance in their federal career might have offered a "Good morning, Director Chase" or a "It's nice to see you again." Not Miss High-and-Mighty. This was going to be more fun than he expected.

"Shut the door," he told her even as he maintained his casual disdain.

Turning, Agent Brinkman slapped one palm to his door and slammed it with a bang. She stalked like one of those dead-faced, long-legged runway models across his office to the window. A smart recruit would have stood waiting front and center of his desk. But that would've required respect for the office, and Brinkman seemed to think everyone else in the world was beneath her. That he owed her something when in fact, it was the other way around.

Tucker pursed his lips and matched her spoiled brat attitude with indifference. She wanted attention. Well, she was going to get it.

Just as she'd smoothed one hand under her ass to sit in the leather chair by his window, Tucker said, "Don't get comfortable. You're not staying here."

Did her nose just flare? Did she shoot him a nasty glare? He could've laughed in her face. The woman was his ex-wife all over again. Spoiled and conniving. Well, he could be conniving too.

By then her hands were on her hips and her nose was definitely out of joint. "What do you mean, I'm not staying? My director said to report to you, that I was officially on loan to the FBI until further notice."

Still stretched out in recliner mode, Tucker yawned to prove how little he cared about how she felt or what she thought. Still looking at the ceiling, he gave it to her with blunt force. "I don't need you and I don't like you. But I do have a job for you if you're smart enough to handle it. That's the real question, isn't it? You can't seem to hold a position long enough to gain any traction, can you? People just don't like working with you."

All Tucker got back was an unladylike grunt. Not that he cared. He offered her the carrot anyway. "I've got a friend in the covert surveillance business. He needs someone to run his office while his Girl Friday is on leave. If you can handle that for, oh, say, six months, I'll put in a good word for you back at FWS, provided that's where you really want to spend your career."

Dead silence.

Tucker wasn't about to waste the time it took to look at Brinkman to judge her opinion of the suggestion. He flat didn't care. The truth was FWS didn't want her back, but if anyone could turn her pretentious ass around and make her an honest broker, it was Alex Stewart. Of course, Tucker still had to call Alex and tell him what he'd done to him, ahem, for him.

But Alex *did* need the help. His admin genius, Sasha Kennedy, hadn't yet come back from the extended vacation she'd gone on after her daughter died. And the Bureau *did* have an agent exchange program with Alex. Kind of. Sort of. That was how Tucker acquired both Ky Winchester and Tate Higgins. Didn't hurt that they were talented psychics. Okay, so that rare talent had made a huge difference. Tucker had been tasked to man the most important FBI directorate in history. He'd all but begged Alex to give him Ky and Tate. Blame it on Eden. She was the one who'd told Tucker they were psychics, untrained, maybe, but still enough to get the Bureau's first psychic directorate up and running.

When Brinkman still said nothing, Tucker turned his head and deliberately stared her down. "Well? What's it going to be? Out the door or upward and onward? Your choice."

"Let me get this straight," she sneered, her razor thin nose flaring, her dark eyes flashing sparks of disgust. "You expect me to work for a private contractor. Me. How is that even legal?"

*Oh, she has a lot to learn.*

"It's legal because the Bureau has a standing agreement with Stewart. We trade agents all the time," he lied. "It's a win/win. You'll get on the job tactical training." *And I'll get rid of you.*

Brinkman snorted.

Leaning forward, Tucker thumped both boots to the floor. "Bottom line, you'll work for Alex or you're off federal payroll. FWS doesn't want you back, and you're not psychic, so I can't use you. If you're smart, you'll knuckle down and do a good job for Alex. He might even decide to keep you."

Huffing, Brinkman averted her gaze to the ceiling as if counting to ten or praying for patience. Tucker doubted that second option. Blink, blink, blink went those bright black eyes. Tap, tap, tap went her expensively clad toes. Tucker didn't want to look at her feet to confirm, but were those purple heels Jimmy Choo's?

It took a minute, maybe because Brinkman didn't know how to count to ten, either, but at last she breathed a drawn out, "Fine. I'll go. Where is this place and what's it called?"

Her snotty acceptance elicited a grin from Tucker. He couldn't help it. Alex and he were not exactly good buddies, but they did have a somewhat amicable truce between them. And Alex *did* need admin help. But Alex was also one tough, ball-breaking DI from the ground up. Miss Entitled had no idea what she was walking into, and Tucker would not tell her.

He handed over Stewart's business card. "Here's the address. It's known up and down the East Coast as *The TEAM.*" That hint should've told her that working for Stewart was a privilege, that she'd be better paid working for him than in the federal sector. But Tucker wasn't about to tell her that. Let Miss Smarty-Pants figure it out. "Stewart's expecting you." *Or he will be as soon as I tell him what I just did for him... err, to him.*

She snatched the card out from between Tucker's fingers with disdain. "The TEAM? Stupid name. Never heard of it."

"Well, yeah, it's *covert surveillance*," he reminded her. "That's what Stewart's good at, never being seen or heard." *Are you sure you graduated from college?*

Another huff. "Do I still get my regular pay?"

"You're a GS-seven, right?" General Service pay scale, GS-07. Depending on her locality and series, she probably cleared thirty-five to forty-five thou a year, which, in the high-priced District, was not enough to live on, not the way she shopped.

"Yes," she hissed, "but I was up for a promotion."

Tucker's mouth twisted at that bold-faced fib. The only raise Brinkman had coming was her cost-of-living increase, and she wouldn't see that until January—if the president signed it into law. But interestingly, her within-grade step increase had been put on hold by her immediate supervisor, which proved what FWS management thought of her. Most within-grade increases were automatic. That Brinkman's boss had taken the time to deliberately squelch hers spoke volumes.

"Unless you decide you'd rather work for Stewart, yes, you'll continue to receive your regular pay and benefits. You'll still be a civil servant."

Agent Brinkman snorted as if that title offended her. But honestly, there was no GS schedule for spoiled bitch. Without so much as a thank you, go to hell, or kiss my ass, she jerked the door open and waltzed out with her nose in the air. Damn. Tucker didn't know whether to feel sorry for Alex or her.

No matter. He picked up his phone, put his boots back on his desk, and rang up his semi-good friend.

"What do you want, Chase?"

"Hey, Alex. I've been thinking. It only seems fair that since I took two of your best operators—"

"You mean stole."

"Well, yeah, but I did loan Isaiah back to you, at least the Bureau loaned him to you a couple months back."

"You mean during that debacle in Vietnam when I had to get your ass out of jail?"

"That's the one."

"Doesn't count. You still owe me, you rat bastard."

Tucker's grin deepened. "You're right. I am a bastard. Comes with the trident, but I thought I'd give you a heads-up. Just sent someone over to fill in until Miss Kennedy comes back."

"She's Mrs. Sandler now."

"Mother got married? Well, err, umm..." That was unexpected news. "When'd that happen?"

"Not sure. I wasn't invited. Who the hell are you pawning off on me?"

*Ouch.* Alex didn't mince words. There were times Tucker wondered if he weren't psychic, too. He did have an uncanny sense for zeroing in on a liar.

Sasha, aka Mother, hadn't been back to work since she'd lost her daughter. After the funeral, she and her lifelong friend, Justice Sandler, had taken an extended ocean cruise that ended at an island somewhere in the Pacific. But not being at his friend's wedding had to have hurt. Alex and Sasha, whom he'd nicknamed Mother, always had one of those love/hate work relationships. She adored him; he tolerated her. But beneath the bluster, they'd been rock solid. Tucker envied them. They were good together.

"I'm sorry," he said sincerely.

"Forget it." Alex brushed him off with his usual gruffness. "When's this genius supposed to show up? Today? Tomorrow? Soon?"

"She's on her way," Tucker said quietly. What had seemed like a good joke on Alex, now felt like a terrible trick. Alex worked his ass off every day. He suffered with his men and women, and he led his TEAM from the front instead of the rear, where chicken shits ruled. If not for the tragedy he'd suffered years ago, he should've, could've, would've made five-star USMC general by now. He had that kind of drive and vision. That kind of honor.

Maybe this wasn't a brilliant idea.

"Thanks for thinking of us," Alex bit out. "Might be hope for you yet."

Tucker had the good grace to wince at that off-handed compliment. "No bother. Just keep her busy. She's a hard worker."

"She got a name?"

"Agent Camilla Brinkman. She worked for the Div—"

"You son of a bitch!"

*Oh, shit.* Alex knew Brinkman. That could be good. That could be bad. Tucker set the smoking hot phone gently back in its cradle. But then he smiled. There were no two ways about it. Agent Brinkman was going to get precisely what she deserved.

# THE END

**Thank you for reading Keller's story!**

**You are the key to this book's success.**

Please tell other readers why you liked ACE
by leaving an honest review
at the retail site where you purchased it.
Recommend it to your friends. Lend it.
Most of all, enjoy it!

**Other Irish Winters' best-selling books/series**

*In the Company of Snipers*

*Alex*
*Mark*
*Zack*
*Harley*
*Connor*
*Rory*
*Taylor*
*Gabe*
*Maverick*
*Cassidy*
*Adam*
*Lee*
*Ky*
*Hunter*
*Eric*
*Jake*
*Seth*
*Beau*

**Coming soon:**

*Renner*

*Beckam*
## Deuces Wild

*King of Hearts*
*Joker Joker*
*One-Eyed Jack*

## Hearts and Ashes

*Smoke*
*Ash*

## SOBs Novels

*Angel*
*Assassin*

## Coming soon:

*Julio's story*

The best way to keep up with my new releases, giveaways, and actionable intel is to sign up for my spam-free newsletter at IrishWinters.com.

# About the Author

# Irish Winters

...is a best-selling author of military romance who, when she isn't writing, dabbles in poetry, grandchildren, and rarely—as in extremely rarely—the kitchen. More prone to be outdoors than in, she grew up the quintessential tomboy on a dairy farm in rural Wisconsin, spent her teenage years in the Pacific Northwest, but calls the Wasatch Mountains of

Northern Utah, home. For now. She believes in making every day count for something, and follows the wise admonition of her mother to, "Look out the window and see something!"

## Connect with Irish online:

### On Facebook
https://www.facebook.com/IrishWintersAuthor/

### On Twitter
https://twitter.com/irishwinters1

### www. IrishWinters.com

www.ingramcontent.com/pod-product-compliance
Lightning Source LLC
Chambersburg PA
CBHW060939190726
48286CB00005B/1336